SHEMI ZARHIN

Translated by
YARDENNE GREENSPAN

NEW VESSEL PRESS
New York

SOME DAY

New Vessel Press

www.newvesselpress.com

First published in Hebrew in 2011 as *Ad she-Yom Echad*
Copyright © 2011 Shemi Zarhin
Published by arrangement with the Institute for the Translation of Hebrew Literature
English Translation Copyright © 2013 New Vessel Press

Library of Congress Cataloging-in-Publication Data
Zarhin, Shemi
[Ad she-Yom Echad. English]
Some Day/ Shemi Zarhin; translation by Yardenne Greenspan.
p. cm.
ISBN 978-1-939931-05-4
Library of Congress Control Number 2013939311
I. Israel -- Fiction.

for Einat

Three Pictures

Two seven-year-olds lie on the roof. A boy and a girl. The boy is Shlomi, the girl is Ella. They lie among the water boilers and watch a dead body being pulled out through a window.

This is the moment when Shlomi's mind begins transcribing.

He transcribes sharp and obscure pictures; writes and collects pleasant aromas and nauseating ones; things that had been and things that were just hatching. Shards of speech and tweets of tears and rustles of laughter and screeches of breath pile up alongside fumes of rage and tight waves of longing. And endless words.

Piles of words.

Before, his head was a puddle of water. Now the puddle is seeping and its few remaining drops are replaced by the details of this picture. It is transcribed so deeply that even if someone shook his head and memories escaped through his ears and scattered in the air of his life, even then, like the sun, like the dawn, it would keep rising each day, never diminishing —

The two of them on the scorching roof.

He, barely breathing.

The haze already piercing his lungs, turning his voice into a whisper.

She, lying at his side, tightly against his body.

Her lips are violently pursed and tears run down her face.

They both look down, to the yard trapped between buildings.

*

Shlomi also looks to the sides. Around them are many small black chunks his mom once referred to as "probably mouse poop, the mice are running around above my head," and immediately shouted at Shlomi's father, "When will you get traps and catch these mice already, what, are you waiting for them to chew my feet off?" And Shlomi's father smiled and said, "If anything they'd probably chew off mine, you always say my feet stink." And Shlomi's mother answered, "I said they smell, I didn't say 'stink.' If your feet stank I'd have kicked you out long ago."

Shlomi clings to Ella, trying to stay away from the mice's disgusting poop. Ella clutches the edge of the concrete, looks with moist eyes at the people trying to pull her father's body out the window. No one knows the apartment key is in her pocket. Those people spent ages trying to break in through the door, then trying to enter from the balcony. Finally they had to break the window, but couldn't open the door even from within, because the key was buried in her pocket and the lock was rusty and stubborn.

In the meantime, more and more people came to escort Ella's father through death, mostly people who never knew him and just wanted to honor him or snoop around. And the sun was a hard sun, the one that usually shines on funerals, and Ella's mother, Hanna, stood on the sidelines and cried in Polish, "Why does it only rain during funerals in the movies, and here the sun is hitting me." No one could understand what she said because of the Polish, but they still held onto her to keep her from breaking down and mumbled, "Poor thing, poor thing, as if what she went through in the camps wasn't enough." Everyone was so focused on her that they didn't even notice Ella wasn't there. Even Hanna didn't notice, or perhaps she did and thought someone was taking care of the little one so that she could cry in peace about what was in store for her now, without him.

Suddenly Ella looks at Shlomi and starts laughing. "Don't laugh," he says. "They'll find us." And she answers, "But it's funny when your thing gets hard, I can feel it through your pants." Shlomi doesn't really understand what she means but is immediately filled with shame and feels his face swell, his lips about to explode. "Don't blush," she says. "It's natural for boys like you to get close to knockouts like me and then your thing gets hard." Shlomi once again doesn't understand but decides to pull away a bit and remembers his mother saying, "Be nice to her because she's a poor little thing, her parents are hard, miserable people, the camps ground them into human powder. They spent all their lives eating frozen potato skins and drinking snow. But watch out for her too, because she's too mature. She's an old child."

Shlomi was completely confused. The nausea from the mouse poop, the shouting in Polish, the burning sun, and most of all Ella's laughter and tears. He didn't raise his head again and so never saw the people wrestling with the body, which folded and drooped till its head banged against the window sill. He just gave Ella one quick look and saw her eyes widen at the sight of the chaos bubbling in the yard, beneath the roof on which they lay, no longer tight against each other, shaking, he with shame, she with terror.

Shlomi asked, "But why did you lock the door?"

Ella answered, "Because I don't want them to take my father."

"But he's dead."

"I know, I'm not stupid."

"Did you want to piss your mother off?" he asked.

"She won't even notice I'm not there," she answered. "Maybe I should jump off the roof so she can finally notice me."

Shlomi said, "Don't jump," and Ella said, "Okay."

*

Two kids on a roof and below, a body emerging from a window.

Shlomi's mind absorbs this image, but also turns back, to older pictures, already faded from the hard punches of the sun.

Like the day the radio said the Sea of Galilee was overflowing and might flood the kibbutz. Shlomi's mother immediately said, "This I have to see, Robert. Get in the truck and take us there." Shlomi's father had a cold and answered in a wet voice, "I'm not going all the way over there just because you feel like watching your hated kibbutz members drowning in the sea."

"I don't hate kibbutz members," she said with an insulted face. "Just because your sister lives in a kibbutz and I hate her doesn't make me a monster who wants to see kibbutzniks drown. Shame on you, the way you talk to me, all I wanted was to see the Sea of Galilee fill up."

He finally conceded, ripped a few strips of toilet paper, stuffed them in his nose to stop the dripping and went to warm up the truck's engine. Shlomi's mother bundled up Hilik, Shlomi's younger brother, who had the sniffles, wore her hair up like she was going to a wedding, cleaned her glasses well and told Shlomi that the sea was so rambunctious that even the fish had begun flying, and you could catch them in midair with a butterfly net.

Then she said, "Why don't you invite the new girl to join us, she's probably never seen such things in her life." Shlomi refused, he didn't even know her, but his mother insisted. "Go and introduce yourself, be nice to her because she's a poor dear, her parents almost burned to death in the camps and in the end the government stuck them in Tiberias instead of giving them a respectable home in Tel Aviv or Jerusalem."

Shlomi walked out the door, down the stairs, across the yard and saw her sitting on the stone wall, as if waiting just for him. And indeed, the moment she saw him she got up and stood in front of him, smiling.

"Hello there," he said in the official tone his father used when he spoke with people who were placing work orders. "My name is Shalom but everybody calls me Shlomi."

One of her eyebrows arched. "Hello to you too Shalom and hello to you too Shlomi," she said. "My name is Israella but I can't stand that name so I changed it to Ella and don't you dare call me anything else."

Ella sat with her parents in the backseat because they wouldn't let her ride alone with strangers, and Shlomi's mother wasn't insulted but happily invited them to join. She asked Shlomi's father to tell some jokes to lighten their miserable souls from all the torture they'd been through. But when they got to the Sea of Galilee they saw that no fish were flying and none of them had a butterfly net anyway. "Who even catches butterflies in Tiberias?" Ella's father asked and went off in rolling laughter, and because he had a beautiful laugh, like a song with a catchy tune, everyone bellowed in unison.

Ella's father, Shmuel, was relaxed. Shlomi's mother's expression and her periodic laughter encased him in comfort and he began spewing jokes, one and then another and another, waves of crazy jokes streamed out of him, and Shlomi's father didn't have to work hard anymore, and everybody laughed a lot, even Shlomi laughed, although he didn't understand the jokes, and only when his mother said, "I'm about to pee my pants," he imagined her wearing pants and finally laughed for real.

Only little Hilik didn't laugh. He fell asleep earlier, on the ride over. "It's better this way," Shlomi's mother said. "He'll sleep away this illness, and maybe it'll pass and he'll finally be able to breathe like a human being."

"I have a cold too," Shlomi's father told her. "But you don't worry about me, instead you take me to the sea in this cold weather." Shlomi's mother smiled. "You're not a child," she said. "You're a big ass. Find someone else to pity you and your runny nose." And he said, "Maybe I will."

Later on, Shlomi's mother let them wander off a little bit and even put their feet in the water, even though it was late January and the water was freezing. Maybe she wanted to be alone with Ella's parents, to feel free to ask all her questions and get to know them better.

Shlomi and Ella sat on two rocks and insisted on leaving their feet in the water, which really was cold. Shlomi tried to ignore her looks and her arched eyebrow. Ella looked at his feet, the back of his head, his elbows, where he could feel her eyes the strongest.

"Why don't you talk at all?" she asked, and he was embarrassed but still answered, "I do too talk," and she said, "You don't," and he said, "I don't have a lot to say," and she said, "Do I look stupid to you?" and he shook his head.

"Did your mother make you invite me because she thinks I'm stupid?"

Shlomi shook his head again, harder.

"Then maybe you're a stupid boy and that's why you don't talk too much."

This time Shlomi didn't answer and didn't shake his head but was a little hurt and stopped breathing and thought she might be a little right.

Suddenly she moved her eyes away. In front of them, in the sea, in a small faraway fishing boat, people were waving their arms, trying their best to get the attention of a police boat sailing loudly nearby. Ella was focused on both boats and Shlomi used the opportunity to take a long look at her hair, her shoulders, the tip of her nose where he counted six freckles. In the meantime, the police boat stopped near the fishing boat. Because of the distance and the sounds of the surf, they couldn't hear the people talking as they tried to reach something that was floating in the water, but their excitement was palpable.

Then, all of a sudden, she looked at him, caught his gaze and said, "But you're handsome. Knockouts like me count beauty over stupidity." Shlomi didn't understand a word she said, but her voice was soft and his face was burning.

The people on the boats finally managed to pull in that thing that was floating in the water, and just then Shlomi's mother came over and asked them to get up right away. "You shouldn't be looking over there, it must be someone who drowned and they're trying to get him out." "Is he dead?" Ella asked. And Shlomi's mother answered, "How should I know? What am I, Deborah the Prophetess? And now come here immediately and don't look over there anymore, and you should get your feet out of that ice water before your toenails fall off." And they never talked about it again, and Ella looked at the boats from time to time, and at the people whose voices couldn't be heard, only their bodies moved in an effort to pull the body out.

A week or so later he heard his mother tell people that the neighbors' daughter was the one to throw herself in the water.

"What do you mean throw herself in the water," said Shlomi's father. "You'd think there were bridges here, with the Danube running under them. It's only the Sea of Galilee."

"You'd be surprised," said Shlomi's mother. "The Sea of Galilee is good enough. You don't have to go to Europe to throw yourself in the water."

"It's nice to know your precious sea is good for something," said Shlomi's father. And Shlomi's mother got mad and said, "You shouldn't get on my nerves too much, or one day you'll find me floating in the water, and then you'll ask yourself why I did it."

"Why would you do it?" he asked.

"Because of you, that you annoy me," she answered.

"Why must you make a big drama out of everything? Why must you threaten me?"

"Because I was just doing you a favor telling you about the girl who drowned because I thought you'd be interested, but you had to be so full of yourself and piss on the whole world."

"Why did she kill herself anyway?"

"How should I know? Maybe she fell in love."

"That one? In love?" he chuckled. "She was as ugly as the night. Who would she fall in love with?"

Shlomi's mother got upset again. "What, ugly girls can't fall in love?" she said, took the laundry and left.

Shlomi went down to the yard immediately and told Ella, who sat on the stone wall, everything his mother had told him. Ella was excited and said, "I see you actually do talk sometimes."

On their way back from the overflowing sea, Shlomi's mother said, "Now you'll come over for dinner." And Hanna said, "No, you should come over to our house." But Shlomi's mother wouldn't give up. "We asked you to go to the sea and people get hungry at the sea, especially today with the water rising. Tomorrow it'll go down and be sad again, because the sea is like a swing, it's moody." And she herself grew sad.

Shlomi's father looked at her and smiled. "That's Ruchama," he explained. "She has a poet's soul. She even takes poetry books to the bathroom instead of newspapers."

Shlomi's mother blushed and hit him gently on the arm. "Watch your language, Robert," she said, shocked. And he laughed. "What do you think, that they don't know you go to the bathroom? Even the Queen of England goes, and you'll be surprised to learn that sometimes she even farts." Then they all burst out laughing and Shlomi's father was pleased to learn that he could also tell a good joke.

Hanna told them she took a dictionary to the bathroom to learn new Hebrew words. Shlomi's mother made an impressed face and Hanna looked her up and down and said, "I've never seen a woman as tall as you."

Shlomi's mother smiled and said, "Now you probably want to know how I can live with a man who's so much shorter than I am."

Hanna nodded, as if pondering what she'd just been told, and never took her eyes off Shlomi's father.

When they got home, Shlomi's mother showed Hanna how she poured a lot of olive oil on hot hardboiled eggs and added salt and pepper and slices of fried sheep's milk cheese. Everyone placed their eggs on thick slices of bread that Shlomi's father sliced for them and took large bites of pretty tomatoes that Shmuel rinsed and cut in two while still joking around and making Shlomi's mother laugh.

"I've never had such good food before, Ruchama," said Shmuel as he took her hand in both of his, like a man holding a firefighter's hose.

When they left, Shlomi's mother said, "He's actually very nice. You can learn a lesson from him on how to be funny, instead of all your long jokes that get stuck in your throat like day-old bread. Look at this man, with everything they did to him, how they ground him into powder, look at him stand on his two feet and become a comedian. I'm not crazy about her, though, she has an unbearable voice, like a broken bicycle horn, goes to the bathroom with a dictionary to learn new words. I think she's an irritating woman."

"She's not irritating," said Shlomi's father. "She's sad."

A few days later Ella turned up in Shlomi's classroom. The teacher introduced her to everyone and told them that she was a new pupil and that her parents had moved to Tiberias from Netanya to work at the Jewish Agency office and help new immigrants, even though they were immigrants themselves, but had come to Israel a while ago, long before Ella was born. She asked everyone to make an effort to help the new girl, and forgot to mention her name. But Shlomi had known her since the trip to the sea and the meetings in the yard and all the days she came over with her parents or he came over with his, and so he signaled to her and she came to sit next to him and showed him that she had a sandwich with a hardboiled egg and a hint of olive oil and some salt and pepper, but no fried cheese because her mother didn't know where to get it, and no tomato slices because she didn't like her bread to get soggy. Some of the children laughed and said the new kid smelled like hardboiled eggs, like the sulfur water in the Tiberias Springs.

Then the teacher led a formation and instructed the children on how to behave and keep quiet when they went to visit the school principal's living room to watch the television broadcast of Prime Minister Levi Eshkol's funeral. Since Shlomi's class performed with distinction in that year's Chanukah ceremony, the principal decided to have them over as a reward. She was one of the only people in town to own a television, which she kept in the center of the living room in her large house, which also had a garden with grass and fruit trees and rose bushes. She used to bring the bad kids over to her fancy garden to hoe and water and sweep it really nice and good, because that was a much more educational punishment than writing "I will never interrupt Israeli history class again" one hundred times or copying down a chapter of the Psalms twice.

All the children sat on the floor and looked amazedly at the strange contraption with the bouncing black-and-white images. The principal gave them watered-down, almost tasteless raspberry juice, and kept telling the teachers who were there, "Our country is going to hell. Without Eshkol we might as well pack up our things and go," and the teachers clicked their tongues and made worried faces and kept looking at the open kitchen and all the shiny appliances the principal's son sent over on a boat from America.

Ella sat next to Shlomi and whispered in his ear, "Half my ass is freezing on the floor, and the other half is sweating on the carpet," and Shlomi was afraid he'd start laughing at that moment, when the prime minister was being lowered into his grave, and so he lowered his head and pretended to cry silently. The teacher saw him and told the principal to stop with her apocalyptic prophecies because she was scaring the children. The other teachers were startled when the teacher dared tell the principal off, and in her big house no less, and were completely quiet until the television went staticky and the prime minister was in the ground.

About a week after the class and the teachers and the principal said goodbye to Levi Eshkol, Shlomi's parents and Ella's parents were already good friends. Shlomi's mother kept commenting on Ella's mother and Shlomi's father kept thinking she was a special, sad woman. "So why don't you marry her," said Shlomi's mother, and he answered with a smile, "I already married you, I missed my chance."

*

And then it happened.

Shlomi's father went over to do a favor for Ella's parents and fix their shutters, because he was handy and fixing things was his profession.

Shmuel wasn't feeling so well. He was pale and grumpy and sighed like an old man climbing up stairs.

Hanna said, "He's upset because Golda was made prime minister instead of Dayan or Alon. He doesn't like having a prime minister with a stronger accent than his Polish one." And Shmuel said, "I don't like people who act like slaves. I don't like someone deciding for me that this old lady gets to be prime minister instead of letting us vote, letting us decide."

Shlomi's father left the shutters for a moment and said, "There'll be an election in a few months anyway, so what's the difference?"

"Who will you vote for?" asked Shmuel.

"Mapai, the Workers' Party," said Shlomi's father. "I've been voting for Mapai my whole life."

Shmuel let out a nervous laughter. "You're a young man," he said. "You're a child, not yet thirty. How many times have you voted anyway?" And Shlomi's father said, "Whenever I voted I always voted Mapai."

"Why?" asked Shmuel.

"Because that's what I always vote, my whole life," said Shlomi's father.

Hanna sensed tensions rising and said, "Why don't I make us something to drink, maybe something cold, because you're very sweaty, Robert."

But Shmuel was getting very heated and said, "Can't you see they're screwing you over, you and all the other Sephardic voters." Shlomi's father blushed, maybe because of the word "screwing," and said that he grew up in Argentina. Shmuel didn't give up and banged his fist on the table. "You grew up in Argentina but you're Sephardic, you're Iraqi. And your wife, it doesn't matter that she was born in

Israel, she's Sephardic too, and you're both naïve like all Sephardic Jews. I say 'naïve' because I can't believe you're stupid enough not to notice when someone is laughing at you and treating you like dogs and abusing your loyalty. What's Mapai ever done for you?"

Shlomi's father went back to pushing the shutter into its base. He was sweating profusely and must have been upset that Ella's father allowed himself to say such a thing. Maybe that's why he didn't answer.

But Shmuel went on. "Look at Begin, for instance. I look at him and want to throw up – he's such an exilic ape. But at least he's dignified, and if you vote for him you'll finally have someone looking at you, and that would be the real revolution."

"I'm happy with things the way they are," Shlomi's father said quietly. "Who's got the energy for a revolution, anyway," and Shmuel banged on the table again and went red until Hanna yelled, "You'll have the heart thing again!" But he kept yelling and yelling, about how even Ben Gurion couldn't stand Golda and refrained from voting, and how it was too bad that Shlomi's father didn't ask his wife for her opinion because she was a smart woman and would probably understand why it was important.

And suddenly he fell.

Shlomi's father and Ella's mother ran over and put him on the sofa. Ella's mother slapped his cheeks and spoke in Polish and Shlomi's father didn't really know what to do. Then Ella pulled Shlomi away and said, "Come help me." She pulled him so hard that Shlomi hit his nose on the doorpost.

In the kitchen she told him, "Don't be scared, it happens to him a lot. Just help me get his Valerian."

Shlomi didn't understand what she was talking about and just touched the bruise on his nose. Ella poured some tap water into a glass, pushed a bottle of dark liquid into his hand and asked him to put exactly twelve drops into the glass, because her hands were shaking. Shlomi twisted the cap off and tried to pour carefully. Ella shouted at him, "Do it quickly, what are you looking at? Are you doing research?" Shlomi started shaking from the pressure and released long sprays of the dark liquid into the glass. "Did you count twelve drops?" Ella asked, because she wasn't looking. Her face was turned towards the living room and the Polish shouts. But Shlomi had no idea how many drops he'd poured, and only managed long, sharp sprays.

Ella poured the water that had turned orange into her father's mouth; he calmed down very quickly and even told Shlomi's father to let go of the shutters, that he didn't need any favors and that he should go home and think about who he was going to vote for. Then he lay down on the living room sofa and closed his eyes; everyone went about their own business, and that night he died.

Shlomi's mother helped take care of everything because Ella's mother had no one but her husband and a few colleagues from the Jewish Agency office.

Shlomi's father sat at home, not moving.

"You're as white as a ghost," said Shlomi's mother. "Don't blame yourself, it's not your fault the man was psychotic and heartsick from all the terrors he went through in the camps and the torture and the snow."

"I don't blame myself," he said. "I just feel bad for her and her daughter who's now an orphan. They've only been here a month and look what happened to them. Look how stupid life is."

He finally had to come help, because people suddenly realized the door was locked and everyone was already outside, waiting for the funeral, and only the body stayed at home, because Hanna insisted it be brought back home after being cleaned and shrouded. "I don't want him sent to the grave from the fridge, I want him to come from his own home." And Ella locked the door and took the key with her and no one knew about it and no one noticed the kid was missing either.

Shlomi's father came but couldn't break the lock because his hands were shaking, and couldn't go in through the balcony, either. Maybe he was afraid to run into Ella's father sitting on the sofa with that look in his eyes that made him feel like an idiot. He stood on the sidelines when they pulled the body out the window and put his big hand on Ella's mother's back.

And Shlomi's mother alone ran the entire operation quietly and efficiently, until finally the body was pulled out the window in front of the eyes of two children lying close together on the scorching hot roof.

Part 1

1969

1

On Wednesday, of all days, the western wind would grow strong and savage, breaking through from between the mountains and coming in to turn worlds over, deafen ears, drown eyes in dust and raise loud arguments that would finally be laid to rest, only to erupt once again on the following Wednesday.

Because everyone always had something to say. Aunt Geula, for instance, Shlomi's mother's sister, would tie an extra scarf around her swollen neck and say, "I'm crazy about the Wednesday wind. It feels good under my scarf, and this way I don't feel itchy in summer." Aunt Drora, Shlomi's mother's other sister, would say, "I don't know what all the fuss is about. That wind blows every day in summer and sometimes in winter as well, and every day I have to spend hours cleaning the dust it spreads all over the apartment." Vardina, the downstairs Romanian neighbor who was Shlomi's mother's loyal confidant, would shake her head in irritation and say, "I wonder who the primitive person was who decided that Wednesday was the day for wind. Why don't you crack open a book or a newspaper, then you'll know that air rises because of heat, so that there's a shortage over the Sea of Galilee and it pulls in all the air from the mountains around it and then there's a western wind that makes it very dangerous to swim between two and four in the afternoon, when everyone should be resting. That's the whole story. It's true on Sunday and Tuesday and any other day, not only Wednesday. People just make up fairytales so they'll have something to complain about."

The kids were terrified of the wind and preferred to stay indoors and do their homework, or bounce a ball on the floor until the downstairs neighbors came up to complain. Everyone knew that when the wind blew the streets and backyards became dangerous. The lid of a trash can would rip off its flimsy hinge, fly through the air and decapitate people as they ran for safety. Clotheslines would tear off poles and spin in the air like flying snakes, shedding dry laundry and wrapping around the necks of high school students who were late to get home. The wind danced around, looking for victims, zooming from yard to yard, circumnavigating buildings, stampeding down pathways and attacking bunches of yellow dates that moaned to surrender and let go of the trunk and landed on the heads of the elderly who stopped to rest under the shade of a palm tree.

Shlomi's mother told him, "All I ask is that you be careful, because you're a trustworthy kid and that's why I'm crazy about you. People exaggerate and invent, telling silly tales about this wind, but where there's smoke, there's fire and we've seen Wednesdays get more dangerous than other days, sometimes even disastrous. Don't ask me why, only God knows why Wednesday rather than Tuesday or Thursday, and if only that were His one bizarre choice."

On Wednesdays, Shlomi would sit at the table and breathe through his mouth. His mother would place a dark, fatty filet on his plate. The filet had the stiff aroma of a fish that did not come from the Sea of Galilee. Beside it was a pile of yellow rice, with brown fried noodles twisting in it, and some salad and a lemon wedge that Shlomi would squeeze with all his might so its juices would conceal the filet's smell. He would swallow it all down quickly, then breathe through his nose again and stand at the window to see how the wild wind broke in the sky over the Arbel Cliff and began blowing away the laundry his mother had just hung out to dry.

His father always welcomed the wind with surprising pleasure. He'd wipe the fish smell that clung to his hands, salute and say, "Welcome back, Wednesday wind." Once he even laughed and told Shlomi's mother, "I sincerely hope your sister Drora isn't walking outside right now. This wind will blow her wig right off." And Shlomi's mother said, "It's not nice of you to joke about her around the children, she's still my sister and their aunt," and stifled a small laugh.

"It would do her well," said Shlomi's father, "to learn from Ms. Aisha. One time I saw her walking down the street on a Wednesday and her wig didn't move an inch. I think she used carpenter's glue, the same kind she huffs sometimes to make her sores stop hurting."

"She has no sores, that one," said Shlomi's mother, her face contorting with loathing.

"You'd be surprised," he said. "Her heart is full of pangs of conscience. It's stuffed like a pepper."

"But she doesn't even wear a wig," she said. "That one can't even pay for food, so how would she afford a wig?"

Shlomi's father was getting a little angry. "How could her hair be so black if she didn't wear a wig? She's like a hundred years old already." And Shlomi's mother explained that Aisha dyed her hair with henna she collected, poking through the garbage cans outside of Kaduri's hair salon, and he insisted that henna couldn't be that black, at its darkest it would be brown, and usually it was red.

"Don't teach me about henna, because I could write you a book about it," she said. "It's true that henna isn't black, but Aisha mixes it with cigarette ashes and the charcoal she steals from Elgarisi's Grill." And her lips trembled as she muttered, "Damn thief, curse her memory."

Only then did Shlomi's father go quiet, because he understood her and knew that the punch Aisha threw to her belly still hurt. She had been seven months pregnant, and Aisha thought she had just gained a lot of weight and told her, "Ruchama, what's going on, you've turned into a pig, what have you been eating?" And Shlomi's mother said, "Are you crazy? I'm pregnant." But it was too late and within two hours her water broke and she gave birth to a crumpled child who was never mentioned in their house; and the crumpling, thieving Ms. Aisha was never mentioned either, with the exception of that one time.

On the other Wednesdays, when the wind suddenly began goofing off, Shlomi's father would finish welcoming it and wiping his hands and then shout, "Close it, close it, there's a draft," and Shlomi didn't understand what a draft was, it could be another expression from the Hershele Ostropolyer folk stories his father sometimes told, about the nobleman and the rabbi and the fishtail and the Sabbath challah. He especially liked to say, "I cannot even afford a piece of challah! I am impoverished and won't even have a fishtail to decorate the Sabbath table with!" and cry out loudly and bang on the table so that Hilik opened his mouth and the spoonful of rice slipped in. Then

Shlomi's mother took the spoon from him and said, "You're giving me a headache with your stories. I might as well feed the children on my own. Besides, where did you hear those Ashkenazi Hershele stories, anyway? Did your Iraqi mother tell them to you?" And Shlomi's father would turn quiet because he remembered his parents, who both died when he was only ten years old.

Shmuel's funeral was held on a Wednesday and the wind began dancing right as he was lowered into the grave. Rain suddenly began pouring and broke the heat wave that awoke that morning and burned the roof Ella and Shlomi hid on. It made Hanna feel a little better and she said, "At least he said goodbye in the rain and we can forget about that sun of yours for a while."

Shlomi's father didn't go to the funeral. He stayed home to take care of Hilik, who was sick, but mostly he couldn't bear being there. Hilik lay in bed with the cold he could not shake off for two months and cotton balls stuffed in his ears to absorb the infection. Shlomi's father sat by him but kept staring at the doorknob and only once moved his eyes to ask Shlomi, "Why don't you make a cup of tea for your sick brother?"

Shlomi was still dirty from the dusty roof. Only after Ella's father was finally pulled out the window did her mother realize her child wasn't there. She started screaming, "My girl, where's my girl Israella?" and Ella had no choice. She got up, shook the dust and black bits off and told Shlomi, "If I don't go she'll keep screaming and her throat will break, I've seen it happen to her once," and ran off the roof and down the stairs and across the yard and clung to her mother. Shlomi kept lying on the roof, and only when the yard was completely emptied of people and of the body and of the shouting in Polish, only then did he get up and go home.

Shlomi handed Hilik the tea he'd made, and Hilik withdrew into his blanket. "I don't want tea," he said in a congested voice. "It burns and when I swallow my ears hurt."

Shlomi looked for a place to put the steaming cup and finally placed it on the floor, near the chair where his father sat and stared. Then he looked for a place to sit. There was a huge pile of laundry on his bed that his mother hadn't had time to fold because she had to go and resolve the issue with the body. Shlomi was about to sit on Hilik's bed when Hilik flinched and said, "Your clothes are dirty, don't sit on my bed. It's bad enough that my ears are sick." Only then did Shlomi notice the whitewash that had gotten smeared on his clothes when he lay on the roof. In the hallway mirror, he saw that his hair had also turned white, and even his face and hands, and he looked like a painting of a ghost. Like in the book he took down from the big kids' shelf in the library where he hid sometimes from the third graders, so that they couldn't grab him by the collar and shake him and take the sandwich Hilik had given him.

Shlomi went out to the balcony and shook his body clean. He shook and shook and thought it was too bad they didn't own a television, because if they did he might have watched Ella's father's funeral the way he watched the prime minister being lowered into the ground, and he would surely see her standing next to her mother, rubbing her arm and calming her down, so that she didn't shout and break her throat.

When he returned to the room he saw his father drinking the tea he'd made Hilik and still staring at the doorknob. Until suddenly he stood up, said, "Shlomi, you'll come help me now," went to the door, and then remembered Hilik and went back and touched his forehead and said, "We'll be right back, and you'll be a hero and wait for us in bed, and maybe you'll even sleep off the disease and get better."

The lock on Ella's front door really was stubborn and annoying. Shlomi's father had to take a big hammer from his toolbox and hit the lock over and over again, until he smashed the rusty bolts and managed to rip the thing off whole. Shlomi stood beside him silently, occasionally taking hold of some tool handed to him. "Watch carefully," said Shlomi's father. "If you watch you'll be a lock expert and when you grow up you can make a great living." And Shlomi really did watch carefully. He was worried that the hammer might break the door, or that it might hit one of his father's fingers and smash it.

"You see how I slowly solve the problem?" said Shlomi's father. "If he'd have only let me focus on the shutters I'd have fixed them up completely, and maybe then I'd have also fixed this lock and some other stuff in his crummy apartment, and none of this would have happened, and they wouldn't have needed to break the window just to get him out. Who ever heard of such a thing? Who ever saw such a rundown home? I'd have fixed everything up if he'd have let me instead of trying to educate me as if I were a stupid little boy."

Shlomi's father sweated so much that water ran down his body and created a puddle outside the door. He took off his blue work shirt and used it to wipe his forehead and arms and absorb the puddle, clean the door and then the new, shiny lock.

"Now let's go in and you'll help me with the shutters as well. I want to have everything fixed by the time they get back."

Like the wild Wednesday wind, Shlomi's father moved around the small apartment, fixing all that was broken. By the time rain started pouring the shutters were sliding on their rails, the leaking faucets stopped blinking, the copper gas pipe was attached to the wall and the doors to the kitchen cabinets were placed back on their hinges. Here and there some sweat puddles formed and Shlomi's father took his pants off as well and worked in his underwear, and then grabbed a mop from the bathroom and cleaned everything up and also washed some dishes that were in the sink and folded two towels and finally mopped the stains left on the kitchen floor by the shattered Valerian bottle.

When they got back home Hilik was deeply sleeping his disease away. Shlomi's father sat in the chair in his wet work clothes and went back to looking at the same spot on the doorknob. By the time Shlomi's mother returned from the funeral his clothes had dried off, but the salt stains on his shirt caught her attention and she asked, "Why did you sweat so much? What did you do?"

"I was at her place. I fixed her apartment."

Her forehead contracted in wonder. "What apartment did you fix?" she asked.

"I fixed her lock and her shutters and everything," he said. "Shlomi helped me."

Her wonder was replaced with shock. "And what did you do with Hilik?"

"Nothing, he slept," he answered, and she became even more

shocked. "You're irresponsible," she said. "Who leaves a six-year-old with an ear infection alone?" And Shlomi's father said, "Nothing happened, but I feel like my lungs are about to explode." And Shlomi's mother saw that he was breathing fast and that his eyes were red. She came closer and put his head against her stomach.

"Robert," she said, "it's not your fault that he's dead, I already told you he was mad from all the torture and beatings his miserable life had given him."

And then Shlomi saw that his father was crying and went to bring him a glass of water. He drank some and told Shlomi, "Don't worry about me, it's just that I'm emotional and Argentinian so sometimes I cry a teeny bit," and when he spoke the Rs rolled in his mouth as if trying to prove his point—Arrrrrrrrrgentinian ... Crrrrrrrrry ... Rolling and mixing with his multiplying tears, not a teeny bit anymore but a roaring flow of Arrrrrrrrrgentinian crrrrrrrrrries.

Shlomi knew this was true. His father would often come home early from work with tears in his eyes and Shlomi's mother would say, "What's wrong? Are you depressed about not having work again?" And he'd answer, "I drove around and around with my truck and no one needed anything." She would nod, cross her arms and say, "You have to specialize. Just because you have good hands doesn't mean you have to do everything, find something to specialize in, be an expert and then you'll have a lot of work, and in the meantime stop worrying because we're not dying of hunger yet."

But it didn't help. For days he'd walk around with that face and those red eyes until Shlomi's mother said, "Stop walking around like a fallen palm tree, bringing bad spirits into the house," and would stroke his cheek and suggest that he go shower and sit for a long time in the water, until he felt better. He'd smile and whisper in her ear, "Only if you come with me and cheer me up." Then she'd sit the children down in front of the aquarium, give them plates of date cookies and go into the bathroom with him.

While they sat silently, watching the imprisoned fish, Hilik would hand Shlomi his cookies and say, "Make up a story about the fish and I'll give you my cookies." "I can't make up stories," Shlomi would answer and Hilik, with his throat infection or ear infection or runny nose would say, "You're just like Mom, that's why you won't make up stories for me. But I'm like Dad and that's why, when I grow up, I'll make up stories."

Then their parents would come out of the bathroom smelling like eucalyptus. Shlomi's mother would look at Hilik's plate and say, "Good job, Hilik, it's good you finished your cookies. That's the way to get strong and healthy." And Hilik would be pleased by the compliments even though he gave Shlomi his cookies because he couldn't stand dates, and Shlomi gobbled the whole thing up in seconds. Shlomi's father would come out with a towel to dry his long, thick hair and walk around completely naked looking for clean underwear in the piles of laundry Shlomi's mother didn't have time to fold. She would look at him, wide-eyed, and whisper, "What are you doing walking around naked like this in the middle of the day in front of the children." And he'd answer, "They're boys, they have the exact same thing." And she'd whisper, "They're children, they don't have the same thing, and this is the example you give them? Walking around naked?" And he would dig into the pile of clean laundry and say, "Don't worry kids, when you get older you'll have one of these too." And Shlomi's mother would smile and whisper in a different voice, "I hope for their wives' sake that they don't have one of those. A little less would be better." And Shlomi's father would be surprised. "You're the only one complaining. All the men are jealous of me." "What do you mean 'the only one?'" she would get upset. "Are there others that I don't know about?" And he would burst out laughing and put on the underwear he finally found, and then stop laughing because he'd see her go to their room and shut the door and she wouldn't let him in until he'd apologize and promise that he was only teasing.

But this time he was sadder than usual. He drank all the water Shlomi brought and said, "How dare he talk to me that way."

"Drop it already," she said. "He's dead anyway, what difference does it make?"

"He can hardly speak Hebrew," he said with anger. "I've lived here since I was ten. It's true I grew up in Argentina, but I was born here and my parents came here long before he did, and he dares to tell me that because I'm Iraqi I should vote for Begin?"

"You really are Iraqi." She smiled at him. "An Iraqi with a South American accent, to confuse the enemy." And she began pulling his shirt off. Shlomi's father lifted his arms like a little boy being undressed before bath time, and said, "How dare he try to own me, like I was his stupid student and he was the big government expert. Maybe he thinks that living through the Holocaust makes him an expert on everything."

Shlomi's mother was done with the shirt and was removing his pants and saying, "All right, enough, you're giving me a headache. The man is dead and this is over. Now go take a bath, sit in the water, it'll make you feel better." And he said, "Just so you know, in the next election I'm voting for Mapai and Golda." "All right," she answered. "You can write her poems and send her flowers for all I care, just go take a bath already."

He started walking to the bathroom and then she stopped him. "Robert, aren't you going to ask me to come with you and make you feel better?"

He thought for a moment before answering, "No need. It's better that you sit with Hilik. We've neglected him enough today as it is." And he went to take a bath. Shlomi's mother stayed where she was with an insulted face and rubbed Hilik's back to wake him up so she could put drops in his ears and give him some food to make him stronger.

The next morning Shlomi woke up early. The sun had yet to conquer the sky and he was cold. He stayed in bed and thought how maybe he should tell his mother what happened the previous day on the roof with Ella, so she could help him understand. And maybe he would ask his father why his thing got hard when he lay close to her and why she laughed and why he was ashamed, and maybe he'd tell them that Hilik really doesn't eat a thing, and gives all his cookies to him and even gives him his lunch at school, and that's probably why he doesn't get better.

But when his mother came to wake him up his thoughts were gone in an instant. She said, "I'm crazy about you, because you're a big boy now and you can be trusted, so when you get back from school I want you to help me. I have a million things on my mind – I have to take Hilik to the doctor so he can look in his ears, and I have to go to the market, and I have to cook a lot of food to bring to that poor woman so she and her orphaned daughter have something to eat, people will probably go over there to console the family sitting *shiva*, and it's important to have something to serve them and she probably doesn't have the strength to do anything and she has no one to help her because her family was burnt in the camps and his family is all gone as well."

At school the teacher said that Ella's father had passed away and urged the children to visit their poor friend. Most of the children didn't know who she was talking about – Ella was a new student and almost no one knew her other than Shlomi, and no one knew where she lived either. The teacher didn't seem too sad herself, and immediately moved on to showing the children how to make non-alcoholic wine from grape juice for Passover. Everyone stood around her as she poured the liquid into the bottles they each brought from home. Shlomi had a bottle of cough syrup his mother had cleaned out well and scratched the label off, to erase all memory of Hilik's illness. Shlomi thought it was a shame he hadn't brought a bottle for Ella as well; she probably had many more Valerian bottles in her apartment, bottles that, drop by drop, were drained into her father's tranquilizer cups. He could have washed and cleaned one of them and filled it with the kids' wine the teacher was making.

When he got back from school the apartment was so filled with the aroma of fried onions and minced garlic and lemon and hot red peppers that it seemed Passover had come early to their home and that at night they would sit down and eat fish in red sauce with their hands, with a lot of parsley and celery leaves, and Shlomi liked to save the celery leaves on the edge of his plate and finally roll them around with whole cloves of garlic, fill his mouth and chew the heavenly taste, the red sauce running down the sides of his mouth like blood and Hilik looking at him disgustedly and saying, "Mom, tell him to stop grossing me out."

A great hunger grew in Shlomi's stomach and rose to his mouth, which was filled with saliva. Since Hilik stayed home from school, Shlomi had only one sandwich for lunch, the one his mother had made him, with soft white cheese and diced cucumber, and walked around school with a growling stomach. And now this smell. But his mother was already waiting with the food baskets.

They took them over to Ella's apartment and then came back and took the rest of the pots and pans and went back to Ella's apartment, where Shlomi's mother transferred the food to Hanna's dishes, and Hanna said, "Ruchama, you're crazy. Who's going to eat all this and what did you go and do that for?" and Shlomi's mother didn't answer, only smiled, but inside she thought that the dishes seemed dirty and didn't smell good and could ruin all the good food she'd made. Then they both sat down in the living room to have tea and occasionally said something quietly, and nobody came.

Shlomi went with Ella to her room. He stayed there even after his mother went home to wash the pots and clean the kitchen and spend time with Hilik, who was feeling better. The new medicine worked right away, just like the doctor said.

They sat on the bed and laughed every once in a while because Ella made a face each time she heard her mother sigh. Hanna stayed in the living room, looking at the fixed shutters, and every so often touching the sides of her head to make sure that her hair-do was holding up and smoothing her blue dress, ready to greet the mourners who never came.

That evening, Shlomi's mother asked if anyone had come. Shlomi told her no one did. She slapped both her thighs loudly and shook her head over and over again, unbelieving.

And then she asked Shlomi, "Did they at least eat the food I made for them?"

"Ella's mother said it was spicy and unhealthy," Shlomi said, "so they didn't touch a thing, and she promised Ella to make her an omelet."

Shlomi's mother went quiet. Her eyes turned into slits. "She said that in front of you? What exactly did she tell her?" And Shlomi answered, "She said it in front of me and looked at me, too."

Now her eyes narrowed as if fire ants had crawled into them. "Are you sure, Shlomi?" she asked, and Shlomi nodded and stormed over his meal, because he was about to faint he was so hungry.

When Shlomi's father returned from work he saw her sitting there with a long face and her eyes still in slits.

"What did you do?" he asked.

"I cooked a lot and baked like crazy," she answered.

"I can smell all of your cooking very well."

"Don't expect anything because I made it all for her and for the orphan, to console them and help with the food for the mourners. For you I made only *shakshuka* and yellow rice."

Shlomi's father looked at her face for a long time. "I see you're having some pangs of conscience, too," he said.

"I'm not having any pangs of conscience," she said. "I just wanted to be a good neighbor and help out."

"So why do you look like you're about to cry?"

"Because my back hurts. Now stop it with the questions and let me rest." And she went to her bed.

But Shlomi's father followed her and she told him everything.

"I told you she was an annoying woman, I think she's a bad woman too, all I wanted was to help her."

Her eyes watered and Shlomi's father stroked her hair and tried to cheer her up, and she did calm down and even grew angry with herself. "What nonsense am I talking, that poor woman, maybe she didn't like the food, maybe the spices really did burn her throat because her whole life she had to eat potato peels or food that had sugar in it but no salt and no taste. How can I be angry with her and insulted by her, her husband died only yesterday and she has no one left but her strange girl, and no one even came to visit and mourn with them even though she did her hair and put on makeup and dressed up as if she was headed to the café to meet friends."

All throughout the *shiva*, Ella's apartment was blue. Maybe because the shutters were almost entirely closed and the little light that came in encountered the blue shades. Maybe because it was the color of the walls themselves. Maybe because of the blue dress Ella's mother wore as she continued sitting in the living room, waiting for guests and every so often placing her fingers on the sides of her head, to make sure that each hair was in its place. One day a man with a long blue face showed up and Hanna gave him a piece of herring and some bread with margarine and they spoke for a bit until he left.

Maybe others came as well, so quiet and thin that Shlomi's eyes and ears had missed them, and perhaps it was only the shadows flickering on the walls when the wind shook the blue shades.

All this time, Shlomi and Ella sat on the high bed in her room and giggled from time to time. Even the air looked blue and cool to Shlomi. It was so nice and still that sometimes he could hear his ears whisper. Only the kitchen was bathed in yellow light because its window had no shade, and the pots of food that Ruchama had made remained on the burner and spread a thick scent, until Hanna threw everything out and washed the pots and the floor and sprinkled some perfume that smelled like flowers that don't grow in Israel.

"You don't have to be with me all the time," Ella told him. "It's enough that you bring me my homework." But Shlomi didn't answer and just kept sitting there and watching her like she was a movie.

One day he brought her candy he took from his mother's sewing drawer. Hard white candy with one almond placed in each piece, and Ella told him, "We have to chew quietly, so that she doesn't hear and come yell at me for ruining my teeth."

Another day he brought her some date cookies and she gobbled them up over her open palm to catch all the crumbs and inhale them all into her mouth.

And one day Ella told Shlomi, "I wrote you a letter," and gave him a folded piece of paper torn from a Hebrew notebook. Shlomi spread open the page and looked at it for a long time, trying to follow the letters that bounced out of their lines and smeared into one another, until Ella realized what was happening and asked, "Can you even read?"

Shlomi was embarrassed to raise his eyes to hers and felt his lips swell again. "You're blushing again. You don't have to be embarrassed around me, Shlomi, because I'm your best friend in the world, and just explain to me how it's possible that you can't read, because I don't think you're a lazy kid at all." And Shlomi shrugged. Ella took the page from him. "Anything you want to read I'm willing to read to you." Then she began reading, quietly, so that her mother didn't hear.

"Hello my dearest Shlomi,"—Ella read without looking at the page, her eyes pierced into Shlomi's—"Lately I've been thinking that

I'm very sick of life and I think it isn't being nice to me at all, and that's why I'm going to throw myself off the roof and it was very, very important to me that you know because you are dear to me and also you are the only one who knows now, because it's a secret."

He was moved by the flattering things she wrote about him, but confused by the rest, and after a few minutes of silence said, "I don't understand anything." She smiled at him and said, "I'm going to commit suicide," and Shlomi asked, "When?" and Ella said, "Tomorrow or the day after," and Shlomi furrowed his brow and asked, "What's suicide? I don't understand," and Ella answered, "Suicide is to die," and Shlomi asked, "You're going to die?" and Ella nodded until the smile disappeared from her face.

"But why?"

"Because I don't know who's going to wake me up for school anymore and help me get ready quietly so she doesn't wake up," Ella said almost without breathing. "And who's going to stir my hot cocoa carefully so that I don't break the glass with the spoon because she only likes thin glasses but then yells when she has to pick up the pieces from the floor, and also I don't know who's going to help me with homework, and I don't know who's going to calm her down at night when she wakes up screaming in Polish till her throat breaks. And I don't know who's going to buy us watermelons and grapes in summer and take out the seeds because you can choke on them, and I don't know who's going to check my hair to make sure I didn't get lice again without her knowing, because if she found out she might send me to get a short haircut like a boy."

Shlomi wanted to tell her that he could help with some of those things, but the words didn't come out and Ella went on and said, "And besides I want people to talk about me the way they talk about the neighbors' daughter that they found dead in the Sea of Galilee."

When he got home he sat in the kitchen, unmoving. His mother gave him a long look and said, "Why are you so worried? Since when does a child your age walk around with such a worried face?" And Shlomi told her right away. "Ella told me she was going to die because she was sick of life." She stroked his hair and said, "Kids don't die because they are sick of life, there is no such thing and I've never heard such nonsense in my life, and you shouldn't worry about her, she probably said it because she'd heard her mother say it so many times because her mother really has many reasons to say that, but Ella is only a child and she's confused now because her father is dead." She ruffled his hair and dried the sweat off his forehead. "When I was your age I was always worried because they laughed at me for being tall, but you are smart and beautiful and I'm crazy about you, so you shouldn't worry too much."

On Wednesday, Shlomi got home from school to a parentless house, only Hilik sitting in the kitchen, drawing with the new crayons he got as a gift for being healthy. "They all went to the fair," Hilik explained. Shlomi didn't know what a fair was but remembered that it was in the city, near the market, and that they did it for Passover, which was just around the corner, and that his mother would probably return with a can of silver paint and maybe this year she'd let him paint the lid of the trash can.

He left the house and ran down the stairs and through the yard to call Ella out to play because her father's *shiva* was finally over. Even before he reached the doorway he heard her call, "Shlomi, Shlomi, look, I'm up here." He looked up and saw her standing on the edge of his building's roof, right by the spot where they'd laid watching the body being pulled out of the window.

"I waited for you to come home from school because I didn't want to jump without you down there."

"But why do you want to jump?" he asked. "It's dangerous." And Ella said, "I already explained it in the letter and today I have to keep my promise." And Shlomi felt his stomach about to explode and tears began streaming from his eyes, and Ella noticed and smiled and said, "It's not like you to be a crybaby, you hardly ever talk."

"Please wait for me to get someone, don't jump," he said.

"You won't find anyone," she answered. "They all went to the fair to buy things for Passover."

"Then I'll get your mother."

"There's no one to get, she went to the fair too, even though she isn't buying anything because we don't do Passover cleaning, but she wanted to get some air."

Shlomi didn't know what else to say and was afraid to breathe and stood down there looking at Ella taking another small step and her shoe already stuck out from the edge of the roof. "Please wait, I promise I'll find someone, I'm sure they didn't all go, don't jump." Finally she nodded.

Shlomi broke into a run, went into his building, flew up the stairs and stopped at every door, knocking and knocking and calling, "Please open the door!" But no one opened. He ran down the stairs and went through the yard. Ella called from above, "You see, I knew no one was here, I waited for nothing." And Shlomi, in tears, said, "Please wait just a little longer, I'll find someone," and flew up the stairs in Ella's building and knocked on the doors and no one opened there either, until finally he had no choice but to knock on the door of Mrs. Katz, of whom everyone was terrified. She was the most famous math teacher in town and everyone tried to be on good terms with her so that she didn't fail their children, because if you fail nothing will ever come of you. In her classes there was always complete silence and all the children had their arms crossed, but everyone knew that once, during a geometry test, she let out a loud fart and to this day when she walked down the street people waited for her to get far enough away and then laughed, hid in the bushes and called, "Mrs. Katz-fart, Mrs. Katz-fart."

Mrs. Katz-fart opened the door and looked at Shlomi with a sour expression. "What is it, young man, why are you knocking like this, you want to break my door down?" Shlomi put his terror aside and said, "The girl from downstairs, the one whose father died, is standing on the roof and wants to jump."

The math teacher knew right away that Shlomi wasn't pulling her leg like kids sometimes did to get back at her for failing them. The lucky thing was that the edge of the roof Ella was standing on was right in front of the window to Mrs. Katz's bathroom. The teacher stood by the toilet and called to Ella through the window, "Little girl, what are you doing on the roof?" And Ella, not surprised at all by Mrs. Katz's appearance, answered, "I want to jump." And Mrs. Katz asked, "Why?" And Ella answered, "Because." And Mrs. Katz said in a soft voice, "Are you being serious, my child?" And Ella was very moved by the tone of her voice and said, "I don't know."

Mrs. Katz convinced Ella to move back a little bit, just a tiny bit, because the Wednesday Western wind was about to begin and it could blow her off the roof. Ella did as she was told and took two small steps back. Mrs. Katz smiled at her and said, "Well done, you are a wise child," and asked, "Will you please wait for me to call the police?"

"What for?"

"So they can come talk to you and so they can find your mother and bring her here. You must want to say something to her before you jump."

Ella thought for a bit and said, "The police station is far away. It would take you a long time."

"I'll call them, I have a telephone. They'll be here in no time."

Ella nodded and promised not to move.

Mrs. Katz, whose phone was one of the only ones in the neighborhood, went to call and left Shlomi standing on the toilet lid, keeping an eye on Ella. "Come on, how much longer?" Ella shouted, and he begged her to wait a little longer for the police to arrive. Ella said, "What do I even care about the police? What do the police care about me?" Then she took a small step forward and announced that she wasn't going to wait any longer.

Shlomi got scared, jumped off the toilet and ran out, passing Mrs. Katz who was busy trying to get a line. Within seconds he was standing in the yard with his arms open wide, ready to catch her if she jumped. "Please Ella, don't jump," he said, and she answered, "I can't wait any longer, Shlomi," and he said, "Then at least jump onto the sandpile," and pointed to a large pile of sand by the building, waiting patiently for the Kurdish neighbors from the first floor, those who never said a word, to finally receive their building permit from city hall and expand their tiny apartment, or at least add a balcony to sit on in the summer because you could suffocate in there.

Ella looked at the pile of sand and then at Shlomi, and although he was three stories away from her, she saw in his eyes something she hadn't seen before. And then the Wednesday wind began rumbling, as if very mad at the child standing on the edge of the roof, blocking its way and stopping it from spinning the entire world around.

At night, when his parents came back from the fair with all the supplies for Passover cleaning, they asked if he'd heard that his friend had fallen off the roof and said it was lucky she fell onto the Kurds' sand-pile and that she only broke her leg.

"From now on," said Shlomi's mother, "I forbid you to go up on that roof or any other roof. It's very dangerous. It was a miracle that nothing worse happened to your friend. And what was she even doing on that roof with all the mouse poop?"

Shlomi didn't tell them that he'd seen her fly with the Wednesday wind, smiling and waving till she landed on the sandpile. He didn't tell them that he'd even seen her ankle go all the way backwards and a small bone sticking out. He didn't tell them that the police had just arrived and that Mrs. Katz made sure to get him out of there so he didn't see Ella, who kept smiling at him from afar and waving and shouting, "I jumped to the sand, Shlomi, I jumped to the sand for you," until she fainted. He didn't tell them a thing, but in the middle of dinner threw up everything on the floor and on himself.

Shlomi's mother took him to the bath and washed him and put his clothes in a bucket of water and laundry detergent, and his father cleaned the kitchen floor and then checked his temperature and saw that he was burning up.

Shlomi's mother rubbed his cheeks and fastened a moist cloth to his forehead. "Your fever is already going down," she said, "because the medicine was quick and because you're a real hero and I'm crazy about you. But tomorrow we'll go to the doctor anyway, so he can take a look at you." And Shlomi thought, how could his mother be so certain that Ella had fallen off the roof rather than jumped. How could she have decided it was the Wednesday wind that pushed her, after he had told her about the letter, and she knew all about how Ella wanted to throw herself off.

And when Shlomi was falling asleep, his father said, "You know, Ruchama, when I was over there fixing their apartment I had the idea of specializing in shutters. You always say I need to specialize so I decided to specialize in shutters. I'm even thinking of taking out a loan and opening a shop. You'll see, I'll make money and make us rich." And Shlomi's mother said, "Money isn't everything but I'm the last person who would say no to being rich." Then she asked him to shut the windows because the Wednesday wind was being especially stubborn, whistling in her ears and interrupting Shlomi's sleep.

2

SHLOMI SLEPT FOR OVER FOUR WEEKS. HIS EYES WERE OPEN, HE ANswered questions, he even painted the lid of the trash can silver, but that entire time he was sound asleep. Once he awoke for a few moments and went to Ella's apartment and knocked on the door. Hanna opened it, her face green, her fair hair no longer up and her blue dress replaced with another, yellow with small brown dots, and said, "Go home, Shlomi, and don't come back because Ella has to rest after her leg surgery." And she slammed the door, and Shlomi went back to sleeping with his eyes open.

The second time he woke up was when he was standing with his mother at the lookout point on the Carmel Mountain in Haifa, and she said, "Look Shlomi, look how high we are. We're on top of the world." And her voice was suddenly happy. She told Shlomi and Hilik about the ships in the harbor and the chimneys in the refineries, and said it was good that we'd taken down all the Arab planes in the war, otherwise they'd have bombed the refineries and all of Haifa would have exploded. And Shlomi's father got mad and said her words were putting fear in the children's hearts. Then she took out a packed lunch and they each got a piece of matzah that she'd moistened until it was soft like pita bread and filled it with schnitzel and diced cucumber. Shlomi gobbled everything up, and even Hilik ate nicely, because the Carmel air gave him an appetite. And Shlomi's father said, "You make me laugh, Ruchama – you stuffed the matzah with unkosher schnitzel, so why don't you decide already if you observe Passover or just pretend to so that people don't make faces at us." And Shlomi's mother answered angrily, "I'm not as hypocritical as you think, the schnitzel is covered in matzah crumbs, not bread crumbs, and it's more kosher than your face, but you're just looking for reasons to make fun of me and spoil my mood and fight with me all the time, even in front of the kids." And Shlomi thought that she probably liked being in such high places because she was tall, and that it was too bad his father had messed it up.

From there they went to the flower show and Shlomi's mother explained how the erect tulips were imported from the Netherlands. Then she said, "I want to go, the air here is wet and it's bad for Hilik, I don't want him to get sick again."

"The air here is great," said Shlomi's father. "You're just making excuses to leave because the mayor had a heart attack here last week and you're superstitious."

"Abba Hushi died?" she wondered. "Where did you hear that?"

"They said it on the radio, we were at home together when they said it on the news."

"What do I care about Abba Hushi, I don't even know him."

"You can't know him now even if you wanted to, he's dead," he said, his eyes piercing her until she lowered her gaze, and Shlomi knew that she'd lost her mood for the trip.

On their way back home they stopped three times to let the truck rest its motor. Shlomi went back to sleep on the way, with open eyes, he even ate an apple his mother gave him and a chocolate covered matzah and peed in the bushes by the side of the road, and slept deep and heavy the entire time.

3

SHE WAS FEELING BETTER ALREADY ON THE WAY TO THE CARMEL. SHE knew the angle the lookout point would give her, onto the slope of the mountain, and onto the sea and the port and the chimneys, that angle would make her feel better and alleviate the heartburn that had been bothering her for weeks. When the truck climbed up the mountain Ruchama tried not to look at Robert. She was worried that the tense smile that had recently clung to his face would poison and ruin everything again. In front of the landscape, her arms holding onto Shlomi and Hilik's, she took big gulps of the wind the Carmel made especially for her, saving up for the moment when everything would be ruined.

And then a thought cut through her mind, it's a shame I'm not like my mother, a joker and a prankster. She turned anything that upset her into a comedy skit, having everyone falling down laughing, and only then was she happy. It's a shame I'm not a little more like her, and all I have left of her is a small yearning, like a desert island in an ocean of heartburn, because she's been dead for a year. It's been a year that there had been no one around to prick Ruchama as painfully as her mother had.

Ruchama's mother died of laughter. Just like that. She choked with the bursts of laughter that blocked her already-weak windpipe once and for all. She was already hooked up to oxygen, her lungs bursting with fluids and her breaths blinking.

Ruchama and Robert visited her daily, bringing her grapes and slices of marzipan that Ruchama had made herself. "You brought enough to feed an army," she'd complained. "It's true that I'm a big fat elephant-bear and eat like a pig and it's true that I'm a sucker for your marzipan, Ruchama, but you've gone too far. I haven't even finished the date cookies and the semolina cake from yesterday." And she showed them that in the box they'd brought the day before there was barely one small piece, and began laughing. The others began laughing with her – Ruchama's two sisters, Geula and Drora, and her two older brothers, Abraham and Yitzhak.

And then Ruchama's mother began reminiscing and told the famous story about the birth of her eldest son, Abraham, when she was only sixteen and didn't know what was happening and thought she had the stomach flu, and about the birth of Yitzhak, who was as hairy as a monkey-baby, and even had black hairs on his nose. Then she had two miscarriages, and when she was pregnant again the whole world was prepared for a third son, who she was going to call Yaakov and have all three biblical fathers. But instead, she had Ruchama.

It took hours to pull her out because she was a long baby. Even the midwife, with all her experience, screamed with surprise and sent her assistant to call the other midwives in the neighborhood and one of the doctors so they could see the miracle. And everyone came and measured her from all directions, and Ruchama's mother looked at her despairingly and said, "Instead of Yaakov I had a praying mantis." And ever since she'd called her Ruchama the Praying Mantis, and laughed and couldn't understand why that tall child didn't laugh at her jokes.

And when Ruchama was twelve, and in Egypt, Nasser – may he burn in hell – took over as president, her mother looked up at her and announced, "God help you, you're so tall. In the end you'll reach all the way over there and scare Him and all his angels. I wanted so badly to have a third son, Yaakov, and in the end I had a praying mantis surprise," and she called her Praying Nasser Ruchama because Nasser also was fond of deadly surprises. And she laughed and laughed, and Geula and Drora laughed too, and their entire small home in the Achva neighborhood in the lower city shook with laughter. And when Ruchama walked down the street the kids would yell "Praying Mantis!" after her and ask her to pull down their rag ball that got caught in the gutters, and the neighbors would mumble "Praying Nasser Ruchama," and spit three times towards the cleavage peeking from their necklines to ward off evil spirits and tell her, "You could work as a ladder and you'd always make a living," and add quietly to themselves, "Because what man other than Og, King of

Bashan, would want a woman whose head can reach the birds."

But along with her mother's pricking laughter came great worry. When Ruchama was as young as ten years old her mother noticed that she blinked like a dysfunctional lighthouse and took her to the eye doctor, who examined her and said it was nothing. But Ruchama's mother wasn't satisfied and took the tall girl to Haifa, where they climbed the Carmel and waited for two hours to see the eye specialist who asked Ruchama questions and examined her and finally said, "The child reads a lot and her eyes are weak. There's no choice, she needs glasses even though glasses would hide her beautiful eyes." Ruchama's mother said, "It's true, Ruchama, what the doctor says. You have your father's eyes, may he rest in peace, and they're the most beautiful eyes in the world. Now you have to decide what's more important to you – do you want to keep reading and not blink like a sprinkler or do you prefer the whole world to see your lovely eyes?" And when she saw that Ruchama was confused and couldn't decide she added, "With your height no one's going to see your eyes anyway, it's best that you be smart and read."

Ruchama's mother placed an order with an optician in Haifa: the newest, most expensive lenses with the ugliest frames, because one should not save on the lenses but one can save on the frames. Thus Ruchama became the Four-Eyed Lighthouse Praying Mantis Nasser Ruchama. The frames made a small scratch on the edge of her nose in the shape of a red bow and when she grew so tall that her head was higher than those of all the men in the neighborhood, she developed a tilt of the head that led her mother to say, "Now you really look like a praying mantis." Then her mother placed a thick book on her head and trained her to walk straight.

She also sent her to a language teacher who taught her French and English. When Ruchama was fourteen she was already fluent in both languages and read books and magazines her mother bought especially for her and knew many things about the world from the teacher, who, in his younger years, had traveled in all sorts of places and saw all the wonders of the universe with his own two eyes. Ruchama never told her mother that during class the teacher sat behind her, put his hand on her shoulder and with the other hand touched himself until Ruchama heard a small moan come out of him, like the chirping of a sick bird. When she was fifteen the teacher's hand came down from the heights of Ruchama's shoulder and slowly crawled down until it grasped at her right breast. Ruchama froze and heard the teacher whisper from behind her in French, "You used to be a child, Ruchama, and now you're a big and beautiful amazon woman." And then he made that chirping sound again and Ruchama took the thick English poetry book and whacked the teacher's head until the book fell apart, and never came back.

All around Julia, Ruchama's sick mother lying in her bed, sat Abraham and Yitzhak and Geula and Drora, bellowing in laughter. Ruchama laughed a little too, but Robert knew it was because she felt bad and that inside she was cringing and it made him mad. Ruchama's mother looked at him and said, "What's wrong Robert? Why did you turn red like a pepper?" And Robert couldn't stop himself and said, "For years I've been hearing this story and I don't get what's funny about it. If I had a daughter I wouldn't call her a praying mantis."

A silence fell. Ruchama's brothers and sisters stared at the spotless hospital floor. Ruchama had a hard time hiding the pleasure his concern gave her. She felt at that moment that she loved all of him. And only Julia kept smiling and looked at Robert endearingly and finally said, "At least I know you love her like her father loved me, even though he was as thin as string and I'm fat as a mammoth, and even though Ruchama is like an electrical pole and you ..." Then she thought and thought, searching for the right word, everyone around her waiting nervously, and finally she pursed her lips, as she always did when speaking French, and said, "You're *petite*." And everyone burst out laughing. Robert asked, "What's *petite*?" And Julia answered, "*Petite* is French. It means you're a tiny midget but I love you because you have a big heart for my daughter, and to love someone her size you really do need a big heart, because as much as I wanted a Yaakov, I ended up with a Praying Nasser Ruchama that went off and married a *Petite*." And then she began laughing and laughing and coughing and choking and Ruchama ran out to call the doctors, who came right away and sent everyone out of the room and intubated her and her heart stopped beating and then began again after several electric shocks, and again she breathed well, and again she began laughing and coughing and then she choked and died.

"At least she died laughing," Ruchama told Robert in tears and kissed his entire body.

When Ruchama was sixteen her mother told her, "I see you're possessed. You're spending too much time with your books instead of going out with girlfriends. Go have fun, go get ice cream or go to the theater, where they have movies and ice cream and lupini beans wrapped in newspaper, buy some corn on the cob or a cinnamon Danish. Just get out of the house already and stop making out with those books." But Ruchama stayed with the books and a year later announced that she'd decided to move to Haifa because the air was good and the libraries were terrific and no one would laugh at her when she went to ask for work, and no one would say, "To hire a girl like you we'd have to raise the ceilings."

Julia cried a river. "You'll be very cold on the Carmel and there are Arabs there who will try to eat you up," she said. But Ruchama insisted. "There are Arabs in Tiberias too and no one's tried to eat me yet, and don't worry about me, anyone who comes close to me will get beaten up so bad they'll be sorry they were even born." And Julia kept crying, because although she'd made fun of Ruchama from the day she was born, she loved her very much, even more than she loved her other children. Maybe that was why she pricked her all the time.

Abraham drove Ruchama to Haifa and helped her find a place. It was a small attic with a triangle ceiling and a bed and a small desk, and Ruchama was happy. Even the sour smell and the loud sighs of the elderly landlords didn't take away from the intoxication that enveloped her. She felt like Rachel the Poetess in that attic, sick with tuberculosis. At night she sat on her bed and, like Rachel, imagined beautiful and painful combinations of words, wrote them down in her notebook, and sometimes coughed and coughed and imagined she had tuberculosis.

She found work at a nearby bakery. The head baker was impressed with her long arms that would knead huge chunks of dough. The other workers would stare at her dancing buttocks and her leaping breasts as she whacked the dough to remove any excess air before the second kneading. In the middle of the night, when the landlords sighed in their sleep and dreamed of their son who was about to finish his studies in a military boarding school and join the navy, Ruchama would go out on tiptoes and skip all the way to the bakery, humming lines of poetry by Alterman and Goldberg and Shlonsky that she'd gathered into one tune that became permanent in her mind, storming over the piles of dough and taking them on a wild dance. When the children in the school near her home played in the yard during the ten o'clock recess, she'd skip back, get a few hours of sleep and wake up to the perfumed air of the Carmel.

A year of tearful yearning went by for Julia, and when she heard the rumor that a storm had attacked the Carmel and that the rain broke through the triangle ceiling and soaked Ruchama's clothes and bedding, she decided to bring her daughter back home before she got tuberculosis or pneumonia. Julia flagged down Robert, a short young man with a strange mane of hair and wide-open eyes, who was driving around in his truck, making repairs and shipments for anyone who would pay. She gave him Ruchama's address and some money and sent him to bring her home.

When Ruchama opened the door she took his breath away. He'd heard about her, perhaps even seen her once on the street, but now she stood in front of him in all her tall glory, shimmering from the bath she'd just taken, her moist hair emanating a sweet scent that made him dizzy.

First Robert fell in love with Ruchama, and a few minutes later Ruchama fell in love with him.

He sat on the edge of her bed and was surprised to find that her room was dry and rainproof and even cozy and protective and not miserable as Julia had thought. He told her he was sent to save her from the eye of the storm and return her to her mother, and Ruchama smiled a small smile and froze in his eyes.

For many minutes they sat, their eyes held in each other and their breaths chasing one another. And then Ruchama asked Robert, "Why are you breathing so fast?" And Robert answered, "Because I've never seen a woman as beautiful as you and my heart is burning." And Ruchama stuttered, "I don't believe you. You've seen me before and I've seen you, and you must remember me because I'm as tall as an electrical pole and I remember you too because you're the only guy in town whose hair falls on his eyes."

"I'm sure you do believe me," he said. "I've never seen anyone like you."

"When you talk your Rs are special."

"That's because I grew up in Argentina, although I was born here."

Again they were quiet, their eyes tied and their gaze cast, and Ruchama thought that even Rachel the Poetess couldn't write what she felt at that moment.

And then Robert said, "I have to sit close to you, is that all right?"

"It's a small room, you're already close," she answered.

"Closer," he whispered, and Ruchama didn't understand how it came to be that she suddenly stood up and took one step in the air and landed by his side and already his hands traveled on her shoulders and ran through her moist hair and her lips drank his honey-candied lips. Robert's hands kept spinning and trembling and removed her embroidered blouse. He detached himself from her and his eyes went to her breasts that were fastened into her bra and he said, "I've never seen such a beautiful thing. Let me see more." And Ruchama wrapped her arms around herself and said, "I'm embarrassed." "Me too, but I don't care anymore," he said, and within seconds took off his clothes and stood before her, wearing nothing but his white underwear, which was inflated like a tent.

Ruchama closed her eyes and Robert asked between frantic breaths, "Have you ever seen one?" And Ruchama shook her head and Robert opened her eyes with a gentle finger and she looked again, and giggled a little, and said, "Your underwear is about to rip." And Robert said, "I've never seen them either, only pictures in magazines you shouldn't read." And his fingers removed the bra and touched the hardened nipples and a small wet spot spread on the taut part of his underwear and his hands rolled down Ruchama's skirt and underwear, and she said, "I'm scared," and he said, "Me too," and removed his underwear and kissed Ruchama all over until her breathing stopped and a small, pretty tweet came from her mouth and her body relaxed, and he kept rubbing up against her legs and his semen broke out and soaked into the blue bedspread.

On the Carmel, with the wind combing her hair and her arms in her children's arms, Ruchama saw Robert send an effortful look to the house she'd once lived in, as if checking that everything was in its place or wondering if the landlords had come back from the dead and were renting the room out again. Ruchama asked herself if Robert loved her now as he did then, when they'd first met and exploded on her bed. She'd remained in her room, flustered, and Robert returned to Tiberias to disappoint Julia. He told her that the triangle ceiling was strong and that the storm had stayed out, and that Ruchama was dry and happy and didn't want to come back. Julia was very angry with him and yelled at the top of her throat, "I want my daughter back by my side, and don't lie to me that she isn't suffering, she can work at a bakery and sing songs here in Tiberias, she doesn't have to stay on the Carmel in the wind and rain just to knead dough." And she sat Robert down and dictated an angry letter to him because she herself couldn't write, only read a little, and only with vowelization. And then she gave him dinner, an eggplant and garlic casserole with pieces of fried sheep's milk cheese, and apologized for taking her anger out on him and asked how a strong and athletic man like him, even though he was short like a midget, walked around with long hair. Then she gave him a few more liras and asked that the next day he go back to Haifa and give Ruchama the letter and bring her home.

When he got to her room they exploded again. Like the day before, the landlords had gone to their club to play cards. Like the day before, her hair dripped and wet his chest. Ruchama put Julia's letter aside and Robert told her that the previous day he'd driven in his truck with one hand on the wheel and the other touching himself until he'd fallen apart, and then he'd touched himself again and fallen apart again, because he kept seeing her face and her neck and her breasts and her waist and her thighs and her eyes and was aroused, and it was lucky he didn't get into an accident.

For ten straight days Julia sent Robert to Ruchama, who persevered in her insistence not to return. He would come at noon, she would wait with moist hair, hungering for his touch. They would explode with love, and at night Robert would eat Julia's cooking voraciously and help her express her anger and pleas in writing.

On the eleventh day Julia decided to join him and went with him to Haifa to make her rebellious daughter return. Helplessly, Ruchama got in the truck with all of her things, and it rattled and grunted all the way back to Tiberias, barely carrying the tremendous weight of the worried mother.

A year later Ruchama and Robert went to Haifa to hand out wedding invitations to her friends from the bakery and to the landlords. On the door of the house she used to live in they saw a sign offering it up for sale. The landlords' smiling son opened the door in his shiny navy uniform. He was happy to see Ruchama and said, "What luck, I happened to come and check that everything was in order just when you came here." Then he told them his parents were no longer alive. About two months before, they'd decided to close their eyes forever, tired of their memories from the camps and mostly of the diseases and all the medicines they'd taken in vain and of the fear that illness would take only one of them, leaving the other one alone. They knew he'd recover quickly and would be all right, he was used to being away from his parents, having spent most of his youth in the military boarding school, now being a soldier on a faraway ship. They had written him a beautiful letter, full of love, cleaned and straightened up the house, swallowed a pile of sleeping pills and sat in the kitchen with their arms folded until their heads dropped.

Ruchama was upset, and tears ran down her face. "No one knows better than you how they suffered in this life," said the landlords' son. "You lived with them for a full year." And Ruchama nodded and was ashamed to realize that, having been so happy, she hadn't noticed how miserable they'd been, except for the sighs and the sour smell. The son smiled at her and said, "They liked you, because when you lived here you gave them a sense of security, maybe because you're tall and they were small and whenever they remembered their past they became even smaller. When I was a child I noticed how on each Holocaust Memorial Day they'd grow smaller and smaller and I was afraid that one day they'd just disappear. And then they did." He laughed to hide his tears and accepted the invitation in his parents' name, and even promised to come to the wedding if the navy allowed it. Then he apologized and said he had to return to his ship, and suggested they rest in the house a little, drink something and regain their strength before returning to Tiberias, and asked that they remember to slam the door shut when they left.

Ruchama and Robert drank tea and washed the cups. "I don't understand those two," said Robert. "Why did they have to send their only son away and how could they have left him like that, he's still a child."

Ruchama smiled at him lovingly. "First of all," she said, "You're more of a child than he is. He's twenty, a year older than you, and just because the army didn't draft you because you're a little thin and short doesn't make you a grownup. Besides, look at you, you've been living without your parents from age ten and you've grown up nicely. I should know." And she caressed his face and his long hair and his neck and Robert leaned into her fingers and said, "What does that have to do with anything? My parents died in an accident, not because they wanted to leave me, and no one sent me away to boarding school."

"He's not really their son," she explained. "When they came to Israel they decided to adopt him, even though they had come back from the camps like human powder and he was a four-year-old orphan. Only later, when he was older, they began fearing that instead of health they were imparting fear to him. They decided it was better if he were brought up by the military and sent him away, even though it broke their hearts."

"They told you all this?" he asked.

"Yes, sometimes they'd talk to me a little, but each of them would do it separately, telling the exact same things and then asking me not to tell the other that I knew. In the end, I'd heard every story twice. They were very sweet, like lines of a poem – they rhymed with each other."

Robert looked at her, impressed, and his entire body was tight with pining. They went up to the little room with the triangle ceiling, took their clothes off and lay on the blue bedspread. Almost a year had passed since the ten days they'd spent exploding here. A year in which they'd managed to steal kisses and fool around in the dark, but always in their clothes and always worried that someone would notice and tell Julia, who kept telling Ruchama, "Watch out for that midget, don't let him think you're easy and that he can eat you up before he puts a ring on you, and be careful not to forget yourself, because you're so in love that you've begun blinking again like when you were small and in the end he'll make your belly swollen and run away without marrying you under a *chuppah*. And what would you do then?"

With her hair spread like a fan on the blue bedspread, Ruchama told Robert, "I'm going to be your wife in a few days anyway. We can do everything now." And Robert said, "Are you sure? You're not scared?" And she answered, "I'm a little scared that your thing won't go in and that it'll hurt." And it did hurt at first and it hurt Robert a little as well, but they moved slowly and gently until it stopped hurting and then came the explosion.

On the way back he asked, "Why are you smiling like that, your cheeks red like roses?" And she said, "Because I was thinking of Rachel the Poetess and I feel a little sorry for her. I know all her poems very well, and I don't think she ever experienced what you and I just had, otherwise she'd have written it in a way I'd recognize."

A cold gust of wind sent a grain of sand into Robert's eye. Ruchama examined the eye that had turned red from rubbing, and said, "There's nothing there, it came out." She really wanted to tell him, "Let's take Shlomi and Hilik and knock on that door, maybe whoever lives there will let us in, maybe the blue bedspread is still there, maybe we'll tell the children how we met," but instead she remained quiet and took the kids to the edge of the lookout point and told them about the harbor and the refineries.

Robert kept rubbing his eyes and Ruchama said with a smile, "It's so lucky we took down all of their planes in the Six-Day War. Just imagine if they'd come over to bomb the refineries, they'd send all of Haifa into the sky." Robert was upset and said, "That's nonsense. They bought new planes ages ago. They have the money, and lots of oil, enough so that the Russians give them everything they need. Why are you making the kids scared?"

"Why are you always mad at me? What did I do to you?" Ruchama asked quietly so the children couldn't hear.

"I'm not mad," he said.

"Ever since he died you've been suffering and blaming yourself and taking it all out on me."

"Stop saying that. I'm not suffering and not blaming and I don't care about him. I hardly knew him."

"So why are you looking at me with hatred?"

Robert smiled a little. "You're really full of nonsense today. You're my love, how could I look at you with hatred? I'm a little concerned about the loan I want to take out and I'm also hungry. The Carmel wind gave me an appetite."

But when she brought out the lunch she'd made, he pricked her again, thinking that the schnitzels weren't kosher and accusing her of being a hypocrite. Suddenly she saw in his eyes the same look her mother had when she pricked her and made fun of her.

When they stood under the *chuppah* Shlomi had already been nesting in Ruchama's womb. Julia made a point of telling all the guests how she hated herself for single-handedly introducing the two. Esther, the elderly aunt, clicked her tongue again and again and finally told Julia off. "Why don't you shut up a little and instead of crying at your daughter's wedding be happy that someone wanted her at all, and even though he's a little short he looks like a movie star, and you, all you care about is that your daughter stays beside you because you only care about yourself."

Julia was insulted and kicked Esther out of the wedding, but Esther wouldn't leave and they began shouting. The next day Ruchama told her mother, "You ruined my wedding and you'll never see me again." But two days later she changed her mind and apologized and Julia forgave her and went on pricking her like before, until the day she died laughing.

A disturbing cloud of tranquility fell on Ruchama the day her mother passed away. For a long time the men worked to lower her body into the grave, and three times they had to stop to dig and expand the hole. The mourners had to fight the desire to laugh each time the burial was halted. Julia's tremendous weight caused difficulties they'd never seen before in the cemetery that looked out onto the Sea of Galilee. Old Esther clicked her tongue and said, "God forgive you, Julia, you've even managed to make a comedy of your own funeral." But Ruchama felt nothing of all this. The cloud of tranquility reminded her of the happy year when she skipped along the Carmel going back and forth from her room with the triangle ceiling to the bakery where she danced with the dough. And then it was quiet again. It even seemed to her that a cool Carmel wind was drying her tears.

When Robert returned from Julia's funeral he made the kids dinner first and then locked himself in the bedroom and laughed for a long time. Like the other men, he'd fought with the heavy gurney, and all the laughter he'd managed to keep inside while they were in the cemetery had piled up and came out at home.

"I feel bad because I loved your mother very much," he said. "Especially since without her I'd never have met you and fallen in love with you and also because of her cooking, but it would have been better if they'd brought a dump truck to carry her to the grave."

"I feel bad too," Ruchama said. "Because suddenly, since she died, I can breathe easier and my mind is at ease."

When the month of mourning was over Ruchama told Robert, "This peace and quiet is hard on me. After all it's my mother and I'm beginning to miss her a little, and that's why I decided to strengthen my relationship with my sisters." Robert was surprised. "But you can't stand them, they only make you feel bad and insult you." But Ruchama was determined and explained that she was going to make this effort for the sake of her mother's memory and most of all for Shlomi and Hilik, because it would be a shame for them not to be friends with their cousins. Robert shrugged. "Do whatever you want," he said. "I don't understand why your sisters are so full of themselves anyway, they should look in a mirror before they even talk about you, maybe their eyes would open and they'd see that they have nothing on you, in every sense of the word." And Ruchama hugged him and said, "That's why I wanted to talk to you and ask that you be patient and not heat up and ruin everything." Robert promised to be a good boy and Ruchama invited Geula and Drora to spend the following Saturday together at the Sea of Galilee. She also invited Abraham and Yitzhak to join them with their wives and children, but the two complained about how the sisters didn't wait for the year of mourning to be over before going out to have fun at the beach, and on the Sabbath, no less.

Shlomi and Hilik stood next to Geula's two sons and Drora's two girls and watched them compete in making stones skip on the water. The adults played cards and then spread all the food they'd brought on a blanket, leek patties and zucchini patties with beef and onions, and a large bowl of mashed potatoes with hardboiled eggs and parsley, and a pot bubbling over with huge red tomatoes stuffed with rice and lamb and dill in a sour sauce, and a green fava bean casserole with chicken wings and pickled lemons and mountains of cilantro and garlic, and quartered sour fennel and a jar of orange jam with mint leaves and a sweet cake made of leftover bread and nuts. They refilled their plates over and over again and ate and even laughed and Ruchama felt that her mission was coming to fruition. No one mentioned Julia or her strange funeral, not a word was said of Abraham and Yitzhak and no one reminisced or told stories from the past. When she went to pee behind the bushes, Ruchama thought that this event was like a first date, an acquaintance with new people whose amiability and good taste she had known nothing of before.

Geula's husband Aaron and Drora's husband Emanuel lay down on the rocks, smoking cigarettes, and when the sun came out from behind the clouds, they shut their eyes and fell asleep with a whispered snore. Considering the sun that was growing hotter with each minute, stubbornly pushing away the clouds, the three sisters conceded to their children's requests to take their clothes off and get in the water. Robert went to the truck to change into his bathing suit and then went in the water to watch the kids and have fun with them. Ruchama and her sisters modeled their bathing suits for each other and giggled like little girls. Geula was impressed by Ruchama's suit that held her ample breasts up nicely, and Ruchama suggested they come over so she could make alterations to their bathing suits, that were a little loose around the waist and let their curves flow out. They sat on the pebbles on the water line and swayed with the small waves.

And then Ruchama saw how her two sisters stared at Robert. He stood nearby, the water caressing his knees, and wrung his long hair, shook it and smoothed it to the sides, adjusted his shiny blue suit and jumped again into the waves to chase the children who ran from him in ringing laughter. When Geula saw that Ruchama was looking she was embarrassed and lowered her eyes and began playing with the pebbles. Drora kept staring at Robert all throughout his chase after the children, and later too, when he walked towards them, shaking his body like a dog in the rain.

When they came home Ruchama asked, "Did you see how Geula and Drora looked at you?"

"Looked when? Looked at what?" Robert asked.

"Don't pretend you didn't notice," she teased him. "They were just about to eat you alive."

"What are you talking about, Ruchama?" Robert asked, laughing. "I thought you were glad it worked out and you had fun."

"I did have fun," she said. "I was even happy, until I saw them drooling over you."

"Over me? What did I do? I don't understand you."

"You didn't do anything, you just ran around naked in front of them in your bathing suit. I told you before that it's too thin and we need to get a new one."

"You're one to talk, Ruchama. You walk around in your suit and your nipples stick out. You're lucky I didn't jump you right there in front of everyone," and Ruchama said, "I'm serious, Robert, I don't like the way they looked at you," and Robert said, "All right, next time I'll wear my wedding suit to the beach, anything to make you happy. And besides, what do you have to worry about your sisters? I've seen them in bathing suits. They can only dream of being half as pretty as you are."

"So you were looking at them too?"

"Yes," he said. "I'm only human, I looked at them a little and at you a lot because you're the most beautiful thing I've ever seen. I've told you before."

"You did a good job with your apartment," Geula told Ruchama. "And your flowerpots blossom so nicely, even though you hardly have any sunlight here," said Drora, and Geula quickly added, "But I don't like flowerpots inside the apartment. I like flowers in the garden, where they belong."

Ruchama spun the wheel on her sewing machine and made another stitch in Drora's bathing suit. She'd already finished with Geula's. "What's wrong with you today?" Drora asked. "You're a little pale," and Ruchama said, "I have a headache," and Geula said, "Maybe you need more blood. You should have some chicken liver from time to time, so that you have enough iron and energy." "I'm fine," Ruchama said and broke the thread with her teeth. Drora touched the altered suit and said, "Maybe you're pale because there isn't enough light in this little apartment, and hardly any air," and Ruchama said, "I like this place, it's my home."

"I feel bad for you, Ruchama." Geula sighed in fake sorrow. "Mom was sure you'd really turn out to be something with all those books you read."

"I'm happy this way," said Ruchama. "I read to feed my soul, not to sell something." She was ashamed to admit that she had hardly read any new books since she'd gotten married. Every once in a while she'd sail into one of the poetry books she loved, touching the words of Rachel, wandering in the familiar lines of Alterman, wounded by Goldberg's rhymes, reaching out a careful hand and immediately returning to her day, to the housework and the difficult pregnancies and the cooking and baking she'd sometimes do for other people's celebrations when they'd ask her—for modest pay—to enrich their holiday tables. Once every month or two she'd go to the public library, browse and borrow a book, promise herself that this time she'd read it and finally bury it in one of the boxes under her bed, where she'd collected many borrowed books from the library that no one ever asked her to return.

"When did you two become such worriers?" Ruchama laughed and covered the sewing machine with a floral fabric. "Don't forget who the eldest sister is. It's true that I don't have a garden because people who live on the third floor don't usually have one, but I have enough light and I eat enough chicken liver and I'm happy this way and don't need anyone to feel sorry for me." Then she made them try on the suits and the two did a fashion show in the living room and laughed and were happy.

Ruchama took them to the small kitchen and showed them how

she fried onion and sprinkled garlic cloves she'd mashed with her hand and seasoned it with spicy green pepper and with ground coriander seeds and squeezed a lemon and placed a pile of green beet leaves that she'd ripped off the stems in the middle, and within seconds the green pile sank into the pot and became an aromatic green sauce, into which Ruchama chopped cubes of sheep's milk cheese and broke three eggs and dripped olive oil, and when everything bubbled and steamed she brought the boiling pot to the table and ripped large chunks of brown bread and the three sisters dipped the bread into the casserole and scooped spoonfuls of the sauce and pieces of the cooked eggs and ate with great pleasure.

"Why don't you tell us why you even married Robert," Geula suddenly said and wiped green sauce from her mouth with her hand.

Ruchama sat up and stopped chewing. "What kind of question is that?"

"Does it bother you that I ask that?" Geula asked, and in her eyes appeared that fake sorrow again. And Ruchama answered, "No, you can ask whatever you want, but ask questions that I can understand."

"Why are you getting so tense?" Drora interrupted. "We're just worried about you."

"Why?"

"Because your husband has been riding around in his truck for years. Fixing washing machines here, moving furniture like some kind of porter. What's going to come of him?"

"And why does he wear his hair so long?" Geula added her own concern. "Who'd want to hire a beatnik that can't be trusted? Why doesn't he get a haircut, so he can look respectable? Who does he think he is, the Beatles?"

The green casserole kept emanating a scented steam that fogged up the kitchen, but Ruchama looked at her sisters hard and clear when she said, "So why did you look at him that way?" And Geula and Drora furrowed their brows, trying to understand her question, and Ruchama went on, "When we were at the beach I saw you swallow him with your eyes."

Drora looked at Geula and said, with a hint of worry, "She's gone mad."

"I'm not mad or anything and don't act innocent, I saw you two drooling and how you were about to pounce, it's all because you're jealous of me that I have this prince who looks like a movie star, not like your Aaron, Geula, whose gut spills all the way down to his knees, or your Emanuel, Drora, whose neck is so hairy that he looks like a human street sweeper."

Geula opened her eyes wide and said, "Maybe your dwarf husband doesn't have a paunch, but he doesn't have a profession either or a penny to save his soul, and look what a shame of a home he's made for you, walking around all day long like a rooster with his crest covering his eyes – he can't see a thing and you've gone blind as well."

"I might be blind but I saw very well how you couldn't take your eyes off him."

And then Drora stood up and said, "You say your husband is a prince? Maybe the prince of dwarfs. Shame on you, having guests over to your disgusting home just to insult them." Geula stood up too, but Ruchama remained seated and said, "You've been mean to me my whole life. You've stomped on my confidence and pushed my face in the mud. All my life you and Mom made fun of me and pricked me for no good reason, just so you could feel good about yourselves, and in spite of all that I tried to make peace with you and forget how mean you used to be. But I guess I was naïve, so take your bathing suits and get your eyes off my husband. And I lay a curse on both of you."

When the two were already at the door, Drora turned back to Ruchama and said, "A curse you lay on us? Just be careful not to lay an egg too, because you look like an ostrich." And she began laughing, and Geula laughed too, and their bellows of laughter resonated in the stairway long after they were gone.

Ruchama didn't tell Robert a thing, but her puffy eyes told her story for her. "We had a little fight and they left in anger, that's all." Robert didn't let go. "But what exactly was the fight about?"

"All sorts of things," she said, dodging him. "What difference does it make?" And Robert insisted, "I want to know what made you cry. Did they insult you? Did they call you a praying mantis?" Ruchama shook her head and her eyes began leaking again, and Robert became angry. "I knew nothing good would come of it. I told you to keep your distance. Some people, even if they're your siblings, you should stay away from them so you don't catch their diseases."

Geula and Drora's diseases were quick to arrive. A few weeks after that wretched meal, Geula noticed that her neck was very swollen. The doctor said she was retaining fluids and advised, "It wouldn't hurt you to lose some weight. You're starting to bloat up like your mother, may she rest in peace, and it's unhealthy." A few days later her neck had transformed into a large quivering pillow, wider than her head.

Robert told Ruchama he'd seen Geula at the market and that from afar she looked like a stork with that sack under her beak.

"You mean a pelican?" Ruchama asked.

Geula's neck kept growing until it finally merged with her shoulders and chin. Her head looked like the top of a mushroom emerging from a large heap of dirt, or like an egg boiling in a pile of green beet leaves.

The tests didn't show a thing. "You aren't sick," said the specialists at the hospital in Haifa. "You're strong like a bull, but we don't know why your neck is swollen. Medicine doesn't have an answer for everything."

That bloated sack didn't interrupt Geula's life. She breathed normally and swallowed normally and felt well, but was ashamed to leave the house in the morning after looking in the mirror, and wore large scarves around her neck even at home.

Drora joined Geula on her visits to the different doctors and on all her tests. One of those days, sitting on a bench outside the examining room waiting for Geula to finish, she suddenly noticed that when she scratched her head, large hunks of hair fell off. Drora looked at the bundle of black locks she'd just picked off her head and leaped to the public toilet, stood in front of the large mirror and was shocked to find that her hair was falling off in heaps.

In just a few days Drora's scalp was almost completely exposed, bald spots scattered among thin remains of her once-flowing hair. Emanuel told her, "Maybe you have some sort of leprosy. Maybe you have a dangerous, contagious skin disease." He took a few articles of clothing and the two girls and went to stay with his parents.

The white scalp was slowly revealed among small islands of left-over hair and Drora's head looked like a motley poached egg. She wrapped her head in a scarf and went to look for an answer at the doctors'. When Geula wasn't getting tested herself she'd join her to hear the doctors say, "You're not sick. Just buy a nice wig and forget about it."

The two sisters stepped heavily, both wrapped in colorful scarves, one covering Geula's humongous neck and the other gripping what was left of Drora's curls. Their eyes were torn open in fear of the plagues that had suddenly befallen them.

When Ruchama opened the door, Geula said right away, without so much as a greeting, "Take back the curse you laid on us. Look what you've done."

Ruchama looked at her two scarf-covered sisters, and what she saw scared her but also brought on a wave of laughter she fought to keep at bay. Only a few weeks had passed since they'd hung out at the beach, comparing bathing suits and splashing water on one another, and now here were two women she could hardly recognize.

"So now you've made a witch of me, too?" she said.

"How do you explain what happened to us?"

"How should I know? I'm not Deborah the Prophetess and I'm no magician either."

Drora broke into a wail and said, "You laid a curse on us and now you take it back because my life is already ruined and even Emanuel is scared to come near me and took the girls away to his mother's."

Ruchama pitied them. She sat them down, poured some cold lemonade, and they sipped it, their tears flowing like the Jordan River after the snow melts down from Mount Hermon. "We're very serious," said Geula. "You have to undo the curse."

"I had no idea you were so primitive, Geula," said Ruchama. "But I'm willing to undo the curse if you tell me how, because I have no experience in undoing curses."

Then Drora screamed, "Just undo it, say it's undone." And Ruchama was a little scared and said, "All right, the curse is undone. There, I said it." And just at that moment the door opened and Robert walked in. Geula and Drora mumbled something and looked down at the floor, and Robert greeted them and went to wash up and on his way winked at Ruchama and said, "You can join me in the shower when you're done." Drora asked Ruchama, "You shower together?" Ruchama answered with a smile, "Sometimes." She looked into their eyes, feeling for the first time that it was her gaze that pricked, and asked, "Don't you shower with your husbands? You should, it saves water."

Geula and Drora said nothing, finished their lemonade, wiped their tears and got up to leave. Ruchama said a warm goodbye and suggested they forget all about what happened and turn over a new leaf, at least for the kids' sake, because it would be a shame for them not to be in touch with their cousins.

But they hardly saw each other after that. Emanuel returned with the girls to Drora, whose hair didn't grow back, only kept falling off until it was all gone under her itchy wig. Geula kept wearing scarves around her neck and hardly left the house.

"Is it true what they say about your curse?" asked Robert.

"Very true," said Ruchama. "You should be careful, because if you get on my bad side I'll lay a curse on you too." And Robert said, "You've already put a spell on me."

When Ruchama told everything to Vardina, the downstairs neighbor who was her confidant, Vardina said, "Can I tell you something very private, Ruchama?" And Ruchama nodded and listened intently.

"You and Robert, all you have on your mind is the body," Vardina said in a singed voice and a Romanian accent that had stuck in her mouth even though she'd come to Israel as a child.

"I don't understand," said Ruchama.

Vardina lit a cigarette. "You fell in love with his body and he fell in love with yours," she said. "And other than that you know nothing about each other."

"I still don't understand, it sounds a little silly to me."

"It's the truth that I've seen all these years I've lived below you, and I'm your friend and sometimes a little bit like a mother to you. You each have your own issues. You, because you're tall as a ship's mast, and he because he's short. You're both like children."

"I still don't understand and you're starting to get on my nerves,"

Ruchama complained.

"Get mad if you want," Vardina answered. "You also have a hot temper, like a little girl. I already told you it was a mistake to go to bed with him less than an hour after meeting him. You fell in love with his body and he fell in love with yours and it was a mistake not to give yourselves time to fall in love with each other's qualities and characters, and now you have a world war with your sisters over matters of the body. What do you care if they looked at him? Look how scared you are when someone looks at his body, because that's all you have, and it's time you both knew that to be a couple you need a soul, too, and to talk sometimes, and laugh, and tell stories and dream together, not just run into bed like rabbits." And Ruchama opened her eyes in rage and said, "What are you talking about? Robert is my soul." And Vardina sighed and moved her head over and over again, up and down, and finally said, "All right Ruchama, do what you want, just remember what I told you, that's not how you last. In the end the body breaks. You can look at me and my old broken body and see for yourself."

The four of them sat together on one bench at the lookout point, Ruchama and Robert, Shlomi and Hilik, bunched up and silently biting into the schnitzels Ruchama rolled into wet matzah with diced cucumber and wrapped in wax paper.

"You seem a little sleepy lately," Ruchama told Shlomi. And he said, "I'm not today." And she thought it was probably because of the reviving Carmel air, and promised that they would go to the flower show soon, where Shlomi would become even more awake and they would all be refreshed by the colors and the smells.

Robert said, "I've also felt lately that Shlomi's been sleeping with his eyes open."

"Maybe I'm a little tired because I threw up and had a fever," Shlomi tried to explain. Ruchama smiled and said, "Maybe you just miss your friend who was lucky to only break her leg."

"Since when does missing someone make you tired?" Robert asked. "If anything, missing someone gives you strength."

Ruchama looked at him sadly and took a deep breath of the Carmel air that no longer revived her spirits. "Don't worry," she told

Shlomi. "Her leg will heal and she'll come back to school, and it's perfectly fine to feel tired sometimes, I'm crazy about you even when you're tired, and you too, Hilik, I'm crazy about you, especially now for being such a hero and already feeling better." And she hugged Hilik and shook the crumbs off his pants.

"Why did you stick with that weird girl, anyway?" Robert asked Shlomi. "What's wrong with the other kids from school or from the neighborhood?" and Ruchama whispered, "Leave him alone, what do you want from the kid?" and Shlomi looked at Robert and said, "I'm not sticking with her, I love her."

Ruchama held her breath. Shlomi's words made her tremble and her eyes grew moist and began blinking like they used to. "What do you mean 'love,' Shlomi," said Robert. "You're only seven-and-a-half-years old, what do you even know." And Shlomi closed his eyes and said, "This I know." Robert told Ruchama, "He's a poet, just like you," and Ruchama said, "And I was just thinking that he turned out like you." And Robert said nothing.

The next day Robert got in the truck and went to Tel Aviv for a third meeting with a friend who had a shutter business, so he could explain to him again what he'd already explained, and especially so he could give him confidence about starting his own business. Ruchama took the forms Robert had left and went to get Abraham and Yitzhak's signatures as guarantors. Her brothers made faces at her and asked questions, but finally signed the papers.

She came home, heated the black saj griddle her mother had given her before she died and piled into it the watermelon seeds she'd collected in summer and had washed and dried in the sun. Over the seeds she poured a lot of salted water and some flour and mixed and mixed until they turned brown and their toasted smell filled the kitchen. She went downstairs and invited Vardina to eat warm and scented watermelon seeds and told her everything.

She told her about Ella's father and about Ella's mother and about the hours they'd spent together at the beach and about the shutters Robert had come over to fix and about the argument they had over Golda and Begin and about Robert's misery ever since and about the coldness and the rage he'd been treating her with ever since and about Hanna's misery, now that she was left alone with her strange child, and about the wounds she had from the camps and about the bug that Robert caught now that he insisted on getting mixed up in a shutter business, and about how Robert didn't touch her anymore and how at nights he turned his back to her in silence and pretended to sleep.

Vardina listened carefully, as was her habit, smoked cigarettes and cracked seeds with incredible speed, and said, "Can I tell you something private, Ruchama?" Ruchama nodded and Vardina said, "I have a big problem with all those Holocaust survivors. I can't stand them." Ruchama was shocked, even though she was familiar with her neighbor's statements. "How dare you, Vardina?" she said. "They're miserable people, human powder, they didn't see daylight in the camps."

"I'm not saying they didn't suffer," Vardina explained. "They suffered to their core. But did you notice that no matter what you do, they'll make you feel bad about it? Here, take your poor husband for example. What did he do? He just wanted to help and in the end he feels guilty for that man's death."

"It's true what you say, but you shouldn't hate them because of it."

"For years I've said that it's a shame they even came here, bringing all of their disease and weakness and spoiling everything," Vardina continued. "We'd be better off without them."

Ruchama was mortified again. "I can't handle you, Vardina, the things you permit yourself to say."

"I'm Israeli and I'm allowed."

"You were an immigrant, too."

"Right," said Vardina. "But we came here because we wanted to. My mother, God have mercy on her soul, didn't run away from anything. And they, on the other hand, your human powder, came here because they do whatever they're told. They were told to go to the camps, so they went. They were told to get into the gas chambers, so they did. They were told to form a line, so they did, and they were shot, and finally they were told to go get their reparation money and they took it, like good kids."

Ruchama looked at Vardina, who continued cracking seeds, and shook her head despairingly. "The strangest thing," she said, "is that you, the old Ashkenazi immigrants, look down on them and talk about them condescendingly and without a hint of pity, while we, the Sephardic Jews who were born here and who've lived here for many generations, treat them with respect and reverence and are even scared because we realize they must know something we never will, and that's why they deserve to live here even more than we do."

Vardina chuckled. "While we're on the subject of who deserves to live here, let me clarify that it's us, because we came here and made the wilderness bloom. What have all your generations made? Wilderness, that's what you've made." And Ruchama began laughing at the things Vardina said, and Vardina kept going and said through a mouthful of shells, "Laugh all you want, I just think of the cream cakes at the café in Bucharest my mother would take me to, I just remember the cherries and I want to die, and you talk about living here like it's some kind of reward. What have we got here, watermelons? Who ever heard of a watermelon reward?" Then Vardina began laughing and a seed shell got caught in her throat and she coughed and coughed until the shell came out.

"It's all nonsense," she said after she'd calmed down. "You're filling your head with nonsense about Robert's conscience instead of just opening your eyes. Since when do men stop grabbing you because they're concerned about a loan? Since when does their conscience stop their thing from getting hard? Open your eyes, he must have someone else."

Ruchama's eyes widened. "This isn't funny anymore, Vardina, I won't have you speak that way about Robert."

"I'm sorry I'm upsetting you, you know I love you like the daughter I never had, but sometimes I have to say things you don't want to hear, Ruchama, and it's not that he doesn't love you anymore, he does, it's just the way it is with men. They still love you, but their thing is looking at someone else."

"You've changed too much, Robert," Ruchama told him that night. "Ever since Shmuel died and you took the blame and turned yourself into a murderer it's like I don't know you anymore." And Robert said, "Not at all, I've just been worried about the loan and the business."

65

"You know I'm right. You don't look me in the eye anymore, your words are as bitter as spoiled almonds and you just keep pulling away from me all the time. I know it's because you're suffering."

Robert was quiet for a long time and then looked up at her with moist eyes and said, "What do you suggest?" And Ruchama said, "That you go see her and ask for her forgiveness."

And Robert was quiet for a long time again, until one day he suddenly said, "All right, I'll go over there sometime."

4

AND THEN SHLOMI WOKE UP. HE SAT ON THE EDGE OF THE RUG IN Vardina's living room, and like everyone else in the room, watched the glaring picture on her new television set. The door to the apartment was open to let the air in, because the living room was stuffy. All the neighbors gathered there, accepting Vardina's invitation, and even added delicacies to her refreshments table – coconut cones and quince marmalade squares and salty sesame cookies and toasted peanuts and watermelon seeds and sunflower seeds and grapes as tart as lemons and orange wedges and sun-kissed dates whose pits were replaced with an almond.

Hanna suddenly appeared at the open door and a moment later was joined by her strange daughter, supported by a pair of crutches, one of her legs in a cast. Vardina got up immediately to welcome her guests, made room on the sofa, sat Hanna down and said, "It's good that you came, I'm sure you'll enjoy the festival, they say this year is going to be special." Ella made her way towards Shlomi, placed her crutches on the floor by his side and sat down on the rug, her bottom touching his and her eyes smiling and lighting him up, waking him from a heavy slumber of four weeks or more.

The day before, a little after the sirens announced the beginning of Fallen Soldiers Memorial Day services in the cemeteries, Vardina came to see Shlomi's mother, her face moist with effort, her eyes sparkling and her heavy chest heaving, and said, "I came to tell you that I'm getting an antenna on my roof. You probably heard the noise the technicians were making, so I came to tell you so you don't get scared." "What do you need an antenna for?" Shlomi's mother asked. Vardina smiled with excitement. "I got a television," she whispered as if sharing a secret. Shlomi's mother raised an eyebrow and said, "Congratulations," and Vardina's face fell. "What's wrong with you, Ruchama," she complained. "Why can't you be happy for me? It's not every day that I get a television."

"It's hard for me to be happy on the Day of Remembrance," Shlomi's mother answered. "Just a minute ago I stood at attention to remember the dead and now you suddenly come and want me to rejoice because you got a television?"

"What do you even care about the Day of Remembrance, as if you lost anyone in a war."

"You're beginning to annoy me again, Vardina, with your nonsense."

"Now you've ruined my mood," Vardina said. "I just wanted to invite you to come watch the Israel Song Festival at my apartment tomorrow. Yoram Gaon is going to sing two songs, maybe even three."

"It's *Yehoram* Gaon, not Yoram Gaon," said Shlomi's mother.

"What difference does it make, as long as you understand me," Vardina answered.

"I'm not so crazy about him," Shlomi's mother added, "but Arik Einstein is going to sing too and I'm crazy about him, and that little one, Rivka Zohar, they said on the radio that she comes from a long established family who've been living in Peqiin for hundreds of years."

"I don't care, as long as Yoram Gaon wins," Vardina said and wiped the sweat from her forehead. Shlomi's mother began waving the kitchen towel, trying to blow some wind on her neighbor's face, and said, "He can't not win, if they're letting him sing so many songs it means they want him to win, it's all politics, you'd think we were out of singers in this country and only Yehoram Gaon was left."

Vardina told Shlomi's mother that she'd invited all the neighbors and asked her to prepare something tasty because everyone would probably get an appetite from the tension of the festival. Before she left she asked why Shlomi was sitting in the living room like a statue, and Shlomi's mother explained that she'd decided to keep him home. Vardina was surprised. "Today of all days you didn't send him to school? They do educational performances on the Day of Remembrance." Shlomi's mother quieted her with a wave and whispered, "He doesn't have a fever and nothing hurts but he walks around like he's asleep all the time." "They say there's a new virus going around," Vardina whispered. "It's best that he rests, and don't forget to tell him and Hilik that I have an antenna on my roof now and that if they go up to play on the roof they should be careful because it can give them a shock."

"Don't worry," said Shlomi's mother. "I don't let them up on the roof anymore ever since what happened to the girl."

"It's good that you reminded me," said Vardina. "Maybe I'll invite her and her daughter, so they could get some air."

Shlomi's mother made a face. "I don't know if the thirty days of mourning has passed yet."

"I'm not inviting them to a ball," said Vardina. "Just to hear some festival songs."

Vardina laid white sheets on the sofa and the chairs, so that the neighbors didn't dirty her new upholstery. A large white tablecloth covered the refreshments table and its edges spilled to the sides. Among the bowls she scattered the plastic roses she pulled from the vases that were set regularly atop the kitchen cabinets and dusted and freshened them with a wet rag. Whiteness covered all, and the red roses and the smell of fruit reminded Shlomi of the *Bikkurim* ceremony on *Shavuot* at the kibbutz where Aunt Tehila, his father's sister, was a member. On *Shavuot* last year he sat by his mother, who pouted all throughout the ceremony. She was especially grumpy when the high priest, a tall man whose body was wrapped in a white sheet with a small beard and a huge mustache stuck to his face, lifted a newborn lamb, bleating thinly, in the air. Shlomi's mother sat up and whispered, "I hope that lunatic isn't going to butcher the poor lamb," and covered Hilik's eyes with her hands just in case. Shlomi's father whispered back, "It's just a show, Ruchama, no one's butchering anything, and maybe you can make an effort to hide your hate for the kibbutz members, we're their guests and no one made us come." She was enraged. "Stop making me into a monster, I can't stand your sister, not all kibbutz members, and besides I think it's stupid that kibbutzes perform temple ceremonies, they have nothing to do with it."

But then the lamb dropped from the priest's arms and ran for its life, pulling the white sheets behind it and leaving the priest almost entirely naked, wearing nothing but gray underwear with holes in them, and all the guests and participants bellowed with laughter and Shlomi's mother's laugh was the loudest, and only Hilik didn't understand why everyone was laughing because she forgot to take her protective hand off his eyes.

A great comfort fell upon Shlomi. Though he felt his lips bursting again and his face as red as Vardina's, his gaze sharpened and he even giggled when he remembered the high priest and the sheet and the runaway lamb. All at once he noticed all those present, his mother examining Hanna's blue dress uncomfortably, his father lowering his eyes and collecting the crumbs of a sweet cookie with a wet finger, the silent Kurdish neighbors from downstairs who both sat in one chair and turned into one body with two heads, Ruti the neighbor whose eyes had been puffy ever since her husband was killed and were doubly puffy in the days after the Day of Remembrance, and other neighbors, loud and excited about the festival that had yet to begin, and Vardina who told Hanna, "Eat some grapes, they're a little tart but they'll heal your soul," and Hanna answering, "I'm not very good friends with grapes because of the seeds, but I like peanuts," and taking the bowl and collecting only the peanuts that didn't have shells.

And Shlomi only avoided Ella's eyes, but she got even closer and blew on his neck and whispered in his ear, "You're blushing again," and Shlomi turned his head to her and was caught in her eyes. Ella whispered, "I'm mad at you, Shlomi," and when he asked why she said, "Because you never came to visit me."

"I came and your mother told me not to," Shlomi whispered.

"I know, but you should have insisted on seeing me," Ella whispered.

"Insisted how?"

"If you wanted to see me you could have broken the window and come in."

"I thought you had to rest because of your leg."

"Who are you rooting for in the festival," she kept whispering, "Arik Einstein or Yoram Gaon?"

"I don't know," he answered, also whispering.

Her eyebrow arched into her forehead. "I hope you're not rooting for Yoram Gaon," she whispered.

"I don't know who that is, I only know you're supposed to say Yehoram Gaon and not Yoram Gaon."

She smiled. "Just so you know, knockouts like me don't like it

when you correct their pronunciation." Then she blew again and Shlomi breathed her air and knew that Hanna made her eat cucumber
and cheese and an omelet and three green olives again.

In the background of Shlomi and Ella's whispers there was a live-
ly conversation, filled with pointed looks, embarrassed coughs and
some sighs of sorrow.

Hanna smiled at Shlomi's mother and asked how she was, she
hadn't seen her in a while. Then she turned to Vardina and the rest
and said, "Just so you know, Ruchama is an angel. She's a true neighbor and has a big heart. She filled my fridge with delicious things,
with cakes and cookies and foods and delicacies that I'd never seen
or tasted in my life. Just so you know, if Ruchama opens a restaurant
there will be a line from here all the way to Afula."

Vardina looked at Shlomi's mother, impressed. "Really, Ruchama?
Good for you, but why didn't you tell me you did such a beautiful
thing, I'd have helped you," and Shlomi's mother lowered her eyes
and her head shook a little when she stopped herself from saying
anything about all the dishes she made that no one tasted until they
went bad and were thrown out.

Hanna looked at Shlomi's mother with squinted eyes and said,
"Ruchama is a good friend and helped me a lot and made sure I had
something to serve the guests at the *shiva*, but no one came, I sat
there alone like a dog." She moved her green gaze to Vardina and
then to everyone else, from one to the other, and they all went silent
and escaped her eyes, until finally she paused on Shlomi's father.
"Even you, Robert," she said, "I thought you'd come, you were the
only friend my husband Shmuel, may he rest in peace, had, and now
he's lying in his grave, being eaten by worms." Her eyes closed and
her lips trembled a bit and all around everyone froze and only the
television kept making noise and Shlomi and Ella kept whispering.

Until Ruti the neighbor got up and sat down next to Hanna, put
her arm on her shoulder and told her, "I didn't visit you because we
don't even know each other, and I never even heard what happened,
only a few days ago I heard about your sorrow and your girl who was
miraculously saved, and if I'd known I'd have come, because I know
very well what you're going through, my husband died two years ago
and the worms must have finished with him already."

Shlomi's mother raised her head and said, "I think you've taken this too far, there are children here and this talk of worms isn't helping anybody. I thought we came here to celebrate our country's Independence Day[1] with this festival, not to speak of horrors." And Hanna answered decisively, "You're absolutely right, Ruchama, I'm sorry about the way I spoke. I just got emotional because Vardina invited me and I remembered all the efforts you've made."

When Yoram Gaon sang his song about the oak tree Vardina said, "Listen to that beautiful tune, it goes straight into your heart and makes you want to sing."

"I actually think the lyrics are stupid," said Shlomi's mother. "What does the oak tree have to do with the sadness in the world? People just put words together with no meaning."

"What are you going to do, Ruchama, not everyone understands poetry like you do," Vardina said, rolled her eyes impatiently and began to sing softly, "Hu-ay hu-ay hu-ay wherefore and why," and encouraged the others with a wave of her hand to join her and Yoram Gaon in the chorus.

When Avi Toledano sang about the high mountains she said, "Toledano has a very nice trill to his voice but I don't think he has a chance because his accent is still strong," and Shlomi's father said, "So what if he has a bit of an accent, what do you care?" and Vardina answered, "Because in the Israeli Song Festival on Independence Day I'd rather hear decent Hebrew from Israelis with no accent."

"This is Israel, everyone has an accent," said Shlomi's father.

"That's right, and I have a Romanian accent like my mother's, but you don't see me singing at the festival," Vardina answered, and Ella whispered to Shlomi, "Your fat neighbor is about to explode from all the nonsense in her head," and Shlomi tried hard not to laugh and whispered, "My mom says she's actually a smart woman," and Ella whispered, "Look at her, her boobs are so big that her neck disappears and her head is attached right to her boobs." And Shlomi looked and they both burst in laughter and Shlomi's mother smiled at them and said, "Good, Shlomi, you're finally awake."

---

[1] Israeli Independence Day is the day following Memorial Day, so that during Memorial Day, ceremonies are held in memory of fallen soldiers and terror victims, and in the evening independence celebrations commence.

No one laughed or sang or commented or even chewed when Yoram Gaon sang the song about the medic saving his friend on the battle-field. Shlomi and Ella watched the grownups and saw they were having trouble breathing. All eyes were fixed on the flickering screen, and all ears collected the words describing the wounded soldier's cries and his savior friend's calming words.

When the song was over Vardina wiped her sweaty face and said, "I've never heard anything like that." Shlomi's mother said, "Thank God Hilik fell asleep and couldn't hear these horrors. I think it's irresponsible to sing songs like that in a festival that children also watch," and Shlomi's father said, "But that's life, Ruchama," and she said, "I know, Robert, and that's exactly why I'm against television. You don't have to see everything." "I'm surprised at you, Ruchama," said Vardina, wiping her eyes, "You didn't like this song either?" and Shlomi's mother said, "I was very moved by it, I'm human too and my heart also breaks over soldiers who are killed in the war, but I don't think it's even a song, it's more like a play than a festival song."

Hanna smoothed the wrinkles in her blue dress. "I completely agree with you, Ruchama," she shrieked, trying to overcome the applause coming from the television, "You don't have to sing about everything in festivals, just imagine they'll start singing about the camps and the march of death and the gas chambers ... Some things you can write poems about but you don't need music and a band and a choir."

Vardina agreed. "I think you said something very important here and that's why I'm rooting for the song about the oak tree, because it's a darling song."

And only then did everyone notice that Ruti the widow was weeping silently, her hands covering her entire face, trying to choke down the wails that rose within her. Vardina cried out, "What happened, Ruti? Why are you crying like that?" and poured her a glass of juice and stroked her hair. But Ruti pushed her away gently, stood up and said with a shaky voice, "Excuse me, I need to go," and left.

Shlomi's mother blamed the song. "Just imagine how many widows like Ruti heard this song and had everything come back to them all at once." Vardina sipped the juice she poured for Ruti. "Ruti's just exaggerating," she said, "after all, her husband didn't exactly die in the war." Hanna was surprised, "Really? She's not a war widow?" And Vardina explained that Ruti's husband indeed was an officer and he indeed died during the Six-Day War, but he died from a disease he'd contracted two years prior.

"And I thought she was a war widow," said Hanna, and everybody was quiet until Shlomi's mother said, "It doesn't matter what he died of, she heard the song and it made her cry." Vardina raised her voice, "Come on Ruchama, everyone here knows she was putting on a show just like she's been doing for the past two years, hiding the fact that her husband died of disease and telling stories to make him into a hero and her into a poor woman, so everyone can pity her and be impressed by her. That's why I could never stand her. That's how Moroccan women are, they always put on a show."

"What does that have to do with anything, Vardina?" Shlomi's mother laughed. "Why do you need to bring the Moroccans into everything, you've built them up into a plague. Ruti loved her husband very much and that's why she fantasizes sometimes. You'd think the Ashkenazis don't have fantasies in this country."

"What happens in this country," Vardina said, "is that you Sephardic Jews die of disease and accidents and we Ashkenazis die of wars." She immediately saw that Hanna was looking at her and was embarrassed and opened her mouth to say something but Hanna beat her to it and said, "My Shmuel died of heart disease," and Shlomi's mother said, "Don't mind her, Hanna, Vardina has a strange sense of humor, sometimes you'd even think she was primitive. But I know her, she's only joking."

Ella put her mouth near Shlomi's ear again and whispered, "I suggest you cover your ears, because I heard once that kids can die if they hear too much nonsense all at once."

Vardina pulled the grape bowl near her. With the tips of her fingers she ripped three large grapes off the bunch each time and put them in her mouth. A thick silence covered the room, on its white sheets and red roses and the people in it, who stared quietly at Arik Einstein dreaming about Prague in the song. The silence brought more attention to the malfunctions that were accumulating in the new set and broke the voice, and also amplified the sounds of Vardina chewing. Everyone felt bad, even Shlomi and Ella stopped whispering. Until Vardina broke the silence and said in a voice wet with grapes, "This song is a disgrace," and Shlomi's father said, "I think it sounds interesting, except that there are reception problems now and they're ruining it." He went to the set, put his hands in the space between the television and the wall and moved his fingers, fastening the connections while everyone looked at him intently. "Bravo, Robert," Hanna said, looking his body up and down, "you really do have hands of pure gold." He sat back down, blushing from the compliments, the picture became clearer and Arik Einstein's voice lost its hoarseness and Vardina said, "I still think it's an unpleasant song and I'm even angry that he's singing about Prague. What do I care about Prague? What's Prague to me?" People nodded and Ella suddenly said, "I think it's the prettiest song."

Everyone turned their heads, surprised. Shlomi thought that what went through their heads is probably what his dad used to tell Hilik sometimes, "When grownups talk children shut up."

And then Ella reached her hand to the table, took a red plastic rose and stuck it in her hair, resting it on her right ear. Hanna said right away, "What are you doing, Israella, put that rose back immediately." Vardina said, "It's fine, it's just plastic." Hanna said, "That's no way to behave," Vardina said, "But Hanna, it's really fine, the girl can take the rose home for all I care, look how many I've got, I have plenty," and pointed to all the roses she'd scattered among the refreshment bowls. "Israella, I'm asking you to put it back," said Hanna, and Ella didn't move, not even an inch, and only said, "I've asked you a thousand times not to call me Israella."

Hanna stood up, smoothed the wrinkles on her dress with one hard motion and said, "Now get up and take your crutches because we're going home," and Vardina said, "Don't go, you'll miss the vote," and Hanna said, "Thank you Vardina, but I'd rather you stay out of this." And then she went to Ella and ripped the red rose from above her ear and Ella began laughing loudly and her mother pulled her up forcefully and pushed the crutches into her hand.

"It's too bad they left like that," said Vardina after the door closed. "Big deal, the girl just wanted to pretty herself up."

"Things aren't easy for her," said Shlomi's mother.

Vardina picked up the rose that fell to the floor. She placed it on her ear. "It's actually a good idea, I feel like prettying myself up a little too," she said, which made everyone laugh. Only Shlomi stayed quiet and felt a small wave of tiredness creeping into his head.

The tension was broken within seconds, and everyone enjoyed the remaining songs and the artistic program and Yoram Gaon's victory. Only Vardina complained that there was no voting point in Tiberias. "Why do they always treat us like we're a different country, like we're in Turkey or Sudan and not part of Israel. If they'd given us a voting point I'd have made sure Yoram Gaon won for that oak tree song and not for the scary song about the war."

When they got home Shlomi's mother said, "I'm worried for you, Robert, she'll give you the evil eye." Shlomi's father didn't answer because Hilik was cuddled in his arms, sleeping deeply. He laid him down in his bed, pulled off his shoes, covered him with a blanket and gently moved a curl off his forehead, careful not to wake him from his dreams. Shlomi tried to imagine what Hilik was dreaming of, maybe *Shavuot* and the high priest running around in his ratty underwear, maybe about a crown of roses adorning Ella's head, redder than the blood that sprang from her broken ankle. And maybe he was dreaming about one of his diseases that appeared every so often and settled in his lungs or throat or ears or all of them together.

"Hilik's breathing heavily again," Shlomi's father said and sat on the squeaky bamboo chair, "and now, Ruchama, tell me what you're so worried about."

"Didn't you notice how she watched you with eyes as narrow as a needle's?" Shlomi's mother said. "You have to go apologize and explain that we feel very badly about what happened and that it's not us who gave her husband the heart attack."

"All right," he said. "I already told you I'd go, and it's not like you to think about the evil eye. Since when are you superstitious?"

And then he looked at the chair he was sitting in, and then at the bamboo sofa, which also squeaked if you moved around too much, and then at the curtains and the potted plants and the bare lamp, and there was something new in the way he looked at them, as if he'd come in for a visit from afar.

"Look, Ruchama, what kind of life is this, we can't even afford a television, and everyone already has one."

"Even if we could, I'm against television," she said.

"I want to go away soon."

"Where?"

"Argentina," he said, and his Rs rolled more than usual, "I have to visit my uncle and ask him for a loan."

"But you already have a loan from the bank," she wondered.

"It's not enough for the shutter business, I have to start big, all at once, it won't do to think about it step-by-step."

"But how will you pay it back, people here aren't rushing to get new shutters. This isn't Tel Aviv, it's Tiberias."

"My sister Tehila said that her kibbutz is building a lot of new units, she can arrange with them to place orders with me."

Shlomi's mother wrinkled her lips. "And you trust Tehila?" she asked, and he answered, "Who else should I trust? And stop it already with the hatred, Tehila loves you." She blinked behind her glasses and said, "Don't give me her honey or her sting,"

"She raised me," he said. "She'd do anything for me." Shlomi's mother nodded, signifying that she'd already heard that before. "I know she's mad about you," she said, "if you weren't her brother she might have made you marry her."

He sighed. "Sometimes you sound so much like a little girl that I don't know what to think anymore."

"You know what I think of her. It's no coincidence she's not married, and don't make me say too much because the kid here can hear everything."

"What does all your nonsense have to do with the shutters? She lives in the kibbutz and she can get me a huge order that'll instantly turn me into an empire. All I need is a bigger loan, that's all," and she got a little scared by his anger and said, "All right, go see your uncle if you must but don't say later I didn't tell you so, your sister is a known dreamer, and because of her opinions no one can stand her at the kibbutz. No one's going to let her create business, especially not with her younger brother who looks like a beatnik."

He smiled. "Then I'll cut my hair," he said, "I've been sick of all this hair for a while."

"Don't you dare." She became angry. "And don't be surprised if the day you go to the barbershop you come back to find me gone," and she reached her long arm and stroked his mane of hair and the back of his neck, but he kept moving his new gaze across the furniture and the plants until his eyes rested on Shlomi and he sent him to bed.

The morning after Independence Day the teacher came into class and asked all the children to get their backpacks and follow her to a different classroom on the bottom floor. "Ella, the new girl, broke her leg and walks with crutches," she explained, "and to make it easier for her we're changing classrooms, so she doesn't have to climb the stairs."

By the ten o'clock recess, the classrooms had been switched. Even the Sabbath corner with the drawing of a woman wearing a headdress reaching for a pair of candles was tacked in its new spot by the drawings of the seasons and the duty board with the changing names. But Ella didn't come. One girl asked the teacher why she wasn't there, and the teacher shrugged and promised to find out during recess. The girl said, "It's too bad, I wanted her to let me have a spin on her crutches."

Shlomi sat in his seat, trying to look around with new eyes, just like his father did the night before. A new look at Ella's ever-deserted seat, a new look at the walls and blackboard and at the Bible on his desk, but everything looked the same. The letters and the words kept bouncing on the pages and Shlomi was once again impressed at how the other children were able to capture them, and even managed to read aloud the stories about Abraham and Sarah clearly. And only occasionally, when the words got too wild, they stopped for a moment, breathed in, and then pounced at the stubborn word again and overpowered it, winning a compliment and a wide smile from the teacher. Shlomi tried looking at the book with new eyes again, maybe this time the words won't recognize him, maybe they'll get scared and freeze in their place, maybe they'll let him overpower them and maybe they'll even be his friends.

During recess the teacher asked Shlomi to escort her to the teachers' lounge. He walked beside her with her heavy arm weighing down on him, just like the wounded soldier leaning on the medic's shoulders in Yoram Gaon's song. "I see you're a little more alert today," she said and rubbed her fingers on the back of his neck. "I was really worried about you, you were sleepy and your head was low like the weeping willow we saw in the pictures from last year, remember?"

and Shlomi nodded but could only remember the fallen palm tree his mother mentioned from time to time. "It's too bad you don't use this alertness more often," said the teacher. "You could put in more effort and participate instead of always looking at Ella's seat." "I was listening but I had nothing to say," Shlomi said, and the teacher crushed the edge of his shoulder and whispered, like she was telling him a secret, "Never say you have nothing to say, Shlomi, because no one has nothing to say," and Shlomi said, "Okay," because he was scared the teacher would crush his shoulder again and lean her arm on him even harder.

She stopped at the entrance to the teachers' lounge. "Are you in touch with Ella?" she asked. He nodded and the teacher smiled. "That's nice of you, Shlomi. I'm proud of you and I hope your parents don't mind your being her friend." "Why?" he asked with wonder, and she made a long face and said, "Because some parents feel differently. Not all the parents are happy she's in our class."

"Why?" he asked again.

"Because," she said. "Some parents are like this and some parents are like that. Not all parents are the same."

"My mother says she's an old child," he said.

"That's because she's mature," she explained, "but that's exactly why she can help you a little. Maybe she can be a good influence because she writes and reads quickly like that dolphin that swims in the sea we saw in pictures last year, remember?" and Shlomi nodded even though the only thing he could think of was the image of the floating body in the Sea of Galilee, waiting to be fished out and onto the police boat.

The teacher pinched the edge of his shoulder a little and asked, "Does it bother you that you can't read yet?" Shlomi nodded and lowered his eyes. She finally moved her arm from his shoulder and said quietly, "Don't worry, Shlomi, the letters and the words grow on a tree above us." Shlomi looked up and the teacher smiled. "It's an invisible tree, there's no use in looking for it or nurturing it or watering it because it grows on its own and all the words grow on it like leaves and fruit and one day they'll fall and land right in your head. I promise you it'll happen. I had the same problem and it only happened for me in fourth grade. For now, just be patient and keep helping me with Ella because you have a heart of gold and the prettiest eyes I've ever seen."

Shlomi saw there were suddenly tears in her eyes, and immediately knew she remembered her two sons who died in the war. His mother once explained to him that a bomb fell on the jeep they were in, and that's why the teacher sometimes started to cry, just like that, for no reason, especially when the children in class were busy drawing and the air was filled with a frozen quiet. Vardina broke into Shlomi's mother's explanation, saying angrily, "The nerve of this country, to put two brothers in the same car and send them to die together. If at least they'd separated them, she might still have one."

On his way back to class Shlomi thought about the teacher's tears and about Ruti the neighbor who wept the night before and went home even before the festival was over. His mother also cried sometimes and his father also shed tears because he was a crrrrrrrry-baby who was born in Arrrrrrrrrgentina.

A small anger rose in his throat. Anger at all those who wept just in the moments when they wanted to say something important. Maybe they knew it didn't matter or they had nothing to say. He decided that even if the teacher directed questions at him he wouldn't answer, he wouldn't say another word till the end of the day.

Shlomi removed the paper wrapping off the sandwich his mother made him, ripped pieces of it with his teeth and swallowed immediately, without chewing. The pieces of bread with white cheese and finely diced cucumber slowly pushed away the anger from his throat. He decided that today he'd go visit Ella, and even if her mother blocked the door, even if she yelled at him in Polish, even if she cried an ocean, he'd go in and sit at her side on the bed and tell her about the teacher's stupid word tree, and that she was right when she told him the night before at Vardina's that sometimes grownups said such nonsense that it could suffocate kids like him to death.

Shlomi wolfed down his lunch with his dad, piling large chunks of chicken and potatoes and sliding them down his throat to finally push out the anger that got caught in there at school. On regular days, when his mother made this stew, he made sure to savor every little bite, taking his time, fervently sucking the sauce that was absorbed by small pieces of bread. His mother first fried the potato

slices until they browned, then fried the chicken thighs and speck-
led them with black pepper she pounded in a copper mortar whose
sound reverberated throughout the neighborhood like a church bell.
In the deep pot she seared the chicken in, she fried a pile of onion
and garlic, smiling to herself and telling Shlomi, "Don't tell grandma
Julia that I make her *sofrito* with onion and garlic, she'd kill me if
she knew I dared change her sacred recipe," and then bellowing in
a witch's rolling and throaty laughter, making scary faces at Shlomi
and scattering handfuls of turmeric on the frying onion and garlic
until a cloud of aroma enveloped the apartment and even the air
turned yellow. Then she poured boiling water into the mix, and when
everything boiled she arranged layers of chicken thighs and potatoes
whose smell met the yellow sauce and was assimilated into it. The
entire time she kept rolling laughter at Shlomi and pretending to be
Snow White's mean stepmother and Shlomi laughed too. In the year
that had passed since Grandma Julia died, she no longer swore him
to secrecy, but that smile appeared by itself whenever she raked the
chopped onions and garlic into the scorching pot.

Shlomi's father followed Shlomi's fork as it rushed between the
plate and his mouth and asked, "Why are you eating so fast?" Shlomi
answered with his mouth full, "Ella didn't come to school again, I
need to bring her our homework." Shlomi's father said, "There's no
rush, I have to go see her mother too, I have something to speak to
her about, so eat slowly and wait for me to get ready, it'll be nice if
we go together." Shlomi nodded and began chewing slowly, floating
pieces of bread in the yellow sauce and sucking them with pleasure.

"You like it?" his father asked as he picked at his plate listless-
ly. "Very much," Shlomi said, and his father asked, "Even though
I burned it a little when I warmed it up for us?" Shlomi said, "It's
even better like this," and his father said, "You're strange sometimes
Shlomi, but I'm glad you're enjoying it, just please don't tell Mom I
burned her *sofrito* a little and don't tell her I didn't eat either, I don't
have much of an appetite today."

Ruchama left the pot with the chicken thighs and the yellow potatoes on the burner, made sure to shut the windows so that a draft
didn't extinguish the flame and fill the house with dangerous gas, left
a note for Robert with the exact time he needed to turn off the stove,
took Hilik and some sandwiches and fruit and the two of them went

to Poria Hospital to meet an acclaimed ear specialist, because it was about time someone serious took a look at the boy.

Shlomi collected the notebooks and worksheets the teacher gave him for Ella and sat on the squeaky bamboo sofa while his father took a long shower and then walked naked around the apartment, looking for clean underwear in the piles of laundry Ruchama didn't have time to fold, smelling like cleanliness and aftershave, completely eliminating the smells of the burnt stew. He combed his moist hair with his fingers and said, "I hope it's all right that we're going in the afternoon. She might be resting from two to four."

Ella heard Shlomi's father's weak knock and opened the door. He said, "I don't want to bother Mom if she's resting," and Ella said, "She told me to wake her up if anyone came."

Shlomi and his father sat in the dim living room, breathing the blue air, until Hanna came and said, "It's good that you came, Shlomi, to help Ella. You two go to her room and do your homework."

Shlomi sat on her tall bed and handed her the notebooks. She said, "Thanks, but I don't need this because I'm not going to school tomorrow either and maybe the day after that."

"Why?" he asked. "I can tell that you can walk well with the crutches and we even switched to a classroom on the bottom floor to make it easier for you."

"Because the psychiatrist can only see me in the mornings," she answered.

"What's a psychiatrist?" he asked.

Ella smiled. "You really don't know? I guess you really are a little silly," and she sat near him on the bed and whispered in his ear, "It's a secret, don't tell anyone because my mother's very ashamed that she has to send me to a man whose job is to help knockouts like me who sometimes act out like I did yesterday with Vardina's rose, that fat neighbor of yours." Shlomi whispered back, "And I thought you were right and that the song was really pretty, and I also thought the rose looked prettier on your ear than on the table with the peanuts, and I don't understand why they don't send Vardina to see a psychiatrist, she said a lot more nonsense than you did."

Ella started laughing and Shlomi caught her laughter and they both rolled around on the bed, which began to squeak loudly, which made them laugh even harder, until Ella said, "My bed thinks it's a person and always has something to say," and she moved on the bed, whose springs screeched with pain, "but that's because it's an old bed. If we go to America I'll get a new bed with a special net to keep out mosquitos and flies."

Shlomi stopped laughing at once. "You're going to America?"

"Maybe. A few days ago this man came to see my mother, someone who works with her at the agency, and he explained that because she speaks excellent English they could send her to work there because what would she stay in Tiberias for, the immigrants don't want to live here anyway."

Shlomi lowered his eyes. "When are you going?" he asked.

"I'm not going, I don't even want to go," she said, "but just so you know, a lot of people in America have color television and everything looks real, not like Vardina's television, where everyone is blue and there are a lot of tiny dots, like flies. And besides everyone eats at restaurants there and if you want a beef patty you get a huge patty the size of a grapefruit and not a small one filled with sweet water, and the ice cream comes out of a machine with special buttons, you press a button and get the flavor you want."

Hanna came in the room and handed them glasses with raspberry juice and ice cubes and said, "Drink and enjoy but keep it down because I have important things to discuss with your father, Shlomi," and she closed the door behind her just in case.

Shlomi drank the juice in one gulp and Ella took the empty glass from him and gave him hers. "Drink that too, I'm not even thirsty." He drank a little and said, "I'll be very sorry if you go to America." Ella didn't answer, just took the glass from him, put it on the desk and lay down on the bed, putting her head in his lap and her thick hair covered his legs and her eyes.

"Why did your father come to see my mother?"

"I think he wants to apologize to her."

She chuckled. "What for?" she asked, and Shlomi said, "I think for everything that's happened."

Ella chuckled again and said, "People are always apologizing to her, she's that kind of person. Even my psychiatrist said so. Some people like apologies like I like chocolate and you like your brother's sandwiches."

Shlomi pricked up his ears. From the living room he heard the sounds of a radio. "My mother," Ella explained, "always turns on the radio when she talks about things she doesn't want me to know, my dad taught her that, especially when they used to argue or when she told him about the dreams she had about her mother and brothers who were burnt alive."

Shlomi asked what she did when she went to see the psychiatrist and Ella told him about strange games with different colored balls, about the drawings she had to make, how exhausted she was because she insisted on not sleeping, days or nights, about the dreams she was afraid of having if she did fall asleep, about the stories she told him with her eyes closed, some made up, some with a few small details changed. The psychiatrist asked her to repeat the stories and she knew he was testing her to see if she was lying, but her memory was excellent and she could pull all those made-up things right out and tell them as if they'd actually happened.

"And sometimes," Ella said, "sometimes I talk about you, too."

"What do you say about me?" he asked, but she didn't answer, and only after a very long silence Shlomi noticed her slow breathing and moved the hair from her eyes with gentle fingers to find them closed.

Ella slept heavily, but her head was light and pleasant in his lap. He wanted to freeze, to turn into a stone statue, so that no muscle moved, no bone squeaked, so that his blood flow stopped and didn't make sounds that would wake her and cause her to lift her head. But the sweet raspberry juice he drank moved quickly down his body and he felt he had to pee or he'd burst.

He held her head carefully, just like that soldier he once saw in a movie, a soldier whose face was sooty and whose eyes shined, who dug carefully in the sand to reveal a landmine and bravely took it apart to save his warrior friends, and Shlomi breathed at the same rate as the soldier and his dad whispered in his ears, "If the movie is scary then close your eyes, and anyway don't tell mom I took you to a movie like this because I didn't know it was a scary movie, I thought we were going to see Tom Thumb."

Shlomi was glad he didn't close his eyes, because that's how he learned to move his hands carefully and hold her head and wiggle his knees that shook from the need to pee. He put her head on a pillow, got up from the bed, opened the door quietly and hurried to the bathroom to get rid of all the juice he'd stored inside of him, working hard to hit only the sides of the bowl and not the water at the bottom so as not to make too much noise.

After sighing in relief and zipping his pants, he stood in the hallway and listened. Sounds came to him from the living room, but those were the voices of people speaking on the radio, not his father's voice or Ella's mother's. The people on the radio argued vehemently about the festival and the winning song, claiming that the dangerous song should be banned from the radio. Shlomi stopped at the edge of the hall, sent only his head forward to peek in the living room and found it empty. Only the radio spoke there, and his father and Hanna weren't sitting and talking and no one was apologizing. He walked over to the kitchen, which was also devoid of people and contrition.

He returned to the living room. On one end Ella's room, on the other Hanna's room, its door closed and muffled voices sounding behind it, like quiet crying. Shlomi stood in front of the door. He felt an intense urge to walk inside and tell Hanna, Stop crying already, your crying is making noise and it's going to wake up Ella.

Without thinking, he found himself going into the bathroom and out onto the adjacent balcony. He remembered that one of the windows of Hanna's bedroom was on the wall shared with the balcony, a small, barred window about which Ella once said, "I stand here and look at my mother through the window. It's nice to sometimes look inside and not only outside." Shlomi held onto the bars of the window and peeked into the room with one eye. Despite the blue darkness he could see his father and Ella's mother, both sitting on the large bed, completely naked, his hand on her shoulder, she holding her face with her hands and crying into them, her shoulders shaking, his hand pulling her head to him, and she continuing to bleat into his embrace.

Shlomi watched them for a long time and thought, here they are, people, crying again. Ever since the festival everyone around here has been crying. He felt nauseous. His lunch bubbled in his throat and he tried hard to swallow just to push the burning away. His gaze stuck to Hanna's nudity, surprised to find the long, slender neck she usually hid behind the collar of the blue dress, her white breasts, smaller than his mother's, with pink rather than brown nipples, and the thicket of fair hair under her stomach.

Ella slept for much longer, never opening her eyes, even when Shlomi returned to her bed and put her head back in its place on his lap. Only when his father opened the door and said, "Come on, Shlomi, we're leaving," only then did her eyes open, a smile stretching across her face. Her arms opened as she moaned and said, "I slept for so long," and Shlomi's father smiled and said, "We thought you were doing homework."

On their way home they stopped by the fence outside of Malka and Geno's house, their tiny elderly neighbors who always looked at his mother as if she were a cloud in the sky, and who, when she asked how they were, stuttered in a weak voice, perhaps afraid that she'd rain on them. Shlomi's father stood in front of a bush of huge red roses, carefully grabbed one of the branches that filtered through the fence and plucked it in one swift motion, brought the three roses on it near his nose and took a long whiff. He said, "Malka and Geno probably wouldn't mind if I thinned their rose bush a little, right Shlomi?" and Shlomi looked at him and said, "Why were you naked?" Shlomi's father erased his smile right away and asked, "What did you say?"

Shlomi didn't move his eyes from his father's narrowing look. "I asked why you and Ella's mother were naked in the room together."

"What are you talking about, Shlomi?"

Shlomi answered faster than usual. "I saw you were naked," and Shlomi's father raised his hand and slapped him, hard.

Shlomi's face burned and his ear sounded a painful ring. Shlomi's father put his face against his son's. "You never saw anything, Shlomi, you're making it up." Shlomi didn't answer, only touched his cheek and felt he had to pee again. "Got it, Shlomi?" His father kept waving his finger. "You made it all up, you saw nothing, little children like you should watch out for what they make up or they can cause a disaster, got it? And don't you dare tell your inventions to your mother."

After he peed and washed his face to calm his scalding cheek, he went to his room, put the notebooks on the desk, sat on his bed and watched Hilik, who lay across from him, bundled, his eyes shut and his ears stuffed with cotton balls. In the kitchen, his mother was telling his father about the day's events, about the long hours they'd spent sitting on the hard wooden bench, waiting for the ear specialist who never showed up, and about how good little Hilik was, sitting still and not complaining even once about the pain in his ears.

"Our life is no festival, Robert," she said, "I ache for this little boy who's in pain, I'm afraid he'll go deaf."

"No one goes deaf so quickly," he said.

"And what's with the roses you brought me? What happened?"

"I felt like surprising you."

Shlomi's mother sniffed the flowers, filling her nostrils with their scent. "So how did it go with her, was it all right?" she asked, and Shlomi's father answered immediately, "It was fine, she said she wasn't angry at all and didn't blame anyone, definitely not us," and Shlomi's mother said, "Good, now we can relax, but let me make it clear to you, Robert, I don't plan on being her friend, as bad as I feel for her that she's human powder and as sorry as I am about what happened to her husband, I still can't stand her."

Shlomi's father stayed silent for a moment before saying, "I bought a plane ticket, I'll go to Argentina in a week. I'm sure my uncle will help and give me a loan and then you'll see, Ruchama, you'll see how our life can become a festival and I'll bring you roses every day, not from Malka and Geno's bush, but proper roses from the florist in the square."

Then Shlomi heard his mother sighing and sniffling and taking broken breaths, and then his father asking her, "What's wrong, Ruchama, why are you crying?" and his mother answering, "I don't know, this whole day suddenly hit me," and Shlomi thought, now she's crying too, maybe I should also cry a little, maybe it'll help me, but not a tear left his eyes.

5

During the long days Hilik spent in bed, his body burning up, his nose running like a faucet and his ears plugged with cotton balls, he'd surround himself with books. Each time his shivering abated and his fever went down, he'd get out of bed and collect books— from the shelves Robert built in the living room, from the drawers in the bottom of the hallway closet, from the three overflowing boxes under Ruchama and Robert's bed, from the wobbly cabinet on the balcony—he'd collect whatever he could carry and arrange the books on his bed: two books on each side of the pillow and one underneath, a long line along the right side of the bed and a long line along the left – the lines met at the end of the bed to create a fortified wall around him – and two other books on his chest and stomach. He'd lay that way for hours, breathing the dust that rose from the books and encompassed him in its thickness. He'd wrap the blanket tightly around himself, pulling its ends to envelope his fort, and crawl inside it, leaving a small crack for the light to seep in.

And then he'd peek in one of the books, discover words and fall in love. Words like fire and duskiness and gloom and treetop and fig leaf and udders and evil and sourness and thrust and torrent and cleaver and darkness and annihilation, mostly meaningless but whose sound he could hum softly until Ruchama would raise the blanket and say, "You built a book castle again? How are you going to get better if you keep breathing that dust?" She'd sit on the edge of the bed, her bottom crushing at least two books, and say, "I'm crazy about you Hilik, that you're not even seven and you can already read." Hilik would say, "I can only read the words, I can't read the stories yet." Ruchama would smile and say, "That's because you keep picking the adult books and there are stories there that I don't always understand either even though I also began reading when I was very young and I loved to read," and Hilik would answer, "I don't love to read, I love books."

"What's the difference?" she'd ask, and he'd answer, "When I grow up I want to be a cover," and repeat the word cover, pronouncing the word with an extra hard k – a throaty kover, scorched and screeching like nails on rough marble, a cover snorting and gurgling with disease. "In my hands I'll carry words words words and hold them very tight so they won't fall, and just so you know, I'll be a colorful cover, not gray and crumbly like with your books."

"You're right," Ruchama would tell him. "It's about time I collected all these old books and returned them to the public library. They've been here for years and none of those airheaded librarians ever noticed they were missing, all they do all day is drink tea and gossip about the whole world."

"Today we begin the new treatment," Ruchama said after pulling the covers off and helping him disassemble the wall of books. "Did you sleep with the books all night? And why did you take your pajamas off?" she asked, and Hilik answered, "Because in the middle of the night I got warm and my pajamas were all wet so I took them off, but then I got cold, so I brought some books." "Then why didn't you wake me? I'd have taken your temperature and given you new pajamas." Hilik shrugged and looked at Shlomi, who stood in the corner of the room in his underwear, buttoning his uniform with eyes glued shut.

"You have phys ed today," Ruchama told Shlomi, "You're wearing that shirt for nothing, you need a sport shirt," and Shlomi said, "I don't have phys ed."

"When are you coming back from school?"

"I don't know."

"What's wrong with you today? You have a long face, maybe you had bad dreams." Shlomi said there was nothing wrong, left the room and shut himself in the bathroom.

Ruchama looked at Hilik and said, "Did something happen to Shlomi? Did he say something to you?" and Hilik said, "Maybe he misses Dad." Ruchama touched her finger to her glasses as if checking that they were in place and said, "All right, get dressed quickly and we'll get ready to go, we don't want to be late to see the doctor."

She went to the bathroom and took a long look at Shlomi, who stood in front of the open faucet, scrubbing his cheeks with soap.

"Why are you scrubbing your face so hard? You'll scratch yourself." Shlomi said, "That's what I want," and Ruchama said, "Tonight I want you to come with me to Mrs. Katz, I made a plan with Dad to call us at Mrs. Katz's apartment when he gets to Argentina tonight."

"I don't want to," said Shlomi.

"Why?" Ruchama asked, and Shlomi answered, "Because."

"Why are you so negative today? Don't you want to talk to Dad?" She helped him pull the towel and dry his reddened face.

"I don't want to go to Mrs. Katz-fart," he said behind the towel.

She grabbed his chin. "You're not allowed to talk that way, Shlo-mi, you're not some brat like those kids who pick on her, she's a kind woman and she agreed to let us use her phone. Do you understand me?" and Shlomi answered, "Yes. Can I pee now?" Ruchama let go of his chin and Shlomi closed himself in the bathroom.

When they sat on the wooden bench near the door of the treatment room, Hilik examined her face up and down. He especially tried to catch her eyes behind the thick glasses, the same way he searched with effort for new words in the books of his fort.

"You have a worry face," he told Ruchama and she awoke from her reveries and turned her eyes and glasses to him and asked, "What's a worry face?"

"I can see worry in your eyes," Hilik explained, "and in your lips that jump like you're chewing gum."

Ruchama smiled, "I am chewing gum." She pulled the squished gum from her mouth, presented it to him and asked, "Do you want a piece?"

"No, chewing hurts my ears."

"Do you worry because I worry?"

"I don't want you to go shouting today like you did yesterday."

"Were you ashamed when I shouted?"

"I wasn't ashamed, I was scared. I never heard shouting like that," and Ruchama said, "But it helped and we're here and you're about to get serious treatment."

The previous day, Robert went on his way with a small suitcase and a fabric pouch Ruchama specially sewed, even adding a belt with rub-ber bands and a zipper so that he could wrap it around his waist and hide the few bills he took and the many bills he'd bring back with him under his clothes.

He left the house before the sun even touched the mountains behind the Sea of Galilee, the blue mountains above which black smoke mushrooms sometimes appeared, and Ruchama would say, "The army is showing off with its bombs again, reminding them that we took the Golan Heights," and Robert would say, "It's just drills, every army does it," and she'd say, "Since when are you such a military expert? You were never even drafted," and without getting upset he'd answer, "It's not my fault I wasn't drafted, it's your fault for casting a spell on me and making me a father at nineteen." "Really?" Ruchama would say, "And I thought they didn't take you because you were tiny," and Robert would threaten, "I'll show you who's tiny," and pull her toward him and wrap his arms around her waist, and she'd free herself from his grip and giggle. "You're a big showoff. It's too bad they didn't draft you, you could have showed off from morning to night like everyone else in that army."

"What do you want from our army, it's thanks to the army that we can live here in peace and not worry about the Syrians stealing the fish from the Sea of Galilee."

"I'd rather have the Syrians steal our fish than have those cocky kibbutzniks take them."

"So now the cat's really out of the bag." Robert would put his hands together and the Rs would roll heavily in his mouth. "You're at them again, you'd think the entire army was made up of kibbutzniks. Look at that hero, Moshe Dayan, with a patch on his eye, he's from a *moshav.*"

"I can't stand him either," Ruchama would say. "He's also a showoff. It's not enough that he only has one eye, but he uses it to look behind our backs all the time."

And they'd continue to giggle and tease until the smoke mushrooms disseminated among the rays of the sun and into the bluish air over the Sea of Galilee.

But yesterday, when Robert went on his way, the mountains were still dark and there were no giggles but only low voices of parting, final coordinating and nervous farewells.

Before he left, Robert went into his sons' room. Hilik sat on his bed, a rectangle of light from the hallway marking his spot, and Robert, smelling of a shower, his long hair pulled back, creating a wet stain on the back of his shirt, sat next to him, took him in his arms and said, "1 hope by the time I get back you'll be healthy and strong and you can even help me with the shutters because I'll have a lot of work." Out of habit, he placed his palm on Hilik's forehead, kissed both his cheeks, helped him lie down and tucked him in.

Then he turned to Shlomi, who was lying with his face to the wall, still and cramped, stood over him and whispered, "Shlomi, Shlomi," but Shlomi didn't move or open his eyes. Robert called his name again, and again Shlomi didn't respond. Ruchama said, "Leave him be, he's in a deep sleep, I'll give him your hug in the morning." Robert stood there a little longer, his eyes fixed on his son's frozen shoulder. Finally he leaned down, kissed him carefully and went out into the night. Aunt Geula's husband Aaron was already waiting for him outside, having come to drive him in his private car to the airport in Lod because he had errands to run in Tel Aviv in the morning.

Hilik waited till he heard the door close and then whispered to Shlomi, "Why are you pretending to be asleep?" and Shlomi didn't answer. "I know you're awake," Hilik continued, and Shlomi whispered back, "You're interrupting my sleep."

"Why didn't you say goodbye to Dad? He wanted to say goodbye to you."

"Shut up, Hilik, or I'll hit you."

Hilik laughed. "You'd never hit me," he whispered.

"Want to try me? Watch out or I'll give you such a ringing slap that your ears will hurt even more."

Hilik kept laughing. "You're funny, Shlomi, how can a slap even ring? Those are just words." And Shlomi didn't answer and a few moments later Hilik heard Ruchama return and Aaron's car drive away and the light in the living room click shut.

When the sun already hung over the blue mountains and Shlomi had already left for school, Ruchama woke up Hilik, dressed him nicely and said, "We're going to put on a big show today." They took the bus to the clinic. Ruchama took Hilik's hand. "If after our show you feel good I'll get us some falafel and we'll have a feast," she said, and they went up the stairs and stood in front of the nurse at the reception desk. To the nurse's amazement, Ruchama reached her long arm, snatched the phone from her ear and banged it back in its cradle.

The nurse stared at Ruchama with wonder and some fear. "You're crazy, Ruchama," she said, "Why did you cut off my conversation?" Ruchama said, "Because I have to see the doctor with Hilik and I can't wait for you to finish gossiping with your friends." The nurse said, "But you don't have an appointment, how can you go in?" and Ruchama said, "Here, I'll show you how I can go in," and pulled Hilik, opened the door to the doctor's office, stood in front of him and began screaming, screams like Hilik had never heard before. The doctor stayed seated behind his desk for minutes, frozen and scared, his eyes gaping at Ruchama who yelled and banged on his desk and made the pins and rods on the pharyngitis instruments shake.

When she stopped for a moment for some air the doctor quickly said, "Ruchama, it's not my fault the specialist didn't come in, and you worry too much. Your son is a little sickly but if he goes deaf it'll be because of your shouting and not the infections."

Ruchama took some more air and then, suddenly, sat on the doctor's desk, lifted her long legs and placed them on a pile of medical files, kicking off the pins and rods and a cup of tea and the phone and pens and pencils and said, "I'm sitting here now and not moving until you get your specialist over here."

The doctor tried to appease her and Ruchama cut him off with blood-curdling screams, "God can't help you now, I'm not moving, and you'd better not call the police because I'll tell the cops how you touch all the poor women who come in for an examination."

Two hours later the specialist appeared, sour and frowning, whispered for a while with the terrified doctor, convinced Ruchama to get off the table and examined Hilik through and through, burrowed into his ears with enlarging devices, trying hard to catch the problem the way Hilik searched hard for new words in one of the books of his fort. At last, after escorting Hilik himself to a series of X-rays and blood tests, he turned to Ruchama and said, "It's good that you made a scene, because things really are bad. Your kid has a secret in his ears. They're built in a special way and can't drain themselves. That's why he has this unending infection and I admire him for being able to take the terrible pain he must feel." He turned to Hilik. "You're a hero, son," he told him, "I'm sure when you're older you'll be a military hero, maybe even the commander in chief, saving your friends, because even Moshe Dayan doesn't have a tolerance like yours."

The specialist hugged Hilik and didn't notice the faces Ruchama made behind his back. She stopped when he turned to her and said with a smile, "And you're a brave mother, and the tallest and prettiest mother I've ever seen. But maybe you should calm your doctor down, you almost gave him a heart attack."

He made an urgent appointment for them for the next day and promised to treat the child himself until he regained his health.

Ruchama and Hilik sat on the bench for ten more minutes until the specialist appeared, bathed and smelling heavily of aftershave, his shirt gleaming white, his nervous hand fastening a blue tie and his Adam's apple bobbing between chin and tie, and his eyes fixed on Ruchama, gobbling her up.

"Good morning, hero," he said to Hilik, "are you ready for our treatment?" Hilik nodded and Ruchama rose to her full height, her face leaning towards the specialist who looked up to her, his neck stretching with effort. "And how is our hero's beautiful mother?" he said and his voice cracked a little. "No need to shout today, because today I'll treat you like royalty, just give me ten minutes to prepare my device."

He went in his room, sending Ruchama another blinking look, and shut the door quietly behind him. Ruchama sat back down, took Hilik in her arms and said, "I'm so happy today," and Hilik said, "I think that doctor is in love with you." She burst out laughing and only when she calmed down and looked at him questioningly he explained that the day before the doctor smelled sour and today he came dressed for a wedding and smelling of a perfume that you could sense even through a stuffy nose. Ruchama tightened her arm around him. "I don't know how I got two strange kids like you and Shlomi, you both have genius hearts that feel things even older people can't feel, it's just too bad that Shlomi has a weak mind and can't learn how to read."

"Is that why you have a worry face today?" Hilik asked. "Are you worried about Shlomi or about Dad?" and Ruchama answered, "I worry about everybody." Hilik asked why Robert went away, and Ruchama explained he had an old uncle in Argentina and he went to ask him for help in his new business.

"How come we've never seen this uncle?" he asked.

"Because he lives in Argentina and doesn't want to come to Israel, not even for a visit, I guess he's very angry at the country."

"Why?"

"Even I don't totally understand," she answered.

"And how come Dad never told us about him?"

"Because Dad doesn't like to talk about things that make him sad."

And though he already knew the answer he asked, "Is it because his parents died in an accident?"

Ruchama looked at him, more and more astonished, as if she'd just discovered a new child. "How do you know that?" she asked, and Hilik answered, "Shlomi told me once."

"What else did he tell you?"

"That's all he told me, but I also heard you talk about how Aunt Tehila raised Dad after their parents died in an accident."

Ruchama sighed and said, "Yes, that's true," and Hilik asked, "Is that why you don't like Aunt Tehila?" and Ruchama got scared and said, "Of course not, I love her very much."

After he lay down on the white bed the specialist explained: "I'm going to put a small tube inside your ear. You'll barely feel it, but when it starts sucking the infection you'll hear a terrible sound, even louder than your pretty mother's screaming. If it hurts too much, raise your hand and I'll stop right away. But I trust you because you're a hero. You can sing a nice song to yourself or think about nice things, maybe think about something tasty your mother makes that you like to eat. Can you think of something like that?" and Hilik nodded and Ruchama laughed and said, "Look who you're asking, the kid eats less than a bird," and Hilik said, "I can hardly feel the taste because my nose is stuffy," and the specialist said, "We'll make you healthy and you'll taste everything."

He felt the heat of the light pouring into his ear, and the specialist's cool fingers, and the tube that introduced a great storm into his ears, crazy gigantic animal screams and roaring seas, waves and waterfalls and floods. All the thoughts were being sucked out and his head was growing empty, all the words he'd collected holding on for dear life, fighting not to flow into the tube and drain along with the infection into the glass jar that hung on a stand by his side. Hilik shut his eyes tightly, trying with all his might to hold onto his words, helping them in their battle against the pulling wind, words like fire and duskiness and gloom and treetop and fig leaf and udders and evil and sourness and thrust and torrent and cleaver and darkness and annihilation; mostly meaningless, their sounds swallowed in the tube's raging shriek as it healed his ears from their pain.

"Won't you at least take a bite? Maybe just one little ball?" Ruchama asked Hilik as they stood at her favorite falafel stand on Ha'Galil Street. But Hilik shook his head and kept holding onto the side of the stand, wavering dizzily while remnants of the noisy wind still blew in his ears.

The vendor put many red slices of lemon over the sizzling balls that filled the pita bread. "I only give extra lemons to you, Ruchama," she said, "because I know you're crazy about lemon even more than about the falafel itself," and Ruchama swallowed and bit into the pile of lemons and her mouth relaxed. Sometimes she'd return from shopping and pull several packed pitas from her basket and tell Shlomi and Hilik with a moist, excited face, "I don't have time to cook today so look what I got you, wonderful falafel from Ha'Galil Street. It's not hot anymore but the pita is completely soaked with tahini and with juice from the pepper-pickled lemon, just so you know this is the food of the Gods, people eat like this only in heaven," and then she'd place the crumbling pitas in small plates and the three of them would sit on the floor by the aquarium and bite into the cool balls. Ruchama would pick ripped slices of blushing lemon from their plates with her fingers and put them in her mouth lustily, and transfer falafel balls from her plate to theirs in exchange, saying, "Whoever gives me lemons will get many falafel balls! You snooze you lose!"

"Are you sure? Not even a little piece of pita?" she asked, her mouth overflowing, and Hilik whispered, "I don't have an appetite at all, I'm afraid I'll throw up," and Ruchama said, "If you have to throw up then throw up, don't feel bad, you were a big hero today."

Hilik smiled and felt his ears part from the last of the noise; suddenly they felt light and hollow and the sounds of the street and the rustling of frying slowly filled them, feeling their way in carefully, like tenants returning home after a long absence.

"And how do you feel other than that?" Ruchama asked.

"My ears feel like new but I'm dizzy," he answered.

"The specialist said that'll happen and it'll keep happening even after the treatment tomorrow and the day after that and until the end of the week," she explained, "but since you don't have a fever anymore he recommended that you go back to school, you've already missed too much. So tomorrow, after the treatment, I'll go to class with you to make sure you're not dizzy and that you're adjusting."

"I want to teach Shlomi to read," he suddenly said. "You think he'd agree?"

"What does that have to do with what I said, Hilik? And why should you teach him? What are you, a teacher? You concentrate on getting healthy."

"Shlomi doesn't have a weak mind at all," Hilik answered determinedly, and a bit of rage even crawled into his words. "He has an excellent brain and it's his teacher who has a weak brain, I saw her at school, all she does is cry in the hallway instead of teach her class to read."

They were at the doctor's office by seven the next morning. The doctor was bathed and scented again, and again his eyes traveled along Ruchama's long body, and again he burrowed into Hilik's ears and filled them with noise and sucked out streams of puss and words.

They walked to school. Hilik felt his legs walking on air and his head turning and turning even when he'd already taken his place in class. Ruchama took the teacher's chair, sat by the door and said, "I'm not interrupting, I just have to watch over Hilik because he's dizzy and it's important to make sure that he can concentrate and doesn't throw up. Ignore me, think of me as part of the wall." But the kids didn't stop looking at her with amazement, even when the teacher placed colorful Legos on their desks and practiced addition and subtraction with them, even when she dictated words with proper Hebrew vowels that she chiseled on the blackboard with red and green chalk, even when they spread doilies on their desks and bit into sandwiches whose sour smells dissipated around the class and emanated from the large windows, and even when the teacher pulled out an accordion and taught them, line by line, how to sing "The Sun is

Burning the Mountains and Dew Still Twinkles in the Valley."

At the end of the day the teacher told Ruchama, "You should come by tomorrow, too. I haven't had such a quiet classroom since the beginning of the school year." Ruchama thanked her and said, "There's no need for me to come tomorrow, I see Hilik's adjusting great," and had no idea that throughout the day he saw large red and green spots floating in front of his eyes and heard strange trickling and chirping sounds that grew louder and louder until they overtook the sounds of the accordion. The growling in his ears was so loud that it even covered Ruchama's voice, as she joined the class in joyous song.

On their way home she asked, "Why didn't you participate? And why didn't you sing? And why didn't you eat your sandwich? Don't you like white cheese and cucumber?" And Hilik said, "Tomorrow I'll do everything, today I'm still a little tired." When they got home he lay down in his bed and fell asleep and woke up a few minutes later, when he heard Ruchama growl at Shlomi, angry that he didn't wait for them and went home alone and devoured more than half the stew she'd made early in the morning, meatballs in a thick soup of lentils and carrots, and then fell asleep again and woke up again a few minutes later, when Shlomi came in and sat on his bed with a long face and sauce-stained fingers, and then fell asleep again and woke up again when he heard Ruchama's pointy voice calling from the living room, demanding that Shlomi join them at Mrs. Katz's again tonight, the phone might ring and it might be Robert announcing that he'd arrived safely and that everything was fine.

The previous night, after the first treatment, Hilik's ears had filled up again. Ruchama told him, "It's going to be this way for a few days now, every morning the doctor will suck the puss out until it's gone. The most important thing is that you don't get a fever." She wrapped a large woolen cap around his head, covering his ears, told Shlomi, "Now get up, you've been sitting in the living room all day like a statue. We're going to Mrs. Katz's to wait for Dad's call and I don't want to hear anything from you about not wanting to come," and together they showed up at the famous teacher's apartment, and she served them round cookies with a red jelly center.

But the phone didn't ring, and when it got dark and Ruchama and Mrs. Katz ran out of conversation topics, Mrs. Katz said, "Ruchama, why don't you call him yourself?" and Ruchama said, "God forbid." "You don't need to be embarrassed," Mrs. Katz insisted, "you have his number in Argentina, just call the international operator and they'll help you."

"Absolutely not, thank you, it's enough that we've been getting in your way for the past two hours."

"Feel free, you're very nice guests," Mrs. Katz assured her, and then looked at Hilik and said, "I think Hilik needs to pee, he's been sitting with his legs together." She turned to Shlomi and suggested he take his brother to the bathroom. "You already know where it is."

Hilik stood in front of the toilet and Shlomi stood by him. "What are you looking at?" he asked, and Shlomi answered, "Our roof, you can see it through the window even in the dark."

"What are you looking for over there?" Hilik asked.

"Ella jumped off that roof and broke her leg," Shlomi answered.

"She jumped?" Hilik wondered, "I thought she fell."

"She jumped, I saw her jump and I saw her bone poke out of her leg."

"You're making it up."

"I saved her. If I hadn't told her she wouldn't have jumped into the sandpile and her whole body would have broken."

Hilik inspected Shlomi's face up and down, wondering if his brother was telling the truth or making up lies. "Why does Mrs. Katz look at you that way?" he asked, and Shlomi answered, "I don't care about her or her farts," and Hilik started to laugh and said, "You're making me laugh and I can't go."

At seven in the morning they'd show up at the suction specialist's. Then Ruchama would walk Hilik to school and leave him there to watch floating spots of color and listen to strange growls. Then he'd walk home with Shlomi and give him his white cheese and cucumber sandwich. Then they'd eat lunch and Ruchama would tell Shlomi, "Try not to gobble down all of Mrs. Katz's cookies tonight, it's enough that we hang around her apartment every day." And in the evening they'd report to her home and sit by the black phone.

It went on like that for four days.

From day to day Hilik's ears drained until there was nothing more to suck out. And only on the fourth night did the phone finally ring and Ruchama burst out crying and told Robert, "I was going crazy with worry," listened to his explanations about delayed flights—it took him four days to reach his uncle's home—and told him about Hilik's successful treatment, said "everything's fine" about Shlomi and praised and exalted Mrs. Katz, especially the way she made Ruchama try and call him herself, though the international operator couldn't get a line, and Robert explained that telephones were problematic in Argentina as well.

And then he said something that made her go silent. Her face fell, her eyes welled up again and she said, "I don't believe you, Robert," and repeated those words three times.

At night, when they lay in bed, listening to the water washing Ruchama who had locked herself in the bathroom, Hilik told Shlomi, "Your girlfriend Ella came to my class during recess and asked me about you."

"What did she ask?"

"She asked why you were fighting with her."

"What did you tell her?" Shlomi sat up in bed.

"That I didn't know anything," Hilik answered.

"I'm not fighting with her and she's not my girlfriend," Shlomi said and lay back down.

"So why aren't you talking to her?"

"Because I have nothing to say."

"Your teacher also came to my class today and asked me to tell Mom to come to school, that she wanted to talk to her about you, I think she's worried about you, maybe because you can't read yet."

Shlomi said nothing and Hilik continued, "But don't worry, I didn't tell Mom, I'm not your crybaby teacher's snitch." Shlomi said, "Are your ears healed?" and Hilik answered, "Almost," and then added, "If you want I can teach you how to read and I won't tell anyone, not even Dad," and Shlomi said, "I want."

Early in the morning, when the sun's rays had just begun discovering the mountains behind the Sea of Galilee, Hilik woke Shlomi and told him, "Look what I made for you." Shlomi sat on the edge of his bed and looked. Multiple paper notes were scattered around the room, attached to furniture and objects, and on each of them was a word or two or three. Hilik said, "That's how you'll learn to read, look at each thing and see how you write its name, it's very easy," and Shlomi said, "But the letters are dancing in my head," and Hilik said, "You don't read letters, you read words."

Then he held Shlomi's hand and led him through the room, walking him between the words. Desk, chair, backrest, doorpost, window, drapes, closet, wall, lamp, woolen cap, book, notebook, book bag, ball, glove, picture, cookie crumbs, sock, socks, shoelaces, stain, dry laundry, Mom's shirt, Dad's underwear, shelf, books, library books, pants, hole, box, nail, windowpane, power outlet, electrical wire, pencil, pencil sharpener, Legos, drawing, paint brush, broken shutters, cover.

"When did you make all these paper notes?" Ruchama asked as they sat on the hard bench, waiting for the specialist who was late. "Last night," Hilik answered and bit into the date cookie she'd handed him, "I woke up and couldn't go back to sleep." "You think it'll help?" she asked, and Hilik answered, "I'm sure it will, but you can't talk about it, I promised Shlomi it'll be a secret." Ruchama smiled, brushed small crumbs from his chin and said, "I'm glad you got some of your appetite back," and Hilik said, "You have a worry face again, what did Dad tell you on the phone last night?"

Ruchama lowered her eyes, rummaged through her brown bag and pulled out a date cookie, bit into it, chewed slowly, swallowed with effort, nodded again and again and then said, "He told me he cut his hair."

6

Robert sat on the hard bench and cursed the entire world. He cursed Ruchama whose blind eyes blinked incessantly and saw nothing beyond her ugly glasses; Tehila, his sister, who'd pricked his heart when he was still soft and young and vulnerable; Shlomi, who stayed silent and whose eyes were evasive and blaming; and his dead parents; and his uncle, who probably didn't understand why he was taking so long to get there; and the fabric pouch sewed to his belt and scratching him; and this airport that stormed and rejoiced around him, completely ignoring his raging spirit and the bitter taste that filled his mouth.

In front of him, he saw a small and polished hair salon, with customers sitting on two of the three high chairs and gabbing in loud French with the barbers in their ridiculous bowties. The barbers circled their customers, clacking their scissors, cutting more and more superfluous hairs and spraying water to overpower the old style and habituate the hair to a new, arrogant look.

On his right, around a long bar, men and women sat in their finest attire, sipping colorful drinks, chatting and laughing loudly and raising clouds of cigarette smoke. One woman sat at the side of the bar, her dress blue and her hair in a tight bun, exuberantly eating a steaming white soup, dunking small pieces of buttered baguette in it. Robert gave her a long look. Her height reminded him of Hanna and so did her fair hair and thin fingers and the movements of her long neck as she leaned over the bowl. Then she looked at her watch, dropped her spoon and got up, put her bag over her shoulder, smoothed her dress and joined the flow of travelers walking towards their exit gates.

He was plagued by hunger. Many hours had passed since the festive going-away dinner Ruchama had made. The four of them sat around a table covered with large baked dough pockets stuffed with green beet leaves fried with onions and cumin; small, golden, flat pastries with a beef, parsley and pine nut center; and a bowl filled with chicken livers and spleens in hot red sauce, a stew Robert was particularly passionate about. He took a spoonful, piled it over the flat beef pastry, covered the pile with a blanket of white, lemony tahini, and devoured the concoction in three large bites. "Don't overdo it with the spicy," Ruchama said. "You have a very long trip, you shouldn't confuse your stomach too much," and Robert said, "So why did you make it? You know I can't stop myself with these things," and Ruchama said, "I didn't say not to eat, I only said not to overdo it. Eat mostly salad so you'll stay light throughout the flight. I'm sure when you get there your uncle will stuff you full of meat," and then she turned to Shlomi and Hilik and explained that in Argentina people ate meat even for breakfast, and some people ate meat at four in the afternoon instead of a piece of cake.

"How would you know?" he said irritably, "when were you ever in Argentina?"

"You told me," she answered.

They were mostly quiet for the rest of dinner. Shlomi put more and more pastries on his plate and swallowed them without chewing, and even when Robert said, "Slow down, Shlomi, you'll choke. You'd think we were starving you in this house," Shlomi did not raise his eyes to him and remained silent. Hilik collected crumbs to fulfill his obligation, his painful ears stuffed with cotton balls and draining his appetite.

When he reached the passport control desk at Lod Airport he was already getting a little hungry, though his stomach was still full, an excited hunger that made him want to pull out one or two of the pastries Ruchama had packed in a bag and placed in his suitcase, saying, "Give them to your uncle, all that meat has probably made him forget the taste of our real food." But the suitcase had already been checked and sent on its way and Robert was left with nothing but the plastic bag inside which he'd placed his passport, the flight tickets, a piece of paper with his uncle's number and address, last weekend's paper, a pack of gum and a sweater and a scarf in case the plane was too cold.

A thick, sleepy police officer welcomed him to passport control. She nodded when he said "Good morning," and began rummaging through his passport. Her eyes grew alert with each passing moment and jumped from the passport to his face and back. Robert asked if there was a problem and she said, "Please wait," and tried making a call on the black phone that was placed in front of her. Then she stood up, asked him again to wait and disappeared. Robert looked at the clock on the wall. Less than an hour to takeoff. He grew worried and his hunger disappeared.

Minutes later she returned with a tall male police officer with red hair and blue steely eyes who asked Robert to come with him. He walked him to a small, windowless room soaked in cigarette smoke. The officer asked Robert to sit and then sat across from him, placing the passport on a pile of papers covered in dense handwriting and red markings. Robert asked, "Is there a problem?" and the officer didn't answer and only kept picking through the papers. Robert wiped the sweat from his forehead and spoke to the officer again. "My flight is in half an hour, could you tell me why I'm being detained?" The officer said, "I don't owe you any explanations," and Robert said, "I don't understand what I did."

"Why are you going to Argentina?" the officer asked.

"To visit my uncle."

"What for?"

"Because I haven't seen him in a long time and he's my only uncle."

The officer blinked as if trying to remove a grain of dust from his eyes, and kept asking, "Why are you flying through Paris and New York?"

"Because that's the cheapest ticket the travel agent could find."

"Are you going to meet anyone in Paris or New York?"

"Of course not, who would I meet," Robert answered.

"Why didn't you go to the army?" the officer asked.

"They didn't draft me, said I was too thin."

The officer chuckled and asked, "Why do you walk around with long hair like a girl's?"

"Why do you ask?" Robert said, and the officer immediately said, "I'm the one asking the questions, you'd better answer because you can already forget about your flight." Robert asked, "Why? What did I do?" and the officer said, "Answer my question."

"That's how my wife likes me, with long hair. At first I was just too lazy to cut it."

The officer looked at him in disbelief. "Do you have any Arab friends?" Robert said, "Of course not," and the officer said, "You look like an Arab yourself, an Arab with a girl's hair and a South American accent."

Robert felt the blood going to his head but held himself back. "What do you want from me?" he said, "do you suspect me of something?" and the officer raised his voice and said, "Get undressed please."

Robert shrunk and froze. He looked at the officer whose curls were dense and red and whose eyes were cold and empty. The officer said, "I asked you to take your clothes off, didn't you hear me?" and Robert said, "First tell me why," and the officer said, "I need to frisk you. You'd better cooperate or I'll do it by force, I'll have to call my guys and they aren't as gentle as I am." Robert wiped the sweat from his forehead again and felt the shirt cling to his body. "Why are you sweating like that?" the officer asked, "are you hiding something?" and Robert begged, "I'm not hiding anything, my flight is about to leave." The officer said, "I already told you, you've missed your flight. If I find out you're a good boy and that you're just a midget with long hair from Tiberias we might help you find another flight, but if I find out you're a bad boy who's sweating because he has something to hide, you won't get on a flight today or tomorrow or ever again in your life."

A sharp thought crossed Robert's mind. Maybe he's being punished now. Maybe that frozen cop with the burning hair and the satanic eyes knows all he's been hiding for months. It's a painful verdict Ruchama sent him from afar. Maybe Shlomi told her, waited silently for him to go on his way with the brown suitcase and the plastic bag and the fabric pouch pressing against his waist and then opened his mouth and his tempestuous heart. And Ruchama laid another curse, like she did to poor Geula and Drora, sent a spell that reddened the officer's hair and blued his eyes, which were shrinking into an evil smile.

Robert got up and began removing his clothes, shaking and sweating, putting his shirt on the chair. His shoes dropped off as if a foreign force pushed them and ripped off the socks and pulled down his pants. Finally he was wearing only his underwear and the pouch on his waist, and the officer asked, "What's that?" Robert undid the belt Ruchama had made and gave it to the officer, who looked through the few bills of money that were hidden inside and said, "Take off everything please." Robert said, "I did." The officer said, "Take off your underwear," and Robert felt his punishment growing more severe and pulled off his underwear in one swift motion, completely nude across from the punishing, enchanted officer's blue gaze. The officer chuckled and said, "Very impressive for a Tiberian midget with a girl's hair, I wish I had one that big," and laughed with a singed voice. "Now lift your wiener," he said. Robert, whose sweat had already begun to dry, said, "I don't understand."

"I asked you to lift your wiener," the officer repeated impatiently. "Why?" Robert asked, "what do you think I'm hiding there?" The officer said, "Sorry, that's the procedure," Robert said, "Are you serious? The procedure is to check under the wiener?" and the officer said, "Depends on the wiener, I once caught a spy who'd taped microfilm to his dick and thought he'd be able to fool us," and Robert, who looked at the clock and realized the plane was taking off without him, lifted his penis in a quick motion and dropped it back and asked, "Can I get dressed now?" "Not yet," the officer said, the smile still stuck to his face, "please turn around and lean on the desk by the door," Robert asked, "Why? Now what do you want?" and the officer, suddenly angry, shouted, "It's not what I want, it's what I need, and I need to make sure you aren't hiding anything in your asshole."

After the procedure had been followed the officer asked Robert to wait in the room and left. He remained standing naked, his shoulders slouched and his breathing tired. If Ruchama had been here she'd probably tell him off for reeling like a fallen palm tree, and Robert would answer her that his treetop was weighing down on him and raising suspicions and leading to humiliation and severe punishment, and that maybe it was time to chop this mane of hair that had already reached the middle of his back, leaving wet stains on his shirt whenever he took a shower.

Long weeks had passed since the day Ruchama pushed him into the truck and made him drive to the Sea of Galilee which was throwing fish up into the air. As soon as they'd sat down on the black rocks on the beach his eyes caught Hanna's long neck and his body was flooded with heat. She sat on the rock, her legs together and her hand holding Shmuel's as if trying to bury her embarrassment inside of it.

Shmuel sprayed jokes. Everyone bellowed with laughter. Hilik slept away his disease. Shlomi and Ella, Hanna and Shmuel's strange girl, went to dip their feet in the freezing water and Ruchama questioned the new neighbors, surrounding them with careful questions, trying to crack the riddle of these human powders.

Hanna shivered whenever a cool gust of wind came in from the sea. Robert wiped his dripping nose and couldn't take control of his glances towards her. Even when the atmosphere was upset by the sight of the girl pulled from the water to the police ship's deck, even then she never let go of her husband's hand, fighting to hold on, battling Robert's eyes which swallowed her and swept her breath away.

When they got home and sat down to eat hardboiled eggs and fried cheese on slices of bread soaked with olive oil and tomato juice, Ruchama spoke with pride of his excellent hands, which could fix and install anything they could think of. She especially praised the laundry drying rack with the special pulleys he'd built and welded to the bathroom balcony's railing. Shmuel said that in America people used electric laundry dryers and every house had one in the basement and there was no need to hang laundry to dry. Hanna asked to see with her own eyes the wondrous apparatus Robert had built and Ruchama suggested he give her a tour of the apartment and show her everything his excellent hands had made.

The bathroom's balcony was dark and filled with plastic pails. Robert and Hanna stood there, almost touching, and Hanna whispered, "Why are you breathing so fast?"

"I'm looking at you and my heart is burning," he whispered back.

"You need to wipe your nose," she whispered, and Robert wiped his dripping nose and said, "I don't know what to do." "Your eyes are shining," she said, "you might have a fever, I don't want to catch it." And then her lips attached to his, her eyes closed and his mouth drinking hers, which tasted like tomato and salt.

After Hanna and Shmuel left, Ruchama spoke highly of Shmuel and his jokes and complained about Hanna. "She's an irritating woman," she said.

Robert wiped his nose and whispered, "She's not irritating, she's sad."

"Why are you whispering?" Ruchama asked.

"Because of the snot," he said. "I guess the cold moved to my vocal cords." Then he went and locked himself in the bathroom and touched himself until he fell apart, and saw her long neck and fair eyes behind his closed eyelids.

The next morning he showed up at her apartment with his toolbox, after he'd promised Shmuel to see what he could do about their shutters that barely moved.

When he walked in, the strange girl sat at the kitchen table across from a plate with a slice of bread with white cheese and three green olives. "My Israella will rest at home for a few days," Hanna explained, "and next week she'll go to school and be in the same class as Shlomi." The girl said, "Make no mistake about it, my name is Ella and not Israella." Robert asked, "Why do you need to rest? Are you sick?" and Hanna explained impatiently, "She just needs to rest, that's all." She looked at Robert with fair eyes and said, "I see you've recovered."

She led him to the living room, slid the two doors shut and turned on the radio, and again her lips drank his, her hands grabbing his wet hair, and his hands mussing her blouse and touching her pink nipples tremblingly, and his mouth groping for them, and his hands pulling down her skirt and the underwear with the small flowers and his tongue venturing into the thicket of blond hair in the folds of her stomach.

Later she told him, "Last night I told Shmuel."

Robert froze. "Told him what?"

"What we did on your bathroom balcony," she answered, "he thinks I'm making it up."

But when Robert showed up at their apartment again with his toolbox to finish fixing the shutters, Shmuel was sitting on the living room sofa, pale and angry and sighing, his large eyes shooting poisoned arrows and Robert surrendering to them like a tormented criminal serving his punishment.

Shmuel punished and punished, banged his hand on the table

and shot different rebukes and insults, about Golda Meir and stupid Sephardic Jews and democracy, and Robert froze in his place, defeated and knowing that this man was fighting against the one who'd stolen his soul.

And Shlomi and the strange girl stand on the sidelines and look on confusedly, and then they run to the kitchen to get Shmuel's medication, after he collapsed mid-sentence, and Hanna leans over her husband and yells in Polish and her voice no longer whispers or caresses, and only sounds like a broken bicycle horn.

And now her shouts filled his ears again, standing naked, his arms drooped in despair, no longer covering his crotch.

Ten minutes passed, maybe twenty, until the door to the investigation room opened and there stood a slender female officer who immediately covered her eyes. "Why are you naked?" she asked, and Robert said, "The cop told me to wait like this," The officer, her eyes still covered, asked, "Who's the one who told you?" and Robert answered, "A cop with curly red hair and blue eyes," and the officer sighed and asked him to get dressed.

She gave him hot coffee, apologized again and again and explained, "Everyone's really nervous because of the plane that was abducted and taken to Algiers last year and the terrorist shooting in Zurich, you probably heard about that." Robert said, "Of course I heard, I'm an Israeli, just like your cop, and I read the papers too and listen to the radio, and I don't understand why he had to humiliate me like that." The officer said, "You're right, and I'm very sorry, but there was a problem with the records and we don't get people with hair like yours every day, and that cop has been on duty for over 24 hours." "That's no reason to act like a sadist," Robert said, and the officer sighed again and said, "We'll clear things up with him. I'll handle it personally."

"I missed my flight," he complained.

"Don't worry," she said. "I'm personally taking care of you now and I'll make sure you'll get where you need to go quickly."

Then she held his hand and together they walked from office to office and got the paperwork straightened out, and she gave him coupons to buy food at the cafeteria while he waited for the next flight to Paris.

The officer sat him down at the coffee shop in the waiting area, placed a cup of coffee with frothy milk in front of him, along with a plate of sliced fruit and a roll stuffed with cheese and vegetables, and left. A few moments later she returned and handed him a bag with two fancy boxes of chocolates and a small bottle of whiskey.

"You shouldn't have," Robert said. "I'm not crazy about chocolate anyway, and alcohol gives me a headache."

"So give it as a gift to the people you're visiting," the officer said.

Robert told her about his uncle, the new shutter business and the loan. He told her about his parents who came to Israel from Iraq with the uncle and about their decision to migrate to Argentina. About the friction that evolved in Buenos Aires, about the frosty welcome they received from the Ashkenazi Jewish community, the big fight following which his parents decided to move back to Israel, and the car crash in which their lives ended only one day after they'd arrived. He told about the difficult life he'd led, he was only ten, and about the difficult life of his sister Tehila, who, though she was only sixteen, decided to raise him by herself and didn't answer his uncle's pleas that they return to Argentina and live with him.

Robert also told her about his uncle's great anger at the State of Israel, whose arrogance and megalomania led to the abduction of Eichmann right under the Argentine government's nose, an operation that greatly harmed the Jews' delicate status and especially the status of the uncle himself, whom his employees already hated for being rich, and whom the Ashkenazi Jews already hated for being Iraqi, and now the anti-Semites reared their ugly heads.

Robert talked and talked, and never spoke a word about Ruchama, Shlomi or Hilik. The officer sat across from him with shimmering eyes, taking in his words, her heart opening to this small, beautiful, sad man. Finally she handed him a note with her phone number on it and said, "I'm so sorry for what happened, next time you're at the airport make sure to call me first, I promise I'll treat you like a king and no one will ever give you trouble again, you've suffered enough for one lifetime."

Over ten hours had passed from the time he arrived at the airport in Aaron's car until he finally took his seat on the plane. Robert thought that, at last, despite the terrible punishment, despite the humiliation he'd felt with the red cop, he now felt good and even loved. That officer had wrapped him in her large heart, she loved him, and Hanna loved him too. Suddenly he was flooded with love, not only Ruchama's. His heart soared with the thought that he could live without her. And then he fell asleep.

When he opened his eyes he found the plane standing still. He looked through the window and saw signs in a foreign language and several airport workers whose appearance was foreign and who wore unfamiliar overalls. It took him a few moments to realize he'd slept deeply and missed the takeoff and the entire flight and the meal and the landing. A few more moments and a few questions asked of the enraged passengers next to him and he learned that the plane had landed in Rome rather than Paris. Some security problem caused an early landing and the plane had been checked and prepared for the past hour before it could continue to its original destination.

Robert was filled with worry. He was going to arrive late in Paris and would possibly miss the next flight and be late to New York and miss his flight to Buenos Aires as well. The plan was crumbling like a house of cards again, and this time the kind officer wouldn't be by his side.

Robert considered consulting the young flight attendant who was pouring orange juice for the passengers, trying to sweeten their anger, but decided to disappear into his seat and not attract unnecessary attention, so that he wouldn't be asked again to join a bitter cop with a soft spot for procedure. He pulled his hair back, packed and rolled it and hid it inside his shirt, leaned his head against the window and closed his eyes, trying to ignore his bladder which ached and begged him to pee.

Another hour went by, and then another. Almost twenty hours had passed since he had entered the airport in Lod and he hadn't gotten to Paris yet. Only when the plane was In the air, the passengers' loud complaints died out and the attendants began giving out sandwiches and high quality alcoholic beverages as a peace offering, only then did he feel safe enough to leave his seat, stretch his legs that were numb and stiff, go to the toilet and pee for a long, calming minute. He ripped through his sandwich and asked for another and for more water. He regretted leaving the roll the officer had bought him at the coffee shop. Only when he tore off a few squares from the chocolate she'd given him and let them melt in his mouth, only then did the hunger begin to subside and his body was filled with a great, uncontrollable sadness and his eyes became wet.

Once a week his sister Tehila would bring him two pieces of chocolate cake she got from Mrs. Berger after she'd finished making sure everything was neat and shiny. Twice a week she'd scrub her house, fighting through the piles of hair shed by the finicky lady's five cats. Twice a week she also cleaned Marco and Adina's house, cooked and baked for them, hurrying from their house to their clothing store on Ha'Galil Street, vacuuming the corners and helping Adina fold the clothes that customers had tried on. On Tuesdays she'd make the stairway shine in an office building adjacent to the movie theater, and then eat a lukewarm hot dog she'd buy at the kiosk outside the religious school, continue to Yiftach, the widower from the insurance agency, wash his clothes, laugh at his jokes, even those she didn't understand, wash and dust and tidy and hurry to the post office in the square to eliminate the filth people had left, polish the counters and wipe away ink stains and congealed spots of glue and sweat.

On Fridays she'd clean the studio apartment they'd lived in ever since their parents had died, cook a Sabbath dinner on the burner and fill the stovetop cooker Wonder Pot that Adina had given her with a braided challah that would rise until it lifted the lid. When Robert returned from school she'd go over his notebooks and help him battle with Hebrew. Then she'd sit at the table, shove the envelope with bills that their uncle insisted on sending them into an even bigger envelope, which she'd mail back to him on Sunday, and tell little Robert, "We can make it on our own, we don't need his favors, I'm not about to help him quiet his conscience for giving Mom and Dad hell and pushing them back here to die. I'm strong enough to take care of us and you'll study well and one day you'll be an important man in Israel." She'd moisten the edges of the envelope with her tongue and glue it shut with a proud look and then write her weekly letter to the secretary of the kibbutz, begging for him to kindly accept them, promising over and over again to work hard and contribute.

At night they'd eat together and Tehila would encourage Robert and promise that if he worked hard he'd be a great student and if he made sure to eat the food she made him he'd grow tall and the kids in his class would stop mocking his short build and his strange accent with the rolling Rs. Then she'd go to bed and sleep till the Sabbath was through. Once or twice she'd get up, her eyes glued shut, go to the bathroom, come out, wash her hands, rip off a piece of challah that remained in the Wonder Pot, chew and swallow and go back to sleep. Once every two weeks they'd go see a funny movie, and once every two weeks she'd sit him down and give him a careful haircut, wash his hair and even spray him with two drops of the perfume Yiftach the widower from the insurance agency had given her.

When he was fifteen and she'd already had her twentieth birthday, Robert would join her at night and help her clean the stairwells. He filled buckets of water and emptied them on the filthy stairs, she'd scrub and he'd collect the black water and fly down the stairs to empty the bucket and fill it up again, making funny noises and loudly singing the Spanish songs they still remembered, and she'd laugh and tell him off, "Stop running, you'll slip and break your neck." And one day he did slip, lose his grip on the banister and roll down the stairs till he landed on both hands and broke his right forearm and his left arm.

When he'd regained consciousness he was already in his sister's arms, and she ran as fast as she could to the nearby clinic, careful not to press on his arms that grew bloated and blue and saying through tears, "We're lucky you're still young and short, otherwise I wouldn't have been able to carry you."

Both his arms were in casts from shoulder to hand, and Tehila told him, "You can yell, don't hold the pain in, I don't need you to be a hero now," and Robert said, "If I yell all of Tiberias will shake," and preferred to swallow the searing pain and count his breaths, letting out a sigh every now and then.

Tehila sat him on the bed, collected pillows from the neighbors and built a wall and watchtowers of soft feathers for him to rest his burning arms on. Adina from the clothing store heard what happened to her devoted cleaning girl's brother and came to visit, carrying baskets of groceries and sweets, and said, "Why isn't he in a hospital? If you want I can raise hell there and make them take care of the child, such a disgrace, putting a cast on him and throwing him to the dogs? Whoever heard of a country that does such a thing?" Tehila thanked her and said there was no need, and Adina asked, worried, "How will you take care of him? He can't even pee by himself," and Tehila smiled and said, "I'll manage, and Robert is a hero."

She gave him hot soup and cold lemonade squeezed from green lemons and wiped the sweat from his forehead. She told him stories of their childhood over and over again to make him forget about his pain. When he was born, she reminisced, on the first day of June 1941, the whole family was distracted by the snatches of news reaching them from Baghdad, about the dozens of Jews killed in the uprising. Their mother was lying unconscious after giving birth to him with great difficulty and their father ran around with his brother, their arrogant uncle, between acquaintances from the British police and secret friends from the pre-state military organization, the Haganah, trying to discover consoling crumbs of information and find out who of their relatives that had remained in the old country was hurt. Baby Robert, swathed in white cloth diapers, was placed in her small hands, and she was not even six years old. He didn't make a sound, only opened his eyes occasionally and blinked at her.

"You were already a hero, even then," she said, "and you waited patiently for three days, until they realized that everyone they knew was on the list of one hundred and eighty casualties, and until our mother was on her feet again and started breastfeeding you, and only then did you begin to scream like a donkey."

Robert screamed for five whole days and quieted down only after he was circumcised, in a small, sad ceremony, surrounded by a small, worried family. The uncle convinced his parents to give him a name that would be convenient for his future, because they'd already determined to leave Israel and make a life for themselves in faraway Argentina. The uncle had begun persuading the parents months earlier. "They're going to build a Jewish state here," he'd say with a long face. "We came here because of the British, who are polite and cultured people who dress well and send their children to good teachers, and also because we thought no one would get in our way when we wanted to observe the Sabbath and fast on Yom Kippur. Who knew people ate each other up here and drank the poor Brits' blood, when all they ever wanted was to put things in order here and make sense of things. Who knew those primitive Communists who'd forgotten what Sabbath songs were would come in from the kibbutz and tell us what to wear and what to eat and teach us what it meant to be Jewish and treat us like we were born in the jungle with the monkeys and the giraffes. And now they want to build a Jewish state here, where everyone can tear each other's eyes out. It would be no more than two days after the Brits leave before the Arabs come in and line us up against the wall. So what did we escape from Baghdad for?"

He'd make his dark speeches repeatedly, telling his naïve brother and his terrified wife about the horrors in Europe, reminding them that his prophecies about the Jews in Baghdad, the prophecies that led them to escape stealthily two years prior, had all come true. "The best place for us is Argentina," he'd conclude. "In Australia everyone's British so they're angry at what the Jews here are doing to their brothers, but in Argentina, those in the know say, everyone's a Spaniard and most of them have Jewish roots from the time of the Spanish Edict of Expulsion and the Inquisition. We can live quietly there, with no one counting our money and no one telling us whether or not to wear a tie."

Tehila told him about their journey on the ship and about the rain that soaked their boxes and the train that moved at a turtle's pace, and about the hard years when their uncle got richer and kept complaining about Juan Peron who gave the Nazis shelter under the noses of his dedicated Jewish citizens. She also told him a little about times that Robert could already remember – their father's arguments with the stern uncle, and the night they decided to return to the place where the Jewish state had already been established and where people had yet to tear each other's eyes out.

Tehila talked and talked and Robert whined and sighed, squirming with pain, searching for new positions for his bandaged arms. Only when he was about to burst did he let her lead him to the bathroom. She'd stand behind him and pull down his underwear with her eyes closed and wait patiently for him to finish and then lean over and clean him, and close her eyes again and wait for him to get up and pull up his underwear and lead him back to bed, wipe the strained sweat from his forehead and caress his head until he fell asleep.

After four days the great pain was alleviated. Robert was able to lie on his back in his bed and sleep for an entire night.

Tehila allowed herself to leave for an hour or two at a time, make up for some of the cleaning work she'd neglected, thank her employers for their patience and go back to take care of Robert.

A week later Tehila told him, "You smell very bad, Robert, we have to wash you or we'll both die of the stench," and Robert said, "I want to take a shower very badly but I don't know how I can do that." Tehila suggested they ask one of the neighbors for help or get someone from his class, but Robert refused. "Absolutely not. I'm embarrassed to ask the neighbors and the kids in class will make fun of me, no one's come to visit me as it is," and Tehila said, "Another option is to ask one of the nurses from the clinic to give you a bath, and a third option is for me to do it myself." He said nothing and looked away. She smiled and said, "You don't have to be embarrassed with me, Robert, I'm your sister. I held you in my arms and changed your diaper when you were a baby, I clean you after you go to the bathroom already."

She took the round chair from the kitchen and put it inside the shower. Then she took off his shirt and wrapped his bandaged arms with plastic bags, tightening them to protect the cast from water. She removed his pants and his underwear and he sat down, embarrassed, on the round chair while the water poured down on him.

When she scrubbed his head, trying to choke down her quick breaths and ignore his shaky ones, she said with an effort, "Your hair is very long, maybe I'll give you a haircut on Saturday," and Robert said in Spanish, "I apologize," and Tehila answered in Hebrew, "What are you apologizing for?"

"That the thing I was afraid would happen, happened," he said.

"You don't need to apologize," she tried to calm him, "it happens and it's natural, you can't control it."

"It's not natural, you're my sister."

"It must be because of the hot water."

Then they were silent, their breathing broken and choked, and when she leaned over him, soaping his stomach and his entire body shaking, she whispered, "If you want I can touch you there, I know boys your age do it to themselves and now your arms are broken." Her face was close to his and her shirt completely wet, and her lips were already clinging to his, her tears pouring down his cheeks and her hand grasping at him and running up and down, and a moment later she took all her clothes off and he got up and laid on the cold bathroom floor and she was on top of him.

An annihilating and quenching silence fell upon their room as they each lay in their bed, trying to fall asleep and pull what had happened between them outside of themselves. Robert felt a burning nausea in his throat, but his body was filled with a sweetness that tormented him. From Tehila's bed came sounds of crying and his heart was overcome with sorrow and regret. With great effort he got out of bed and sat next to her, feeling her body contract as she pulled away and clung to the wall. He said, "I'm sorry, Tehila," and she said through tears, "I have to kill myself now," He said, "I promise to forget everything," and she said, "I deserve to die for what I did." He placed one bandaged hand on her. Streams of pain pounded through him and he said, "Don't talk that way, you're the only one I've got," and she cried and shrunk again and he laid beside her and whispered in her ear, "I love you and I don't care about anything," and she let him kiss her wet face and rub up against her with his penis that was hardening and again they became entangled and moved in a storm, sucking each other in, until a silence annihilated the room again.

The next day Tehila got up, left without a word and never returned to the small studio. That very morning she went to the kibbutz and showed up at the office of the secretary to whom she'd sent begging letters every week. The secretary listened patiently to her prayers, gave her water when she wailed, and finally agreed to accept her for a trial period.

Robert waited for her in their apartment for an entire day, pale with worry and his entire body taut and aching, until at night Adina appeared and told him that Tehila had phoned from the kibbutz and announced that she'd moved there and wouldn't come in to clean the clothing store anymore. Adina tried to get explanations from Robert, but he sat silent and after she'd left took a kitchen knife and began taking apart, piece by piece, the cast that had entrapped him, until he felt that he could move his arms enough to eat and drink and clean himself. Two weeks later he'd taken the rest of the cast off, left his apartment and visited each of Tehila's regular employers, asking to take her place. Adina reprimanded him for endangering his arms and not letting the bones heal properly, but agreed to hire him and even ordered more and more work from him. He built new shelves for the store and fixed the vents and painted the changing rooms and replaced the electric wires that had decayed. Adina would make him eat from the boxes that came every day at noon from the restaurant next door, filled with steaming, overly-spiced dishes, and would praise and laud his vigor and say again and again, "I've never seen a man break his bones and get such good hands."

A year passed before they had a chance meeting on Ha'Galil Street. Tehila told him that she was a full member now, everyone voted in her favor at the member council. Robert showed her the truck he'd bought for almost nothing from Yiftach the widower and told her that he worked as a handyman and made enough money and no longer went to school. Tehila said, "I see you've stopped cutting your hair, too," and Robert smoothed the mane of hair that almost touched his shoulders and said, "I didn't have time, maybe I'll go this Friday." Tehila said, "How can you drive a truck, you're barely sixteen," and Robert said, "This is Tiberias, no one asks questions, everyone knows I do it to make a living." They said nothing about what had happened before they parted ways and made a plan to meet once in a while, and Robert promised to visit her at the kibbutz.

In the heart of the Paris airport, across from a chatty hair salon and a busy bar, Robert sat on a bench and cursed the entire world. Over forty hours had passed since he went on his way and his journey already seemed to be taking forever. When the delayed plane had finally landed in Paris, Robert clung to the young flight attendant and begged her for help. She escorted him to an office and left him there, impatient. He sat there for hours, waiting until a solution was found and his itinerary was reestablished. In a moment of despair he asked the clerk about canceling the entire trip and returning to Israel, but the clerk encouraged him and even offered to let him rest for a few hours in one of the nearby hotels. Robert refused and remained sitting there, punished and rebuked until a way was found – ten more hours waiting for a plane that would stop in Toronto for an hour and then continue straight to Buenos Aires.

After things had been settled and his updated tickets were in his hands, Robert exchanged one of the few bills he'd packed in the fabric pouch into local currency, made some change and called his uncle to announce his delay. The uncle slowly wrote down the new details and the coins were quickly swallowed and pushed his already low spirits even lower. He cancelled his plan to call Mrs. Katz and ask her to calm Ruchama and also decided to forego the coffee and sandwich he was going to buy to quiet the thirst and hunger that bothered him. In his mind's eye, he could see Ruchama sitting by the black phone in Mrs. Katz's living room, her face taut with worry and her glasses covering with dirty fog. A great anger filled him.

The day before he went on the unending journey, he and Ruchama stood in the bedroom, Ruchama folded his clothes and he carefully arranged them in the suitcase.

"Vardina told me a while ago that all we have, you and I, is the body," she said with an awkward smile.

"Your Vardina is full of nonsense as usual, one day she'll explode she's so full of it."

"Don't disrespect her, Robert, she's a smart woman and lately I've been feeling she might be right."

Robert grew alert. "Why?" he asked. "What's happened lately?" and Ruchama said, "You hardly come to me like you used to." Robert said, embarrassed, "It's because my head is full of shutters," and Ruchama said, "I look at you and see only a body, and I love your body but I don't know anything else about you, I don't even know if you have a soul and what it looks like."

"Vardina's made baba ghanoush of your brains," he said, trying to restrain his anger.

"Why don't you think about it before you reject it," she answered, "because I'm talking about what I feel now, not about Vardina."

They continued to arrange the clothes silently and Robert thought that maybe she was right. When he met Hanna, he felt Ruchama being pulled away from him all of a sudden, just like when he'd met Ruchama and the sight of her body on the blue bedspread in the attic in Haifa completely erased the memory of Tehila's touch. The hole that had opened inside of him when his sister left for the kibbutz was instantly filled and was overflowing with Ruchama. When they rode his truck to the kibbutz to give Tehila a wedding invitation and introduce the two, his heart beat so fast that he almost lost control of the wheel and veered out of his lane. Ruchama said, "You're pale, stop worrying, I'm sure I'll love your sister," and Robert nodded and didn't tell her that the worry that had filled him was for his own heart, not hers, that he feared that the moment the two of them would stand before him his heart would skip back to Tehila and a hole would again open within him and Ruchama would be pulled out of him. When Ruchama went to the bathroom and he was left alone with his sister in her room in the kibbutz, she looked straight at him with moist eyes and said, "You needed a huge woman to erase me, but I, even if I meet Og, King of Bashan, I won't be able to erase you, and for that I can never forgive you and I can never forgive myself."

When she was finished balling the socks and underwear and stuffing them in the corners of the suitcase, Ruchama asked, "What exactly happened there with Hanna?" and Robert became alert again and said, "I already told you, I apologized and she said she wasn't angry and didn't blame anyone."

"I mean with Shlomi," Ruchama said. "What happened to him there? Ever since the two of you returned his mouth has been shut and his eyes are on the floor."

"He played with Hanna's girl and nothing happened," Robert answered.

"So why is he acting this way?"

"Don't know," he said. "I wish I understood why he's even glued to that strange girl and why he doesn't have any other friends. He's always shut inside the apartment or he goes to her apartment instead of playing outside with normal friends," and Ruchama said as she closed the suitcase with her long arms, "Most kids stay indoors, we only think that normal kids play outside. I think if you checked you'd find that most kids don't even have friends. Childhood is a shitty thing you just have to go through as quickly as possible."

These words floated in his thoughts and strengthened his anger at Ruchama. All at once he got up from the hard bench, pulled a bill out of the tight fabric pouch, walked quickly to the salon that was already empty of customers, and sat on one of the chairs. A barber with a purple bowtie looked at him imploringly and Robert pointed to the scissors and then undid his long mane, which had still been rolled and packed underneath his shirt. The barber widened his eyes at the thick hair that draped all the way to the middle of Robert's back. He frowned and protested loudly, in French. Then he tried using sign language, holding Robert's hair and looking impressed, begging not to destroy the spectacular mane that had accumulated on his head for over ten years. But Robert insisted and pushed the bill into one of the barber's hands and the scissors into the other.

A few minutes later he stood in front of the mirror in the public bathroom and inspected his new head with satisfaction, buzzed and leveled and perfumed. Tiny strands stuck to his back and the back of his neck and created an irritating itch. Sticky sweat collected on his body during the countless hours of waiting and humiliation and delays and pleas. It was night; the airport was almost empty of people, the bathroom stall spacious and vacated and the stream of water raising a warm steam that awoke in him a yearning. Robert took the sweater out of the plastic bag, put it on the corner of the sink, opened the pouch, which now contained only one bill he'd use in a moment to buy himself a nice meal, removed all of his clothes, grabbed handfuls of warm water and began washing his body, soaking his new head, squeezing more and more soap from the dispenser near the sink, scrubbing his shoulders and neck and stomach and armpits and his penis that had hardened a bit, giving himself a thorough cleaning.

He dried his body scrupulously, tearing off more and more paper towels, folded the shirt and placed it in the plastic bag and put on the sweater. Then he tore off more paper towels and dried the puddle of water that collected on the floor as best he could. Bathed and buzzed, he looked at himself and said aloud, "That's it, Ruchama, you won't see that crest on my head anymore and no one will call me a Tiberian midget with hair like a girl's. You can scream and rage and threaten all you want."

Many hours passed until he finally presented himself at the door to his old uncle's house, and then he broke out in wild, bitter cries, his tears wetting his uncle's shirt as he hugged him and cried as well. And many more days passed, more than what he'd planned when he left Israel, before he came home, the pouch tied to his waist concealing many bills.

7

AT NIGHT SHLOMI DREAMED OF MANY PAPER NOTES INSCRIBED with Hilik's words. The paper notes fell and gathered and finally stuck to his fingers. The words stained him until they were absorbed completely, without a trace.

When he woke up he moved his fingers and felt that they were sticky. He sat up in bed, wiping his hands on the blanket. Hilik was still asleep, cuddled among his crumbling books, his mouth open and his breath rising and falling through a quiet wheezing. All the paper notes that had filled their room in the previous weeks were collected the night before by Ruchama, who said, "I've had enough of these paper notes, the walls and the furniture are covered in glue stains."

After she turned off the lights and left, Shlomi told Hilik, "I'm not calling her Mom anymore." Hilik asked, "Why?" and Shlomi said, "If you stuck a note to her, what would the note say – Mom or Ruchama?" and Hilik laughed and said, "How can I stick a note on Mom? You think she'd let me?" Shlomi said, "Starting tomorrow I'm calling her Ruchama and when Dad gets home I'm calling him Robert, that's what I want." "They'll get mad," Hilik said worriedly, and Shlomi answered, "I don't care, it's stupid, just imagine that I called you Boy or Brother, anyone can be a brother but only you can be Hilik and that's why I call you Hilik and that's why, starting tomorrow, I'm calling them Ruchama and Robert."

After he finished bathing, combing his hair and putting on the school uniform, Shlomi stood in the kitchen and said, "Starting today I'm calling you Ruchama and when Dad comes home I'm calling him Robert." Ruchama asked, "Why?" and Shlomi answered, "That's what I want."

"You've said that's what you want too many times lately," she said, "you're becoming a little brat and I'm not crazy about you at all."

"That's what I want," Shlomi repeated, "you're Ruchama and he's Robert, those are your names and that's it."

"I don't have any patience for you, Shlomi," she said, "call me whatever you want, you can call me Golda for all I care, just leave me alone."

"I won't call you Golda because you're not Golda, I'll call you Ruchama."

And Ruchama said, "Fine," and put a sandwich with white cheese and finely diced cucumber wrapped in wrinkled wax paper in his lunch box and said, "Don't forget to put the wax paper back in your lunch box, it's expensive and I can't afford to buy new paper every time."

At school, Shlomi sat in his place and watched the crybaby teacher and the other children, some of them rehearsing for the end-of-the-year play, others drawing happy pictures about the experiences they were going to have over the approaching summer, pictures of multicolored popsicles and ice cream cones, pictures of multi-shaped balloons, pictures of the beach with parasols and small boats where Moms and Dads and smiling children sailed. When the teacher asked him, "Why aren't you drawing?" Shlomi answered, "I don't have anything to draw." The teacher tried to entice him and said, "That's too bad, Shlomi, you're very talented in art, why don't you draw us a beautiful beach with a sand castle." Shlomi said, "There's no sand in the Sea of Galilee, only rocks," and the teacher smiled and suggested, "Then draw a rock castle."

Shlomi didn't answer and his face burned when he saw Ella standing in the corner with the other kids in the play, sending him an angry look. Then he got up, took his bag and moved to the last seat by the window.

The teacher came up to him immediately. "Why did you sit here, Shlomi?" she asked.

"This place is free because Ofir didn't come to school today," he answered.

"But I didn't give you permission to sit here, did I? Then why are you sitting here without my permission?"

"That's what I want," Shlomi answered, and the teacher shook her head, sighed loudly and returned to the play participants.

During recess, he sat on the stone wall by the drinking fountain and finished his sandwich in two bites, scrunched the wax paper into a tiny ball and flicked it into the nearby trash can. A moment later Hilik was by his side, handing him his own sandwich, which Shlomi also gobbled down in two bites and whose paper he also threw out.

"Mom will be angry at us for not bringing the paper back," Hilik said.

"I forgot we had to," Shlomi said. "When the bell rings I'll take the paper out of the trash."

"They'll find out you've been eating out in the yard instead of at your desk."

"I don't care, I want to eat here."

"Our neighbor asked me again to ask you to talk to her."

Shlomi didn't answer and Hilik shrugged and left. A moment later Ella stood in front of him.

"At least explain why you're fighting with me," she said. "Did I do something wrong?"

Shlomi didn't answer again.

"So I guess you're fighting with me because you're stupid and an ass and lazy and ugly and your head is dumb and numb and made of gum."

Shlomi didn't even raise his head, only focused his eyes on a drop of water that collected at the edge of the rusty faucet, swelling until it fell and crashed into the basin and made room for the next one.

Ella sat next to him and said, "My mom said to ask if you know when your dad is getting back." Shlomi's throat contracted for a moment. He looked at her and said, "Tell her it's none of her business." Ella said, "At least you're talking, I thought you'd swallowed your stupid tongue," and Shlomi said, "You're stupid." Ella said, "I thought you loved me, you promised me things, you promised you'd come to me and be with me and you didn't do it," and he said, "So what, that's what I want."

They both stared at the drop of water renewing on the edge of the faucet until Ella said, "Two weeks ago your dad called my mom." Shlomi pulled his eyes from the faucet, looked at Ella and said, "How is that possible, you don't even have a phone," and Ella said, "He called her when she was at work at the agency."

"Why?" he asked.

"He asked her if she wanted him to bring us milk jam."

"What's milk jam, that's not a thing."

"There's milk jam in that place your dad is in. There are all sorts of strange places where they make strange jams, once I even heard of jam they make out of eggplants and jam they make from tomatoes and roses."

"You're making it up," Shlomi said.

"I'm willing to swear so you'll believe me," she answered.

"Why would my dad bring you jam? Who are you, anyway?" he grumbled.

"Maybe he bought a lot of jam and wants to give it to people he knows, and he knows my mom very well."

His throat contracted again and Ella said, "One time I even saw them naked together. I peeked through the living room doors." She smiled. "They were naked on the sofa and your father put his thing inside my mother."

Then Shlomi raised his hand and slapped Ella, hard. A surprised Ella put her hand on her stinging cheek. Her burning eyes fixed on Shlomi and her mouth was open. Shlomi whispered, "You didn't see anything like that, Ella, you're making it up, you're a bad, old child who makes stuff up."

When the bell rang, she wasn't sitting next to him anymore. He got up tiredly from the stone wall, his hand burning, pulled the wax paper balls from the trash can and went back to class. He sat in Ofir's seat again, and this time the teacher only looked at him and returned to the other children. Shlomi smoothed the wax paper, shook off the crumbs, folded it carefully and put it in his lunch box. Ella sat in silence, her hand still on her cheek and her eyes shining. The kids around them tried on their costumes and others tacked their cheerful drawings to the walls. Ella pulled a pen from her bag and began drawing on her cheek, tracing her hand with a blue line. When she was done she moved her hand and a drawing delineating the red mark of his slap remained. The teacher looked at her with wonder and said, "What are you doing, Ella? Why are you drawing on yourself?" and Ella said, "That's what I want." The teacher looked at Shlomi and Ella and spoke to both of them. "I guess you decided to drive me crazy today. Did something happen? Why don't you explain why you're acting this way?" and they were both silent.

"Why are you walking so fast?" Hilik asked Shlomi on their way back home, trying to keep up with his brother, "you're almost running." Shlomi said, "I'm starving, my stomach is sticking to my back," and kept walking quickly, avoiding Ella's looks as she walked silently behind them, the tracing of his hand still on her cheek and her eyes pricking his back. He grabbed Hilik's arm and pulled him forward, helping him keep up, ignoring his strained breaths.

"Why are you running from her?" Hilik asked. "What did she do to you? And why does she have a drawing of a hand on her face?" and Shlomi sent a quick look back, recoiling from her fiery eyes, pulled Hilik's bag and said, "I'll carry your bag, that way it'll be easier for you and we'll get home soon and Ruchama will give us *sofrito* and my stomach will relax."

A few yards from their building, Hilik bumped into a stone and fell flat on the ground. Shlomi had to stop his flight and help Hilik get up and shake the dust off his clothes. Ella stood at a distance, her eyes and lips pursed and the drawing on her cheek melting into the blush and sweat. She dropped her bag on the path and said, "You can't run away from me, and you'll pay for what you did." Then she picked up a stone and threw it hard towards Shlomi. The stone cut through the distance between them, drawing an arc of dry dirt clumps through the air until it landed on Hilik's shoulder. He let out a small cry of pain and grabbed his shoulder. Ella grabbed her bag and ran off, jumping over the stone wall she was sitting on when Shlomi invited her to come see the Sea of Galilee throw fish up in the air.

Shlomi leaned over Hilik and pulled his shirt gently, revealing a red bruise adorning his shoulder. Hilik choked down the tears and said, "Don't worry, it doesn't hurt too much and I won't tell Mom anything," and Shlomi said, "She threw it at me but she's an idiot and she hit you by accident instead of me. I'm very sorry,

Hilik." Hilik said, "I know, it's not your fault." Shlomi said, "Wait and see, I'll get back at her," and Hilik said, "You don't have to get back at her because of me," and Shlomi said, "Yes I do."

Ruchama sat at the kitchen table, her eyes red, the edges of her glasses covered in steam and two plates across from her, one filled with a pile of rice and the other with a pile of brown lentils. She looked at Shlomi who stood in front of her and asked where Hilik was. Shlomi looked at the piles of rice and lentils and said Hilik went to the bathroom. "Straight to the bathroom? Without saying hello?" she asked, "What's wrong, does his stomach hurt?" Shlomi shrugged and kept looking at the piles.

"Why didn't you make *sofrito?*" he asked.

"How do you know I didn't?" she asked back.

"Because there's no smell. On Mondays it always smells like *sofrito*," he said sadly.

"I didn't make it today, we'll eat something else."

"Why?"

"I don't owe you any explanations, Shlomi, you'll eat what I give you."

"My stomach is sticking to my back."

"I need you to help me sift through the rice and the lentils, my eyes are burning today and I can't cook them without sifting first."

Shlomi washed his hands in the kitchen sink and sat at the table. "You do the rice and Hilik can do the lentils," Ruchama said and wiped her moist eyes with her hands. "It's a lot harder to sift through the rice, and you have to watch Hilik so he doesn't leave any grit that'll break our teeth."

Shlomi and Hilik sifted quietly, their fingers digging through the piles of rice and lentils, transferring them grain by grain to the corner of the plate and pushing away sand and damaged grains. Ruchama sat in the living room, frozen and still. Shlomi whispered to Hilik, "How's your shoulder?" and Hilik whispered, "It doesn't hurt anymore, but there's a black and blue mark, I'll tell Mom I fell during recess." Hilik pricked up his ears when heavy steps sounded from the stairway and said, "It must be Vardina, she walks like an elephant," and a moment later the door opened and Vardina walked in, huffing and puffing, two cups of steaming coffee in her hands. She put one of them in front of Ruchama, sat across from her on the squeaky bamboo chair and said, "I brought you some coffee, I hope you'll at least let me give you that."

Ruchama looked at the cup without moving. Vardina sighed and said, "You're so stubborn, like a mule, at least send your kids over to have lunch, you want them to starve?" and Ruchama said, "I'll manage, I still have some rice and lentils, I'll make them *mejadara*." Vardina widened her eyes. "That's what you'll give them? Rice and lentil stew? Poor man's food?" and Ruchama went silent again.

Vardina tasted her coffee. "Did you talk to Baruch?" she asked.

"I have nothing to talk to him about," Ruchama answered, "he said he won't let me use my grocery tab anymore and he doesn't want to see my face again until I pay my debt. What do I have to talk to him about?"

Vardina sighed again and said, "So why won't you let me give you a small loan, you can pay me back when Robert returns," and Ruchama answered, "I've taken enough from you." Vardina said, "I don't understand him, doesn't he know the money he left you is gone? How can he just leave like that and not come back, he could at least send you some money from there."

"Enough, Vardina, I'll start crying again, my eyes are spent."

"At least drink the coffee, get some liquid back after shedding all those tears," Vardina beseeched her and pushed the cup into Ruchama's hands.

Ruchama sipped the coffee that was already lukewarm. The two sat like that, quietly, for a few more minutes, only the sounds of Vardina sucking the coffee and Ruchama swallowing deeply broke the silence.

Before she left Vardina said, "I don't know what to do about my legs anymore," and she raised her dress a little to reveal swollen knees. "If only the Kurds from downstairs were willing to switch apartments with me, I could live on the first floor, it would be easier for me to climb the stairs and I wouldn't suffer so much." Ruchama looked at Vardina's bare knees and said, "I don't care that he's staying longer, I know he'll come back soon and open his business and everything will be okay. What I don't understand is why he decided to cut his hair all of a sudden." Vardina dropped the edges of her dress and said, "You're thinking of nonsense."

After Vardina left, Ruchama got up, complimented Shlomi and Hilik on their help, washed the rice and lentils well, drained the water, chopped a small onion that was left in the basket, fried it with some oil and cooked everything until the mix softened and absorbed all the water and salt. She took only one large spoonful for herself and gave the kids the rest. They ate the rice with gusto, the lentils and onions having melted into it and filled it with the salty taste of wet dirt. While he chewed and swallowed many questions ran around in Shlomi's head – why was Robert held up, why was Ruchama crying and mourning over his haircut, why did Robert call Ella's mother, why did he waste money on milk jams instead of sending it to them, what will they eat tomorrow instead of Tuesday's beef patties, what will they eat instead of Wednesday's smelly fish and yellow rice?

At dusk, Vardina's elephant steps echoed in the stairway once more. She came in and without a word sat in the kitchen and placed a large jar full of a yellowish substance on the table.

"What is that?" Ruchama asked.

"Mayonnaise."

"I know it's mayonnaise," Ruchama said impatiently, "but why did you bring it?"

"Because I found you some work," Vardina answered, "so enough sitting at home and crying over your husband's haircut, it's time you got up and took care of your children, I'm sick of hearing you whine, that's not the Ruchama I know."

Ruchama twisted her lips with disbelief. "What job are you blabbing about?" she asked.

Vardina smiled, "I went to town to get long socks to warm my knees, and I met Adina at the clothing store, you know her?"

"Of course I know her," Ruchama answered, "Robert used to work for her, everyone shops at her store."

Vardina lifted her dress to show Ruchama the thick socks she bought and said, "Those are quality socks, they hold my fat legs nice and tight, maybe they won't hurt so bad now."

"I don't see what your socks have to do with a job, is that why you brought mayonnaise? What does mayonnaise have to do with socks?"

"You're so impatient, Ruchama," Vardina shouted. "Hear me out and then talk."

Vardina let the edges of her dress fall back into place and hide her legs that were embalmed in the new socks and said, "Adina told me they were having a henna ceremony before her granddaughter's wedding tomorrow, and they'll have around a hundred guests. She ordered food for a hundred and twenty people from the restaurant next to her store, but today municipal inspectors shut the place down because they found mice in the yard where they throw their trash. Long story short, Adina and Marco are in trouble, so I suggested she ask you to cook, you're known for the food you sometimes make for events, and she agreed. She'll pay you very well, she has no shortage of money, what with all those overpriced socks."

Ruchama wrinkled her forehead, her eyes began blinking incessantly. "But how will I cook for a hundred and twenty people in one day?" she asked in a cracked voice, and Vardina answered, "I'll help you and the kids will help you."

"But how will I get all the shopping done and carry everything?"

"Adina will send her Arab workman," Vardina answered, proud for having thought in advance of every hitch and having found solutions. "You just have to make a list of everything you need, meat and chicken and vegetables and oil and flower and dishes, Adina's workman will be here in an hour to pick up the list and he'll get you everything by tomorrow morning."

A scared Ruchama looked at Vardina, her eyes working hard to stop the burst of blinking.

"Stop looking at me like a chicken at a slaughterhouse," Vardina shouted. "A little gumption and you'll be on your feet in no time."

"So why did you bring this mayonnaise?" Ruchama asked.

Vardina smiled secretively. "The only thing Adina asked is that you serve modern food," she said. "Adina said she ate once at an event you catered and that the food was good but too traditional. She wants to treat her guests to some modern food. She has people coming especially from Haifa and even from Tel Aviv, she can't afford to serve them home cooking, it has to be modern, classic elegant food like they serve at wedding halls, and not too spicy,"

Ruchama shook her head. "What's modern wedding hall food? How should I know? When did I ever eat at a wedding hall?" she asked, and Vardina said in a calming voice, "I told Adina to count on me, that I'd teach you exactly what to do." Ruchama laughed in desperation. "You'll teach me? How? You can hardly crack an egg, when you make patties they fall apart in the oil and turn into mush, since when are you and Adina such close friends that she trusts you, what a pair, Vardina and Adina."

Vardina frowned. "Do you want to insult me now or do you want to let me help solve the problems your bratty husband left you?"

Ruchama went quiet and lowered her eyes. Vardina took a deep breath and continued. "All you need to do is make what you know, and when you're done just add a few tablespoons of mayonnaise, and that's it." Ruchama raised a questioning look to her and Vardina explained, "Trust me, my patties may turn into mush but I know modern food, and that's the whole secret in event halls, they make eggplant salad and add mayonnaise, they make charred peppers and add mayonnaise, they make spicy carrots and add mayonnaise, and they do the same to the red beets and the egg salad and the white coleslaw and the red coleslaw, you name it. You can even make something up. Two years ago I was at a wedding and they served a salad made from chopped celery mixed with slices of sour apples and canned pineapple and they poured a bunch of mayonnaise and raisins over the whole thing and everyone was impressed by how modern it was."

Ruchama listened to Vardina and blinked repeatedly. "All right," she said, "but that's only for the appetizers and the salads. What about the rest? You want me to cook chicken and beef and pour mayonnaise over it? Should I put mayonnaise in the rice and potatoes, too?"

"God forbid," Vardina cried out. "Chicken with mayonnaise sounds disgusting."

"So how do you make modern chicken?" Ruchama wondered.

"Chicken is chicken," Vardina announced. "You don't have to make anything up there. You can just add some orange juice to the sauce."

"I can make my mother's chicken with raisins and quinces and cloves," Ruchama said, her eyes beginning to light up behind the glasses and barely blinking anymore.

"Excellent idea." Vardina ran a finger on Ruchama's cheek. "They'll go mad for it, just you wait and see how many offers you'll get, you'll end up opening your own event hall."

Ruchama got up, pulled a spoon from the drawer, opened the mayonnaise jar in one motion, dipped the spoon in and tasted. She called Shlomi and Hilik from the living room, where they sat next to the aquarium and listened intently to the conversation. They each got a spoon of mayonnaise to taste. Shlomi said, "It's good." Hilik barely swallowed it, twisted his face and said, "I think the word mayonnaise is made up of the words milk and nasal, milk comes out of your nose and you get mayonnaise, and that's why it's gross." Vardina said, "I didn't get it, explain it again, slowly," and Hilik said, "A lot of words are made up of other words, like glasses, which is glass and is, or dusk, which is dark and husk, that's how it works." Vardina and Ruchama laughed a long, liberated laugh and Vardina said, "Your little boy has been reading too many books."

Ruchama pulled out three double pages from Shlomi's math notebook. She took a pencil from his pencil case and sharpened it quickly with a kitchen knife, spread the checkered pages before her and began running her sharpened pencil over them. On one page she wrote a menu, on the other the groceries she needed, and on the third the preparation and cooking plan.

Shlomi, Hilik and Vardina watched her silently, following the pencil's bitten tip and her wrinkled forehead and her eyes, which no longer blinked. By the time Adina's silent workman came, the plan was ready. Ruchama gave him the shopping list, he gave her a little bit of cash Adina sent in case she thought of other ingredients she wanted to buy herself. The workman went on his way and Ruchama handed Shlomi the shopping basket and one bill and sent him to Baruch's grocery store to get flour and yeast and some oil and sugar so she could set some dough to rise that evening.

Baruch from the grocery store told Shlomi, "Tell Mom I'm giving her the things she asked for even though she still hasn't paid her debt, I don't want her to think I'm heartless." He put the groceries in the basket, smiled at Shlomi, gave him a yellow gumball and sent him on his way.

Shlomi carried the overflowing basket with great difficulty. He climbed up the alley that led to the main road and stopped, huffing and puffing, next to a tall palm tree. The treetop moved from side to side in the wind. Shlomi leaned on the squeaking trunk and watched a heavy bunch of yellow dates that hung from the praying treetop. And then, all at once, the bunch detached and landed loudly at Shlomi's feet, and date juice smeared over his sandals. He looked at the bunch with wonder, tried to move it, thought of dragging it home and surprising Ruchama. She might wash the dates, chop them, mix them with mayonnaise and surprise Adina's guests with a modern dish they'd never seen before. His mouth filled up with saliva and he tried as best he could to drag the unwieldy bunch, until he gave up and let go. Once again he picked up the basket, looked one more time, saying goodbye to the yellow dates, and thought, how lucky, if I'd stood two centimeters to the right, the bunch would have landed on my head and finished me.

While he walked with the basket hanging off his shoulder, Shlomi shook the juice off his sandals. The basket was heavy and his hands stung but his head was light. He felt that since his ears heard the thud of the bunch hitting the sidewalk his head had emptied of hard thoughts, his sight and hearing grew clearer and everything around him became focused and bright.

He stopped at a street corner, discovering a new bulletin board. His eyes reviewed the signs, clumping letters into words and words into sentences. There was a sign announcing future infrastructure work intended to improve the sewer system. Another implored the members of a certain union to attend a meeting where pay and terms of employment would be discussed. Two colorful signs presented the movies that would be played that week at the Gil and Chen movie theaters. Shlomi put the basket down carefully and continued to gather words – piping, sewage, salary, discount, matinee, adults only, family comedy, Chitty Chitty Bang Bang. He took one bag from the basket and looked at the words printed on it with pale ink – wheat flour, strictly kosher, produced and packaged. His eyes traveled to the signs on the board again and found new words – member cards, cafeteria is open, strike, water flow cutoffs, critically acclaimed, Tiberias Municipality, resident welfare, early sale.

He returned the bag to the basket. His body shuddered and his eyes were pulled everywhere, picking words wherever he could. Egged Bus Company, Stop, No Parking, Café Elite, Excessive Baggage, Zehavi Family, Tamar Hotel and Guesthouse, Children Crossing, Two Rooms for Rent, Discounted School Books, *Ma'ariv, Yediot Ahronot*, Dubek Cigarettes, Fresh Carrot Juice, Sarah Cohen has Passed Away, No Longer with Us, the Family is in Mourning, Lost, Finder, Generous Reward, High Voltage.

Shlomi picked up the basket and raised it until it felt comfortable on his back. He thought about his crybaby teacher who told him that one day the words would fall on his head from a tall tree. He began walking home quickly, his eyes coveting each word he happened across. He only stopped when he reached the path to Ella's building. The window through which they once removed her father's body was shut, the new glass sparkling in the setting sun and blinding him. Without putting the basket down he squatted, picked up a small rock and with great momentum threw it at the window. The glass shattered noisily and Shlomi hurried away with the basket dancing at his side.

When the sun had already been swallowed deep behind the Arbel Cliff and the street lights shone with an electric chirp, a huge mound of dough stood on the kitchen table, and Ruchama beat it, rolled and raised and kneaded it, her body dancing and vibrating, until her face was covered in white dust and the dough was placed in a large pail to rise. Adina's Arab workman kept bringing in boxes of groceries despite the late hour. Shlomi ran around the apartment, fulfilling Ruchama's requests with speed and accuracy, until she told him, "Tomorrow you'll stay home to help me, I'm crazy about you today, the way you do things like a big boy and

I can trust you," and Shlomi told her, "Anyway all they're doing at school is rehearsing for the end-of-the-year play and I'm not in it, and anyway I already know how to read." Ruchama asked, "Really? Since when do you know how to read?" "Since today," Shlomi said and picked up one of the bags of flour and read Ruchama all the words printed on it in one flood of speech. She opened her eyes wide behind her flour-reamed glasses and said, "Good job, Shlomi, and your brother did a good job, too," and Hilik smiled while sifting through a huge pile of rice and said, "When Dad gets back he'll have a surprise when he finds out Shlomi can already read."

And then began the march of the neighbors. One after the other they came from all corners of the neighborhood, carrying large pots, deep bowls and laundry pails so that Ruchama would have a place to put all the ingredients and the dishes. Vardina conducted the march with authority. She'd called Ruti the widow beforehand and assigned her to visit all the neighbors and ask for their help and their kitchenware. And they agreed. Perhaps because they liked the tall Ruchama, perhaps because they worried about the tears Ruti would cry if they refused, perhaps because they feared Adina's grumbling, and that she would overcharge them at her clothing store.

Vardina gathered the dishes, listed them carefully on a page she pulled out of Shlomi's thinning math notebook and said, "The school year is over anyway, and you didn't write anything in this notebook."

Even Hanna came, carrying a slender glass pitcher decorated with tiny blue flowers. Ruchama thanked her but refused when Hanna offered to help with the preparations. Before she left she asked Shlomi, "What are you doing over there?" and Shlomi kept stirring the bubbling tomato sauce, looked at her through slitted eyes and muttered, "Making milk jam." Hanna ignored his answer, or maybe she never heard him, since the apartment was filled with squeaks and screeches and thumps and drags and spraying water and bubbling pots. "Maybe you know what happened to Israella today?" Hanna asked, and Shlomi shrugged and stirred faster.

"And why don't you have a drawing on your face?" she continued, "Israella told me everyone had to draw hands on their faces for the school play."

"I'm not even in the play," Shlomi answered dryly.

Hanna turned to Ruchama. "Have you ever heard of such a thing?" she said, "they have a play and ask little children to dirty their faces, what kind of a school is this?" Ruchama didn't answer and only kept dissecting chickens with a large butcher's knife Malka and Geno sent her and prayed for Hanna to leave her house already and let her work in peace.

But Hanna went on, "And what do you think about how they shattered my window today?" Ruchama asked, "Who did?" Hanna said, "I don't know, some punks probably, there are too many punks in this city, acting very uncultured," and then Vardina told her, "There was a strong wind today, almost like on Wednesday, maybe the glass shook with the wind until it broke," and took the pitcher from Hanna and said, "Thank you so much for your help, goodbye."

After she left Ruchama told Vardina, "God help me, I can't stand that annoying woman. Did you see what she brought? What could I possibly use that ugly vase for?"

They worked into the night.

Vardina and Hilik had already fallen asleep on the bamboo sofa in the living room and Ruchama and Shlomi kept running around.

Ruchama dissected the chickens and removed their skin. She showed Shlomi how to insert a thin knife into the legs and gently separate the meat from the bone. Shlomi operated on dozens of legs, Ruchama pulled the bones out of them and stuffed them with a mixture of fried onions, olives and chopped almonds, parsley and toasted bread crumbs. The overstuffed legs she arranged in pans, covered with the soup she made from the bones and baked them in the oven. She fried the thighs and then cooked them with diced quince that Shlomi sliced and boiled in water and mixed with raisins and honey and cloves. Around the breasts of the chicken Ruchama tied thin strips of lamb fat and glazed them with a paste she made of crushed garlic, lemon peel and dried mint leaves. She taught Shlomi how to connect several slices of chicken and roll them into a loaf that contained broken pistachios and whole hardboiled eggs. Shlomi rolled over ten loaves, tied them carefully and anointed them with oil and spices until his palms were redder than Vardina's plastic roses. Ruchama baked the loaves and cut two fragrant slices from one of them and said, "Look what beautiful sausages we made from the chicken." They ate the slices with their hands and Shlomi said, "This is the most delicious thing I've ever eaten in my life."

While Ruchama made dozens of balls from the risen dough, flattened them with her hand and stuffed them with green beet leaves fried with onions and cumin, Shlomi peeled boiling potatoes and mashed their insides, mixed them with eggs and vegetables and packed patties from the mixture, and then fried them carefully until they browned. Ruchama demonstrated each thing before he did it himself. She made sure he didn't come too close to the sizzling oil and held the knife safely. "There's genius in your hands," she said again and again, impressed with his accurate movements and his quick mind. "Your hands are smart like your father's and your eyes are gorgeous and you're tall like me." Each time she complimented him his cheeks burned. Whenever he was done with a task he asked, "What should I do now, Ruchama?" and Ruchama smiled and said, "When will you explain to me why you decided to stop calling me Mom?" and Shlomi answered, "Because that's what I want." He squeezed tomatoes, peeled peppers that Ruchama burned, lopped the ends off green pea pods, chopped onions and garlic and hills of green leaves and occasionally scrubbed the dishes that piled up in the sink and dried them with a towel.

When Ruchama finished stuffing the dough pockets, tightening their edges, spreading an orange mixture on them and baking them in the oven, she went over to the large chunks of beef, set them on the table and sat down.

"Now I don't know what to do," she told Shlomi. "I have to make something up for the beef and my head is all out of ideas."

Shlomi sat by her side. Together they stared at the bleeding chunks until Shlomi said, "Why don't you just make *sofrito*?" and Ruchama said, "I know how to make *sofrito* from chicken, not beef, and besides I need it to be modern, *sofrito* is home cooking."

They stared in silence again. The sound of running water came from the sink, rinsing the beans in the strainer, and Vardina and Hilik's measured snores sounded from the living room.

Shlomi said, "You can grind half the beef and make patties, if you put something surprising inside the patties it'll be modern, like jelly inside of doughnuts."

"That's a great idea," Ruchama said, "Maybe I'll put dried figs inside and cook the patties in a sauce made of lemon and garlic and celery and sugar and turmeric."

"That sounds tasty and modern to me."

"How do you even know what modern means?"

"I really don't," he answered, and Ruchama laughed and said, "Tomorrow I'll send the workman to buy figs and lemons and we'll make these patties. I think it'll go great with white rice, and we'll pour over it a pile of fried dried fruits, almonds and raisins and pine nuts and figs." She put a hand on his head and caressed his hair. Her hand had the pleasant smell of garlic and spices.

"And what should we do with the rest of the meat?" she asked. "We can't only serve patties."

"The other half of the meat should be prepared with lemons as well," he answered after some thought, "so that there's a connection between the dishes."

"You're right, I'll make a roast with pickled lemons and tomatoes and coriander, people will go crazy for it."

At three in the morning Ruchama woke up Vardina and walked her from the sofa to her apartment. Shlomi helped Hilik get up and falter to the bed with his eyes closed. He tucked him in, making room between the old books that filled his bed. "How's your shoulder?" he asked, and Hilik yawned and said, "Hurts a little, but I don't care." Shlomi said, "Thank you, Hilik, for teaching me how to read." Hilik said, "You learned it, so you should thank yourself," and Shlomi said, "All right." Hilik said, "I'm afraid Dad isn't coming back," and Shlomi said, "Don't be afraid, he'll be back, and even if he doesn't come back, Ruchama and I are here with you and we'll take care of you." Hilik said, "You're not a father, you're a kid, like me," and a moment later he was asleep.

Shlomi took off the stained and floured clothes, turned off the light and burrowed into his bed. His hands smelled of spices and vegetables and chicken fat. Ella appeared before his closed eyes. He knew she was lying in her bed now, thinking about him, the floor of her room covered in glass shards, and her heart beating so loudly it didn't let her sleep. He was filled with worry, what if she got out of bed in her bare feet and cut herself on the broken window. Her cast had only been removed a week before, and her crooked walk still retained the memory of her drop into the pile of sand, and now she'll cut herself on the shards of the window he'd shattered and her blood will spray everywhere again. A great sorrow filled his stomach and flooded him with longing for the old girl he'd loved and hurt. He fell asleep and woke up less than three hours later. It was six in the morning and the sun was sleepy and pale. He got out of bed quickly and went to wake up Ruchama.

8

RUCHAMA KNOCKED ONCE MORE ON VARDINA'S DOOR. SHE'D BEEN standing there and knocking for a long time. Worry snuck into her heart, maybe something happened to her beloved neighbor. Maybe she got out of bed, her heavy legs bumped into a chair and she fell and hurt herself. Maybe she was lying there, unconscious and in need of help. Ruchama banged on the door with her palm, shaking the whole stairway, but then the door opened and Vardina stood across from her, wrinkled with sleep, her eyes glued shut. "I was getting worried," Ruchama said, sighing with relief, and Vardina said, "I'm sorry, Ruchama, I slept like an elephant, I promised to help you but I was falling-down tired, my legs are killing me." "It's all right," Ruchama said, "I just wanted to get some coffee from you because I'm sleepwalking too and I still have a lot to do." Vardina opened the door wide and signaled to Ruchama to come in. "Come take whatever you want, I'll just take a shower and I'll come up to help," and Ruchama said, "There's no need, really, Shlomi's helping me. You should come just to watch him, I've never seen anything like it, such a young boy who does these things better than I do, I think he's a wonder boy."

With steaming cups of coffee in their hands the two stood and looked at Shlomi with amazement, the way he glossed sheets of skin Ruchama had pulled off the chickens with a halved lemon, scraped them with a knife until they turned thin and pink, piled a mixture of rice and chicken livers and chopped spleens onto them, tightened and rolled and handed them to Ruchama to stitch with a needle and thread and cook in a thick garlic and red pepper sauce. Vardina smelled the sauce and said, "It smells delicious but it might be too spicy for Adina's spoiled guests," and Ruchama smiled and said, "Don't worry, if they complain we'll pour some mayonnaise on it."

When Adina's workman arrived with the remaining groceries, Ruchama began preparing the patties stuffed with figs and the pot roast cooked with pickled lemons. Then they cleaned and packed and prepared the mayonnaise dishes. Eggplants were seared, cabbages were sliced, carrots were steamed, beets were baked, and they were all covered with generous blankets of mayonnaise. Ruchama opened one jar after another and emptied them into the bowls.

The radio was on the entire time. The announcers spoke about Apollo 10's successful journey and the preparations for the next spaceship that'll attempt to land on the moon, and Vardina said, "They're mad, those ones, they've got nothing better to do, I can't imagine what they think they'll find on the moon, maybe they think they'll find some treasure there." The radio announcers spoke of the War of Attrition between Israel and Egypt and Vardina said, "We can't get one day of peace in this country. At least if we had some oil we wouldn't have to beg for charity from all the anti-Semites." They also spoke of the upcoming elections and Ruchama said, "Golda can forget about me, I won't vote for her even if she jumps through hoops."

"Why?" asked Vardina. "What did she do to you?"

"She's an expert on ruining people's lives," Ruchama answered. "I even heard she had an affair with Zalman Shazar, even though she's a ragged old lady who looks like a fairytale witch."

"Who's Zalman Shazar?" Shlomi asked and Vardina said, "He's the president, how can you not know, what do they even teach you in that school of yours?"

"He was even in Tiberias a few weeks ago," Ruchama said, "and the school kids stood on the sidewalk and waved state flags when he drove by. Didn't you see that, Shlomi?" and Shlomi said, "He was inside a black car and we couldn't see a thing, and I didn't know that was his name, I thought his name was The President."

Once in a while, between announcements, the radio played Judy Garland songs, and Vardina said, "Look at that, we were so busy yesterday we never even heard that poor Judy Garland died." She broke into tears.

"What are you crying about?" Ruchama said. "What's Judy Garland to you, what do you care about her?" and Vardina wiped her tears and said, "I feel bad for her, she was a great singer and actress, even though she wasn't Jewish."

At noon Ruchama said, "This is giving me a headache," and

turned the radio off. She took four plates, put a little of each dish on each plate, set the table and sat everyone down. "We deserve a royal feast," she said. Hilik ate a little, Vardina and Shlomi swallowed the whole thing up with great pleasure. Ruchama tasted a drop of each dish, forcing herself to push away the excitement that blocked her appetite. "I think Adina's going to have a big problem today," Vardina said, "her guests might go mad with deliciousness; they'll end up eating the plates and then hunting down Adina herself." Ruchama smiled and Shlomi asked, "What do you think, Ruchama? Are they going to like the food?" and Ruchama said, "I don't have a clue, what do I look like, Deborah the Prophetess?" and Vardina said, "Why does he call you Ruchama? Why doesn't he call you Mom? It isn't healthy."

When they finished eating Adina arrived, accompanied by her silent workman, her hair done up and smelling like a salon. She equipped herself with a spoon and moved between the pots and bowls and pails, tasting each dish, clicking her tongue and licking her lips. Ruchama followed her movements closely, her heart adding a beat each time Adina opened her eyes wide and pursed her lips with wonder. Finally she said, "I'm going to burst in a minute, I'm bloated now from eating so much, I won't be able to fit into the dress I had made."

She put down the spoon, went to Ruchama, embraced her in her heavy arms, Ruchama's head floating over her rigid hairdo, and said, "You're an angel, you're a genius, I'm so lucky city hall found mice in the restaurant's yard." Adina kissed Vardina's cheeks, ran a soft hand over Shlomi's head and turned to the workman. "Now go and get all the kerosene burners from the restaurant, tell them not to cause any trouble or I'll take them to court over the mess they made." Then she told Ruchama, "I need burners, my two ovens won't be enough to warm up all the delicacies you made."

Ruchama gave the workman three pastries. He lowered his head in gratitude and was on his way. "You shouldn't have spoiled him like that," Adina said. "These Arabs, you spoil them a little and they start with their demands." Then she drank from the coffee Vardina served and her face glowed again when she told Ruchama, "Now you're going to take a nice long shower and go down to the hair salon, have them give you a nice do, it's on me, and then drop by the store, I'll give you something nice to wear, also on me, and then come over and watch the workman, make sure he doesn't overheat the food and ruin your art, and make sure he arranges the food nicely, because you eat with your eyes first and it should look good."

Adina stayed for a little longer, telling stories of the days when Robert used to work for her, about his good hands that had healed so quickly after breaking, about his strange sister who disappeared to the kibbutz one day, never to return. At last she kissed Ruchama and Vardina again and left, leaving behind the smell of hairspray.

"Why are you being a sourpuss all of a sudden?" Vardina asked. "Not enough compliments?"

Ruchama's eyes moistened. "I suddenly thought how I don't even care if Robert comes back," she said, "I can do just fine without him."

"You're talking nonsense again," Vardina replied.

Under the flow of water that washed off all the smells and flavors covering her body with a sticky film, Ruchama kept shedding tears, her shoulders shaking and her lips choking down the sounds. The last time she spoke with him, over a week ago, she held the black phone's receiver, covered her mouth and the mouthpiece with one hand so Mrs. Katz wouldn't hear, and said, "Robert, you said you'd be back in a week, it's been over a month, I'm starting to worry," and Robert said, "There's nothing to worry about, my uncle needs me here right now, I'll tell you all about it when I get back." "What does he need you for?" she kept asking, "doesn't he know you have a family?" and Robert said, "Patience, Ruchama, it's important for my shutter business." Ruchama didn't let go. "What do I care about shutters, I'm out of the money you left me, even Baruch won't let me use our tab anymore." "Figure it out," he answered, "ask your sisters for a loan, I'll pay them back, don't give me a hard time now."

Ruchama said nothing. His voice had a dryness that hurt her ears.

"These calls are very expensive," he said, "just wait till I get back and we can talk about everything."

"You worry me, Robert."

"Why?"

"Because if I didn't know it was you I'd think it was a stranger on the phone. Your voice is different, I don't know you anymore."

"Please Ruchama, don't start talking to me like one of your poetry books, I'm too tired for that."

"Why did you cut your hair?" she asked and Robert raised his voice. "Because I'd had enough."

Then there was static on the line and a moment later they were disconnected.

Ruchama waited a few minutes more in case he called again, stopping herself from crying in front of Mrs. Katz. Finally she thanked her and went out to the stairway, walked past the door to Hanna's apartment and went home, where she locked herself in the bathroom and cried for a long time.

The water washed off the smell of cooking and the tears of anger. She dried her body with a towel, inspecting it in the mirror, touching her breasts as if to check if they were still round and firm, and her thin waist and her smooth belly. Her three pregnancies hardly left a mark. The first brought Shlomi, the second brought Hilik, the third ended because of Aisha the coal thief's fist. Ruchama ran her hand between her thighs and a longing for Robert's body rose in her. Her breaths galloped and her eyes closed with passion. A moment later she opened her eyes, embarrassed and ashamed of the lust she was overcome with.

When she got out of the shower she told Shlomi, "Go take a quick shower, I want you to come with me, you deserve to be spoiled by Adina too," and she told Hilik, "You'll have to stay here alone until we get back. I trust you to be a big boy and take care of yourself," and Hilik said, "Don't worry."

"Start with Shlomi, give him a nice haircut, he deserves it," Ruchama told Moti the hairdresser who was already waiting for them, smiling. "The whole city is talking about the wonderful smells coming from your apartment," he said while massaging Shlomi's head, adding more and more fragrant shampoo and washing it with warm water. "Adina already paid and threatened that if I didn't pamper you and make a beauty queen out of you it'll be the end of me."

Ruchama followed his movements as he wrapped Shlomi in rustling red fabric, moved around him like a cat, clicking his scissors and spinning the small comb, and felt her body filled with lust again. Once in a while he sent her angled looks and said, "Take this time to think about what you'd like me to do with your beautiful hair, because I already have plans of my own." Each time he looked at her, Ruchama blushed. A great embarrassment ran through her as she fought her eyes, trying to restrain them from wandering over Moti's body, coveting it. He brushed the back of Shlomi's neck with a soft brush, pushing away strands of loose hair, dusted it with white powder and sent another prickly smile, perhaps already noticing her quick breathing. He told Shlomi, "Look how I made you look like a kid from a magazine," and Shlomi got up, shook his shirt a little and went to sit on the bench, trying to keep his head steady on his neck, refraining from any quick motions that would spoil his haircut.

Ruchama sat with her back to the sink, entrusting her hair to Moti's hands as he applied and massaged and rinsed, his breath warm on her face and his waist rubbing against her shoulders, sending chills through them.

After he wrapped a tower of towels around her head, she asked for his permission to go to the bathroom, where she sat on the toilet, trying to steady her breathing, telling herself off again and again, what's wrong with you today, Ruchama, you're acting like a slutty girl. She closed her eyes and tried to imagine Robert in his short hair, and that aroused her even more. She sent her hand again to touch herself, her chest rising and falling, longing for his touch. Then she got up suddenly, flushed the toilet, looked at her reflection in the small mirror and told herself silently, you should be ashamed of yourself Ruchama, you were this close to losing it and jumping Moti and giving Shlomi a shock. You should get a hold of yourself immediately.

Moti raised the rustling fabric like a bullfighter, wrapped it around her neck, pressed the pedal to lower the seat and told Shlomi, "You see those shelves in the corner, the ones with the shampoo and conditioner bottles? You know who built those?" Shlomi shook his head with small, careful motions. "Your father built them for me with his good hands," Moti said, and then turned to Ruchama. "My dream is that Robert will come in and ask me to do something with that hair of his, I've never seen anything like it. But I'd hold my horses and convince him not to do a thing." Shlomi said, "He got a short haircut," and Moti froze and said, "It can't be, I don't believe it," and

Ruchama said, "It's true."

"When? Where?"

"He went to visit his uncle in Argentina and got his hair cut there."

"I'm shocked," Moti said. "How did you let him do a thing like that?" and Ruchama shrugged and said, "I haven't seen it because he isn't back yet, maybe it looks good," and Shlomi told Moti, "You're the only one who likes Dad's hair, everyone else laughs at him." "That's because they're jealous," Moti explained and sighed deeply. "It's a shame he cut his hair. Everything's changing. This city isn't what it used to be."

He ran his fingers through her moist hair, looking at her reflection in the large mirror and his forehead wrinkled in thought. "What are we going to do with you, Ruchama, maybe we should just smooth it and comb it nicely, I like your head this way," and Ruchama surprised herself and said, "Make it short."

Moti let go of her hair and asked, "What do you mean?"

"Give me a buzz cut," she answered. "I'm sick of this pile of hair on my head."

"Did you go crazy, too?" he cried, and Ruchama said, "That's what I want."

Moti looked her in the eyes through the mirror and said determinedly, "So go to someone else, I won't give you a buzz cut even if Adina paid me a million lira."

Blood raced through Ruchama's face. She felt it beat in her temples. "Don't argue with me, Moti, and don't get on my nerves either," she raised her voice. "Walking around like some artist in a museum, dancing like a cat around a trash can, all I asked you was to cut it, and if you can't do it I'll do it myself." All at once she raised the blue fabric and her hand jumped to the scissors on the dresser, but Moti's hand was quicker and he blocked her hand with his soft touch, holding her fingers and caressing them.

Ruchama was quiet. Her eyes caught Shlomi who sat up on the bench. Moti brought a chair near her and sat down, continuing to hold her hand and not letting go of her eyes. He said, almost in a whisper, "I understand you're tired and probably nervous about Adina's night, but it's important that we think rationally. You're a beautiful woman, but you're also very tall and you wear huge glasses.

If I give you a buzz cut you'll look like the Tower of David. I want to keep you pretty and preserve your femininity."

She breathed in deep, lowering her eyes to the blue fabric that fell on the floor. "Let me cut it, but only to the shoulders," Moti suggested. "I'll give you a gorgeous modern haircut. Trust me."

On the grass in Adina's garden, rows of tables were already set with white tablecloths and cutlery and centerpieces. Rows of colorful lights shone among the lemon and guava trees and on the wide steps stood musicians brought in especially from Nazareth. When Ruchama arrived, one arm linked with Shlomi's, clad in his new outfit, the other nervously running through her head that rested mischievously on her shoulders, the pots were already sitting on burners and the pans were warming up in the ovens. The silent workman smiled at Ruchama and his eyes escaped shyly when she complimented his efficient organization. Adina received her brightly, praised her haircut and said, "Now you look like a young, beautiful woman instead of a Bedouin worker, look how the dress I chose for you flatters you, you're glowing like a flower," and Ruchama smoothed the striped dress awkwardly and said, "I look like a zebra with all these stripes," and Adina said, "What zebra are you talking about, black-and-white stripes are the most modern thing in the world right now. It's an Italian pattern, just so you know." "I'm not used to wearing sleeveless dresses and such revealing necklines," Ruchama said, and Adina answered, "So get used to it because you should flaunt it."

Ruchama turned to the kitchen to run a final inspection. She added salt to one stew, some water to another. Then she fried a large pile of almonds and raisins and pine nuts and scattered them generously over bowls filled with white rice.

A little after the guests arrived, Shlomi fell asleep on a living room chair. Ruchama covered him with a blanket, surprised by his deep sleep. The air was full of the sounds of the band, trilling song, cheerful violins, drum strikes and strumming ouds and qanuns, and sounds of revelry and clapping from the guests. She spent most of the party in the kitchen, piling more and more dishes on the platters the silent workman handed her and then carried back to the tables. She went out to the raging garden only once, Adina and Marco made her come out so they could show her off to their important guests from Haifa and Tel Aviv and so she could have a glass of arak with their granddaughter, the blushing bride. Vardina, who was a little late, wearing a red lace dress whose puffy edges disguised her aching legs, held her close and whispered, "Everyone's going crazy over the food, I've already heard about five events they want you to cater, and I gave them a much higher price than Adina's paying and they didn't make a peep," and Ruchama said, "Don't go crazy, Vardina, I don't know if I'm going to do this again, I'm not sure I can," and Vardina said, "Shut your mouth my child and let me handle your business in peace."

Ruchama began making rounds among the local guests she knew. Even her sister Geula was there, wrapped in her scarves and her bursting mouth chewing delightedly. At the edge of one of the tables, she noticed the specialist who treated Hilik's ears, sending her bashful looks and loosening the tight blue tie around his neck. Ruchama received great praise and returned to the protective kitchen and the emptying pots. Marco came into the kitchen to get some more arak and said, "I've never seen anything like this, Ruchama, people are eating like pigs, they'll end up eating me." He peeked in the pots and said, "When the food is gone I demand that you come out and dance with us, you deserve to have fun." Ruchama nodded with a smile, but when the pots emptied she fastened an apron around her waist and began scrubbing them in the sink, filling it with warm water and soap, removing the remnants of her victory.

Suddenly she felt warm air blow on the back of her neck. She turned around quickly, alarmed when she found the specialist standing near her, almost touching her, his shiny eyes staring at her, his shirt collar open and the edges of his shirt untucked and almost reaching his knees. The doctor noticed her alarm and took one step back, leaning on the table to stop his body from shaking.

"I apologize if I scared you," he said, his eyes not letting go, "you ruined my life, Ruchama."

"Why? What happened?" she asked, and he said, "I'm a little drunk from the arak and from your good food, but even if I were completely sober I'd still tell you I'm in love with you."

Ruchama stood against the sink. Blood filled her face. The doctor's eyes sparkled and he said in a small, begging voice, "Ever since I saw you with your son, when you sat on the desk and made a scene, ever since then I've loved you desperately. Sometimes I pray your son gets that infection back so I can see you again, just imagine how heinous I've become."

Ruchama had a hard time breathing. Her eyes attached to his graying temples, his tightly pursed lips and his fair eyes, beseeching her.

"Even at work I keep getting confused," he said in a trembling voice, "I can barely sleep at night, sometimes I find myself sitting in the dark, in the middle of the night, writing you poems."

"Why?" Ruchama whispered, and the doctor whispered back, "Because I love you."

He closed his eyes for a moment and said, "I'm sorry for putting this on you all of a sudden, but I couldn't stop myself. I always thought I was a strong man and took pride in my self control. I'm thirty-five years-old and I'd never been in love until I saw you. If I could and if you'd let me I'd kiss your entire body."

His tearful eyes cut through hers, his soft voice caressed her ears and she felt her body filling with longing again. She said, "You can't talk to me this way, I'm a married woman, I have children," and the doctor said, "I know, that's why my heart is ripped to pieces, and if I could I'd murder your husband." Ruchama said, "You're crazy and you're scaring me," and he said, "Don't be scared of me, I'll never hurt you in any way, shape or form."

"I think you're completely drunk, you'll wake up tomorrow and remember nothing," she said.

"Maybe that's why my body's betraying me this way, the moment I saw you I had to take my shirt out of my pants so people wouldn't see what's happening to me." He raised the edges of his shirt to bring her attention to his swollen pants and she closed her eyes with embarrassment. "I apologize for my rudeness, but my whole body is begging for you."

The water filled the sink stacked with dishes, spreading warm steam everywhere. Ruchama shut the tap and turned quickly to the nearby pantry, turning her back to the doctor and pulling dry kitchen towels from a drawer. But the doctor followed her to the pantry. She said, "Go away, don't make me yell and embarrass you." The doctor didn't move, standing silently and looking at her and not letting go. She handed him a towel and he wiped his eyes and cheeks and returned to looking at her silently. Their quick breaths filled the small room and a moment later she clung to him, her lips searching for his, drinking the taste of arak and the tears that kept falling. His hands held her waist, moving up and feeling her chest through the zebra dress. And then she pushed him and left the pantry, returning to the sink and polishing the pots. The doctor looked at her for another long moment and then left.

And she didn't say another word. Even when Vardina came to say goodbye because her aching legs demanded that she go home, Ruchama only nodded silently, working hard to smile back at her excited neighbor and keeping her mouth shut, trying to erase the image of the doctor's tearful eyes and the taste of his mouth which filled her with passion and pangs of conscience. Even when Adina came to reproach her for doing the dishes by herself, and to give her more and more compliments and to hand her a roll of bills, her fees and a generous tip, even then Ruchama only replied with shy nods and effortful smiles.

As they made their way home Shlomi asked, "Why aren't you talking?" and Ruchama answered, "I'm out of words," and returned to her silence, which continued even when they opened the door and were surprised to find Robert, who'd returned home.

He sat on the squeaky sofa in the living room, his eyes tired but excited, all smiles, Hilik cuddled in his arms, clinging to him and not letting go and saying, "Look, Dad's home." Shlomi and Ruchama stood at the doorway without moving. Ruchama looked at his new head, his temples almost shaved and the crown of his head covered with prickly, carefully shorn hair, his entire appearance thinner and younger, unfamiliar to her. She sat across from him. He reached his hand and pulled Shlomi to him, hugging and kissing, embracing both children and never taking his eyes off Ruchama.

"Why are you looking pale?" he asked and Hilik answered immediately, "She's tired, Shlomi's tired too, and they're probably also surprised by your new haircut."

"Hilik told me all about you," Robert said. "He told me about the operation you carried out for Adina's party and about the ear treatment that helped and now he's healthy, he even told me that Shlomi can read." He kissed Shlomi's head again and again and said,

"I missed you so much it almost killed me."

"I actually like the haircut," Shlomi said, "but you sound strange now," and Robert laughed, wiped his eyes and said, "It's because I spoke nothing but Spanish for a month and a half, my mouth almost forgot Hebrew."

Ruchama remained silent, her eyes fixed on Robert's head, wondering where that mane went and who the man was who was revealed beneath it.

Robert finally released himself from Hilik's grip, went to the suitcase and began pulling out new clothes, plaid shirts for Shlomi, shorts for Hilik, dresses for Ruchama, pajamas and socks and belts for everyone. He carried one of the dresses to Ruchama like an offering and said, "You cut your hair too, Ruchama, it looks very nice," and leaned in to kiss her cheek. She took the dress from his hands, ran her hand over it and took a long look, avoiding Robert's eyes. She wanted to thank him, she wanted to stand up and hug him, she wanted to smile at Hilik and Shlomi and send them to bed because it was already late, she wanted to compliment Robert on the pretty clothes he'd brought, tell him something comforting about his short hair. She wanted to show him the stack of bills she'd earned in sweat and tell him about her exhaustion and the waves of passion that had gripped her, but she remained seated in silence.

Robert walked the children to their room, hugging their shoulders, and told Shlomi, "Hilik told me you've decided to stop calling me Dad, tomorrow you can explain to me why you've decided such a strange thing."

Ruchama listened to the laughter coming from the children's room while Robert put them to bed, tickled them cheerfully, tucked them in, kissed them, turned off the light and locked himself in the bathroom. She listened to the sounds of the shower that broke the silence of the night. She got up with great effort and went to the bedroom, took off the zebra dress and her glasses and sat on the edge of the bed. Robert finished showering and went to the room, his naked body wet and wrapped in a towel. He sat next to her and asked, "Why are you quiet all the time, Ruchama? Are you surprised I'm back? I told you not to worry." He put his head on her shoulder gently and shut his eyes. Ruchama leaned her head against his moist head, breathing in his smell, finding it difficult to recognize the new feel of his buzzed head. She put her hands on his shoulders and pushed him slowly until he lay on his back, removed her underwear and bra and lay beside him, caressing his neck and arms, tasting his lips and eyes. Robert whispered, "I missed you too, Ruchama, but I'm so tired, I've been on flights for two days." She didn't answer. Her body rose and her lips and tongue went to Robert's chest and stomach. Her hands removed the towel. His penis was limp and she put it in her mouth, sucking it and running her tongue over it until it hardened, and then she put it inside of her and moved on it, her mouth linked to his, stopping the sounds that wanted out, breathing with passion, his eyes shut and hers gathering the waves of passion that shook her all that day, until they exploded. First Ruchama exploded, then Robert kept moving his body gently until he exploded too.

When she opened her eyes to a gray morning she saw Robert sitting on the edge of the bed and looking at her, his eyes smiling and his body nude like hers. She pulled the blanket from the edge of the bed and covered herself, shivering in the morning chill, embarrassed by his smiling eyes and his hand that caressed her foot.

"Yesterday I met Vardina in the stairway," Robert said, "I got here just as she got back from Adina's celebration and told me about the wonders you and Shlomi did there. I helped her up because her legs could barely move and I told her I was willing to buy her apartment from her."

Ruchama blinked with confusion and Robert smiled. "Everything's going to be different now, Ruchama," he said. "Look what I brought." He pulled out the fabric pouch Ruchama made him before he'd left from under the pile of his clothes. The bag was stuffed and engorged. Robert pulled out a wad of bills, and another and another, and then smiled. "That's a little money my uncle gave me, but now I'll show you the real thing," and then he pulled from the pouch four small bags, opened one and gave it to Ruchama to show her its contents. It was full of little diamonds, shining happily and reflecting the pale light of the morning into her surprised eyes.

Robert laughed quietly and said, "The money my uncle gave me will be enough to buy materials and pay workers and professionals, but these diamonds are going to make us rich, they're worth a thousand times more than the money, I need to sell some of them and then we'll have enough to buy a nice big place for the new business, and enough to expand the apartment and buy a new car and a television and anything else we want. When I heard Vardina wanted to move to the first floor because of her legs I thought it would be best to buy her apartment, with the money I pay her she can buy the Kurds' apartment downstairs, they want to move anyway because city hall won't approve their expansion, and we can attach our apartment to her old one and make a palace, we'll make a huge living room and a big balcony for your plants and an open kitchen because that's what's modern, and we'll build rooms upstairs, everyone's going to have their own room, and we can even make a big bookcase for all your books and a huge bathroom and an extra bathroom for guests. I have a whole plan in mind. At first I thought we should buy some land and build a house on the mountain, where we can see the Sea of Galilee, but I know you like the neighborhood and it's convenient because the kids' school is nearby, it would be a shame to drag them and ourselves to a new place, and what are you going to do without Vardina. That's how I got this idea, we'll all be happy. Imagine, Ruchama, you won't have to cook for others anymore, we can finally replace your old glasses, we'll get a little room for all your books and if you want we can make a triangle ceiling like you had in Haifa, maybe you can even sit quietly and write all the poems you used to think up."

Ruchama followed his movements, his thin body running around the small room as if inside an imaginary blueprint, pointing his hands and buzzed head towards the small dreams he'd collected and now wanted to purchase and create. Her face was sealed and he sat on the edge of the bed, touched her foot again and said, "Say something, Ruchama, you haven't said a word since I got back. At first I thought you were mad but after what you did to me last night I can't believe you are. Please say something," and Ruchama pulled the blanket again to cover her shoulders and asked in a whisper, "Where did you get all that money and diamonds?"

"My uncle gave them to me," he answered. "He's very rich, who would he give it to if not me, he has no one else."

Ruchama got up and got dressed, went to the bathroom and took a quick shower in cool water, woke up the children and sent them to school, avoiding his eyes that waited for a response, cleaned and straightened out the mess her cooking left, and remained silent the entire time.

Ruchama was silent for many more days, even when Robert began
acting on his plans in a storm. In a matter of days he became the
entire area's shutter expert, hiring more and more workers, getting
more and more orders and sending work teams to seal the windows
and balconies of the city's residents and the kibbutz members and
people in the moshavs around the Sea of Galilee and the new ones in
the Golan Heights. Robert's workers moved in waves towards Mevo
Hama and Merom Golan and Givat Yoav and Ein Zivan and the
large bases the army had erected after the Six-Day War. Tehila's nearby kibbutz was the first to purchase shutters that soon covered the
members' rooms, the schools and the dining halls. But the majority
of work took place in the neighborhoods of Tiberias, whose residents
no longer chuckled when they saw the young, energetic guy who had
cut off his long hair and won their hearts over with tempting offers
of pull shutters and silent rods and folding blinds. The houses were
slowly shut, the smells of cooking and sounds of parents yelling at
their children remained locked inside and no longer scattered in the
air of the neighborhoods.

And Ruchama stayed quiet. She said nothing even when Robert
equipped the apartment with new furniture and a new television,
and even installed a white phone in the corner of the living room,
and even when Vardina thanked him tearfully for saving her legs
from terrible pain. Two or three times a week Ruchama would give
in to the pleas of her culinary admirers, call in Shlomi, who was
already on summer vacation, and cook dozens of dishes, inventing
delicacies, conducting experiments and raking in a great fortune, the
majority of which she deposited in a new account she'd opened, some
of which she used to buy new sleeveless dresses at Adina's store. People got married and gave birth and celebrated, and Ruchama would
cook for them, she and Shlomi working silently and listening sourly
to radio broadcasts about the War of Attrition, about air raids and
shootings of Egyptian planes, about man landing on the moon and
Moshe Dayan and his fans' political plans. Most of the time Hilik
sat with them, rummaging through his books and looking impressed
at Shlomi's quick fingers, now that he'd become an expert in gutting
the fish of the Sea of Galilee, removing their insides and shaving

their bodies of scales. Hilik's ears were dry and his breath healthy and only slightly wheezing at night. Ruchama took him in for a checkup, silently ignoring the specialist's red eyes and his hands that trembled as he said, "I hope you forgive me for losing control, but everything I said was true."

Once in while Robert would say, "When will we talk, Ruchama, I still haven't told you anything about my trip, and we haven't decided how to connect the apartments, I can't start renovating until you tell me what you think of the plans." But Ruchama stood firm in her silence, another day in and another day out, and at night pushed Robert onto his back and swallowed his body with great passion and went back to not speaking. Until once, when they were nude and sweaty in bed, she suddenly opened her mouth and said:

"In the first days of your trip, when I still sat at Mrs. Katz's and waited for you to call, I tried to imagine what you did over there, at your uncle's, and I couldn't picture it. Maybe because I don't have an imagination anymore, maybe I never had any and only wanted to. I look at Shlomi and Hilik and see what it means to have an imagination. Shlomi uses his to invent recipes and Hilik cooks words up like a little poet. Days later, when you postponed your return again and again and we were left waiting here without any money and without understanding anything, I started feeling that only my body missed you, Robert, but I don't want to be just a body anymore, I want other things too. I look at you and think that I don't know you at all, and not because you cut your hair, and not because you have three or four gray hairs above your ears and two hairs on your chest. I know your body perfectly well and I don't care about anything else. I don't even want to get to know the rest. I don't want to hear about what you did there, I don't want to know what your uncle wanted in return for the treasures he gave you, I don't want a triangle ceiling or a room for my books, those books belong to the library anyway and it's time I gave them back, I'm sick of my house looking like a graveyard for books I used to read and haven't touched in years, I'm sick of Hilik putting them in his bed and breathing their dust, I'm sick of watching all the dreams I used to have hiding between the pages of these crumbling books. I don't want a television to bring all the neighbors swarming into my house, and I don't want another apartment to clean, I don't want a modern kitchen, I don't want to write poems because I'm not a poet, I don't want new glasses, and if I did I'd use my own money, I have plenty, and I don't want shutters on the balcony, I hate all these shutters the whole world is suddenly donning like shrouds."

Robert looked at her for a long moment, his ears still processing her voice that they'd almost forgotten, and then said, "I don't understand anything, I don't understand what you're saying," and Ruchama said, "I'm saying I don't need you anymore. I'll need you sometimes at night, but you don't have to accept me, I'll be fine without that, too." Then she covered herself with a blanket, shut her eyes and said nothing more till she fell asleep.

9

MINUTES BEFORE HE LEFT ON HIS WAY BACK HOME, ROBERT FOUND the note on which the kind officer had written her phone number. Her name was written in tight handwriting that was hard to decipher, maybe Ofira, maybe Sophia, maybe Shifra, and Robert decided to answer to her beckoning and call her, let her know his expected arrival time at Lod Airport, maybe she could help him avoid threatening inspections and meetings with suspicious cops with red hair and cold eyes. The wads of bills his uncle gave him were already hidden in the fabric pouch on his waist, and the tiny bags of diamonds were concealed in the folds of his underwear. He prayed his excitement wouldn't raise unnecessary suspicions. The uncle promised to escort him to the airport and push bills into the hands of the local police at the right moments, so that they would jump over the first hurdle easily.

Ofira recognized his voice right away. Her voice was excited and cheerful, as if she'd been sitting and waiting intently for him to call, and she laughed when he apologized and asked for her name because he had trouble understanding her handwriting. "You're right," she said, "my handwriting's a little retarded and a lot of times people don't understand what I mean." She wrote his flight details down and promised to wait for him and try to make him forget again about the event that brought on their first meeting. She told him that the cop had been fired and that the lesson had been learned. The short conversation dispelled his fears.

When he hung up he exhaled with relief and zipped up the suitcase overflowing with new clothes he bought for Ruchama and the children, among which he'd placed some jars of dulce de leche. The pouch filled with bills pressed down on his stomach and the diamond bags in his underwear tickled his testicles. He laughed loudly and told his uncle, "Look what you've made of me, a little diamond smuggler," and his uncle hugged him and said, "Don't worry, no one will suspect you, you look like a cute kid going on a trip, no one will know you're smuggling your future in your underwear, and even if they find something, it's not as much as criminals carry, tell them it's a gift from your uncle who loves you, the worst they'll do is confiscate them and then I'll come over myself and bring you twice as much." And together they went into the taxi that waited for them, hugging and tearful in expectation of their upcoming parting.

When Robert arrived at his uncle's house six weeks earlier, they both burst into tears. The uncle hugged and kissed him and said, "You look so much like your father, small and beautiful like him, how did I let myself stay away from you all those years, I deserve to be punished." Robert was exhausted from the long journey. His ears found it difficult to reunite with the Spanish language, his eyes wanted to close and his head almost dropped on the table of delicacies his uncle prepared for him. With his remaining energy he called Mrs. Katz and briefly spoke with Ruchama, explaining why his journey was prolonged and listening to her silence when he told her he'd gotten his hair cut. Then he washed himself in a steaming bath drawn by the servant, trying to listen to his uncle's deluge of stories as the man sat on the edge of the tub and wiped tears of excitement and guilt from his eyes. When the uncle noticed his closing eyes he said, "You'd better get out of the water so you don't drown." He handed him a robe and led him to the fancy guestroom. Robert burrowed into the blankets in the large bed and slept for almost twenty hours. Once or twice he opened his eyes and saw the contours of his uncle, sitting on a chair in the dark, watching him, as if guarding him from evil. When he awoke, new clothes waited for him by the bed and the unfamiliar smell of a large city wafted through the window and caressed his shaved head.

They hardly spoke of the past. The memory of Robert's parents, who drove to their death after their relationship with the uncle grew rocky, was only mentioned sporadically, in shards of words, in random bits of blurry and tormenting remembrance. The uncle asked about life in Israel and about Robert's shutter plan and about the approaching election. He insisted on leading Robert around Buenos Aires, walking into alleys, climbing onto the roofs of tall buildings to look over the city and showing Robert its face which had changed only a little since his childhood. Once in a while they went into small eateries, hidden inside residential buildings or alleys at the edges of the city, and the uncle would ask the servers to fill their table with dishes and encourage Robert to eat more and more, shocked by his thinness.

His uncle gave long speeches about the country he'd left and to which he'd never return, mocking the universal admiration of Israel for winning the war in six days. "One day they'll realize Israel had no one to fight," he said. "Because of the state the Arab army was in, anyone would have beaten them, even in five days, even in four. Even the corrupt Argentine army would have beaten them easily, because the Argentine army is vicious and not self-infatuated. But the Arabs aren't stupid, I know them very well because I grew up in Iraq, I'm a little Arab myself. They've learned their lessons, and they won't sign a peace agreement until they can strike your cocky country to the ground. The world will stop being impressed very soon, because the world has always been anti-Semitic and always will be, and Jews have always been stupid and always will be and Arabs have always had oil and always will."

Once in a while he'd urge Robert to change his mind and come live there. Robert would smile with his mouth full and shake his head no, and his uncle would say, "You've become stupid like all Israelis and stubborn, like your sister. At least you're not as arrogant as her, you still have your modesty, like your father, may he rest in peace." Then he'd tear up and say nothing, until suddenly his hand banged on the table, his other hand wiped his tears and he said loudly, "Let's continue our walk, there are a lot of other things I want you to taste."

In the evenings they'd lock themselves in the kitchen. His uncle would send the servant to her room and cook a delightful dinner himself, roasting bleeding pieces of meat, cutting small slices off them and feeding them straight into Robert's mouth, filling and re-filling his wine glass, opening more and more bottles he'd collected in his cellar. Robert's suitcase stayed closed for three days because his uncle bought him so many new and beautiful clothes. When he finally opened it, Robert found the pastries Ruchama sent with him to give to the uncle. They were stale. Robert threw them out and never mentioned them to his uncle.

In the morning of the fourth day his uncle said, "Today we're going for checkups, I made an appointment with a terrific dentist and with a famous professor, both Ashkenazi Jews, neither can stand me, but for the money I give them they'll do a perfect job." "What for?" said Robert. "I'm as healthy as a bull," and the uncle said, "For my benefit."

The dentist poked and did an X-ray and was impressed with Robert's strong teeth. The other doctor asked dozens of questions and measured and checked every bone and every muscle, filled beakers with his blood and one jar with his urine and was satisfied and even proud of the results, and only advised Robert to eat a little more.

When they returned home, his uncle surprised Robert by introducing him to Rochelle, who'd just returned from a visit to her family in France. She sat at the kitchen table, smiling awkwardly, and only when she stood up to shake his hand did he notice her height.

The uncle said emotionally, "Robert, I'd like you to meet Rochelle, my wife, though she looks more like my daughter or granddaughter."

"I didn't know you were married," Robert said, "I've been here for almost a week and you never said a word."

"I wanted to surprise you," the uncle answered with a shy smile.

Rochelle went to her room to unpack, and the uncle told Robert they'd gotten married a year ago. "It's hard, being lonely," he said. "No one here can stand me. It's because I'm rich and Jewish and Iraqi and only tell the truth and don't kiss anybody's ass. Rochelle is a good and pretty girl, an orphan, she only has an aunt, in Paris, and despite all she's been through in her life she makes me laugh and fills my house with light." He looked at Robert and his eyes sparkled. "I know she loves me like you do a father, or an uncle, she has her own room and sometimes she goes out with her friends. I don't care. I don't ask her many questions. I'm grateful for what she gives me."

Tears ran down his face again and Robert, still surprised, asked, "Why didn't you tell me until now?"

"You didn't tell me much about your family, either," his uncle answered. "I barely know your sons' names. I guess you and I had to take care of ourselves first and cure our longing. Besides, I think I was a little embarrassed."

The three had dinner in silence. Rochelle had a healthy appetite and she smiled each time the uncle refilled her plate. When Robert lay in bed, his head spinning from the great amount of wine he had, trying to avoid her shy looks and her beauty, he suddenly thought of Ruchama and her image went blurry, her face replaced with that of Tehila and her neck growing thin, like Hanna's, her glasses disappearing and her lips smiling Rochelle's wide smiles.

The next day the three of them crowded into Rochelle's little car and went touring the city's streets. The sun was generous and washed over the Avenida Nueve de Julio and the Avenida de Mayo. The uncle explained at length about the governor's pink house, detailing the benefits of the tango clubs on Avenida Córdoba and enthusing over the colorful houses in La Boca district, impressed as if seeing them for the first time. Robert drank in the sights and once in a while sent careful looks towards the silent, smiling Rochelle.

At night she went to visit a friend and Robert and his uncle remained sitting in the large living room, the television screen flickering across from them in silence. "Do you have a television at home already?" his uncle asked, and Robert smiled and shook his head no.

"I'll make sure you have the newest television," the uncle said.

"Ruchama is against televisions," Robert said.

"I'm sure when you have enough money she won't object anymore."

He was silent for a long moment and then asked, "What do you think of Rochelle?" and Robert said, "She's very cute." The uncle sipped his wine. "You must also think it's ridiculous that someone like her married an ancient old man like me," he said, and Robert smiled and said, "Of course not, I'm very happy for you."

"Everyone here laughs at me," his uncle said. "Most of the time I don't care because I'm happy to have her here. Sometimes we even sleep together, but that happens seldom, I don't have the strength for it anymore and I can't always do it."

Robert lowered his eyes. Suddenly the uncle was gloomy. "Am I making you uncomfortable?" he asked, and Robert said, "A little."

"If I could only have a child with her things would be different, all the mean people would shut up and stop smiling behind my back."

He sipped more wine and said, "I've postponed your flight back home." Robert was surprised and looked at him in wonder. The uncle smiled calmingly and said, "I did it because we've hardly had any time, you have so much more to see and you haven't told me anything about yourself and your family yet." Robert said, "Ruchama's alone with the kids, how can I?" and the uncle, decisive and frozen, asked, "Why do you only have two children?" Robert said, "Ruchama was pregnant after we had Hilik but it didn't work out," and the uncle asked, "Why? What was the problem?" Robert answered, "There was an accident, Ruchama got hit in the stomach and after that we couldn't."

The uncle looked down and said, "I'm sorry." He put his glass on the table. "Tell me a little about Ruchama," he asked, and Robert felt his throat contract and her image undo in his mind again. He said, "She's very tall," and the uncle laughed and asked, "As tall as Rochelle?" and Robert said, "Much, much taller than Rochelle."

"Do you love her?" his uncle asked.

Robert looked at him, surprised by his directness. A burst of tears suddenly rose in his eyes and his voice broke. He put the wine glass on the table and his face in his hands, trying to stifle the damn tears that suddenly shook him. The uncle said nothing, waiting patiently for Robert to calm down, but Robert kept bellowing, fighting the flood of tears and the trembling of his body.

His uncle placed a soft hand on his shoulder and said, "I've been looking at you for a week now and my heart is breaking. If I could only turn back time, I'd have never let you have such a hard life, growing up the way you did, orphaned and lonely, with no one but your messed-up sister. But from now on, everything is going to be different. I'll treat you like a king. I'll give you the money you need for the shutters, and even twice as much. Maybe you can finally grow up, maybe you can stop being a ten-year-old kid whose parents are suddenly gone, maybe you can start feeling like you're worth something and can really love yourself and your wife, without feeling like she's doing you a favor."

Robert slowly settled down, wiped his eyes and said, "Thank you."

The uncle hugged his shoulders, handed him the wine and said, "I want to ask you for something too." He breathed deeply before going on. "All I ask is that you stay here a while longer and make sure

Rochelle gets pregnant," he said.

Robert froze. His eyes dried in an instant.

"I can imagine you're shocked by my request," his uncle said, "and I won't be surprised if you decide to get up and leave."

But Robert remained seated, breathless, trying to understand the man who suddenly looked elderly and helpless, almost like Hilik on days when his fever skyrocketed and his eyes begged for the medication to relieve his aching ears.

"I'm grateful to you for giving me a chance to explain my strange request," said the uncle. "It's not a condition or a demand, I'll give you the money for the shutters anyway, and if you decide to say no I'll understand and you'll never hear another word about it." He paused for a moment, trying to gather his strength for the difficult task at hand. "I lied to you before when I said we sleep together," he said. "I can't anymore, and even if I could it wouldn't work. When I was young I had enough opportunities to understand the truth. Rochelle isn't my first wife. God took away my ability to have children but not the dream or the longing for someone who'd let me give them everything I can. You're the only relative I have left, you're young and healthy and strong, you can help me. I promise you no one will ever know about this, I promise to repay you. The money for the shutters is nothing. I'm a very rich man. It would be my way of expressing my gratitude for the gift you might agree to give me."

He took another deep breath and said, "I'm relieved now. I didn't believe I'd be able to say all that."

Robert's mind was racing. His eyes ran around the living room, collecting images from other worlds that flickered silently on the television screen.

"I don't expect an answer right now," the uncle added. "Why don't you go to bed. If you want I'll change your ticket back again tomorrow, and you'll go home with the money I already have ready for you and we won't discuss it again. But if you choose to stay I'd be the happiest man in the world."

Robert stayed. The next day the uncle packed up a small suitcase, said goodbye to Robert and Rochelle and disappeared for a week.

The two remained alone in the large house, the servant was also sent on a sudden vacation. They talked very little. Had dinners together in the evenings. At nights she'd come to his bed, her face dark and unsmiling, her breaths fast and quiet. Robert liked her long body, her thick hair and the touch of her lips on his shoulders. He'd wait for her, naked and chilled, and when his excitement turned into horror and paralyzed his body, Rochelle would caress and calm him until she'd gather him into her, silent the entire time.

A week later the uncle came back, smiling and cheerful and full of plans for shared activities. He didn't ask and didn't wonder, did not even insinuate, his eyes were devoid of fear or suspicion, his cheeks blushed and his wrinkled skin stretched as if a sudden youthful spirit blew through him.

Robert and his uncle began taking long drives. They'd sleep in small hotels on the beach, get rowdy at tango clubs like two mischievous children and return home, devour the delicious feasts Rochelle made for them and then go out again until morning. Once, the uncle made Robert take a puff of a marijuana cigarette and Robert coughed and giggled for a long time. Rochelle didn't join them. Even when they ate her cooking together they never mentioned the week they'd spent alone.

Except for the one evening when the phone rang and the uncle answered and turned pale, and after he hung up he fell on Rochelle's shoulders and mumbled excitedly that the test results were in and that she was pregnant. Robert watched the two of them hugging and weeping with happiness and his throat contracted. The uncle wiped his young wife's tears, kissed her eyes and then went to Robert and hugged him for a long time.

Six weeks after embarking on his journey, Robert sat down in a plane again, wads of bills clinging to his stomach and bags of diamonds rubbing against his underwear. The plane's windows were covered and the long neon lights were turned off and darkness spread around him. He leaned back in the wide first-class seat, another surprising gift from his uncle, and pleasure spread over his body, washing him with small, confusing waves of yearning. A yearning for Shlomi, who might have forgotten his anger and the stinging slap to his face by now, a yearning for Hilik, whose ears may already be calm and his breathing peaceful, a yearning for his giggling uncle who seemed to have gotten his youth back, a yearning for Rochelle's smiles and her quick breaths, a yearning for Hanna's cool and slender neck. Robert worked hard to think of Ruchama and her face melted again. He wondered how he'd present the expensive luggage his uncle gave him, how he'd brighten her dark gaze with his plans, weave happy dreams and ignite a new fire in her. Robert thought he might keep the diamonds a secret and surprise her only a few days later, call her out to the laundry balcony and tell her to look down to the street, where a moving truck would be waiting, filled with furniture and appliances and gifts. He might take some of the diamonds and embed them in a special piece of jewelry, surprising her by placing it around her neck. Maybe he'd offer to get a new apartment. Spacious and well-lit. Maybe he'd build her a special room with a triangle ceiling and install shelves with his good hands and pile her books on them.

A bitter taste came to his mouth, his eyes began to close and he thought, all these plans are really intended to buy her love. Suddenly the plans seemed weak and pale, a small gust of transparent haze that burned the eyes and scorched the soul.

In the airport in Paris, Robert sat on the same familiar bench, across from the hair salon. He waited for his second flight to take him back home to Israel. Only a three-hour wait. This time everyone was polite, giving him the respect deserved by first class travelers with shorn hair and clean, expensive clothing.

A great anger crawled and searched until it filled him through. An image of his uncle and Rochelle hugging and crying tears of joy was imprinted in his mind. His semen was absorbed into Rochelle's body and became a small fetus that was his own and which he'd never see. That was his agreement with his uncle. That was his gift and he'd erase it from his mind forever, but it would not be erased. How could he eliminate it when it kept coming back to him? And Ruchama, she'd look at him through her old glasses and see a secret in his eyes. She'd ask and he'd stutter. And Shlomi and Hilik would wish to break a path through the walls he'd need to build around himself now. He must bury his secret in the ground and cover it with a headstone to which he will keep returning, even if he doesn't want to, to place small stones on it and grieve. His seed was already sprouting and Rochelle was rocking it and placing it in the uncle's warm arms. Ruchama told him he was a body and that the rest of him was unfamiliar. Bills of money and tiny diamonds scratched his body now. Suddenly they were light and frivolous, superfluous, an annoying burden, proof of his smallness. He felt smaller than ever, growing smaller and shrinking and becoming an invisible fetus. If Julia, Ruchama's laughing mother, were alive, she'd probably give him one of her pricking laughs and say, "You're petite, I always knew you were a petite, stupid little Tiberian midget, going off and selling his sperm to the highest bidder. I once thought you had a big heart, now I see your heart's petite too, small and clumsy like a praying mantis, handing out forbidden gifts so he can cover himself with diamonds."

A great anger flooded him.

I'll never speak with my uncle again.

Tehila was right all along, holding a grudge and blaming him for our parents' death.

I hurt Tehila too. I killed her and said nothing.

And now I'm asking her for help again, asking her to influence her kibbutz members to let me install shutters.

And Rochelle.

I gave in to her silence. I caught her foolishness.

And Hanna. And Shmuel, who collapsed because of me and left her fluttering in my hand.

A fool, just like me.

I call her at her work at the agency and offer her dulce de leche. She yearns for me and doesn't know I've been selling my sperm.

And Shlomi with his big eyes. And my hand slapping his cheek, trying to erase what his eyes saw.

You can't erase. I can't erase their image.

Hugging and crying.

Like Ruchama and I hugged and cried when the pregnancy ended and we had a crumpled child.

I won't be able to erase it from my eyes and Ruchama will see.

She's blind but she can see. She's a witch and a sorceress.

She'll lay a curse on me. I'll have to wear a scarf like her poor sisters.

Instead of poems she'll write curses. She'll sit under the triangle ceiling in the room I'll build her and write curses.

My uncle is old and crumbly, like the books in Ruchama's boxes. One day he'll die. Soon.

Rochelle will go visit her aunt in Paris. She has an aunt, too.

She'll land in this airport. Maybe she'll walk by this bench, carrying my son or daughter. She'll come show her aunt the baby before she dies.

Maybe she'll stop at the hair salon.

Maybe she'll ask the hairdresser with the purple bowtie to chop all her thick hair off.

Maybe she'll sit down and order soup and dip small pieces of baguette into it. Dip and soften and put them in my son or daughter's mouth.

Maybe I'll keep sitting here. Stay here for years.

And one of these days I'll meet her. We'll have soup together, feed our small child together.

I gave my uncle my word. He'll die without knowing that I broke my oath.

Send terrible curses from his grave. Disown me of his diamonds.

He'll summon mean red cops to strip me of my clothes and tear the money and diamonds off me, taking away my labor fees.

How can I return home with nothing?

I've been gone for six weeks and now I'll return empty-handed.

How could I tell Ruchama about the small hotels on the beach? About the marijuana cigarette that made me happy. About Rochelle's cooking that tasted better than all the pastries she'd made for me. How can I explain why I cut my hair?

My hair looks now like my dead father's hair in the pictures my uncle still saves.

My uncle is small like me, like my father, we're all petite. Ruchama is tall and so is Rochelle.

Rochelle has an aunt to go to. I have an uncle to return from.

You see, Ruchama, my life suddenly looks like those poems you used to like and read to me and point at the recurring words, at sentences that reflect and flip, at rhyming syllables. I didn't understand and was impressed by your intelligence. And now pieces of our lives rhyme. We are the poems you wanted to write and may now write in your new room. I feel like one word that doesn't understand the poem. Like Hilik told you once, I can read the words, but not the stories, and you laughed and were impressed with his wisdom. He wants to be a cover. I'm a word, you're a word, and so are Shlomi and Hanna and the late Shmuel, and my uncle and Rochelle, hugging and crying and happy because they just received a new word, an invisible one.

You see, Ruchama, we are all words and Hilik will be our cover. Write a pretty poem. Don't ask me to explain. I'm a new word that isn't in the dictionary. I'm a short and shorn word, small of stature and meaningless.

I'm sorry I left. I'm sorry I'm back. I'm sorry I cut my hair.

Robert got up from the bench, sat at a small table at the nearby café, ordered a steaming white soup, softened lumps of fresh baguette inside it, chewed and swallowed, paid, got up and sat on the chair of the barber with a purple bowtie. The barber recognized him right away, washed his hair, corrected and shaved and trimmed what had collected in the last six weeks. Robert added an extra bill and asked for another wash, so he didn't have to wash himself in the public toilet again.

Ofira waited for him beside the stairwell that was attached to the door of the plane. He recognized her the moment he came out – blushing, wearing nice clothes, made-up face and combed hair, standing and waiting for him excitedly. Only when he stood before her did she recognize him, open her eyes wide and say, "It's you. You've cut your hair. I thought I'd recognize you by your long hair." Robert asked, "Are you disappointed?" and she giggled and said, "Of course not, you're even more beautiful now," and her cheeks reddened even more. She took his hand and walked him to a car that waited by the bus the rest of the passengers boarded. She quickly drove him to the terminal, cut through the line and had his passport stamped, collected his luggage. Within minutes they were in her car again, leaving the airport and starting their way up north. Ofira said, "You're in luck, I'm going to see my family in a kibbutz in the Galilee, so you have a ride home," and Robert said, "Are you sure? I don't want to be a burden," and Ofira said, "I'm completely sure, I would have killed you if you hadn't called."

She drove very fast. Twice Robert asked her to slow down and said, "I'm in no rush, it's very dark and you should be careful," and Ofira laughed and said, "Trust me, I can drive by heart." She told him about the cop who had been fired and also about her name Ofira, that used to be rare and now, since it was the name of a city captured from Egypt in the Sinai Peninsula, had become fashionable. He told her about Buenos Aires and his reunion with his uncle, making sure not to mention Rochelle, trying hard to erase her from his mind.

Right before they reached Afula, Ofira veered off the road surprisingly and drove into a side thicket, raced on the dirt path and stopped the car in the shade among the pine trees. Robert looked at her, surprised, she breathed heavily and her eyes shone, and he asked, "What's wrong? Why did you stop here?"

He felt a shiver in the back of his neck when she turned to him and said, "I'm sorry if I'm scaring you, but it's all because of you, Robert, it's your fault," and the chilled Robert asked, "Why? What's wrong?" She answered, "I've spent the last six weeks since we first met sitting by the phone, praying for you to call. I'm a wreck, I can't concentrate at work, I can't sleep at night, I jump every time the phone rings."

"You barely know me," he whispered. "It's insane, you're scary."

"I'm sorry," she said, "I promised myself I wouldn't say anything, just drive you home and forget it, but I couldn't." She looked down and her hands gripped the wheel like it was a life preserver.

"You think I'm only a body too," he said sadly, and she looked at him, not understanding, wiped her tears and said, "I apologize, forget the whole thing, I'll drive you now and it'll all be over. Promise me you'll wake up tomorrow and remember nothing." Robert sent his hand to her wet face, helping her wipe the tears, trying to stabilize her breaths and alleviate her shame.

They were silent for the rest of the drive, their eyes fixed on the dark road, and Robert couldn't understand why a sweetness had spread in his body. When they reached his street, he stepped out of the car without a word, pulled out his suitcase and shut the door silently. Ofira drove away quickly, leaving him outside his home.

Robert dragged the suitcase to the stairway and was surprised to find Vardina leaning against the wall, wearing a red lace dress and heavy makeup. Vardina saw him and yelled. Maybe she was happy to see him, maybe she was frightened, maybe surprised at his new look. She fell on his shoulders and gave him a long hug.

"What are you doing here, Vardina, in the dark?" he asked. "Why aren't you going home?"

"I can't climb the stairs," she answered. "I have an old elephant's legs. Each step makes me want to die."

Robert hid his suitcase behind the stairs, leaned Vardina on his shoulders and said, "Slowly, I'll help you, and don't talk nonsense, you're not that old yet." They took each step at a time, Vardina sighing with pain and grateful for his strong shoulders. On each step she told him about a different matter, about Hilik's ear treatment, about the cooking operation for Adina's event, about Shlomi's wonders in the kitchen, about Ruchama's bravery and inventions, about the silent Arab workman, the neighbors' generosity with the dishes, Hanna's stupid glass vase, the mayonnaise that makes everything modern, her aching legs, her loneliness and her longing for her mother who'd died years ago and left her alone, her great love for Ruchama, her wish to switch apartments with the Kurds on the first floor, the excessive price they asked for, and about Judy Garland who died and broke her heart.

When they reached her apartment Robert said, "Tomorrow I'll take care of the apartment issue for you, I'll offer the Kurds to buy their apartment from them and let you live there and we'll take your apartment and build a palace." Doubt rose in her eyes and she said, "But where will you get the money? You can hardly afford food, Ruchama had to come and ask me for coffee because you left her penniless." Robert said nothing for a moment, embarrassed by her accusing look, and then said, "Starting today we're rich, you'll see, everything is going to be different."

After she thanked him and went home, Robert went downstairs to get his suitcase. He knew Ruchama and Shlomi hadn't returned from Adina's event yet and couldn't wait to walk home quietly, surprise Hilik, hug and kiss him, listen to his breathing that was no longer sickly and wheezing and wait for Ruchama and Shlomi. But his feet carried him to the path that led to the adjacent building, to Hanna's door.

He knocked on the door and Hanna opened, standing silently before him, staring at his buzzed hair as if at a ghost, wearing a short-sleeved nightgown, her slender neck moving towards him and asking for him and his lips. But Robert detached himself from her and said,

"I just got back, Hanna," and Hanna said, "I can see that, I can also see you've cut your hair, it looks nice, come in, why are you standing outside, Israella's asleep," and Robert said, "I'm not coming in." Hanna asked, "Why not?" and Robert said, "Because Hilik's home alone, and I miss him, and Ruchama and Shlomi are going to be back soon." Hanna whispered, "Then why did you come?" and Robert said, "I wanted to see you, I wanted to tell you we won't be seeing each other anymore." "Why?" asked Hanna, and Robert said, "I can't do it anymore."

Hanna touched his face and neck and caressed the stubble of his head. Robert's throat contracted, her hand was cool on his face and neck and chest. He held her hand gently, as if asking to stop the pleasure spreading through him and pulling him inside, into her blue apartment. She whispered, "I don't understand," and Robert whispered, "I don't completely understand it yet myself, but we can't do it anymore." "Don't you love me?" she asked, and Robert didn't answer.

"You've ruined my life," she said, and Robert said, "I'm sorry."

"You must be tired from your trip, why don't you rest up and come by tomorrow, or even the day after that."

"I won't come again," he said.

"I won't have it, I'll ruin everything for you, you don't know what I'm like when I get crazy."

"Stop it, Hanna, you have to understand."

"How can I understand when even you don't? All I know is that Israella and I are alone now, you killed Shmuel, you've burned my heart."

"Don't talk like that, I didn't kill anyone."

"Come back tomorrow, please," she said, and tears flooded her face, and Robert said, "No," and turned to go home.

He stood and watched Hilik sleep, the boy's breathing quieter than before but still wheezing. He sat carefully on the edge of the bed and Hilik opened his eyes immediately, jumped up and clung to him with his entire body, his head on Robert's neck and his small hand traveling on the crown of his head. "I knew you'd come back," he said.

They sat on the bamboo sofa in the living room. Hilik told him everything he'd already heard from Vardina, and when Ruchama and Shlomi stood in the doorway he said, "Look, Dad's home." Robert sent his hand and pulled Shlomi to him, and his eyes kept going to Ruchama, wondering, can she see secrets in my eyes, will she try to understand, will she see that I'm a new word that isn't in the diction- ary, short and shorn, small of stature and meaningless.

10

On Thursday, January 15th, 1970, Leah Goldberg[2] died. The next day Shlomi returned from school to a silent apartment. Hilik welcomed him with a whisper, "Keep it down, Mom's in mourning." Shlomi asked, "Why?" and Hilik answered in a whisper, "Because Leah Goldberg died."

"Who's Leah Goldberg?" Shlomi wondered.

"She's a poet and she had cancer, she died yesterday," Hilik continued whispering.

"But why is Ruchama in mourning?"

"She loved her and her poems very much."

Shlomi examined his younger brother's wide eyes for a long time, trying in vain to find a trace of a smile or a shadow of a prank, and raised his voice, "I'm sick of your lies, you're just a little lying kid," and Hilik got scared and whispered, "Don't shout, she's been crying all morning, her bed is like a puddle. And don't call me a little kid, you're a little kid just like me."

Shlomi dropped his bag to the floor. The thump spread in the standing air of the apartment like ripples around a pebble. Hilik was scared by the noise and opened his eyes even wider. Shlomi ignored him and went to the kitchen.

Boxes of groceries sat there, just as they'd been placed yesterday after he'd gone shopping with Ruchama.

Fifty people were to come to the Kurds' new home the following day to celebrate their first grandson's *bris*. Only a few months ago the silent neighbors cleared their apartment for Vardina and

---

[2] 1911-1970. Goldberg was a prolific Hebrew-language poet, author, playwright, and literary translator known for her modernist, lucid, and straightforward style. Goldberg's poetry, composed with a tragic intonation, deals with her intimate relationship with her mother, Israel, nature, as well as loneliness and the breakdown of relationships.

migrated to the end of the street, where they could see the Sea of Galilee and municipal approvals for expansions were easy to obtain. Ruchama and Shlomi took it upon themselves to nourish the guests. For a Saturday lunch Vardina charged extra, since preparations had to be completed on Friday, before the Sabbath, and burners had to be procured for warming the food up, and an appropriate recipe, suitable for the Sabbath's complexity and beauty, had to be designed.

The preparation plan was posted on the board Ruchama had installed over the dining table. She posted a work plan on the board each time they were hired to cater. After Adina's celebration the orders began rushing in. While Robert established his successful shutter business, Ruchama and Shlomi became a small factory that turned any event into a feast that was etched into the mouths of the guests, exciting their senses and turning into an enthusiastic conversation the next day. As promised, Vardina booked the orders and set high prices from which she took a small, satisfying percentage. Ruchama designed the plans, assisted by the inventions Shlomi wrote down in math notebooks. Vardina composed the grocery list and gave it to the Arab workman, to the great chagrin of Adina, who kept complaining to Robert, "Your wife stole my workman, drugged him with her delicious cakes, confused him with her spicy cooking. I'm not surprised at him, he's an Arab, they have no loyalty, but her – I wouldn't expect this behavior from her." Robert set her up right away with two other silent workmen, younger and more vital. Adina kept complaining, but when Ruchama came to her clothing store she'd serve her jovially, show her the best dresses she'd ordered specially from Tel Aviv and lower her eyes when Ruchama pulled out a bursting wallet and said, "Charge extra commission, you deserve a lot after you opened my eyes with that strange zebra dress you gave me."

Most of the shopping was done by the workman in the Nazareth wholesale market and in the nearby Arab villages, where produce was fresh and inexpensive. In the morning of the cooking day, at sunrise, the workman would pick up Ruchama and Shlomi in his old truck and together they'd go to the butchers and fish vendors. Ruchama would sniff each piece, run her hands over the chickens, raise the fins of fish and check that their gills were blushed enough. The workman would help the vendors wrap up the bleeding goods and place them in boxes packed with ice. Then, as Ruchama napped in the truck, Shlomi would walk among the fruit and vegetable stalls, gather the groceries that were still on the list, choose tomatoes, tap his fingers on the zucchini, weigh eggplants in his hands and pick only the light and meaty ones, shake bundles of parsley and coriander in the air and take in their wet scent, taste olives, smell spices that had just been ground and tell off the vendors, forcing them to succumb and lower their prices. The vendors, who already knew him, would smile and say, "It's better to haggle with this *akrut,* this clever bastard, than with his scary mother with her head in the clouds." While the workman brought the loaded boxes up to their apartment, Shlomi would put on his school uniform, pack the sandwiches Ruchama made, with white cheese and diced cucumber, into his and Hilik's lunchboxes, go over the preliminaries that had to be done in the morning with Ruchama, and walk to school, holding his little brother's hand.

And now the boxes stood in the silence of Ruchama's grief. The potatoes hadn't been peeled, the hunks of meat had not been unpacked, even the legumes remained in their bags rather than being soaked in water. Shlomi was filled with a great anger. It was noon, and they had to finish everything before the Sabbath and make sure the workman took the pots to the Kurds' apartment and placed them on the burners.

Shlomi went to Ruchama and Robert's room, Hilik's wide gaze following him there. The door was closed and Shlomi opened it wide to discover Ruchama bundled in a blue blanket, her head dug into the pillow and the edge of the blanket pulled up to cover half her face. He stood over her and she stared at him with big, moist, naked eyes.

"Get up right now, Ruchama," he said, and Ruchama didn't answer.

Hilik stood at the doorway, holding onto the doorpost, and whispered, "Leave her alone, she's sick."

"Are you sick?" Shlomi asked Ruchama and she didn't answer

again, only continued to breathe under the blanket.

"You're really not all right," he told her off. "You did none of the things we agreed on, if you don't get up we have no chance of finishing the cooking before the Sabbath, we promised them," and Ruchama said, "I'm sitting *shiva* now, don't interrupt me."

Shlomi raised his voice. "You're talking nonsense," and Ruchama said, "Don't yell at me, Shlomi, I'm your mother and you're a kid, you have no right to yell at me, and now get out of my room and let me mourn."

"What do you even care about Leah Goldberg?" he said angrily. "Who is she, anyway?"

"Get out of this room, Shlomi, right now," she answered, her voice muffled under the blue blanket, and Shlomi muttered with anger, "I hope all your poets and all your writers die and I hope all your stinking books burn," and left the room, slamming the door with a sound that spread in tight waves over the house and outside.

Shlomi sat down in the kitchen, quickly piled the dry beans at the edge of the table and began sifting. "Now tell me exactly what happened," he asked Hilik, who sat across from him and began describing the chain of events, making sure to whisper, as if talking to a librarian:

"When we waited for the specialist we met Nurse Dina, who Mom knows from childhood, and Dina said, 'Didn't you hear Ruchama that Aisha died yesterday?' And Mom said, 'Really? Aisha the coal thief? She finally croaked?' And Dina said, 'Yes, they found her yesterday sitting on the beach near the cemetery and they called an ambulance but she was already completely dead and smelled terribly,' so Mom said, 'Very good, I hope she burns in hell till there's nothing left,' and Dina said, 'Listen to the way you talk Ruchama, and the kid is sitting right next to you and can hear your scary words,' and Mom told Dina, 'I don't care if he can hear, if that stinking Aisha had died a long time ago Hilik and Shlomi might have had a little brother, if I could I'd burn her myself,' and Dina was shocked and told Mom, 'You've changed Ruchama, ever since you got rich you got a foul mouth.'"

Shlomi, his hands flying automatically through the beans, pushing out small pieces of grit, looked at Hilik and said, "Aisha is the woman who punched Ruchama in the belly when she was pregnant."

"I know," said Hilik, "you don't have to explain it to me."

"But what does that have to do with the poet?" Shlomi asked and Hilik said, "Then we went into the office of the doctor who checks my ears, and he had tears in his eyes again, every time we come for a checkup he has tears in his eyes and sometimes Mom even says 'Stop it, doctor, you promised me you wouldn't cry.'"

"Why does he cry?" Shlomi asked, already confused by his brother's convoluted tale.

"Mom says he's emotional because my ears are healthy," Hilik answered.

"Or he's just a crybaby," said Shlomi, "like my second grade teacher and like Robert," and Hilik said, "Maybe."

Shlomi swept the pile of beans into a colander and began washing them.

Hilik stood at his side and continued his flow:

"And then the doctor told her he was crying because Leah Goldberg died, and Mom said, 'When? What do you mean she died? She's not even sixty,' and the doctor said, 'She died of cancer yesterday, it was in the news, didn't you hear?' And Mom began crying and said, 'I didn't hear, I was out shopping all day.' And then we went home and Mom went to bed and told me to shut the door and not bother her for a week because she was mourning, and that's all, until you got here and began making noise."

Shlomi transferred the washed beans into a large pot, filled it with water, put it on the stovetop and said, "I don't understand anything, why does she need to mourn someone she doesn't even know," and Hilik answered, "Because she loves her words, her heart is broken."

Shlomi shrugged and went to the phone at the corner of the living room. He dialed the shutter factory's number and when Robert answered he told him, "Ruchama decided she's in mourning over her poet, she won't get out of bed and we have to cook for fifty people for tomorrow and it's almost Sabbath."

"I don't understand," Robert wondered, "she's mourning over Rachel the Poetess? But she's been dead for a long time."

"It's a different poet who died of cancer yesterday," Shlomi explained. "Her name is Leah."

Robert sighed. "Is she crying?"

"No," Shlomi answered, "she's just lying in bed and saying she's sitting *shiva.*"

"Maybe we should call a doctor," said Robert, and Shlomi answered, "She's not sick."

Robert sighed again. "I don't know what to do," he said, "I don't know anything about your cooking."

"Why don't you talk to her?"

"You know she won't talk to me at all, it won't help, Shlomi, why don't you call Vardina over to talk to her."

"Vardina can't come upstairs, her legs are swollen."

"So I'll talk to the Kurds and explain the situation, do you agree?"

"What will you tell them?" Shlomi answered angrily. "You'll ask them to cancel their *bris*? Tell them Ruchama can't cook because she's sitting *shiva* over a poet? What will you tell them?"

"You're right," Robert said, "but maybe they'll let me buy the food for them at a hotel or a restaurant."

"It'll ruin everything for them."

"You decide, Shlomi," Robert gave up. "I'll be home soon and I'll do whatever you tell me. Even I can peel potatoes."

Shlomi went downstairs to Vardina's apartment. Her elephant legs were resting in a pail of boiling water and salt. She clicked her tongue and said, "You shouldn't be mad at your mother. I can understand her, it's not an act."

She pulled the phone to her and dialed. Hilik answered. She asked him to call Ruchama to the phone and Hilik said Ruchama locked the door and won't come out and won't talk to anyone. Vardina clicked her tongue again and told Shlomi, "We have no choice but to call the Kurds and cancel the order, I'll compensate them," and Shlomi said, "Don't cancel it, we made a commitment." "So what are you going to do?" she asked worriedly, "I can't stand, I can't help you, what will you do?"

"I'll make *hamin*," he said.

He went back upstairs. Hilik sat on the floor, his ear against the locked door, behind which Ruchama quietly lamented the words she'd loved. "I need your help," Shlomi said, and Hilik whispered, "I'm watching over Mom now, that's more important than the Kurds' silly *bris.*"

Shlomi went into the kitchen. He removed the foam that covered the boiling beans in the pot, his mind roiling and searching for solutions. He explored the corner where Ruchama piled the pots and pans and giant bowls she'd purchased over the previous months and extracted five deep pots. He oiled them well and lined them with slices of potatoes, fried onions and bones from a cow's leg. He piled the boiled beans in two of the pots and added whole chickens, peeled potatoes, onions, garlic and fabric bags filled with rice. In two other pots he piled dried chickpeas, and large chunks of beef on top of them, carrots, heads of celery and fabric bags filled with wheat. The last pot he filled with macaroni he'd cooked till it was slightly softened. In the macaroni he submerged turkey legs and throats.

The pots were heavy but he was able to pick them up off the floor and put them on the stove. Three pots crowded the old stove and the other two sat on the new one Ruchama had recently installed. He transported water from the sink to the pots in a jug until their contents were completely covered. Then he scattered spices, each pot had its own mix, and then some dates and dried figs and some onion skins to brown the stews. Shlomi lit the fire and sat, waiting for everything to boil and begin cooking.

Clouds of steam began to rise from the five huge pots and swirl through the air, spreading hard smells, burning his eyes. He followed the swirls and wondered why the steam didn't spread in waves. Not long before, he'd asked Robert, "Why does the Jerusalem Broadcasting Authority's logo looks so strange?" and Robert said, "It's a symbol that shows how television broadcasts come out of a giant antenna and scatter in waves through the air till they meet our antenna on the roof and bring the shows into our new television."

"Why can't we see these waves?" Shlomi kept asking. "Maybe they're dangerous?"

"They're invisible waves," Robert explained and smiled, "and they travel through the air, which is completely transparent."

Hilik listened to their conversation carefully and suddenly

smiled and said, "That symbol looks to me like a confused man who has a terrible headache and a very thin body."

The smells kept swirling and Shlomi felt nauseous. In less than two hours he'd put the entire meal together, all by himself. His eyes itched a little and his shirt was stained, but the mission was almost accomplished – the pots would boil exactly when the workman came to take them to the Kurds' and put them on the burners. Shlomi wondered where the joy that was supposed to fill him now was, and why instead of feeling proud of his accomplishment, he felt nauseous. If he could he'd invite Ella to sit next to him and watch the pots. Maybe they'd hold hands. Maybe the smell of her vinegar-washed head would spread in waves and push away the sickening steam. Maybe he'd tell her, "Look at how I managed to cook for fifty people without Ruchama," maybe she'd laugh and say, "But it's no big deal, you just made *hamin*," and he'd answer, "It's three different kinds of *hamin* that I invented, now say I'm not a stupid kid like you thought," and she'd say, "You don't have to work so hard to prove it, I forgave you a long time ago."

Over six months had gone by since he'd last seen her. In that time he'd grown tall and his hands strengthened and became skilled and confident. The new third grade teacher told him, "Are you sure you're only eight? You look like a fifth grader," and Shlomi thought to tell her, "It's a waste of time for me to even attend third grade, I already know how to read and write, I'm wasting my time here instead of cooking at home with Ruchama."

In class he'd sit with his eyes almost shut and think of Ella, imagining her in the faraway land she'd gone to with Hanna. Once in a while he'd write down ideas for new recipes in his notebook and the teacher thought he was copying from the blackboard and studying well and concentrating. Then he'd run home and read them to Ruchama and she'd pull out the page, put it in a special bag, smile and nod silently. Two or three times a week they'd cook together and she'd pull one of the ideas from the bag, add it to the recipe and say, "This will be our surprise this time." Sometimes they'd finish late at night when Hilik was already dreaming in his bed, buttressed with books, and Robert had already turned off the light and fallen asleep on the new sofa. Shlomi would ask, "Why is Dad sleeping in the living room?" and Ruchama would answer, "Because he loves sleeping on the new sofa he bought, and you don't have to ask about everything, Shlomi, you're just a kid."

Sometimes they'd already be finished in the evening and then he'd turn on the new television and wait a minute or two for it to warm up and begin playing. One time he called Ruchama. "Come look, they're showing how to make fried eggplants on television." Ruchama said, "For fried eggplants I need a television?" and to make sure Robert could hear she raised her voice and added, "One day I'm going to throw that television out the window," turned on the radio to full volume and added, "It's better to hear all this talk of the war in Sinai than watch some guy named Sami talk to his ugly puppet on television." Shlomi would sit in front of the television and gobble the pastries Ruchama saved for him from their preparations. Hilik would sit in front of the aquarium and say, "I prefer the fish because they're colorful and they don't look me straight in the eyes."

Ella didn't make it to the second grade end-of-the-year party. Ruchama and Robert didn't make it either. Ruchama felt weak after cooking for Adina's event, Robert was tired from his trip to Argentina and busy establishing the new shutter business. Hilik came with Shlomi. They sat on the floor, at the feet of the parents who came to cheer for their kids who were dressed in strange costumes and recited flowery lines on the beauty of the land, the Jewish National Fund forests, agriculture and water sprinklers, the army and its heroes, the distinguished leaders and the kibbutzes, which were the crown of creation and the wreath of Zionism. Hilik whispered to Shlomi, "It's lucky Mom didn't come, she'd get angry and yell that they were sucking up to the kibbutz again." Shlomi didn't answer and only kept wandering with his eyes, maybe they'd run into Ella, maybe she'd come late, maybe she'd hurry up and put on her pioneer outfit and her tembel hat and join the children at the last moment in singing, "The Sun is Blazing in the Mountains."

But Ella didn't come. At the refreshments table, his mouth filled with a stiflingly dry chocolate cake, he heard the crybaby teacher ask Mrs. Katz, "Did you hear anything about Israella? Do you have any idea why she and Hanna aren't here?" And Mrs. Katz, looking refined in a brown suit she wore especially to receive the Exceptional Teacher Award in light of her retirement, nodded worriedly and said, "I haven't seen her in a few days, but at nights there are terrible screams coming from their apartment, I'm very worried," and they both clicked their tongues in sadness until the teacher said, "Some people's lives are one big curse," and wiped two or three tears that suddenly left her eyes. Shlomi took another piece of cake, wrapped it in a blue napkin and told Hilik, "Let's go, I have to bring Ella some cake from the party." Hilik said, "I thought you were fighting," and Shlomi said, "You can bring someone cake even if you're fighting."

After he knocked repeatedly, the door finally opened. Hanna stood there, staring at him as if at a ghost, wearing a short-sleeved nightgown, her thin neck moving backwards and her face, which was swollen and red, twisted as if she'd smelled something foul. She looked only at his eyes, ignoring his extended hand and the cake, ignoring Hilik who stood aside and scratched his head.

"What do you want?" she asked.

"I want to see Ella and ask why she didn't come to the party."

"Israella's sick and you'll never see her again," she said. "Tell your father not to dare ever send you here again, if he wants he can come here himself."

"He didn't send me," Shlomi said. "He wasn't even at the party, I just want to bring Ella some cake."

But Hanna slammed the door in his face.

The steam kept swirling above the pots, hitting the greenish porcelain tiles and turning into heavy drops. Hilik stood at the kitchen doorway and said, "There's a bad smell from your cooking, I can hardly breathe," and Shlomi looked away from the steam and said, "It's like that in the beginning, the smell will slowly get better and in the end it'll be very tasty." Hilik pulled the edge of his shirt over his nose, creating a mask to filter the smell. He said from behind the shirt, "I'm hungry," and Shlomi got up immediately and said, "I'll make you an omelet and salad and when I'm done making the Kurds' meal I'll make us a nice dinner, maybe Ruchama will even agree to stop her mourning and eat and get stronger."

"Don't make an omelet," Hilik said. "I'm hungry but I'm nauseous from the smells, if I eat I'll puke right away."

"Are you sure? Maybe a piece of bread with cheese or jam?"

"Nothing. I feel like throwing up just thinking about it."

Shlomi sat back down and looked at the steam again, yearning for the moment when the pots would boil and the workman would come to take them to the burners, and Robert would be back by then, probably glad that the preparations were over and he didn't have to peel potatoes, maybe he'd agree to try and talk to Ruchama, maybe he'd convince her to stop her mourning and see how in two hours Shlomi fixed the problem and the Kurds wouldn't be disappointed.

Hilik tightened the shirt around his nose and asked, "You like it? You really like all this cooking?" And Shlomi was surprised by the question, thought for a moment and said, "I like inventing, I like it when it gets tasty."

"Your shirt is covered in stains, it's all ruined," Hilik said.

"So what," Shlomi answered, "Ruchama will buy me a new one."

"Sometimes you smell, too." Hilik wouldn't let go. "You smell like spices and gross fish."

"That's not true, I scrub myself with Ruchama's special soap."

"That soap smells disgusting too, like foul jam, even the kids at school say you smell."

"I don't care about them."

"Lately you've become like one of those kids in stories who are sent to work in a coal mine and their hands and cheeks and clothes are covered in dirty stains, or they're sent to an orphanage and barely even get soup or gross porridge with worms."

"What's a coal mine, anyway?" Shlomi asked.

"It's a place in the ground where they have piles of coal."

"How do they get the coal out of there?"

"They cut it out of a hole," Hilik answered. "That's why it's called coal. Because you cut it out of a hole and you burn it."

Shlomi shrugged. "Are you sure you don't want a sandwich?" he asked, and Hilik nodded and went back to guarding Ruchama.

The day after the graduation party, Shlomi didn't go to school. Ruchama told him, "It's the last day of school anyway, we'll get your report card from your teacher, instead of wasting time in class you'll come help me buy dishes," and Shlomi was glad not to have to sit for a whole day and stare at Ella's empty seat while the other kids cheered and passed around their excellent report cards.

He walked Hilik to the school gates and then ran back home to join Ruchama. Together they walked from store to store, stuffing pans and wooden spoons and mixing bowls into their woven baskets to use for future cooking projects. One of the salesmen told Ruchama, "If you want bigger pots you need to go to Tel Aviv or Haifa or check hotel warehouses, because we only have small and medium pots, here in Tiberias people cook every day because they like fresh food, not like in Tel Aviv, where they cook for the entire week or go out to a restaurant." But Ruchama pulled out the bills of money Adina gave her, handed them to the salesman and said, "I'm paying you in advance, with commission, if you order everything I need from Tel Aviv."

Shlomi carried one of the woven baskets. The wooden spoons hit his legs again and again. He wanted to tell Ruchama about the night before, about the door that was slammed in his face and shook Ella and Hanna's stairway, but knew Ruchama would ask questions and his answers would reveal all secrets – about the window he'd shattered and the rock Ella threw that hit Hilik's shoulder and the milk jam and about Robert and Hanna naked on her bed and about the slap Robert gave him.

Shlomi asked nothing and told nothing. When they got home he took the piece of cake he'd been saving since the previous night, peeled off the blue napkin, which was already moist and stained, wrapped it in a fresh piece of wax paper he took from the kitchen drawer and left the apartment.

He knocked on the door again, more insistent than the previous night, his gaze already pointing up, waiting for Hanna's blazing eyes. A moment later she opened the door, still wearing the thin nightgown, her eyes narrow and tired and her face even more swollen and red. Shlomi didn't wait before saying, "I just want to give Ella her piece of cake from the party, I have to give her this cake today or it'll go bad."

Hanna looked at him, her eyes moving up and down from his gaze fixed on her to his hand holding the piece of cake. She sent her hand to grab his shirt collar, wrapping her fingers tight around it, wrinkling the shirt, shaking him again and again, and saying, "You're a shit kid, you're like your father, stinking dog shit, you're like your mother, you're all Arab punks, I wish you'd go back to your stinking countries, I hope the Arabs make dogs out of you, I hope the Arabs butcher you and drink your black, smelly blood, you've ruined my life enough, and if you ever dare show your face back here I'll butcher you myself," and only when she was done talking did she let go of his collar. His face reddened, his throat closed up and a sharp pain shot from his neck down his back. But his hand rose in the air as if to protect the cake, which remained whole, while the other hand fought her choking, shaking arm.

The door slammed in a loud noise that spread in waves within his ears. He stayed standing in the stairway, hardly breathing, his ears ringing and every little movement of the neck launching waves of pain to his back and legs.

After he calmed down his legs carried him from the stairway out to the path. He stood across from Ella's window. The new glass shone in the sun and blinded him. He stood there for a long moment, his eyes fixed on the window, trying not to blink, hoping his gaze would penetrate the glass and spread in tight waves inside her room. He summoned all of his power, for one moment and then another, till he noticed her hand searching at the window, her head rising and appearing and her eyes smiling at him tiredly. Ella opened the window quietly and reached out her hand. Shlomi raised his hand with effort and gave her the piece of cake, suddenly unbearably heavy. Ella took the cake, peeled off the wax paper and began eating in small bites, gulping down its sweetness, licking the chocolate that had smeared on the paper and on her lips, her eyes linked with his the entire time.

His throat relaxed completely and the waves of pain evaporated. She finished collecting crumbs with her tongue and handed

him the wax paper. Then she whispered, "I forgive you for everything and you forgive me too, knockouts like me always forgive,
even kids like you," and Shlomi whispered, "Summer vacation
begins tomorrow, will your mother let you come out?" and when
she shook her head he asked, "So how will we see each other?"

"I'm going with her to Brazil soon, anyway," Ella whispered.

"Where's Brazil?" he asked.

"Far," she answered.

"How long are you going for?"

"A long time."

Shlomi whispered, "That's too bad," and Ella smiled and
whispered, "I'll write you letters, but you'll have to learn how to
read if you want to read them," and Shlomi whispered, "I already
can."

They hadn't seen each other since. Shlomi'd gone back home and
buried the wax paper that was stained with chocolate in the trash,
He didn't tell Ruchama anything. Even when, once in a while,
sharp pain shot from his neck down his back, even then he said
nothing and waited patiently for the pain to subside.

A week later, he went to the crybaby teacher's home to get his
report card. He sat in her living room, his eyes staring at the pictures of her killed sons hung tightly together on a side wall. The
pictures overlooked a small, polished chest upon which objects
were placed in an ordered queue – a stained military cap, a letter
in a wrinkled envelope, a ping pong paddle, a black recorder, a
chewed red pencil, a yellowing booklet whose cover was torn off
and two identical tiny leather wallets.

The teacher gave Shlomi a glass of lemonade and asked, "Why
didn't you come to the last day of school?" And Shlomi sipped
and said, "I had to help my mother with her shopping and I
wanted to bring Ella a piece of cake from the party." The teacher
smiled and asked, "You brought her cake?" And Shlomi didn't
answer and his eyes suddenly filled with tears.

"What's wrong, Shlomi?" the teacher asked. "Why are you
crying?"

"I'm not crying," he said.

"You have tears in your eyes," the teacher said.

"The lemonade is a little sour."

"Feel free here, tell me what's bothering you, whatever you tell me stays here, only you and I will know."

Shlomi sent another quick look to the eyes of the killed boys in the pictures and wondered if they could hear him too. He sipped some more, wiped his eyes and said, "Ella's mother sent me away."

"Don't be mad at her," the teacher said. "Her life is very hard, when she was your age she was in the camps, an orphan, alone with the Nazis."

"I know," Shlomi said. "My mom says she's human powder." The teacher nodded and Shlomi continued, "but that's no reason to send away kids who bring her daughter cake, and it's no reason to hurt me."

"She hurt you? Did she hit you?" the teacher asked.

"I don't care about that," he answered, "as long as I got to give Ella her cake."

The teacher took a deep breath and said, "Ella won't be in your class anymore."

"I know," he said and his eyes went to the killed boys again and noticed one's small smile and the other's large, toothy grin. "Maybe you can explain to me why she's going," he asked, and the teacher explained. "Because her mother got a job in the embassy in Brazil and because she thinks it'll do Ella good to go someplace new."

"Why?" he asked.

"Because Ella is a special girl who sometimes does dangerous things," she answered.

"What did she do?"

"All kinds of things," the teacher said. "It's not important. What's important is she's healthy now."

Shlomi raised his voice. "It is important, I want to know. You told me to feel free, you told me only you and I will know what we say here, so I want you to tell me what she did."

The teacher lowered her eyes, escaping his, and then said, "Ella was confused, she accidentally thought the medicine they had at home was candy and she accidentally ate it and it poisoned her." Shlomi looked at her rushing eyes and said, "I know it wasn't an accident, I know Ella," and the teacher said nothing.

Then she made him finish all the lemonade and gave him his report card. Shlomi told her about the day the bunch of dates fell and smashed at his feet and that since then he'd known how to read. The teacher looked at him doubtfully and handed him the day's paper. He read her the title about the air raid in the Golan Heights, seven Syrian airplanes taken down, and the teacher put her hands together excitedly and, as was her habit, burst into tears.

A thin rain fell outside and knocked on the kitchen window. Shlomi went to the pots. The steam kept swirling but the liquid had yet to boil. He sniffed each of the concoctions and wondered why their smell made him nauseous too. He opened the small window. Drops of rain sprayed the marble and the steam swept out the window, escaping outside and mixing with the rainy air. Shlomi thought about the medicine Ella had swallowed. Was she trying to poison herself or did she really have an accident, like the teacher said? Did she step on the shards of glass from the window he broke and drink from the bottles of dark liquid that were left over from Shmuel's death to alleviate her pain? Did she want to punish him? Maybe she wanted to punish Hanna and Robert and make herself forget their image, naked in the blue living room. Many months had passed since she told him she'd forgiven him and he'd yet to receive any sign of life. Hilik found him a book that described Brazil, the carnival and the soccer games on the streets. Maybe she's dancing at the carnival, maybe playing soccer with kids who taught her to read and write their language, maybe she'd forgotten how to write in Hebrew and that's why she hasn't been sending letters, maybe she'd forgotten his address, maybe the letter was lost in the ocean, maybe she found new bottles and managed to poison herself completely.

Over six months ago, walking back from the teacher's house, he walked the path across from Ella's building. He climbed the stone wall, the report card dropped from his hand, he stood on the tips of his toes and looked into her apartment through the fixed window. The place was empty, the furniture had been removed and the blue drapes had been taken down. While Robert filled his home with new furniture, Hanna removed her furniture and possessions and migrated to Brazil, taking Ella with her and escaping to a new world. Shlomi looked at the empty room and the naked walls and felt time standing still. And now, against the boiling pots and the bad smell, the image returned to float around his mind.

A window, a floor, bluish walls, complete emptiness.

Shlomi thought, that image is like a small stone pulled out of the water. When a stone is pulled ripples also begin surrounding it, but maybe they flow inward, towards it, and not away from it.

The moment he saw Ella's empty room and realized she was far away, that was the moment time stood still. Though life kept flying around him, coming at him in waves, a wave of cooking with Ruchama, and a wave of a new school year. A wave of Robert's complaints of the pots and pans overfilling the apartment, and a wave of Ruchama's silences. A wave of books Hilik begged him to read, and a wave of lists of new recipes in his notebooks. Time has flown around him for over six months, hitting him, touching his frozenness, almost waking him from his slumber of yearning, then being pushed away and making room for the next wave. Once a day he went downstairs to the mailboxes and stuck his hand inside, looking for a letter from her, and then returning to his slumber and to frozen time.

Many days after Ella went to Brazil and disappeared from his world, there came an especially large wave. It moved and shook until it almost hid his longing from him. Summer vacation was over, the high holidays had passed and winter had begun announcing its arrival. This entire time Ruchama stood in front of Robert, silent. Ever since he returned from Argentina he'd tried again and again to revive the silent lunches and dinners. He'd ask questions, tell stories, try to make jokes, but she remained enshrined, shaking her head a little, sometimes nodding it or answering him in one or two words, and mostly quiet and never raising her head to look at him. Her eyes would wander to Shlomi and Hilik and the pots and bowls, but not to his eyes or his carefully cut hair. Until one day, as they sat around the new dining table and ate steaming lentil soup, Robert tried to get Ruchama to talk and said, "Tomorrow's the election, did you decide who you're going to vote for?" and Ruchama nodded, her eyes concentrating on the bowl of soup, and Robert, trying as usual to get her to speak, asked, "Who will you vote for?"

Ruchama raised her head suddenly, looked straight into his eyes and said, "I'm voting for Begin." Robert was surprised by her look, blinked a little and said, "Why? We always vote for Mapai. How come Begin?" and Ruchama said, "That's what I want. I don't have to vote the way you vote, you'll vote for the labor party and I'll vote for Gahal."

Shlomi and Hilik ate slowly, careful not to make any noise and interrupt the conversation that was suddenly rolling and breaking Ruchama's long silences. Robert looked at her, either raging at her intentions or excited about the fact that she'd answered.

"I thought you hated Begin," he said.

"I hate Golda more."

"Why? What did she do to you?"

"She didn't do anything to me and Begin didn't do anything to me and I didn't do anything to them."

"So what happened all of a sudden?" he asked, and Ruchama put down her spoon and said, "What happened is, I suddenly remembered what Shmuel said before he died." Robert went a little pale and said, "How could you remember it, you weren't even there when it happened and I can no longer remember a thing," and Ruchama said, "I remember perfectly well what you told me, word for word I remember it, and you remember it very well too, don't pretend." Robert said, "I just remember he was yelling," and Ruchama said, "That's right, and to this day I'm still trying to understand why he was so upset at you, like you stole something from his miserable life, all you did was say you were voting for Mapai and he got so mad that he died."

Robert said nothing, put the spoon down and then said, "What are you trying to say, Ruchama?"

"I guess he had other reasons to get mad at you," she answered, "otherwise he wouldn't have screamed that way and died."

"What reasons? You weren't even there, what are you talking about?"

"I don't know, you tell me, just don't think I'm stupid because I'm not stupid."

Shlomi kept eating in silence, careful not to look up at his parents.

"A week after you got back from Argentina she went to Brazil," Ruchama said.

"So what? What does one have to do with the other?" Robert asked, the Rs rolling in his mouth, spraying out.

"Why did she go without saying goodbye? She never even came to get that ugly jar she lent me."

"How did you expect her to come say goodbye, you can't stand her."

"I expected her to come say goodbye to you, or at least let her strange daughter say goodbye to Shlomi, they were friends, she just took her and disappeared."

"I'm sure you've heard the rumors about her daughter and what she tried to do."

"I already told you I'm not stupid."

Robert closed his eyes for a moment as if trying to push away the burbling that threatened inside him. "Explain the connection to me, and what you're accusing me of right now," he asked.

"You explain it to me," she demanded, firmer than him.

"Again you're putting together things that aren't related," he said, "I already told you, life isn't one of your poems, you can't make things connect with force. I have no idea why she left and I have no idea why she didn't say goodbye."

"Don't try and teach me what life is and don't try and teach me what poems are," she said, and Robert smiled with an effort, trying to look amused, and said, "And that's why you're voting for Begin?"

"No," she answered, "I'm voting for Begin because I thought about what Shmuel told you then and that's what convinced me. I'm voting for Begin to remember poor Shmuel, who was human powder. That's what I want. And you can keep voting for whomever you want, it suits you to vote for Mapai, keep sucking up to the kibbutzniks."

"I'm sucking up?" he asked in fake wonder.

"We saw the chocolates you gave them for the holidays and

the wine bottles and candy," she hurled at him, her eyes blazing behind the glasses and the steam rising from the soup.

"Those were gift baskets," Robert explained. "They give me work, it's only thanks to them that the shutter business is successful."

"They give you work because you suck up to them."

"For months I've been trying to talk to you and you barely answer," he said, his voice suddenly cracked. "When you finally decide to open your mouth such poison comes out that I just can't understand, I can't understand any of it, what does Begin have to do with Hanna and Brazil and chocolates and kibbutzes? What's the connection?" and Ruchama said, "Think about it, you'll get it," and picked up her spoon and returned to her soup and her silence.

Robert went silent too. The silence between the two moved in a big wave and shook Shlomi from his longing. Suddenly he thought, maybe I have to awaken the block of time I've become frozen in, maybe my longing for Ella is creating dangerous waves. Her face floated in front of his, framed in the fixed window, her tongue licking the chocolate from the wax paper. Then the vision faded and her face reddened and swelled. Her neck became slender and was sent back and she looked like Hanna. Maybe I need to stop missing her. Maybe if I forget Ella Robert will forget Hanna and Ruchama will forget Shmuel and the silence won't hurt so much. Shlomi looked up from the soup bowl and a sharp pain flew from his neck down his back. I cannot forget. I won't forget. I love her. I love you, Ella.

A few days after the election, the silence of the house was broken. Tehila, Robert's sister, came to visit. Equipped with an old suitcase full of clothes and possessions, she stood at the doorway, put the suitcase in the corner of the living room and fell on Ruchama's neck. Then she gave Ruchama a bag full of clementines and attacked Shlomi and Hilik with kisses, raving over Shlomi's height and little Hilik's shining eyes. Ruchama looked at her with a long face and asked, "Are you healthy, Tehila?" and Tehila answered, "Why? Do I look sick to you?" and Ruchama said, "You're thin like a skeleton, you're less than half your old size," and Tehila said, "My life is no picnic," and then sat wearily on the new sofa, looked at the turned-off television and said, "Good for Robert, you can tell he's working hard and earning well."

A worry rose in Ruchama. She sat by Tehila and said, "You surprised me. I didn't know you were coming, Robert never told me."

"I surprised myself too," Tehila said.

"What's wrong?" Ruchama asked. "There are clouds in your eyes."

"I'm in trouble," Tehila answered, "I need to stay here for a while. I'm sorry, Ruchama, if I'm in the way, but I have no choice."

"You can stay here for as long as you want."

"I'll tell you everything in a minute, but first I have to take a shower, I haven't showered in four days."

"Why?" asked Ruchama, her worry growing with each moment.

"Because they disconnected my hot water." Tehila smiled with an effort.

"Who disconnected it? Why?"

"Please, Ruchama, I'll take a shower and rest first and then I'll tell you everything."

Ruchama gave her a towel and sent her to the bathroom. Then she dialed Robert's number. "Your sister's here," she said, and Robert said nothing, perhaps surprised by Tehila's sudden arrival, perhaps surprised that Ruchama called him herself rather than asking Shlomi or Hilik. Ruchama continued, "She looks very sick, something bad's happened."

After hanging up she went into the children's room, quickly changed the sheets on Shlomi's bed and said, "Shlomi, I'm giving your bed to Aunt Tehila, she has to rest. At night you can sleep with Hilik, and in the meantime you can help me and make her a cup of tea with mint leaves." Shlomi said, "I thought you couldn't stand her," and Ruchama said, "Stop thinking so much, Shlomi, make her a cup of tea."

Tehila came out of the bathroom, wrapped in a towel and shivering. Ruchama helped her open the suitcase and get dressed and put her in Shlomi's bed. Tehila lay on her side, her shaking body folded under the blanket and her black hair spreading wet stains on the pillow. Ruchama put a hand on her forehead and said, "You're burning up," and Tehila said, "I'll just sleep for a little while, your hand feels good," and fell asleep.

Tehila slept for many hours, and when she awoke she saw Ruchama and Robert sitting on Hilik's bed and looking at her with worry. Tehila smiled at them, sat back in Shlomi's bed and sipped from the cup of tea Ruchama served her. Ruchama put a hand on her forehead again and said, "Your fever's gone down," and Tehila said, "I needed a bath and a nap, I'm not sick." Shlomi looked at Robert's face, which had grown long and gray. Once again he felt a great wave swelling in the distance, threatening to get closer and shatter his stagnation. Then too, when Robert slapped him so hard his ears rang, then too, his face had been long and gray.

Ruchama asked Shlomi and Hilik to sit in the living room, even turned on the television for them. Hilik stared at the aquarium and Shlomi listened intently to the conversation between Tehila and his parents in the children's room. Tehila told them she was asked to leave the kibbutz. "You were kicked out?" Ruchama asked, and Tehila said, "Not exactly, they told me I'd better leave." "Why? What did you do?" Robert asked, and Tehila answered, "They found out I voted for Begin in the election."

"Is that true?" Robert wondered. "Did you vote for Begin?"

"Yes," Tehila said. "And I don't regret it."

"But you're a kibbutz member," he said. "What's Begin to you?"

"I am a kibbutz member," she answered, "but I don't have to be another sheep in their flock, I don't have to vote according to their decisions."

"I voted for Begin too," said Ruchama.

Then they were quiet for a few moments and Shlomi lowered the volume of Sami and his puppet chatting and joking and listened closely.

"It's been fifteen years since I joined and they still call me the Tiberian. I'm the dark girl from Tiberias to them," Tehila said. "So I told them I'd rather vote for Gahal, where they don't ask their members to get blood tests."

"I didn't know you were unhappy there," Robert wondered.

"I'm not unhappy," said Tehila, "I like my solitude, I like it there, except for when they expect me to salute them for every little thing."

"But how did they even find out who you voted for? The polls are confidential," Ruchama said, and Tehila laughed and said, "Because when they counted the votes there was only one for Gahal. They suspected me and when they asked me I didn't deny it, I'm not ashamed."

There was another silence, until Robert asked, "Why did you leave, anyway? You said they only suggested you leave and you said you were happy there, so why did you leave?"

"I didn't," Tehila said. "I came to be here for a while and ask you about it because it has to do with you." He looked at her, amazed, and she said, "They're threatening that if I don't leave they'll cancel all the shutter orders they placed with you."

Another silence, this time longer and more burdensome. Shlomi lowered the volume even more and heard Ruchama say, "Now you see why I can't stand the kibbutzes?" and Robert ignored her and asked Tehila, "What do you want to do?" and Tehila said, "It's your decision, you tell me," and Robert said, "The parts are all ready, if they cancel the order now I'll be stuck with them, it'd a terrible loss for me." Tehila was quiet for a moment and said, "You decide. I joined the kibbutz because of you, and if I leave it's going to be because of you. You tell me what to do."

"You went to the kibbutz because of him?" Ruchama asked with amazement, "Why?"

But Tehila didn't answer, and only after several minutes Robert said, "I have to speak with them first, they can't behave that way to you after you gave them your soul, and they can't cancel the order." Then he got up and left the apartment.

Ruchama sat Tehila down in the kitchen, put a plateful of food in front of her and asked, "Why did you say you joined the kibbutz because of Robert?" and Tehila started eating and said with her mouth full, "It doesn't matter, you'll see they'll tell him stories about me, like in *Arabian Nights*, and convince him how right and noble they are," and Ruchama said, "So why do you stay there? How can you stand it?" and Tehila said, "Where else would I go?"

Robert returned two hours later. This time the kids were seated in the kitchen, and Ruchama placed omelets and salad on the table and asked them to eat quietly. Tehila sat on the carpet in the living room, Ruchama and Robert sat on the sofa across from her. Shlomi whispered to Hilik, "Chew quietly, don't interrupt me, I'm trying to listen to them," and aimed his ear at the living room.

"I sat with the kibbutz secretary," Robert told them. "He told me he didn't have a choice and that it wasn't because you voted Gahal."

Tehila started laughing. "You see, Ruchama?" she said, "I told you he'd come back with stories from *Arabian Nights*."

"What did he tell you?" Ruchama asked Robert, and he answered in a small voice, "He said Tehila was involved in different things that hurt the kibbutz."

Tehila bellowed in laughter again, this time irritated and short, and said, "What things exactly?"

"He said you had relationships there," Robert answered, "with married men, for instance," and Tehila said, "That filthy dog." Ruchama said, "So why don't they kick the married men out? Why are they picking on her?" and Tehila laughed again and said, "You're naïve, Ruchama." Robert said, "The secretary also said they knew you had private money that you didn't report and you sent it to the Black Panthers."[3]

Tehila's laughter stopped. "You send money to the Black Panthers?" Ruchama asked.

"Yes," Tehila answered.

"Where did you get the money?" Ruchama asked, her voice more and more incredulous.

"Robert gave me some when he got back from Argentina," Tehila answered. "He forced me to take it because I didn't want a cent of our uncle's money, but ultimately I thought it could help

---

[3] An Israeli protest movement of second-generation Jewish immigrants from Middle Eastern countries. One of the first organizations in Israel with the mission of working for social justice for Mizrahi Jews (descendants of Jewish communities from the Middle East and parts of the Caucasus).

them, they buy bread and milk for the poor."

Robert raised his voice and said, "If I'd known that's what you were going to do I wouldn't have given you the money. What do you have to do with the Black Panthers? What do you care about them?"

"I'm a bit of a Black Panther myself," she said.

"This isn't funny, Tehila," Robert said.

"I'm not kidding, I'm completely serious."

"The secretary says you voted for Begin just to tease them."

"So what, they deserve it," said Tehila and her rolling laughter caressed their ears.

"I'm surprised at you," said Robert. "You're acting like a little girl."

"You're right," she answered, and her laughter died in an instant, "I'm growing smaller every year, I used to be big, I had the strength to raise you and take care of you when you broke both your arms, I guess you've forgotten all that."

Robert went quiet, got up, took a few steps, sat back down and said, "What do you want me to do?" and Ruchama said, "She's your sister, cancel the deal, don't let them blackmail you and her." Robert said, "What for? So she can go back there and be eaten alive? It doesn't look like she has it too good there," and Ruchama said, "So invite her to come live here, you can give her the apartment you bought from Vardina, I have no intention of connecting the apartments like you wanted, anyway. You can hire her to work in your company, she's a Black Panther, she can do a great job haggling with your kibbutznik customers, she won't let you suck up to them." Then Robert raised his voice, "Why are you interfering? How come you're talking to me all of a sudden?" And that was the first time Shlomi could recall hearing a shout leave his father's mouth. Ruchama said, "Don't yell at me, Robert," and Robert said, "So stop making her offers at my expense," and Ruchama yelled, "She's your sister! Why don't you explain to me once and for all why you're so afraid of her, what do you care if she moves here and works with you?"

Tehila stayed three days. At night she'd turn over in Shlomi's bed, and the bed squeaked and woke him up, but Tehila ignored his looks. Hilik kept sleeping, dreaming of the stories Tehila told him in the afternoon when he returned from school. In the mornings she helped Ruchama with preparations for her cooking and then watched Shlomi's quick hands cutting and chopping and stuffing and frying, impressed, and each time she put her hand on his shoulder and caressed his neck he'd curl up in her arms and sharp pain would wash over his body.

Robert went to Tel Aviv to buy materials and equipment. He stayed there until Tehila left.

One night, Shlomi heard stifled crying from the kitchen. He couldn't decide which of the two was crying, maybe it was Tehila and maybe Ruchama and maybe both of them together. Even Hilik woke up and whispered, "What's wrong? Why are they crying?" and Shlomi shrugged and said, "Aunt Tehila is telling Ruchama stories in whispers, all I can hear is crying," and Hilik whispered, "She's probably telling her about Dad and how miserable they were when their parents died."

In the morning, Tehila's suitcase was by the door. Tehila was bathed and dressed but her eyes were red. Ruchama was as white as a wall. Tehila hugged Hilik and then Shlomi, who curled up in her arms again. Ruchama took a big wad of bills from her purse, placed it in Tehila's hand and said, "I'll send you more in two weeks, don't worry." Tehila clung to Ruchama and said, "I know you could never stand me, I hope now you understand and that you'll forgive me," and Ruchama didn't answer, only hugged Tehila and then helped her pick up her suitcase and sent her on her way.

When the door closed Shlomi asked, "Where is she going?" and Ruchama said, "She's going to Jerusalem, she'll find work there and maybe even join the Black Panthers." "Who are these panthers?" Shlomi asked and Ruchama answered, "People who don't think only about themselves all the time."

That night, Robert returned from Tel Aviv. He didn't ask about Tehila, hardly said a word. Shlomi was alert. The apartment was awash with tight waves that closed around him in circles, and he sat in the dark on his bed and listened.

He heard Robert sit by Ruchama, who was lying in bed, and ask, "What did she tell you?" Ruchama didn't answer and Robert coughed a little and said, "She's a fantasizer, don't believe her, we were little kids, it doesn't matter anymore."

"You've been lying to me our entire life," Ruchama said.

"I haven't been lying."

"You lied to me about Hanna," she said, and Robert didn't answer.

"If I could at least understand what you saw in her," she said, "what dragged you toward her, maybe her white skin, maybe the long thin neck and the straw hair with her stupid hairdo. What did you think, that she was the Empress of Austria? The Queen of England? She's nothing but a Polish clerk with a voice like a broken bicycle horn and an annoying personality."

Robert coughed again and said nothing. Ruchama sniffled repeatedly and finally said, "You ran from your sister to me and then you ran from me to her, who else did you run to?"

Now Shlomi could only hear his coughs and her breaths. Then she continued and said, "From now on I want you to sleep in the living room, your new sofa will be very comfortable," and Robert said in a hard voice, "Don't kick me out, Ruchama," and Ruchama said, "I didn't, you're the one who ran away." Robert said, his voice choked, "I'll go to the living room, but just so you know, I'm waiting, I'll wait for you my entire life, until you tell me to come back."

When he opened his eyes, Shlomi saw that the pots had boiled and the swirling steam continued fighting the drops of rain outside the open window. The sharp smells surrounded him and woke him from his sudden slumber. He covered the pots and lowered the flame. A moment later the silent workman came in, wrapped towels around the pots and cleared them out. By the time Robert got home the smells had evaporated and Shlomi had closed the window.

Robert got Hilik up from his perch by Ruchama's closed door and said, "Why are you sitting on the floor? Your butt is like a popsicle, go to the living room and warm up." Hilik sat by Shlomi in the living room. Robert knocked on the door and begged Ruchama to open it. "Open up, Ruchama, you're scaring the children." Finally the door opened. Ruchama came out,

passed by Robert and went to the living room, stood in front of
Shlomi and Hilik and said, "Don't worry about me, I'm mourning Leah Goldberg, please respect that and give me a few days to
think about her and about her poems that I loved so much." Shlomi said, "But what about the cooking? We have orders for next
week," and Ruchama smiled and said, "Vardina will take care of it
and cancel the orders, it's not a big deal, I'm too sad now to make
other people happy." She took a glass of water and returned to her
room, shutting the door in front of Robert's silent eyes.

On Sunday afternoon the Kurds knocked on the apartment door.
Shlomi opened it. They asked to speak with Ruchama and he told
them she was sick and led them to Vardina's apartment that used
to be theirs. In small, polite voices, they told Vardina about the
bris that was ruined. The pots of *hamin* stew were placed on the
burners and all night long bad smells emanated from them, until
they had to be emptied into the trash. When the guests came,
a cloud of nauseating smell still lingered in their home. They
couldn't open the windows because they worried that the winter
air would come in and give their newborn grandson a cold. The
neighbor said, crying, "We so looked forward to this moment,
why do we deserve this punishment, all these years we were good,
quiet neighbors, no one heard a peep out of us, all these years we
respected Ruchama and helped her when she needed us, I don't
understand why she made us a spoiled meal."

Vardina put her hands together in sorrow and looked at Shlomi who stood in the corner of the living room, his face blank,
deep in his frozen state and his slumber of longing.

"I apologize," Vardina told them. "Ruchama didn't do it on
purpose, everyone gets sick sometimes, I'll compensate you well,
instead of you paying me I'll pay you and I'll also leave you the
five big pots."

"What am I going to do with those pots?" asked the neighbor.
"They're too big, I cook fresh food every day."

"Then I'll think of another compensation, I promise," Vard-
ina said, pulled a few bills from her purse and gave them to the
Kurds. "This is for now," she said. "When my legs stop hurting
I'll go to the bank and get more money and send it to you."

After the Kurds left, she told Shlomi, "You shouldn't feel guilty for what happened, you did your best, no one expects an eight-and-a-half-year-old boy to do magic instead of his mother." Shlomi shrugged and went home. Ruchama had just left her room to refill her glass with water. Shlomi told her, "The Kurds came to complain that I cooked them smelly food," and Ruchama said, "It really did smell here a little on Friday. No matter. I'm crazy about you anyway and next time I'll show you how to make *hamin*."

"Are you still in mourning?" he asked.

"Yes, until Thursday," she answered.

"What kind of stupid mourning is this, no one comes to comfort you, no one prays," Shlomi said, and Ruchama smiled and returned to her room.

On Tuesday afternoon Robert came home from work, took a large blanket and piled his clothes and some towels and dishes inside of it, tied the ends of the blanket together, hoisted the large bundle on his back and told Shlomi, "Come help me." They went down to the apartment below, the one that used to belong to Vardina and was now filled with the old bamboo furniture. Robert had been storing it in the empty apartment since the new furniture arrived, as if he knew that one day it would be used again.

Shlomi and Robert poured water all over the apartment floors, polished, soaped, collected the dust that gathered throughout the previous months. Robert opened the bundle and arranged his clothes in the closet. When the sun was almost gone, a small truck appeared in front of the building, and from it were pulled, one by one, a fridge, a stove, a heater, a fan, a washing machine and three large televisions. Within minutes, Robert put the new appliances in their place and plugged them in. He installed the televisions in the living room and in the kitchen and in the bedroom, which contained only an old mattress. Shlomi asked, "What do you need three televisions for?" and Robert said, "Because I like watching television and you and Hilik like it too."

Then they went back upstairs and Robert stood at Ruchama's door and said, "I'm moving downstairs, Ruchama, I'll wait for you there, until you tell me to come back."

On Thursday at noon Ruchama rose from mourning, went into the kitchen and began cooking and baking. The apartment was filled with pleasant smells of cinnamon and burnt sugar. She packed three large bags of warm cookies and asked Shlomi to give one to the Kurds, the other to Vardina and to place the third in the kitchen of the apartment Robert had moved into.

When he finished delivering the bags, Shlomi stood in front of the mailboxes in the wall near the doorway to his building. As was his daily custom, he reached his hand inside. He pulled out a bluish, wrinkled envelope. His name and address were written on it in Ella's handwriting. One after another, sharp bursts of pain shot from his neck down his back. Shlomi held up his head. The pain stopped and suddenly his breathing was calm. In the envelope, he found a colorful postcard with a picture of a strange, pointy cliff, a sort of giant mountain surrounded by a few small hills and endless green trees, all overlooking a quiet surrounding body of water. The postcard was attached to a sheet of paper on which Ella wrote:

Faraway Shlomi,
The picture is of Sugarloaf Mountain. I don't know why they call it that. Maybe people think it's sweet. Once I wanted to climb up and then jump off of it. But there is no pile of sand below and you aren't below either. It was only because of you that I jumped on the sandpile. It's only because of you that I'm not jumping here. It's very hot here but cold. Freezing. Wait for me.
Ella

He read it again and again, his eyes clinging to the tight waves that burst from the end of the cliff in the picture and flooded him with yearning. He turned the paper and the envelope over, searching for her address again and again, but couldn't find it. How will I answer her? How will I tell her I'm waiting for her? How will I tell her I'll wait for her my entire life, even when I'm grown up, even when I'm old, I'll wait for her and never stop.

Shlomi went up to the roof, the letter in his hand, held tight. He stood among the antennae and water boilers. The roof was moist with rain. He looked down at the path leading to her home. Almost a year had passed since they lay here, watching the people pulling out her dead father's body through the window. That year, the Sea of Galilee overflowed and threw fish up in the air, and Ella's father died, and Ella jumped off the roof and broke her leg, and Yoram Gaon sang frightening songs that shouldn't be played on the radio, and Robert slapped him and went to Argentina and came back with milk jams and tons of shutters. That year, the words fell on his head, and Hilik's notes gathered inside of him, and the food he cooked with Ruchama stained his clothes. And one man even landed on the moon and bounced around in his white puffy clothes, and his bouncing spread tight waves from the moon to the antennae on the roof and the new television in the living room.

How will I tell her I'm waiting for her? Maybe I'll jump down like she did. But the pile of sand was long gone, cleaned up when the Kurds moved to the edge of the neighborhood and Vardina moved one floor down. If I jump I might break my arms and then who would help Ruchama with her cooking? Maybe I'll bounce on the roof like that man on the moon. Here I am trying to bounce. I'm climbing on the boiler. I'm jumping down to the roof that is still covered with many black bits that might be mouse poop. I'm jumping to the roof but I'm staying put. Why aren't I floating like that man on television? Why am I not moving up and down and making waves that would spread like in the Jerusalem Broadcasting Authority's television logo and reach all the way to Sugarloaf Mountain and to her? What's keeping me on the ground? How can I tell her I'll wait a lifetime for her, how can I tell her not to jump? I can see the Sea of Galilee. It looks calm and isn't throwing fish up in the air anymore. Maybe I'll toss in a large rock, right in the center, and the rock will sink quickly and spread waves and more waves and more waves and they will rise to the air and cross the ocean and reach all the way to Sugarloaf Mountain and to her.

Part 2

1975

1

THE DAY ELLA RETURNED, A BOILING PAIL WAS OVERTURNED ON THE city. A heat wave erupted in the streets and wandered between the houses, carrying clouds of yellow desert dust and smearing it on balcony shutters. Within moments, the lower city was covered in wet, still, unmoving air, the few people outside walking like divers at the bottom of the sea, one measured step and then another careful one, fighting their shopping baskets, clearing their throats and spitting out lumps of sand, their breath scorched. In just a short while, Ha'Galil Street became a spittoon.

The previous day, when the heavy heat had just begun pushing winter away, Ruchama told Vardina, "God has gone crazy, sending us desert heat in January."

"I told you there was no God a long time ago," Vardina said derisively. "Maybe there used to be one, and one day He just died, may He rest in peace."

Ruchama continued stuffing Vardina's fridge with boxes packed with food, leftovers from her latest catering event, and said, "There is a God, He's just a little crazy and mean. One time He dropped by and invented bread, and since then He's been sitting and watching us as if He were in a theater, laughing away, sometimes throwing a curse or a tragedy at us like peanuts at monkeys, watching how we get into trouble with His peanuts and laughing to high heaven."

Vardina propped her aching legs on the edge of the sofa. "You've become quite the philosopher," she said. "You should write for the paper, you're wasting your time in the kitchen."

"Are you making fun of me?" Ruchama asked.

"Sure, I'm making fun," Vardina answered. "How do you know your God invented bread and then ran away? Have you spoken to Him? Do you have a thing going with Him? You're being a witch again," she said, and laughed and laughed.

Shlomi stood to the side, handing Ruchama the boxes and holding the fridge door with his other hand, making sure it didn't close
on her fingers, following her nervous movements and praying they
didn't fight again, that they didn't start yelling at each other and then
go silent for two days and then soften and answer his pleas. Each time
a commotion broke out between them, Vardina entrenched herself in
her insulted state and refused to book orders, and Ruchama locked
herself up in her anger and refused to cook. Then they would recon-
cile and make peace. Ruchama would lean down and hug Vardina
who was already having trouble getting up from her chair, and say, "I
love you even though you're a mean woman," and Vardina would say,
"Just so you know, I'm only willing to forgive you because of Shlomi,
your child is worth putting up with your face."

Ruchama waited for Vardina's laughter to subside and said, "I
don't need to talk to God to know, it's enough for me to smell the
bread when it comes out of the oven and I immediately know it's the
only gift He's ever given us before He started playing games."

"Really?" Vardina wondered as she twisted her face in ridicule.
"And who exactly made people? Did bread make us? And who made
God? Maybe my grandmother, deep in the grave, made Him, or
maybe you made Him, witch."

Shlomi let go of the fridge door and said, "You're going at it
again, I can't handle this," and the door travelled on its hinges and
slammed on Ruchama's fingers.

She screamed, he opened the door immediately, she blew on her
fingers and told Vardina, "Look what you did," and Vardina yelled,
"What *I* did?" and Ruchama yelled, "Yes, you did, you only bring me
pain," and Vardina shouted, "You should thank me for all I did for
you, I made you rich," and Ruchama said, "You got rich too, sitting
here all day, just talking on the phone and charging money."

Vardina began tearing up. "You stick me with all your leftovers,"
she wailed, "and because of you I can't stop eating, I'm like a mammoth, I can hardly get up to go to the bathroom, and you complain
that I talk on the phone?"

Ruchama pierced her with a sharp look. "Go on a diet," she said
quietly, "and stop blaming me for being fat like a mountain," and she
took her basket and left in anger.

Vardina wiped away some tears and told Shlomi, "Don't worry, pal, it's because of the heat that suddenly attacked us in the middle of winter and made puddles of our brains, tomorrow we'll calm down and forget, and it might even rain."

But the next day, the day Ella returned, it didn't rain. The heat worsened and clouds of haze kept whitening the heads of passers-by. Ruchama pulled down all the shutters. Darkness fell on the apartment but it was still burning with heat. "I don't care about the heat," she told Shlomi, "and I'm not cancelling our appointment, you're coming with me now to the doctor so he can take a look at you." Shlomi stretched on his chair by the kitchen table and said, "As long as I don't have to go to that shit school with the stupid teacher," and Ruchama told Hilik, "Maybe you should stay home today too, you should take a handkerchief from the drawer and breathe through it, the last thing I need now is for your lungs to fill up with sand." Hilik finished buttoning his green school shirt and said, "I'm not missing school and I don't want to breathe through a handkerchief, I'm completely healthy, stop worrying about me." Ruchama said, "What kind of stupid request is that, stop worrying, it's like asking me to stop breathing, and what's going to happen if you miss one day?" Hilik said, "Today we're handing in our papers about the Bedouins in Israel, I have to go," and Ruchama said, "All right. Just don't be surprised if you're the only one who shows up, I'm sure the teacher is going to stay at home too, there are more important things than the Bedouins in Israel." And she went out into the hallway.

Hilik opened the shutter a little, looked through the cracks and called Shlomi over. "Come look, there are people swimming through the street air." Shlomi stood by him, pulled the shutters farther apart and peeked out. Two people crossed the street slowly, their hands pushing the thick air and their feet almost sticking to the scorching ground. The image reminded him of a movie they'd once seen on Robert's television, a movie about a group of mountain climbers. When they reached the top they breathed hard and had trouble talking, and Hilik had said, "See how they can barely breathe, the air is thin and there's no oxygen, if I were up there I'd die in a minute."

Ruchama came back into the kitchen. "Close the shutters," she said, "I don't want sand getting into the house, I don't have time to wash the floors today." She handed Shlomi a white shirt. "I don't know what to do with you anymore," she said. "I buy you new shirts every week and within two days they have sauce stains all over them. When will you learn to use an apron?" Shlomi shrugged and put on the shirt. Ruchama looked him over and said, "And it's time you stopped walking around in your underwear, you're too old for that." She left the kitchen. Hilik smiled at Shlomi and said, "Mom's talking about the little beard growing on your balls." Shlomi looked down and saw a few wild hairs that escaped his underwear. He blushed and Hilik laughed.

Over the summer vacation, Shlomi had gotten so tall that the kids hardly recognized the electrical pole that had entered the classroom. He was one head taller than the teacher Reuma, two heads taller than Robert, three heads taller than Hilik and shorter only than Ruchama, just by a little.

On the first day of the eighth grade, loyal to his resolution to participate more, Shlomi raised his hand to answer the teacher's question about the green color of leaves. He remembered how he showed Hilik the green water that the beet leaves dribbled after he'd poured salt over them and kneaded them until they became soft and flattened-out. Hilik looked at the green water and explained all about chlorophyll, the plants' lungs, as he called it, and Shlomi understood how the grains of salt scratched the leaves and how they spilled their lungs out into the water. A green plant lung soup, nothing like the red spicy cow lung stew Ruchama taught him how to make for one of their events years ago. Shlomi remembered the explanations and wanted to answer the teacher's question. But once he began talking she burst into great laughter until tears appeared in her eyes, and said, "I'm sorry, Shlomi, for laughing, you've gotten so tall but your voice is still chirpy, I apologize," and she burst out laughing again. This time everyone in the class echoed her laughter, waves of laughter hit Shlomi, who sat at the end of the right row of chairs, by the wall, his head towering over everyone, watching like a lighthouse. During recess, the teacher walked up to him and said, "I'm truly sorry, I didn't mean to laugh, and please don't tell your mother, I don't want her making a scene."

The speedy growth had surprised him as well. His legs reached forward to take small, familiar steps, but their new length sent his feet three times farther, escaping his hips and arms that hung back, ashamed, his hands wandering and hurrying to regain his balance. "You look like you're about to fall down any moment," Robert told him. "Maybe we should get you a walking stick." Ruchama frowned and said, "Don't listen to him, Shlomi, I think it's beautiful, you move like Rudolf Nureyev." Robert asked, "Who is that, anyway?" and Ruchama answered, "He's a great dancer, his body moves like a poem," and Robert said, "Again with the poems, I thought you'd forgotten about them." Ruchama put her spoon in her plate and said, "Just because I ask you here to eat with us sometimes doesn't mean I'm going to discuss art with you, or anything else," and Robert went quiet and finished sipping the soup and sucking the bones. He washed his hands, winked at Shlomi and Hilik, invited them over to watch Simon Templar on television and went down to his apartment. "Is that what you do over there all the time?" Ruchama asked, "watch that Simon Templar nonsense?" and Hilik answered, "Simon Templar hasn't been on television for a long time, that's just how Dad calls all the shows," and Ruchama cleared the table and said, "One day that television is going to swallow you up."

Back at the end of seventh grade, the teacher moved Shlomi to the back of the row so he didn't block other kids' view of the blackboard. He sat there during recess too, his back against the wall, leaning on the map marking Alexander the Great's conquests and the pictures of flowers in the Judean Desert that bloom only one night of the year.

He kept growing over summer break. Three hairs curled on his chin and a thin and silky mustache darkened above his top lip. When he kneaded dough, doing the dancer's moves Ruchama taught him, beads of sweat slid down from the tip of his nose and stopped at his mustache. Thin hair also grew in his armpits, but his voice remained chirpy. Hilik said, "Shlomi has a sick bird in his throat and it's chirping."

A week before Ella returned, Shlomi announced he wasn't going to go to school anymore. Ruchama raised an eyebrow over her glasses and asked, "What exactly does his honor mean, if I may," and Shlomi answered, "I don't need it anymore. I cook and I work and I manage our events, I even do your bills, what else can they teach me." Ruchama let her back fall into the seat and said, "I've yet to hear of an eighth grader who decides to drop out of school." Shlomi told her that Albert Einstein, the genius, didn't go to school either, and she said, "What do I care about Einstein, maybe if he'd gone to school people would be able to understand his nonsense. People think he's smart because no one can even understand what he says." Shlomi said, "Hilik teaches me what I need to know. He's much smarter than my teacher Reuma-Dumba."

Ruchama gently wiped the sweat off his mustache fuzz. "Are the other kids picking on you?" she asked.

"Are you crazy?" he shouted. "Kids beg me to hire them to cook and work the events, I'm their king."

Ruchama knew it was true. Before each big catering event, Shlomi would recruit a few of his classmates, instruct them and manage them in the kitchen while she gave in to exhaustion and desperation, locked herself in her room and closed her eyes. Two of the kids, Moshik and Genia, already knew how to quickly scrape the insides of vegetables until they became thin sacks in their hands, ready to be stuffed. They fulfilled his quiet orders, chopped and swirled and kneaded and rubbed and rinsed. Then they'd help the loyal silent workman with carrying and setting tables and creating cooking areas, and finally give Shlomi a grateful look when he handed over a generous amount of cash.

Ruchama didn't let go. "But you only talk to them when they come to work for you," she said. "Why don't you play basketball with them? You're a tall kid, you could be a great ballplayer," and Shlomi answered, "I can't stand basketball and I need to be careful with my hands." Ruchama sighed. "Do they laugh at you because you're tall?" she asked. Shlomi didn't answer, and only lowered his eyes. "Do they call you names?" she went on, "Do they call you Electrical Pole? Giraffe? Praying Mantis?" and Shlomi was annoyed and chirped, "Enough Ruchama, I'm sick of your irritating questions. I just don't want to go to school," and a voice so high and screechy left his mouth that she let out a giggle. And when she saw the insult on his face she realized it was time for her to act.

And so it was. On Friday, Robert came up to eat with them. They had stuffed fish and a green soup with lots of fennel and lemon and coriander and dill and small potato cubes, the sour soup Ruchama made when someone was sick or when she wanted something refreshing to accompany the spicy fish. Robert clicked his tongue with pleasure and his eyes shone, because this time she even talked with him a bit, even asked if his backache had gone away and warned him not to forget to only take Muscol on a full stomach, or it would cut holes through his belly.

Finally she said, "We have a problem with Shlomi, he doesn't want to go to school anymore."

Shlomi nodded with approval.

"I don't think it's so bad," Robert said. "What does he need to go to school for anyway? He's making more money than I am."

Ruchama looked at him, surprised and disappointed. "You should be ashamed of the lousy way you bring up your kids," she said.

"I stopped going to school at a young age, too." Robert smiled.

"And that's the example you want to set for them?" Ruchama was furious. "He's only thirteen and a half."

"Judging by the scene you made last year, I thought you were against that school," Robert said and began to laugh.

Shlomi and Hilik caught his laughter. They also remembered the bar mitzvah celebration the class held at the end of seventh grade. All the boys stood on stage, dressed like yeshiva students with taped-on *peyot* and *shtreimels* made of cardboard and loose fur. They danced the *sherale* to a familiar Chassidic tune. The excited parents hummed along with the accordion, the little Chassids put their arms together and spread their hands to the sides, their heads raised to the ceiling as if in prayer, and only Shlomi, who was already taller than everyone else, struggled with the wide socks Reuma-Dumba had procured especially for him, pulling them up so they didn't run down his ankles, trying to ignore the bursts of laughter his movements gave rise to. And then, like a sudden storm, Ruchama rose from her seat, walked determinedly to the teacher who orchestrated the ceremony from the side of the stage, stood in front of her and shouted into her shocked face, "What's this stupidity? Stop this nonsense right now!"

The sounds of the accordion faded, the tiny *Chassids* ceased their praying, the parents' humming and laughing fell away at once. "What does any of this nonsense have to do with us?" Ruchama kept screaming at the terrified teacher. "Did we come from Poland? Did we grow up in a ghetto? What're all these ya-ba-bam-bam-bam and these stupid *shtreimels* to us? What right do you have to turn my children into Chassids?"

Reuma-Dumba went pale. "Ruchama, it's our tradition," she stuttered, and Ruchama leaned her head closer and closer to the teacher's and screeched, "Really? And what exactly are you going to serve us, calves foot jelly?" And then she turned to the audience of parents – they all knew Ruchama made piles of fragrant refreshments for the party herself—Moroccan cigars and her famous green beet pastries—and thundered, "I'd like to know, whoever feels that this is their tradition, please raise your hands."

No one breathed. Even standing below the stage, Ruchama was taller than the dressed-up kids who froze in their place. Only Morduch Levy, Sigal's father, raised his hand and said, "I actually know this song from our childhood." He began laughing and singing, "*Sherale* dances ballet, ya-ba-bam-bam, and then comes Moshe Sharet[4] ..." and some of the parents joined his singing, "and the Labor Minister is churning, she's in bed all day, her ass is burning ..." and they continued and laughed endlessly, and the accordionist joined them with a cheerful tune with no ululation, and even the children joined in and clapped along. And then Rachela, Yossi the athlete's mother, stood up and said, "Ruchama is right, we have a tradition too and we don't need cardboard hats to celebrate it," and then she began singing an ancient poem in a pleasant, trilling voice, "*Dror yikra leben im bat*," *Freedom will beckon to the son and the daughter*, and everyone joined in great song, and three mothers from the parents' committee brought in the huge trays of food Ruchama had made, and the children got off the stage and joined their parents' dancing circle.

Ruchama leaned over the wide-eyed teacher again and whispered in her ear, "If you turn my son into a joke one more time I'll lay a curse on you, you should be careful," and went over to help with the refreshments, leaving the horrified Reuma to check her neck and make sure all the hairs on her head were in place.

When they went home, Robert said, "You made a real Independence Day parade for them, it's too bad we didn't have fireworks and toy hammers." Shlomi held Ruchama's hand and felt it tremble. "They should learn their lesson," she answered Robert. "They don't

---

[4] Israel's first Foreign Minister.

have to follow all the orders they get from the kibbutzes." Robert said, "Again with the kibbutzes? What's that got to do with it, they get their orders from the Ministry of Education," and Ruchama said, "And who's sitting in the Ministry of Education? Open your eyes a little, it'll do you good, I don't see the kibbutzniks being too good to you lately, I don't see them ordering any work from you, I guess either you've stopped sucking up to them or they found another sucker to make inexpensive shutters for them."

"And I see Tehila's had a great effect on you," Robert said, trying to shoot an arrow at her in return for the one she'd pierced him with. "She'll make a Black Panther out of you yet."

Ruchama took Hilik's hand too. "It wouldn't hurt you to call your sister sometimes," she said, "or at least come up to say hello when she visits me."

Shlomi tightened his grip around her warm hand and she whispered in his ear, "Next time tell me before you agree to participate in that sort of nonsense, no one's going to turn you into a joke."

Only after their laughter died down did Ruchama say, "Laugh all you want, I don't mind, as long as others don't laugh at you." And she looked at Shlomi with stifled worry. They kept eating in silence. Robert tore large pieces of the black-raisin challah that Shlomi had baked, handed them to Shlomi and Hilik and Ruchama and dipped his in the remainder of sauce from the stuffed fish, wiping his plate with it, fighting for each red drop. Hilik pulled the raisins off his piece and piled them next to Robert. When Robert's plate shone, he chewed the pile of raisins and told Ruchama, "This is the best meal I've had in my life." Ruchama smiled. "You always say that," she said.

"So what do you want to do about Shlomi?" he asked.

"I've made an appointment with a doctor to look at him," she answered.

Shlomi asked why he needed to see a doctor, and Ruchama explained, "Your glands are going wild, I want him to see you, your head is about to reach the door frame."

"What's there to check?" Robert said. "He came out like you, that's better than a midget like me."

Ruchama got up to clear the table, stood in front of the sink and piled the plates in it. Robert stood by her and whispered, "What's it going to be, Ruchama? When are you going to let me back in? I've been waiting for you for five years," and Ruchama whispered, "You'll even wait an eternity."

On the morning Ella returned, Ruchama stood in front of the mirror by the apartment door and drew inside her eyelids with black eyeliner. Hilik, his book bag already strapped to his back, asked her, "Are you going to wear your contacts?" and when she said yes, he said, "I think you should wear your glasses. The air is full of sand that can get under your contacts and scratch your eyes, and they're very red as it is." Ruchama obeyed, said, "I can't stand makeup anyway," cleaned off the black line, put on her glasses, said goodbye to Hilik and told Shlomi, "Let's take a taxi. I'll ask them to send us one with air conditioning. The world has gone mad and put us in a Turkish bath in the middle of winter."

"What's a Turkish bath?"

"It's like a sauna," she answered.

He thought "Turkish bath" sounded like the name of a festive dish, a pigeon stuffed with rice and pine nuts and pistachios and baked in a sweet sauce.

"But what's a sauna?" he asked, and Ruchama explained it was a room people went into so they could sweat and get healthy, God knows why.

Then she said, "You're a strange boy, Shlomi. On the one hand, you do my bills, but on the other hand, you don't know what Turkish baths are. On the one hand, you're big like a man, and on the other hand your voice is chirpy like a seven-year-old's. You're like a poem. Each line comes from a different tense, and all the different tenses live together, like eternity," and Shlomi sighed and said, "You're giving me a headache."

As they sat in the taxi and Ruchama scolded the driver for skimping on the air conditioning, a large truck was already parked in front of the adjacent building. A group of porters unloaded furniture and boxes and carried them into the empty blue apartment – its windows were wide open, letting in wet and sandy air and letting out the thin steam that had been collecting for the past five years.

Ruchama and Shlomi didn't see the truck, nor did they see Hanna and Ella, who stood there in awe, watching the reddish sand clouds float in the sky. "It's lucky we haven't cleaned the place yet," said Hanna. "We'd better wait for this haze to disappear and then do a thorough job." But Ella didn't hear Hanna. The sound of the passing taxi muffled her words.

For a moment, they were close again. Two thirteen-and-a-half-year-old kids. A boy and a girl. One sitting by his mother, who was scolding the driver and fanning a handkerchief in front of her burning face, the other standing by her mother, wiping grains of sand from her watering eyes.

She, looking at a window that was once familiar and now seemed small and distant.

He, looking at the taxi's dusty windshield and wondering why he was feeling an old, sharp pain running down his neck and along his body and filling his mouth with the taste of blurry yearning.

The old family doctor laughed and said, "Look in the mirror, Ruchama, and you'll see for yourself why he's so tall. You're just trying to make trouble."

Ruchama wiped her glasses. "At least if he were an average of both of us," she said. "Who needs all this height?"

The doctor brought his head closer to hers and looked into her eyes. "But it's good that you came," he said, "because I'm going to send you to an eye doctor to check why your eyes are red like peppers."

"It's because of the sand in the air," she said.

"That's not true," Shlomi said. "Your eyes have been red for a while, even before the heat wave."

Ruchama ignored his words and his look and returned her glasses to their place. "Don't try to get rid of me," she told the doctor. "I don't care about the red in my eyes right now, I want you to give Shlomi a full checkup. I'm not going anywhere before you find out what's going on with the kid."

The doctor grew alert and pulled his face away. "I'll look at him, but you should watch it, Ruchama. If you're going to mess up my desk again and protest like a hoodlum, like you did that time with Hilik, I'll call the police." Ruchama smiled and said, "*Yalla, yalla,* doctor, I'm not impressed." The doctor smiled too and asked her to leave the room but she insisted on staying. The doctor said, "Shlomi has to take his clothes off, let me check him in peace." Ruchama straightened her back and said, "You think I'm going to see anything new?" and Shlomi said, "Enough, Ruchama, go." "Are you embarrassed by me?" she asked, and then she got up and told the doctor, "Check his throat too, you might find a sick chirping bird there you could take care of," and she left the room.

The doctor smiled at Shlomi and said, "Now tell me everything and don't be embarrassed. Do you mind being tall?"

"No."

"Do people make fun of you?"

"A little, sometimes, I have a chirpy voice."

"That's perfectly normal, your voice hasn't changed yet."

"I know."

"In the meantime, just talk less, talk only when you have to, no harm will come from being quiet."

"I don't talk much, I don't mind shutting up."

Shlomi ran his eyes over the naked walls, the one with the window covered in sand-colored drapes, and the one with the locked door in its center. He thought, Ruchama must be sitting outside, waiting for the fat nurse to be occupied so she could put her ear to the wall or the door and listen to what's going on inside. But even if she put her ear to the keyhole she wouldn't hear anything, because Ruchama had bad hearing and there were no glasses or contacts for her to wear on her ears. Maybe there'll be something like that one day, maybe Hilik will invent it when he grows up and becomes an inventor, he has so many ideas. But Hilik wants to be a book cover. Strange kid. He also grew a bit lately. He also has a tiny beard on his balls. But his face is clear of hair. He can hear perfectly. Maybe all the infections and the treatments have improved his hearing. Ruchama can't hear and she can't see, obstructed by a sand cloud. Maybe that's a tall person's problem. Maybe I'll also have to walk around with huge glasses because I won't be able to see or hear, I'll grow taller and become a bespectacled lighthouse, work on the beach, catch fish and cook them in hot sauce that'll make everyone tear up. Ruchama's outside and can't hear my answers. Even if she puts her ear to my body, even if she puts it in my throat to check on the sick bird and find out why it's chirping.

"So what's wrong, Shlomi?"

"Nothing's wrong, Ruchama wanted me to come because I don't want to go to school anymore."

"Why?"

"It's boring."

"And why do you call her Ruchama rather than Mom?"

"Because."

The doctor's smile widened with every moment. He said, "You look a lot like your mother. Your eyes are like hers, and they're a little red too." Shlomi blinked and said, "It's the sand."

It's not the sand, he thought, his eyes traveling the walls again. So why shouldn't I tell him? I could tell him about the moments I stand on the roof trying to see into the distance, but the blue mountains block my view and the white skies burn my eyes. That's why they're red, from trying to see far away. And what are they trying to see anyway – I ask and ask and feel there are answers in my throat, but I can't cough them up. People ask me questions and I think for hours until finally I chirp a whisper and they start laughing. My throat hurts. Even now. Maybe I should tell the doctor, so that he can poke my throat with one of those sticks on his desk and help the bird fly out. When it hurts I jump in. Maybe I should tell the doctor. I didn't even tell Hilik. I have a small place inside of me where I look for recipes. They're arranged on long shelves, and each shelf has a name, a smell and a taste:

The fried fish shelf, the cooked fish shelf, the slow-cooked beef shelf, the stuffed pastry shelf, and another one for unstuffed pastries and another for pastries with a new smell, and many shelves for red sauces, green sauces, transparent sauces, recipes for sickness, refreshing recipes for heat waves, celebration recipes, Friday night recipes for when Robert comes upstairs to eat, dough you have to knead through dance, dough for hitting, dough for kicking, dough for ringing slaps.

And there's another shelf for recipes that have yet to be invented, and that's my favorite. People ask me difficult questions and I go to my shelf and invent:

How are you Shlomi? – Yellow rice with grapes that are melted in it and only their seeds squeak between your teeth …

How was school? – Fried potato patties with lots of lemon peel and burning hot black pepper …

Why don't you go out and play basketball with your friends? – Tomato soup with beets and lots of chopped dill and small cucumber and pickle cubes and you serve it cold in the afternoon or when your eyes burn …

"Do you cry a lot, Shlomi?" the doctor asked.

"No, of course not, I don't cry at all."

"Do you miss someone?"

"Who?"

"Does anything hurt?"

"Sometimes my neck hurts. It hasn't for a long time and then today it did."

"It's called growing pains. Your body is having a hard time getting used to itself, that's why it hurts. It'll pass."

Shlomi nodded. He wanted to tell the doctor that the pain had begun long before his body grew, but before he could open his mouth the doctor asked, "And does your mom cry a lot?" and Shlomi said, "No, she has no time for nonsense, we work hard."

The doctor kept staring at Shlomi's face, perhaps searching for his next question. Shlomi thought, ask already, I'm enjoying this, the answers are coming quickly and chirping out and I don't mind, only my throat hurts a little.

I should build a new shelf – recipes for yearning, that's how I'll call it.

But how do you make those up? Maybe I could ask Robert, he's an expert at yearning. He eats it up and gobbles it down, he even has a little potbelly, a tiny one, you can't see it when he has clothes on, a belly that makes Ruchama smile and say, "Your father has become a man, he even has some gray in his hair, and if you look closely you'll see he has a cute little belly." Not a fat belly like Vardina's. She has a huge belly, a huge everything, she has a swollen belly under her chin and under her arms and in her legs. She's become a belly. Maybe I should ask her, she's the one who eats yearning up in enormous portions, like the piles of food they feed to elephants at the zoo. Hilik and I saw it on Robert's television, and Hilik laughed and said, "Vardina would love it there." Every day Ruchama packs her boxes of yearnings and stuffs them in her fridge and she eats and expands.

Maybe I should ask Ruchama. She cooks and packs, and I cook too. We're all yearning experts. We could have a contest, and the winner would help me make yearning recipes and put them on the shelf.

"And how's Hilik? Is he healthy?"

"Yes, sometimes he still gets ear infections, but he hasn't had one for a while."

"Good. Your mom probably takes him in for a checkup once in a while, right?"

"No, the ear doctor comes over himself to check him and stays around to talk to Ruchama."

"What do they talk about?"

"I don't know, they talk in the room. Hilik says the doctor teaches her how to treat infections."

The doctor nodded again and again, sipped some lukewarm tea and asked, "And how's your father?"

"Fine, he spends most of his time in Tel Aviv. I only see him on the weekends. Sometimes Ruchama asks him over for dinner."

"What does he do in Tel Aviv?"

"He's learning about air conditioners. He wants to change his business, shutters aren't so hot anymore."

"Your father is a smart man, with good instincts."

"Yeah?"

"It's too bad your mom is torturing him like she does, the whole town is talking about it, but that shouldn't interest you, you're still a kid."

I guess I'll ask Robert ... I guess he's the winner of the expert contest ... I'll ask him for ideas for yearning recipes.

But he'll probably laugh and say again, "What's with you, Shlomi? Your head almost reaches the ceiling, and you can cook better than Grandma Julia, may she rest in peace, and you're doing Ruchama's bills like a veteran banker, but you still have a little boy's mind." And then he'd stop laughing and say, "You need to grow up and decide how old you are," and Hilik would tell him, "What you said now makes no sense," and Robert would say, "We each have our own sense."

And then the doctor had him take off his clothes and checked him thoroughly, tapping his knees and taking his height and weight and pressing his spine and gently shaking his neck until a little click sounded, which made Shlomi feel that his head was suddenly light and his neck was nice and loose. The doctor asked him to take off his underwear as well, looked him over, felt his testicles and said, "You can get dressed, everything's fine, you're just very developed for your age."

Shlomi got dressed and sat across from the doctor again. The doctor said, "Is there anything else you want to tell me?" and Shlomi said, "Like what?" and the doctor said, "I don't know, anything you want, just as long as your mother doesn't blame me for not giving you enough time or not looking at you carefully enough." Shlomi said, "I have nothing more to tell," and the doctor asked, "Do you whack off yet?"

"Whack off what?"

"You don't know what whacking off is?"

"I don't understand what I should whack."

"Your genitals."

Shlomi went quiet and a little red. The doctor said soothingly, "You shouldn't feel embarrassed, Shlomi, kids your age whack off, especially those who are developed like you, and there's nothing wrong with it, on the contrary, it's fun and it's healthy and don't believe anyone who tells you otherwise."

"I don't understand anything," said Shlomi.

The doctor's face grew long and he said, "Your dad never talked to you about it?" and Shlomi asked, "About what?" and the doctor sighed. "Tell your dad I asked him to talk to you about it a little," he said, "and don't worry, it's not a disease, it's just a man's secret, and you're almost a full man, and that's why I ask you not to say anything about it to your mother, or she'll kill me."

"Now I'm relaxed," Ruchama said on their way to her favorite falafel stand. "Even though I know that doctor is a prattler and sometimes he's really stupid as a man, I trust his diagnosis." She hugged Shlomi and said, "There's nothing we can do, you're sentenced to be an electrical pole. You'll have to learn how to live up there. There are a lot of positive sides to it, especially for a boy."

She asked to pack up the pitas with extra-extra spicy lemon slices.

"We'd better eat at home, the air is so humid you could drink it, we could make air soup." Shlomi looked at her angrily and said, "You wasted our morning for nothing, I could have started prepping, we have a bar mitzvah with eighty guests tomorrow and we haven't even decided what our special dish is going to be." "Don't worry," she said, "I'll be ready in two hours, you can take the day off, maybe go outside and play, maybe go to the library with Hilik," and Shlomi said, "You won't get it done on time by yourself."

The taxi dropped them off by the grocery store. Ruchama bought some groceries and they walked up the street, past the bulletin board and towards the house, making their way among the billows of moisture and dust. When they reached the path leading to Ella's building they stopped in their tracks.

The small yard was strewn with furniture. A sofa. Three chairs. A dining room table with a pile of chairs on top, and a large bed leaning against the building's wall. The furniture was covered in sheets of plastic that barely hid their blue tone. Hanna sat on one of the chairs with a cup of coffee. In her other hand she put a handkerchief to her mouth and nose to filter the sand out.

Ruchama and Shlomi stood there, wide-eyed. It took Shlomi a long moment to realize he'd stopped breathing. He took in a loud breath of air and Hanna turned her head towards them. Her eyes rested on Ruchama and she smiled and stood up.

"Ruchamaaaaaa," she drew the word out in a twittering tune, as if finding a melody that had picked at her brain for a while and suddenly emerged. She wrapped her arms around Ruchama, who stood there, breathless, not even noticing the drops of coffee spilling from Hanna's cup and staining her sleeve. "I'm so glad to see you."

Ruchama looked down at her, her body stretching and her lips searching for words, until she said, "I didn't know you were coming back," and Hanna said, "Really? Vardina didn't tell you? She helped me book the movers from the port." "How?" Ruchama asked, and Hanna told her how she'd worked hard to get Vardina's number and had spoken with her several times and had asked for her help booking the movers, because before returning to Israel they'd spent some time in America and Hanna bought everything new, "Furniture and an oven and a fridge that doesn't make noise." Hanna pulled away from Ruchama's stiff body and said, "Look at the welcome I've got with this weather, straight into a heat wave. The sun's hitting me over the head and the whole apartment is filled with sand."

Ruchama moved slowly backwards, keeping a distance from Hanna's smiles. "Why are you sitting outside?" she asked.

"The movers decided to take a break, so they made a living room for me in the yard and left. Why don't you have some coffee with me? I have excellent Brazilian coffee. They have real coffee there, not like here, and anyway, everything is different abroad, the air is good and the people are nice."

"Then why did you come back?"

"Because it got a little tough there after the war and they needed me here in the Immigrant Absorption Center."

And then she looked at Shlomi and went quiet, even pale, her gaze drowning in his eyes and then traveling over his long body. Her neck stretched back as her eyes went to his again. She said, "Are you Shlomi?" and Shlomi didn't answer, the sharp pain seared through his neck again and his arms sweated and almost dropped the falafel and the grocery basket.

"I can't believe it, I thought he was just someone helping you with the groceries."

"Why?" Ruchama asked. "You think I have slaves who carry my basket for me?"

Hanna's paleness was replaced with patches of blush. Her eyes remained fixed on Shlomi's. She'd hardly changed. Her straw hair still protected her blue eyes, and only under her chin her skin loosened a bit and a small bag clung to her slender neck and vibrated whenever she opened her mouth.

"Israella's grown a lot as well," she said and moved her eyes from Shlomi to Ruchama with an effort. "And how's Robert?" she asked, and Ruchama said, "Robert's fine, I still owe you a jar," and reminded her of the flower vase she'd brought over to help with Adina's catering event, but Hanna remembered nothing.

Only after they walked past the stone wall did Ruchama tell Shlomi, "I knew there was sand in the air for a reason. That woman is like a phoenix in a sandstorm, falling and rising, falling and rising and raising dust."

She kept complaining, but Shlomi didn't hear her. He was so

excited he'd forgotten how to control his limbs. His head crashed into tree branches and his elbows hit a rusty laundry pole. Ruchama stopped, took the bag and the basket from him and said, "Relax, your body's all over the place and your cheeks are about to burn up."

Before they went upstairs they went into Vardina's apartment. Ruchama put the bag and the basket down and stood with her hands on her hips, her eyes fixed on her friend sitting in her chair and her face gloomy.

"I hope for your sake that you came to apologize for the disgusting things you said to me," Vardina said.

"Why didn't you tell me she was coming back?" Ruchama asked.

"Who?"

"What do you mean 'Who?'" Ruchama huffed with anger. "The sandstorm phoenix. The Polish empress."

Vardina moved a little in her chair, searching for a place to put one of her bellies. "I didn't want to upset you," she said, her eyes lowered.

"And why did you help her?" Ruchama asked.

Vardina looked up tiredly. "Because that's who I am, if people ask me for help, I help," she answered. "She called me from America, I couldn't say no."

"I don't understand," said Ruchama. "If she'd called from Haifa or Jerusalem, would you have said no? So what if she called from America?"

"What do you care about her?" said Vardina. "You can finally return her ugly jar."

The two were silent for a long moment. Finally Vardina asked, "What's with Shlomi? Why is he red like a beet?" and Ruchama answered, "He's hot." Vardina moved some more in her seat, blinked and said, "I'm willing to make peace with you." Ruchama burrowed into her bag, pulled out one pita and handed it to her. Vardina sniffed the paper bag and her mouth filled with saliva. "If this heat wave doesn't kill me," she said, "I'll probably drop dead from all the food you stuff me with."

When they came home Ruchama went into the kitchen, opened the top cabinet and rummaged through it until she pulled out the floral vase. She looked at it for a few seconds, shaking her head, and then threw it forcefully into the sink. The sounds of the glass smashing grated Shlomi's ears. "Now go take a shower," she said. "Cool your body off, stand under the water until you calm down, I don't want your face exploding."

Shlomi shut his eyes under the cold water. Even as his body cooled off, he felt the sweat continuing to spill out of him in waves. He tried to summon her image, which had faded by now, only slivers of sights remained – the chocolate staining her cheek, drops of blood spraying on the sandpile, one eyebrow arching into her forehead, six freckles on the tip of her nose, maybe five, maybe four. Her face was blurry but his heart was full. A forgotten picture of Sugarloaf Mountain and words sketched on the back of a postcard that had since gone missing. She must have grown. Perhaps she stretched taller like him, perhaps a small quivering bag appeared under her chin, perhaps she wore glasses, perhaps she'd become a large belly. He tried to dive into the corner with his shelves, to look up recipes or make up new ones, anything to steady his breathing. Slowly he opened his eyes and looked in the mirror in front of the shower, trying to recall when he'd last looked at himself that way, maybe never, surprised by his height, staring at the few hairs curling under his arms, at his long neck. His breath had calmed. He felt his testicles as if trying to decipher what the doctor was looking for down there, looked at his penis and wondered how to whack off and why he should and when he'd do as the doctor instructed and ask Robert and what he'd do if Robert laughed again.

A small knock was heard and then the door opened and Hilik peeked inside. "I have to take a shower," he said. "Hurry up because my head is on fire, one more minute and I'll burn up from all the sweat." Hilik came in and began taking off his wet school uniform. "How did it go at the doctor's?" he asked. "Did he give you anti-height medication?" and Shlomi laughed. "Leave the water running," Hilik said, handed Shlomi a towel and stepped into the shower right as Shlomi stepped out.

Shlomi began drying himself, watching Hilik moan with pleasure under the cold water. Hilik saw Shlomi's furrowed look and asked, "What's wrong, Shlomi? What's on your mind?" and Shlomi answered, "The doctor asked if I whack off," and Hilik said, "Really? What did you tell him?" Shlomi said, "I didn't answer because

I didn't understand what he was asking. He told me to ask Robert to explain what I needed to do."

Hilik moved over a bit so that the stream of water didn't wash over his hair and cover his eyes. He looked at Shlomi, astonished. "Shlomi, are you kidding me? You don't know what whacking off is?" and Shlomi said, "No, maybe you can explain it to me." Hilik opened his eyes wide and said, "There's no way, I've seen you wake up with a hard-on like a rocket and run to the bathroom, I thought you go there to whack off," and Shlomi said, "I go to pee."

Hilik sighed. "All the boys do it," he said. "They touch themselves until the semen comes out and they relax, it's a lot of fun." And he showed Shlomi on his body where the semen came out.

"How do you even know how to do it?" Shlomi asked. By this point there was anger in his voice.

"I saw Dad," Hilik said. "One time I went in his apartment and he didn't hear me. I saw him sitting on his bed and rubbing his wiener."

"Did you ask him? Did he teach you?"

"Are you crazy? I ran away. Then I found a library book and read about it."

"I don't understand anything."

"It's really simple, Shlomi, you can imagine things too, I even imagine this one girl in my class who already has a little bit of boobs."

"Who is it?"

"You don't know her. You can imagine whoever you want, just close your eyes and imagine, next time we're at the library I can show you a book, it's a book the librarian won't let us borrow because it's for adults, but when I take it to the corner to read she looks the other way. There's all sorts of things in it that you can imagine, and that's it, then the semen comes out."

"Maybe I don't even have semen."

Hilik laughed. "No way, you're older than me and I have it."

"Show me."

"Are you crazy?"

"I won't get out of here until you show me."

"Why are you so upset?"

"Because."

Hilik put his head under the water for a moment, shook his hair and said, "I can't, Shlomi, I'm embarrassed," and Shlomi said, "Since when do you get embarrassed with me? We've been showering together our whole lives." Hilik said, "It's not the same," and shook his head again and asked, "Why are you crying?"

"I'm not crying," Shlomi answered.

"Your eyes are red."

"Because you're annoying me."

"And what if Mom comes in?"

"She won't come in, she never comes in."

Hilik got out of the shower, leaving puddles behind him, locked the door and returned to stand under the stream of water. He said, "Promise you won't laugh at me," and began stroking his penis. A moment later he stopped and said, "I can't, Shlomi, I can't get it hard when you're watching me like that," and Shlomi said, "You're just teaching me something, you always teach me, everything I know you taught me, except for cooking," and Hilik sighed and said, "I'll close my eyes and try to imagine, I can't promise you that I can do it, but if I open my eyes and see you laughing at me, you're finished." Then he closed his eyes and ran his hands up and down his penis. Shlomi waited at attention. He wondered, Who will I imagine when I learn what to do? Maybe I'll meet her today. Maybe her face is pretty. Maybe I'll read a book and think about her.

Hilik began moaning quietly. His penis was swollen and his hand ran over it, gripping, sliding and releasing. His chest rose and fell and his body moved back and forth at a quickening pace. Shlomi followed his motions and thought that that was what he himself must look like when he was beating egg-whites with the curved hand mixer, turning them into a white, fluffy cloud.

The choked moans reminded him of sounds he'd heard coming from Hilik's bed at nights. Hilik would lie covered in his blanket and his books and moan, and Shlomi thought his breath was scorched by the dust of the crumbling books, or that sickness came to haunt him at night. Now Shlomi realized what Hilik did under his blanket. And that's also what Rani and Menashe from his class did in recess when they rubbed themselves against the soccer goalposts in the yard until a strange serenity spread over their faces, and then they'd doze off in class.

A shudder went through Hilik, his motions stopped and a stream of white drops came out of his penis. He slowly opened his eyes, took a few deep breaths and showed Shlomi the drops that had collected in his hand. "You see? It's not so complicated." Shlomi said, "You moaned like you were sick," and Hilik said, "Don't be afraid, Shlomi, at first you might feel a little sick but in the end it's fine, maybe you can try it later, maybe at night, but first get some toilet paper from the bathroom so you can wipe yourself, otherwise Ruchama will ask you about the stains on the sheet."

When they sat at the kitchen table, Ruchama put the plates of falafel in front of them, after having taken the slices of lemon when she'd eaten hers. She poured cold lemonade and Hilik downed it in one gulp. She filled his glass again and he downed it again and asked for more. Ruchama raised an eyebrow and asked, "Why are you both as red as beets?" Shlomi didn't answer and Hilik only shrugged, blushing more and sending Shlomi terrified looks. "Did you take a hot shower?" she asked, and they nodded. Ruchama sighed, filled Hilik's glass again, turned the fan towards them and said, "You must be completely crazy, at least get plenty to drink, the falafel is a little spicy today," and she went downstairs to consult with Vardina about the following day's catering job, or to scold her again for not telling her about the Polish empress, or to tell her she'd shattered the ugly jar.

In the quiet she'd left between them, Hilik said, "Now I'm afraid you're going to make fun of me," and Shlomi said, "Stop your nonsense, I won't make fun of you because it isn't funny," and Hilik said, "I feel ashamed every time you look at me."

Shlomi drank some lemonade and said, "You have nothing to be ashamed of, I wish I could teach you something." He put the glass down and wiped the sweat that dripped from his head to his forehead. "I don't understand it," he said in a hoarse voice, "I'm a year older than you, I'm much taller, how could I have known nothing about this."

"It's really too bad," said Hilik, "you missed out on a year of whacking off," and he laughed as he pounced on his falafel, chewing voraciously, licking the tahini spilling from the pita, and added with his mouth full, "But you can make up for lost time now, do it in the morning and at night, you can even do it during lunchtime at the school bathroom, lots of kids do it, but if you ever tell anyone what I did I'll kill you, and don't you dare interrupt me or laugh at me if you can ever tell that I'm doing it, and don't even dare say a word or even cough or you'll ruin my fantasies, it's my private thing."

"All right, calm down already," Shlomi said, "you'll choke on your falafel. You have such an appetite all of a sudden."

Hilik stopped chewing. "Why is your voice so hoarse?" he asked, and Shlomi said, "I don't know, maybe because of the sand," and Hilik smiled and said, "Maybe the chirping bird died." Shlomi shrugged. "And why aren't you eating?" Hilik asked. "You've got red eyes again, and some tears," and Shlomi said, "She's back."

"Who?"

"Ella."

"Yes, I know," said Hilik.

"How? Did you see her?"

"No, but Vardina said they were coming back and she was helping them."

"When?"

"A while ago."

"Why didn't you tell me?"

"Because I didn't want you to get too excited, your whole body falls apart when you're excited," Hilik said and put the rest of the pita in his mouth.

Shlomi pushed his own pita towards him and said in an even hoarser voice, "I don't know what to do now."

Hilik bit into Shlomi's pita. "Have you seen her?" he asked.

"No, only her mother."

"Now I understand why Mom broke the jar."

They were silent, Shlomi drinking a little and Hilik swallowing the falafel down almost without chewing. Finally he said, "Go to her," and Shlomi answered, "I can't move my legs."

When the sun began to set, Ruchama flooded the apartment with water. She filled bucket after bucket, poured the water on the floor and said, "This is the best air conditioner. We'll give the apartment a cold shower." The desert dust had settled, and only a thin scent of smoke could still be sensed in the air. "God really has gone crazy," said

Ruchama. "It's not enough that there's no rain, but now His stupid heat wave is burning up our forests." Then she pushed out the water, mopped the floor dry and polished it, refusing Shlomi's continuing efforts to help her. "You have the day off today. I'll do everything myself."

And when the streetlights turned on, she went to bed and set an alarm to wake her in the middle of the night to continue cooking. Hilik also burrowed into his bed, diving into an old book, and Shlomi put on a clean shirt with only few stains dotting its edges and went downstairs to the yard.

A moment later she arrived and sat next to him on the stone wall.

Shlomi raised red eyes to her, careful not to blink too much, worried that the beating of his heart might hurt her ears. She'd grown a lot. Her long hair ran over round shoulders, some of it touching her chest, as if protecting her breasts, which were already held by a bra, the rest of it pulled back with a pin, revealing a forehead into which one eyebrow now arched, accentuating her sparkling eyes.

"Did you wait for me?" she asked, and Shlomi nodded.

The voice of Chaim Yavin, the newscaster, rumbled from the windows, announcing the break in the sudden heat wave and the efforts to put out the fires in the forests of the north. A truck drove by in the next street, bottles shaking in its cargo bed.

"And if it had taken another five years for me to come back," she asked, "would you have still waited?" and Shlomi nodded.

And then she said, "Now we'll say nothing. We'll talk tomorrow or the day after," and Shlomi said, "All right, the doctor said I shouldn't talk much anyway." "Why?" asked Ella. "Are you sick?" and Shlomi answered, "No, it's just because I have a chirpy voice." Ella said, "You're voice is hoarse and beautiful," and Shlomi said, "Because of the sand," and Ella said, "And now we'll be silent."

And they were silent for hours.

Ella looked away, examining the yard and the buildings and their roofs and thus allowing Shlomi to take a long look at her. At her neck that wasn't slender like Hanna's, at her bitten nails, at the tan triangle of her neckline, at the freckles on the tip of her nose, he counted only five, and at the scratches on her wrists, as if someone chiseled lines into them, trying to turn her arms into notebooks. When he looked there she felt his gaze and folded her arms between her thighs, protecting them.

Then he closed his eyes and froze in his place, allowing her to send a curious look towards his face and arms and stained fingernails and his hands that were scarred from cooking.

When he opened his eyes they met hers. Their eyes tied into each other and didn't let go. Even when tears came to her eyes, even when his eyes burned and reddened, even then, their gazes remained entwined, trying to read what could not be read. Five long years passed between their eyes.

And only after window shutters banged shut, and wind blew over the strains of the national anthem resounding from television sets, only then did Ella get up from the wall. Shlomi stood up too. She said, "You've gotten very tall," and sent her hand to the back of his neck, lowered his head towards her, kissed his cheek and left.

Shlomi went home. Hilik lay in his bed with his eyes shut. Shlomi wanted to ask him if he was awake, but only a hoarse whispered murmur left his throat. He tried again, and this time no sound came out at all, only a breath of hot air. Shlomi cleared his throat, coughed with an effort, but his throat was completely silent, not even a sigh emerged, not even a squeak or a chirp. The bird had died, or perhaps flown away, gone to nest elsewhere.

He ripped off a piece of toilet paper in the bathroom, undressed silently, got into bed and under the covers. He began touching himself, gently pulling on his penis until it became hard. In his mind's eye he saw her new face and the smell of her breath came to his nose. His hand moved and his eyes were closed, his breath swelled and he wondered what he should do now. He almost woke up Hilik to ask him, but no sound left his mouth and the white drops refused to emerge from his penis.

He kept moving until he fell asleep, the toilet paper in one hand, his penis growing limp in the other, his breath calm and his eyes looking into hers.

2

"I THINK MOM IS GOING TOTALLY MAD," HILIK TOLD SHLOMI. "THIS morning when I went shopping with her instead of you, she asked the butcher to grind a piece of meat for her, and he did and put it on an old newspaper, and Mom picked it up with her hand and chewed it with her mouth open, and all the blood spilled out from the side of her mouth, like a lion eating a zebra in a nature movie on television." Deep shock appeared on Hilik's face. "I thought she only ate raw fish and today I realized she was actually crazy, I want to throw up just from remembering the blood leaking from her mouth."

Shlomi shrugged. It had been like that for a while. Ruchama would ask for a piece of meat from the butcher to make sure she wasn't buying spoiled meat that would stink up her cooking, like what happened with the *hamin*. He wanted to explain this to Hilik, but his throat had been silent for almost a month, not a sound came out, and all the doctors who looked into it found no answers and only said, "Maybe his voice is changing and it's gone for now, has taken a break." Until his voice came back from its break, Shlomi had to make do with hand gestures, and sometimes, when there was no choice, he whispered with an effort, exaggerating his lip movements. Hilik looked at Shlomi's mouth and his hands cutting circles through the air and said, "Don't try so hard, I can understand you by looking in your eyes," and Ruchama said, "I won't have you whispering, that's the worst thing for your vocal cords, it's better that you write down what you want to say, or just don't talk."

So Shlomi didn't talk. In class he sat at the end of the row, his back against the wall decorated with autumn leaves and rain clouds made of Bristol board and crepe paper, his leg touching Ella's. Sometimes she reached out and tickled his thigh, and he laughed soundlessly and crossed his legs, trying to hide the bump stiffening in his pants. Not even a chirp left his mouth and so none of his classmates laughed mockingly or even looked at him, only Reuma-Dumba looked sometimes, but most of the time she ignored him and the strange girl that had joined her class, shrugging and continuing to write exercises and quandaries and rhymes on the blackboard with white chalk that cracked the skin of her fingers. When Ella looked away from him he sent covert looks at the hair covering her shoulders and hiding her neckline. When he leaned his head a little he discovered more and more freckles above her breasts and up her neck. Then she fixed her blue eyes on his and whispered, "Stop looking down my shirt, you pervert," and Shlomi laughed soundlessly again.

And even when they sat on the stone wall, Shlomi said nothing, and Ella said, "I didn't mean for us to be quiet for so long." Shlomi made a funny face and pointed at his throat. Ella laughed. "I didn't know you were such a clown. I really liked your hoarse chirping," and then told him of Brazil, demonstrating soccer plays with her fingers, singing songs with a melancholy melody and faraway words and sometimes touching his knee or adjusting a curl that fell on his forehead. And when he'd return from the grocery store with the baskets he'd stop at the old bulletin board whose posts were already rusting and with the paper notices ripped off, and think, I'm so glad I've run out of words.

Hilik blinked, trying to erase the vision of the blood dripping from Ruchama's lips. Shlomi tried to catch his eyes, trying to calm the storm. How could he explain to him that more than enjoying the taste of blood she liked protecting her diners' health, just like the armor-bearer in one of the books he gave him to read. He was a short, loyal armor-bearer who would taste his master's food and drink to prevent him from being poisoned, until one time he dropped dead, a piece of accursed meat stuck in his throat.

When Ruchama went to the fresh fish store to put aside her selections she told the vendor, "God have mercy on your soul if you give me yesterday's fish, and God have mercy on your mother's soul if you sell me tilapia that smells like oil," and the vendor would say, "My mother's been dead for years, Ruchama, what do you want from her life?" and Ruchama would ask, "Slice me a little piece." She'd hand the vendor the little knife she carried with her in case of a sudden terrorist attack, the vendor would wipe the knife on his stained apron, remove the skin from the fish in one motion, cut a thin slice of the meat and say, "I wish I had such a fine knife," and Ruchama would say, "If you give me some money I'll buy you one in Haifa," and take the piece of meat from him with two fingers, hold it in the air, squeeze some lemon over it and add some salt, give Shlomi half and put the rest in her mouth, closing her eyes and chewing and smacking her lips and saying, "Only heaven tastes like this." But sometimes she opened her eyes, spit the fish out and told Shlomi, "Spit that out and don't you dare swallow, this fish drank a lot of oil," and then fixed the vendor with a searing gaze and said, "You should be ashamed of yourself, giving me poisoned fish." The vendor would lower his head and apologize, "What can I do, Ruchama, fishermen these days want to have it easy, they put some oil in the water and collect the dead fish, and that's what they sell me."

A week before, they went to Haifa together. "I want a venerable doctor to see you this time," said Ruchama, "I'm sick of the nonsense the doctors in the hospitals here tell us, they can't tell the difference between the measles and angina." She made an appointment with a doctor whose name was spoken with reverence by all the nurses and medical secretaries she'd grilled, begged Hilik to agree to skip school that day and join them on a visit to her favorite city, and that very morning they were already on the bus, Shlomi sitting quietly, Hilik devouring one of his books and Ruchama scolding the passengers lighting cigarettes again and again. "At least blow your smoke out the window, I have a sick child here, he doesn't need to breathe in your stench."

When they reached the lower city, she said, "We have at least two hours before we have to see the doctor, why don't I take you to a terrific fish shop, it's time you see some real fish from the Mediterranean." They followed her down Ha'Atzmaut Street, Ruchama stopping once in a while and sniffing and saying, "I don't remember where it is exactly, but my nose will lead us there." When they arrived she said, her eyes sparkling, "It's exactly the same, nothing's changed." Hilik said, "I've never smelled anything this bad in my life," and Ruchama leaned down and whispered in his ears, "So breathe through your mouth, Hilik, you don't know anything about fish anyway, and try to speak quietly, I don't want you embarrassing me."

The elderly vendor recognized her right away. "It's been so many years," Ruchama said, "how can you remember?" and he smiled and said, "No one could ever forget a lady as tall as you, I tell you, it's a shame the Olympics don't have a height contest, you could have finally gotten us a medal. They'd make you into a hero and put you on television and make a stamp out of your beautiful face." Ruchama's cheeks reddened and she said, "Give us a little taste of something, it's time my kids knew what a dream tastes like." The vendor pointed her to the ice trays along the wall and she smoothed her finger over the large fish, pressed on their meat, peeked at their gills and marveled at their beauty. The vendor sliced a few pieces and placed them on a piece of bread he'd ripped from a large loaf and soaked in olive oil and tomato juice. Shlomi chewed and his mouth spun with the flavors of the sea. The fish squeaked between his teeth. Ruchama shook her head as if trying to swirl the tastes inside of it. And only Hilik stood in the doorway, his fingers pressed against his nose, his stomach rippling in cramps and his throat fighting off the nausea.

Later, as they walked down one of the Carmel's green streets and almost reached the doctor's house, Hilik told them he'd once read a book about an old fisherman who was lost at sea and had to eat the giant fish he'd finally been able to catch. "He ate it alive," Hilik said and became nauseous again. Ruchama said, "That's the only way to eat fresh fish," and Hilik suddenly stopped and ran to the bushes, leaned over and threw up. Ruchama found a tap, helped him wash his face and said, "You have to stop reading books that disgust you, I think I read that book once and it disgusted me too." Shlomi was surprised, he thought she never remembered any of the many books she'd once read and put in boxes, some of which now filled Hilik's bed with dust and yellowing paper crumbs, though three times a year she recalled fragments of lines from the poets she'd loved and mourned, lying in her bed for seven days for each of them, soaking the pillow through with tears. Three times a year she lit a candle for their souls: a candle for Leah Goldberg, a candle for Alterman, a candle for Shlonsky, and each time she added two more, one for Rachel the Poetess and the other for her laughing mother. Each time she stood in front of the trembling flames, her eyes glittering under her glasses, her shoulders slumped and her head swaying like a fallen palm tree.

The venerable doctor looked inside Shlomi's throat and said the cords were a little swollen and that it would pass. He wrote down a prescription, signed it quickly and handed it to Ruchama. Ruchama asked, "Is that all you have to say?" and the doctor said, "I don't see anything unusual here." Ruchama frowned. "So why did you give me a prescription?" and the doctor said, "To calm you down. I can see you're anxious."

She gave the prescription back and stood up. "You might think you can fool us because we're from Tiberias, but with this kind of attitude I won't pay you a lira," and the doctor said, "We're neighbors. I'm originally from Kibbutz Degania." Shlomi and Hilik followed her eyebrows as they went up into the sky and counted down the seconds to the explosion, but to their surprise she said nothing, even pursed her lips tightly as if holding back the words bubbling inside. "Don't be mad at me," said the venerable doctor. "You have nothing to complain about, you should check with your son why he doesn't talk, I see no physical reason other than some swelling," and Ruchama mumbled, "Go to hell," put some money on his desk and left, urging Shlomi and Hilik to follow.

Then she took them in a taxi to a restaurant in the lower city. She ordered the three of them roast beef covered in a sweet brown sauce with prunes and a big pile of mashed potatoes with an earthy smell and sweet carrots cooked with raisins, and for dessert, a thick, cold fruit compote. Hilik said, "The main course tastes like dessert and the dessert tastes like a main course," and ate almost nothing. When they were finished she said, "Let's take a stroll, walk this heavy food off."

They crossed the Arab neighborhood of Wadi Nisnas on their way to the Hadar neighborhood. Ruchama pointed at the houses and said, "Look, see how much these houses look like Grandma Julia's house, where I grew up," and then she told them about the nearby Wadi Salib and said, "Next time Aunt Tehila comes to visit I'll ask her to explain everything that happened there, it's important that you know that her Black Panthers didn't invent anything new." A wailing song rose from one of the houses and Ruchama stopped and said, "Listen, they're listening to Umm Kulthum, she's a lauded Egyptian singer and each of her songs is about a year long." The screeching sounds merged with the howl of the cold wind that had begun blowing. Shlomi zipped up his sweater and helped Hilik with his stubborn zipper. Ruchama continued to listen with her eyes fixed on the balcony from which the singing came. "They're listening to her because she died last week," she said. "They must be mourning her, she was their national singer, even Grandma Julia was crazy about her, even though everyone knew she was an anti-Zionist and she always held a handkerchief full of sniffing drugs she'd breathe in to relax." Then the singer's voice began jumping and Ruchama said, "Their record is broken," and the three of them laughed at the jumps that instantly turned the melancholic song into a crazy joke. "Even her record is on drugs," Ruchama said and laughed.

When they reached Hadar, Hilik said, "I don't know why they call this place Hadar, because that means splendor and there's nothing here but dirt and noise and shouting," and Ruchama said, "Now I have a surprise, I'm taking you to a real movie theater, not like the one we have in Tiberias that smells like pee and mold." She bought tickets to the movie *The Man with the Golden Gun*, gave them each a small bottle of grape juice and said, "Drink it all quickly, I don't want you to be thirsty." But Shlomi and Hilik knew she was going to roll the bottles again. She used to go into movie theaters with three or four empty bottles hidden in her bag, and every time something exciting or suspenseful happened in the movie and the audience was silent, she'd pull out a bottle and roll it on the floor. The bottle would roll down the stairs and hit people's legs, its sounds reverberating and awakening the viewers immersed in the movie, and Ruchama would say, "Very good, it's time they woke up from their imbecilic dream and remember they're nothing but little people with no air conditioning and hardly anything to eat."

But the empty grape juice bottles remained in Ruchama's bag this time, because a few minutes after the movie had started a hard rain began pouring. The drops hit the roof of the theater and drowned out the actors' voices and the sounds of shooting and the screeching of brakes on their modern cars. "It's good the rain is so noisy," Ruchama said, "now nobody can get lost in the movie and think there's anyone real who's as perfect as that James Bond." Then she said, "I think this James Bond looks a little like your Simon Templar on television," and Hilik said, "It's the same actor," and Ruchama said, "I prefer the old James Bond, his smile was less annoying."

When they returned home, Hilik's ear doctor came to visit and told Ruchama off, "You took him to every doctor in the world but me, I'm really insulted." Then he looked and checked and investigated and finally said, "The doctor in Haifa wasn't lying, there's really nothing but some swelling."

Before she locked herself in her bedroom with the doctor, Ruchama asked Shlomi, "Is it all an act? Tell me the truth," and Shlomi cut the air with wide hand gestures and whispered with an effort, "No way, are you crazy?" and Ruchama said, "All right, don't strain your voice. I'm fine with you keeping quiet until you get better."

But Shlomi didn't get better. Almost a month had passed since Ella had returned and his voice had gone still. It seemed the world had gotten used to his silence and that Shlomi himself had given in to it, and only rarely did his throat contract with frustration, like when he wanted to calm Hilik and push away his trepidations with words that wouldn't come out.

And so, against Shlomi's silence, Hilik continued to collect proof of Ruchama's insanity. His eyes grew worried as he told him again about the blood from the raw meat dripping from her lips, and about her frequent fights with Vardina, and about the memorial candles, and the hiding drills she ran them through in case terrorists broke into the house, and the torment she put Robert through, and the bottles she rolled at the movie theater. "Yesterday I even heard two teachers talking about her," he said. "Everyone at school thinks she's a psycho because she was arguing with the principal and said it was a shame Israel didn't lose the war." Hilik took a deep breath and continued with fervor, like the defense lawyer they'd seen speaking in front of a jury on Robert's television. "And today," he said, "while she was eating the meat, she told the vendor all sorts of things that angered him, about the Agranat Commission[5], and about how she

---

[5] A National Commission of Inquiry set up to investigate failings of the Israel Defense Force in the prelude to the Yom Kippur War, when Israel was found unprepared for the attack on the Egyptian border and a simultaneous attack by Syria in the Golan — the first phase in a war in which 2,812 Israeli soldiers were killed. The commission called for the dismissal of a number of senior officers in the IDF and caused such controversy that Prime Minister Golda Meir was forced to resign. Yitzhak Rabin was elected in her place.

prefers Golda's annoying accent to Rabin's sleepy voice. She even told him she thought they should disband the Maccabi Tel Aviv basketball team so we wouldn't have reasons to enjoy this country anymore, she thinks everyone should be grieving and thinking about their miserable lives. The vendor got upset at her and turned red. I think she's decided to become Deborah the Prophetess." He nodded vigorously, and only when he raised his eyes and saw Shlomi looking at the doorway, only then did he turn his head and see Ruchama standing there silently.

"What's wrong, Hilik?" she asked. "You've turned white as a wall."

Hilik turned even whiter and whispered, "Did you hear what I told Shlomi?"

Ruchama sat across from him. "You don't have to worry about me, I'm not going crazy and I'm not a prophetess or anything," she said and caressed his forehead. "Don't listen to every piece of nonsense that comes out of your stupid teachers' mouths."

"Do you really think we should have lost the Yom Kippur War?"

"Yes." She smiled. "I was just trying to explain to your principal that if we'd have let the Arabs win and occupy their stupid land, they might have relaxed."

Hilik swallowed. "The paper said the Syrians made it almost all the way to Tiberias," he said. "What would we have done then? Where would we have gone?" and Ruchama said, "What do the Syrians have to do in Tiberias? Since when are you a politician? Stop it, Hilik, you're too smart to be thinking about this rubbish." She was quiet for a moment and then said, "Don't worry about me, Hilik, I'm not going crazy, I'm just worried because I get the feeling someone's put a curse on me."

In the evening, when they sat on the stone wall, Ella told Shlomi, "It's really cold, the stone is making my butt freeze, why don't we go into my house?"

Shlomi shook his head, rejecting her suggestion, and then pointed to his knees. Ella smiled. "Are you offering me a seat on your lap?" and Shlomi blushed a little and nodded. "Why don't you ever want to come to my place?" she asked, and he shrugged. "Your silence is beginning to get on my nerves," she said.

Then Hanna came out of the building and walked towards them, her eyes on Shlomi. "Why are you sitting out here in the cold? You'll be sick," she said and her eyes were still on his, shifting occasionally to run over his body.

"Because we feel like it," Ella answered.

"Is your voice still lost, Shlomi?" Hanna asked, and Shlomi nodded. "I've never heard of anything like that," she added. "You're a true phenomenon."

Again her eyes moved to inspect his long legs and his shoulders and his panting chest. Then she pointed to a nearby parked blue car.

"Did Israella tell you we bought a car?"

"I didn't tell him," Ella said angrily. "He doesn't care about your car."

Hanna ignored her. "Tell Mom that if she needs a ride somewhere she can ask me, I'll gladly drive her."

"How will he tell her?" Ella said with even more anger. "Did you forget he's lost his voice?"

Hanna laughed thinly and said, "He can write her a note."

Then she turned to leave, stopped, said, "You'd better come in, I'll make you some tea. It's about to rain," and went on her way, the sack of skin under her chin bouncing with each step and her straw hair bristling in the cold wind.

"Did you see how she swallowed you with her eyes?" Ella said after Hanna disappeared into the stairway.

Shlomi looked at her with his forehead furrowed, trying to understand. "Watch out for her," she added, "I know her swallowing looks very well. Sometimes she's like that snake that lives in the jungles in Brazil: it can swallow an entire animal and then digest it slowly for months." And once she was finished talking, the sky began spraying a thick rain. Ella got up immediately, smoothed her hand over his dampening hair and ran home.

When he got inside, his clothes were wet but his face was on fire. Hilik looked at him from his seat in front of the television, bundled in a woolen blanket and enveloped in the red light from the space heater. "You're all wet," he said. "Go change your clothes before you get a cold and give it to me, too."

A puddle of water grew at Shlomi's feet. He quickly took off his clothes, left them by the door and sat on the sofa in his underwear, as far away as possible from the heater. "Have you gone crazy now, too?" Hilik said, and Shlomi waved his hands, fanning his blushing face, signaling that his body was burning up. Hilik looked at the pile of clothes and the expanding puddle and said, "At least pick up your clothes, Mom's going to kill you," but Shlomi kept waving even as Ruchama came in from the kitchen and said, "Why are you naked? You want to catch pneumonia?"

The rain grew stronger, hammering the windows and making even more noise than when they were at the movie theater in Haifa. Ruchama went from window to window, closing the shutters. "God has lost His mind," she said. "Just a month ago He suffocated us with a heat wave and now He's bringing us Siberia. Why don't we turn on another heater, the apartment is like a freezer." She looked at Shlomi staring at the television and fanning his face. "Dry that puddle you made right now and go get dressed before I get mad," she said, and Shlomi didn't even return her look. "Besides, I've already told you I don't like you walking around naked, you're too old for that," and she picked his clothes up off the floor and went to the bathroom.

Hilik looked at Shlomi, smiled and whispered, "You're a little hard," and Shlomi made a derisive face, folded his legs and kept staring at the news in Arabic. Hilik said, "Maybe that's why you're so hot, you should go whack off and imagine Ella." Shlomi raised a threatening finger and Hilik said, "You don't scare me, Shlomi." Shlomi pulled back his hand and closed his legs tighter. His eyes tried to focus on the newscaster with the big hair. In throaty words full of sorrow, she described the mourning in Egypt over the singer who used to carry a drug-infused handkerchief. But in his mind he saw Hanna's straw hair blowing in the wind, making a light halo around her blue eyes and the sack vibrating up her neck.

And then thunder and lightning took over the world.

They broke out at once, flashing through shutter cracks, cutting a blinding light through the living room and shaking the house. Ruchama stood in the living room, her eyes fixed on the light bulbs that had begun flickering, their yellow light dancing on her face. The television screen flickered as well, as if lightning had invaded the set and was now trying to break out. And indeed, a moment later the

television sounded a grating hum that grew louder until it was interrupted by a small explosion. Fire began burning, searing through
the television set, blowing sparks that caught on the nearby window
curtain. It ignited into a red flame in seconds. Hilik jumped from his
seat and began beating the shade with the woolen blanket. Ruchama
yelled, "Get away from there, I'll get a bucket of water," and Hilik
yelled, "Don't you dare, you can get electrocuted by the television,
it's dangerous," and Shlomi kept staring at the television blowing
sparks and at the fire in the curtain that Hilik's beating had choked
down and turned into a thick smoke.

"Get up already and go unplug the electricity," Hilik shouted,
but Shlomi froze in his place. Ruchama ran to the kitchen and returned with a towel, prepared to beat the burning television. "Are
you crazy?" Hilik yelled and pushed her away from the television,
"The towel is wet, we have to unplug it first." He ran to the stairway
and quickly switched off the fuses in the fuse box.

Darkness descended on the apartment, and only the flashes of
lightning and the fading red light of the space heater and the small
flames rising from the television set broke the darkness and turned
the living room into a mysterious, deceiving cave. Hilik ran back inside. He slipped in the puddle Shlomi had left and his body slammed
loudly into the floor.

A shout escaped his mouth.

Ruchama threw the blanket on the television and the fire died out
immediately. She unplugged the set and ran to Hilik, searching for
him in the dark by the sound of his cries. She leaned over him and
he yelled, "Don't touch me." She asked, scared, "What's wrong?" and
Hilik answered, "I think I broke my arms."

Ruchama went out into the stairway and switched the fuses back
into place. The lights went back on, no longer flickering, illumi-
nating frozen Shlomi, the television covered in a sooty blanket, the
smoking window curtain and Hilik, sprawled on the floor, shaking
arms at his sides and tears washing over his face.

Ruchama leaned towards him and said softly, "Let me help you
up, hold up your arms, I promise not to touch them." She put her
hands on his chest and pulled him to a seated position. A choked
cry burst out of his throat, his face went pale and he rolled his eyes.
"Don't you dare pass out on me now," she said and shouted at Shlo-

mi, "What are you doing, sitting like a statue? Throw me a pillow, get him some water and get me the scissors from the sewing drawer."

Shlomi awoke from his stagnation. He threw Ruchama a pillow and went quickly to the kitchen. She gently placed the pillow under Hilik's shaking arms. Then she took the scissors Shlomi brought her and cut Hilik's shirt sleeves in one swift motion, exposing his arms. They swelled within seconds. Ruchama looked at them with worry – the elbow of his right arm grew twice as large as normal and his left hand was also swollen and distorted. Shlomi handed Ruchama a glass of water and she made Hilik take two small sips. "Don't worry," she said, "I'm calling an ambulance," and she leaped to the phone, praying for a dial tone that never came. Then she ordered Shlomi to get dressed and go out to the road to stop the first car that went by.

"It's pouring out there," Hilik bawled. "No cars will be going by now." "It'll be all right," said Ruchama. "A car has to go by." "But how will Shlomi stop it?" Hilik kept bawling. "He's lost his voice," and Ruchama said, "He'll manage." She gave him more water and mumbled, "Your father just *had* to be in Tel Aviv, if he were here we'd already be on our way to the hospital. You can't rely on him."

Shlomi put on his wet woolen pants and flew down the stairs without shoes or shirt, working hard to catch up with his legs and arms that flew every which way. Feelings of guilt and anger at himself rose inside of him. Stupid, mute, idiot, coward, mean, baby, retard, imbecile, shit, scoundrel, lousy lighthouse with a dead bird in the throat, ugly fallen palm tree, whacks off with no white drops, asshole, butt face.

The cold wind scratched his shoulders and his bare feet carried him to Ella and Hanna's door. He knocked loudly, ignoring the pain that had begun shooting from his neck down his back.

Ella opened the door and was shocked by his appearance. Shlomi panted and shook. He opened his mouth to explain, his hands cutting through the air, but not even a whisper left his throat. Hanna stood by Ella, her eyes wide with worry. She pulled him inside and shut the door. Her arms gripped his shoulders tightly and led him to the living room, where she sat him down and covered him with a blue blanket. His eyes ran around the room, taking in only fractions of the familiar home's new look: new furniture, bluish drapes, no more screen doors.

"Try to explain what happened," Hanna said, her hand on his knee. "He can't talk," said Ella, looking at Shlomi's lips that opened and closed. A lump of silence blocked his throat and tears broke out from his eyes. Ella ran back to her room and returned with a notebook and pencil and shoved them into his hands, her hand crashing into Hanna's, which was caressing and trying to calm him. Shlomi held the pencil tightly, forced the trembling in his hands to stop and wrote. Ella took the notebook and read out loud, "Hilik broke arms, need car for hospital."

Hanna stood up at once, ran to her bedroom and returned with a heavy coat on her shoulder and her large, rustling purse in her hands.

Shlomi and Ella followed her down the path. "Careful not to slip," she said and grabbed both their arms, affixing them to her sides.

When they reached the stairway, they found Ruchama leaning against the wall, holding Hilik's small body folded in her arms, one of her arms hugging his shoulders and the other serving as a seat for him. Hilik shook, his swollen arms placed on a pillow and his face white, his teeth biting his lips, drawing blood.

Ruchama looked at Hanna and froze. "Come," said Hanna, "I'll take you to Poria Hospital." She looked at Hilik's arms and added, "We'd better hurry." Then she clung to Ruchama, gently placed her arm under Hilik's butt and said, "We'll carry him together, the car is parked a bit far." Without a word Ruchama unlatched from the wall. They moved together as one, step by step, Hilik moaning in their arms. "You stay here with Shlomi," Hanna told Ella, "and make sure he gets dressed, he shouldn't get pneumonia so that Ruchama has to take care of him as well, one is enough." When they reached the building's entrance Ruchama said, "Thank you," and Hanna said, "Don't mention it, I owe you a ride, you took us to the Sea of Galilee once, when Shmuel was still alive."

When they disappeared into the path's darkness Shlomi collapsed on the steps. Ella turned on the light and said, "Let's go upstairs," but Shlomi remained in his place, drained of power, his arms and legs unwilling to oblige. Ella put her hands on his shoulders. "You're like a block of ice, you have to put on a shirt and change your pants right now," she said and pulled him up. And like that, with her arms around his waist, they climbed the stairs.

Ella looked at the scorched curtains, at the blanket on the television and the puddle that had spread out when Hilik slipped and fell. Her eyes pieced everything together. Shlomi sat on the sofa, his body slumped and his gaze hanging on the cloud of smoke that still hovered in the living room.

"Please go get dressed, I'm worried about you," she said, but Shlomi didn't move. She walked towards the bedroom and returned a moment later with a towel and clothes. "I found these pajamas on one of the beds in your room," she smiled. "Judging by the length this must be yours." She leaned towards him and wiped his head and face and shoulders and stomach, and then laid him on the sofa, unzipped his water-drenched pants and gently pulled them off. Shlomi lay there, following her motions. He was surprised to feel his breath relax and a pleasant calm flowing through him. She said, "Your underwear is wet, too," and Shlomi nodded. "I'll get you some from the closet," she said shyly and went to the room again. Another wave of pleasantness crashed over him, his eyes almost closed, his breathing quiet and his body warming up. Ella returned and placed the underwear on his stomach. "Your mother folds underwear very weird," she said, and Shlomi didn't move, only kept looking at her through half-open eyes. "You want me to dress you?" she asked in a trembling voice, and Shlomi nodded. A long moment passed before she put out her arms and removed his wet underwear in hesitant motions, her eyes trying to escape the image of his groin. There was silence between them. Her compressed, choked breaths, his clam breaths. She pulled the clean underwear gently up his legs, trying to cover his penis quickly. Her hand went on to rub his stomach, climbing up to his neck and caressing his face. His eyes closed a bit more. Her hand eliminated the remaining cold from his cheeks and forehead. She pulled her hand away, took a deep breath, and then grabbed his pajama pants, put them on his body and, in motions that became quicker and sharper with each moment, she helped him up to a seated position, put his shirt on, buttoned it up and said, "I'm touched that you aren't embarrassed and that you let me help you." A small smile appeared on her lips. "You didn't even blush when you got hard."

Then she went to the living room, folded the charred blanket and put it in the stairway, ripped off the scorched curtains and put them in the trash, removed the remaining burnt fabric from the furniture, collected it with a broom, wiped the puddle with a rag, cleaned the floor, opened a window and aired out the cloud of smoke, brought the space heater closer to Shlomi, covered him with a blanket, leaned towards him, said, "I really didn't mean for us to be quiet for so long," and left.

Shlomi remained alone with her words whispering in his ears. She returned with truth in her words, he thought. Her touch is truth, her blushing smile is truth. Her eyes are good, loving. Maybe I really don't need to be quiet for so long. A sharp pain is tickling my throat, announcing to me, and I announce to it, that words will come out soon.

Shlomi awoke when Ruchama and Hilik returned. He got up from the sofa immediately and helped Hilik sit and set the pillow under his arms, in casts. His right arm was put in a cast from the shoulder to the tip of the forearm, and on the left only his hand was covered in a hard, puffy cast. Shlomi hugged Hilik and kissed his cheeks again and again until Hilik laughed and said, "Stop, you're tickling me, and I'm in crazy pain as it is," and Shlomi whispered, "I'm sorry." Hilik said, "It's not your fault, if you hadn't called Hanna my arms would have exploded, it's thanks to you we made it in time, and thanks to Hanna, who drove like crazy and screamed at the doctors and made a scene so they treated me right." Shlomi looked at him questioningly and Hilik said, "You want to know why she had to make a scene?" Shlomi nodded and Hilik whispered, "Because Mom couldn't get a word out, I've never seen her silent like that."

Ruchama brought a plate with slices of bread covered in white cheese and finely diced cucumber. She sat by Hilik, pointed one of the slices at his mouth and said, "You have to eat something, it's not good for you to have an empty stomach with all that pain medication they gave you." Hilik obeyed, took a bite and chewed it, and Ruchama told Shlomi, "Check if the phone line is back, we have to tell Dad what happened, and make sure Vardina didn't have a heart attack from the thunder, I'll go down to see her later, she must have been scared."

Then she bit into one of the slices herself. "I'm sure of it," she said with moist eyes, "someone's cursed me."

3

Towards the middle of December 1974, in the midst of Chanukah, the phone rang in the shutter factory and awoke Robert from his slumber.

He was sitting at the edge of the factory floor, across from the piles of merchandise, carefully arranged and growing dusty alongside the silent machines. He sat there for hours on a stool, his eyes almost shut and his ears taking in the sounds of a miserable trapped pigeon flapping its wings and trying to escape, fluttering from pile to pile, leaving droppings on the plastic sheets covering the orphaned shutters. Hundreds of shutters of different sizes and colors, only waiting to be loaded onto trucks and assembled as planned.

Robert had invested a fortune in this canceled order. He'd taken on huge loans, recruited more and more workers, working them in shifts, day and night, until the plan had been fully executed, and even finished before the agreed-upon deadline. Only then, when everything was already packed and ready, the kibbutz suddenly cancelled the order. "We're in very bad shape," the secretary told him, his face yellow. "Many members were killed in the war and we can't get our bearings." Robert was quiet for a long moment before saying, "But everything's done, I'm in terrible debt, you never even made a down-payment." The secretary opened his arms in apology and said, "There's nothing we can do, it's *force majeure*," and Robert raised his voice, "What *force majeure*, you've committed to this and you'll pay every last lira." The secretary sat up and said, "Don't yell at me, Robert, it's not my fault the coffers are empty." Robert raised his voice, "If you don't pay me, I'm finished," and even threatened, "I won't let you kill my business." The secretary got up and said, "You can sue us if you want, but you'll waste a few years doing that. We're a large, historic kibbutz; no court will take your word over ours. It's because of our members who were killed in the war that you can sleep quietly in your house in Tiberias. It won't hurt you to contribute a little to the war effort, you live in this country too, you don't live on the moon."

"You should have signed a proper contract with them," the lawyer he consulted with said. "The technical specifications they gave you have no legal merit and they never signed your price quote." "But we'd made a deal," Robert said tiredly, and the lawyer said, "I can start working on this, but you have to be ready, it's going to take a long time and cost a lot of money," and Robert said, "I'm too tired to do anything." The lawyer said, "You're a young man, you even look like a kid, take a deep breath, I believe we'll win in the end." "When?" Robert asked hopelessly, and the lawyer answered, "God knows."

With no other choice, Robert sent all his workers home. He paid back some of the loans after using his savings and selling most of the assets he'd accumulated – two apartments he'd bought for Shlomi and Hilik, some plots of land he'd purchased as a long-term investment and which were eating up tax money and two trucks used for shipping goods and equipment. He kept the old truck, the factory with the machinery and the small apartment he'd bought in Tel Aviv.

These were bad days. The bankers frowned at him and the orders stopped coming in. The entire world was covered in shutters and what little work that remained was divided between himself and his competition in Afula, Beit Shean and the Krayot. And since these were meant for new buildings whose construction had been halted till things got better, shutter factories had stopped their activity altogether. "Shared trouble is half a consolation," Robert told Ruchama once when he was invited to dinner with her and the children, and she answered, "Shared trouble is a fool's consolation." Robert sighed and whispered, "What am I going to do now?" and Ruchama said, "You keep studying air conditioners and you'll be all right, you don't have to worry about me, I make enough money to help you if you need it."

The days were bad and hard. Northern Israel was covered in deserted construction sites. Naked plaster skeletons were fenced in with wooden planks and on them were signs warning off infiltrators. In spite of the signs, groups of adventurous children turned these sites into backdrops for games of hide-and-seek, running among the scaffolding, hiding behind barrels of congealed concrete and piles of bricks, making jolly paths with forgotten ladders, competing in pushing wheelbarrows filled with ghostly whitewash, dismantling the planks and building carts and scarecrows and nail guns, or throwing gravel at each other. Not a day went by without injuries. Rusty nails penetrated their feet, arms were broken when kids fell from the second floor to a rain-drenched sandpile, heads were banged on loose fallen blocks. Scratched and bleeding, they'd return home, clean their wounds in hiding, smear stinging iodine on them and conceal their pain from their parents' tired eyes.

And so, for months, the shutters just sat there, gathering dust. When Shlomi came to help clean the place up a bit, Robert told him, "Look at these shutters, from a distance they look like a huge monument for the Yom Kippur War dead." Then he said, "Let's have some fun, I'll teach you how to sing the national anthem in Spanish," and he burst into roaring song while pushing the broom around and raising clouds of dust. Shlomi tried to avoid it, but Robert made him repeat each line, emphasizing teeth-breaking words and happily rolling his Rs: *Errrretz Zion VeYerrrrrrushalaim.* Shlomi sang a little and mainly laughed. This was a long time before the sandy heat wave fell upon the city, before Ella and Hanna came back, before his throat went still.

Once in a while, Robert would go to the factory, sit there and stare at the piles. Occasionally, he'd be called to fix jammed shutters that he'd assembled in the past, or to grease squeaky pulleys. On Saturdays, he'd sit with Shlomi and Hilik in front of the television, trying to receive transmission from Lebanon or Jordan, but most of his days were spent in Tel Aviv. He cleaned and tidied and furnished the small apartment on Gordon Street that he'd purchased a few years before. It had one large room and a balcony Robert had enclosed with shutters and which served as his bedroom. He would arrive early in the week and go to the Ministry of Labor's air conditioning engineering class each day. On Monday nights, he'd go to English lessons, and on Tuesday afternoon he participated in a Hebrew poetry class at the public library. He'd sit at the edge of the room filled with made-up older women, his back against the wall and his mind battling with the stern teacher's musings. He didn't tell Ruchama about it. Maybe one day he'd surprise her with the insights he was working hard to collect, maybe he'd wake her with a quote from one of the poets she used to love and now mourned three times a year, perhaps he'd even be able to come up with some rhyming words of appeasement himself and win her heart back. But the words kept their distance, hitting the bare wall behind him, echoing through the perfume-drenched room and scattering before he was able to grab and understand them. Every once in a while the teacher would turn to him for his opinion. Robert would squint as if pondering, try to avoid the eyes of the blushing women who were staring at him, some of them veiled in mystery, and then he'd say, "There's a secret in this poem, I think the source of its beauty is in the fact that the secret is indecipherable and I'd hate to ruin it. It's better kept this way, in secret." The teacher would nod with enthusiasm and the women would blush more and bat their lashes, as if trying to imprint his face on their irises before they returned their attention to the teacher and his musings. During breaks, he'd go outside and look at the sculpture exhibition, chew an apple and ignore the women's attempts to engage him in conversation. Once, one of them sat down beside him, offered him some gum and said, "We suspect you're a poet, maybe someday you'll bring your own work to the class – we're sure it's very moving." A shudder went through her body when Robert looked at her, nodded lightly and remained fortressed in his silence.

On other nights, he'd open the shutters slightly, sit on his bed, bite into some bread and cheese and look at dark Gordon Street. When he couldn't sleep, he'd go for a short walk – walk to Ben Yehuda Street, buy a bottle of juice and a bag of peanuts at the kiosk, head north and turn on Arlozorov Street, walk slowly down Dizengof, past the famous café where Ruchama's poets used to congregate. Once he even met the scholarly teacher there. The teacher bought him a cup of coffee and asked, "What do you do, really?" and Robert answered, "Shutters." The teacher smiled and said, "Tell the truth, I won't tell your fans, they think you're a serious poet and you'll be discovered some day, and the truth is I suspect it too," and Robert said with embarrassment, "I'm telling the truth, I do shutters." The teacher said, "I've never thought about that metaphor before, poems really are like shutters sometimes." Robert sipped the boiling coffee and said, "But I'm switching to air conditioners now," and the teacher burst out laughing and said, "You're killing me with your metaphors. I'd love to read some of your shutters and air conditioners sometime."

Then he'd return to his small apartment, sit in front of the open shutter for a while longer, calculate the loans he'd still not had a chance to pay off, and yearn for Ruchama. Sometimes the yearning burned his eyes and he couldn't shut them to fall asleep. His finger would dial her number hesitantly and his ear would wait to hear her voice. She'd say, "It's so late, you woke me up," or she'd say, "I can't talk right now, I'm kneading dough and my hands are covered in flour," or, "These long-distance calls are so expensive and you know I don't like talking on the phone." Robert would answer, "You hardly speak to me when I'm home, either, I've been waiting for you for almost five years," and Ruchama would whisper, "You'll even wait an eternity."

Once he suddenly told her, "I won't give up on you, Ruchama; *I'll wait for you like your shoes.*"

Ruchama was silent for a long moment and then said with wonder, "How do you know that line?"

"I read poetry sometimes too," he answered.

Ruchama laughed. "I don't believe you, you must have seen it in a newspaper."

Robert became determined and said, "It's from a poem you like by Alterman. If you'd like I can recite all the lines I remember."

Ruchama was silent. Robert listened to her breaths being swallowed in the static on the line, surprised by the teacher's distant and meaningless words that suddenly rose in him.

And then he said in a cracked voice:

"*You fall asleep, and I'll enter and sit. Sit on the floor to watch you. Silent and strange, in your peaceful room, I'll wait for you like your shoes.*"

Ruchama said nothing for a long minute. Then finally she said, "You reminded me I need to get Shlomi new shoes." She giggled a little, said "Good night" and hung up.

Robert would lie in bed and close his eyes, images from her small room on the Carmel floating in his mind, the triangle ceiling and the blue bedspread, her body twisted around his and her wet hair dripping on his face. His body would fill with longing. He'd touch himself until he exploded, clean himself and fall asleep. For five years he hadn't been with her, or any other woman.

And when he felt his heart would burst with yearning, he'd decide to skip school and return to Tiberias early, gladly taking her up on her invitations to join them for dinner, filling and refilling his plate, absorbing the spicy sauce in the bread Shlomi had baked, compensating himself for all those cheese sandwiches he ate while watching the street from his Tel Aviv balcony. Or he'd go to the factory first, open the doors, turn on the radio, sit on the stool and stare at the piles of shutters. Once in a while more words the teacher had quoted from Ruchama's favorite Alterman poems would float in his head:

"I wanted her to think me light, and my hands pure and my mind clear."

Or:

"Even an old vision has a moment of birth."

Or:

"Today the pigeons fill with frothing."

And then, in the middle of December 1974, the phone rang and woke Robert from his reveries, paving a new path in his destiny.

The ringing was loud and grating. Robert had connected the phone's ringer to a special speaker so that he could hear it even when the machines were working and the workers were banging, drilling and sharpening. Now the ring echoed among the piles of shutters, sending the trapped pigeon on another terrified wandering dance between the windows. Robert walked quickly to the office cubicle. Perhaps it's the lawyer. Perhaps he has news. Perhaps it's Ruchama, maybe she'll invite me for a Chanukah candle lighting to eat the small, honey-glazed donuts she fries for the holiday.

He went into the office. The radio was playing softly and before he turned it off he caught another report on the two killed and dozens wounded in the previous night's grenade attack. A terrorist had thrown grenades into the audience at the Chen Movie Theater in Dizengof Square in Tel Aviv. Robert had walked by there many times on his nightly prowls, and only once did he buy a ticket and go in to watch a movie, but fell asleep instantly, exhausted from the effort to focus on the subtitles that moved by too quickly.

"Hello?" he answered, breathless.

"Hello, Robert."

He froze in his place. It wasn't the lawyer. Nor Ruchama. It was a woman's voice, speaking Spanish, choked with tears. He recognized it but still asked, rolling his whispered Spanish words, "Who is this?"

"It's me, Rochelle, I'm in Paris."

It had been a long time, five long years, but her voice was crisp in his memory, maybe because she'd barely spoken, barely said a word that week. She'd visited his bed each night, gathering him into her in silence, her face dark and unsmiling, the touch of her lips on his shoulder, her thick hair. Her eyes had evaporated from his memory and only her voice remained sharp, even now, choked and crying, even within the noisy medley of this long-distance phone call.

"Your uncle died," she said. "It's a shame you two hadn't talked in so long. He wanted to hear your voice very much before he closed his eyes. I think he knew he was dying. He loved you very much."

"What did he die of? Was he sick?" Robert whispered after a long silence.

"No."

Again they were silent.

Finally she said, "I'm coming to Israel tomorrow. I'm bringing your uncle. God knows how I've managed to get him out of Argentina. He requested to be buried in Israel."

Robert wanted to ask many questions, but remained still. Through the glass partition he saw the pigeon still banging its wings against the closed windows, until it changed directions and flew to the partially open doors, deserting the room and taking off elsewhere.

"I need help," said Rochelle.

The image of his uncle and Rochelle embracing and crying tears of joy returned to Robert's mind. His semen had already been received in her body, becoming a fetus.

He'd never asked. In the few conversations he'd had with his uncle since, he'd made sure to report about the success of the shutter factory, and nothing more, and the uncle hadn't said anything either, not even through insinuation, about the fate of the pregnancy he'd left behind when he'd returned from Argentina. Had the child been born and grown up? Was she bringing him along on this burial mission? It might have been a girl rather than a boy. Or perhaps it wasn't born at all. Or perhaps she'd left it in Buenos Aires with the quiet servant, or with her only aunt who lived in Paris.

"I hardly have any money left," said Rochelle. "I need you to help me make the arrangements and find a place for me to stay until my life becomes clear again. Right now it's covered in sand."

Robert locked the factory doors, surprised by his confident movement and steady hands. Surprised also by the terrific hunger that had suddenly hit his stomach. I have to prepare, I have to get a car, the truck won't make it to the airport, maybe I'll ask Aaron, Ruchama's brother, but then I'd have to explain, Ruchama would ask questions, I never told her about Rochelle, I need to check her flight again, bringing a coffin with her and maybe a child, too, asking to stay here until her life becomes clear. I have to find out what the arrangements are, maybe I can speak to the man from the *Chevra Kadisha* burial society, I did a shutter job for him once, I made a donation, an anonymous one, I'd have to explain to him too, what if he's tempted to insinuate something to Ruchama, people love how powerful they feel when they reveal secrets, and Ruchama would catch on and ask questions, her senses are sharp, I can't bury him in Tiberias, strange man, asking to be buried in the country he hates, sending himself along with his young, quiet wife, his son or daughter, or maybe the baby was never born, or maybe she left him in Buenos Aires, why did the money run out, maybe she's carrying diamonds in her underwear, I have to buy a plot, I'd have to explain to Ruchama and the children why I'm returning to Tel Aviv even though it's almost the weekend, it's Thursday, what Chanukah candle is it today, I won't taste the honey-glazed donuts, I'll be on the road, maybe I'll rent a car, I'll take the bus to Haifa and rent a large car with a trunk big enough for a coffin, a small coffin because he was a small man, and he probably shrank even more, people grow old and small, really I'll need a medium-sized car, not too expensive, I'm out of money too, so many loans, I can't ask Ruchama, I'll have to explain it and she'll ask questions. You'll even wait an eternity. *Even an old vision has a moment of birth.* Here it is, being born right in front of me.

Robert sat down in the nearby bakery, at a small table at the end of a room filled with scents of singed sugar, cinnamon and yeast, his back leaning against the wall and to his right a window overlooking the street. Hunger had crumpled his stomach. He ordered a piece of cake, a cylinder of fluffy dough filled with cream and covered in chocolate. The cake was tasty, the cream was fatty and satisfying, the chocolate smeared into a moist mustache above his lip. Through the stained window, his eyes followed the people walking down the street, most of them familiar to him, their houses covered in his shutters. Outside it was wintry and inside it was warm. What if I met Ruchama now? What if she walks into the bakery to buy honey to glaze her donuts, or a bottle of citrus water to add to the honey, to make it taste fresh and blossomy. What would I tell her? How would I explain that I just got here today on the early bus and already I'm planning to leave? It's too bad, she'd say and scrunch her face, I wanted to invite you to light the candles with us and eat honey and citrus-water donuts.

The elderly baker brought him a cup of tea and handed him a paper napkin to wipe off the chocolate stains. He asked her permission to use the phone.

The kibbutz secretary, the one with the yellow face, recognized his voice immediately. "The Argentine accent gives you away," he said, laughing.

Robert said, "I need help, it's urgent."

The secretary said nothing for a moment, and then, "Come over, I'll wait for you in my office."

Thirty minutes later, he was already sitting across from the secretary's yellow face, and the latter listened patiently and then said, "Don't worry, my driver's down in Tel Aviv anyway, I'll send him over to the airport, he'll take care of everything, we have enough contacts there and it's not the first time we've had to handle coffins. You'll go to the airport on your own and wait for him."

Robert nodded silently.

"Where do you plan on burying him?"

"I don't know."

"In Tiberias?"

"No."

"Where did he request to be buried?"

"I don't know."

"You'll have to buy a plot."

"Yes."

"If you want, I can talk to the secretary of a kibbutz near Hadera, he can easily arrange for a plot for you there."

"How much would it cost?"

"Don't worry about it, I'll take care of it. I do owe you a little money, after all."

Robert mumbled his thanks and lowered his eyes. The secretary placed a warm hand on his shoulder and said, "I'm flattered that you turned to me for help, in spite of everything that happened with the shutters. I'm sorry for your loss."

That evening he was already in Tel Aviv, and in his pocket was the money the yellow-faced secretary had put in his hand after laughing and saying, "It's all right, think of it as a Chanukah gift." Before they parted the secretary asked, "Why did you call me, of all people?" and Robert said, "I don't know, it was the only thing I could think of." The secretary smiled and said, "You could have called your sister, I hear she's doing great things in politics in Jerusalem, she must have some connections," and Robert said, "Tehila hates our uncle, she wouldn't lift a finger for him, even though he's dead now," and the secretary laughed again and said, "Your sister is an expert in hating, maybe that's why she's making it with the politicians."

At the last moment, before it closed for the night, Robert managed to visit the neighborhood grocery store and buy some things, bread, milk, cheese, eggs, oil, sausage, sardines and some candy, in case Rochelle didn't come alone. Only after he'd finished stuffing the groceries in the fridge did he call Ruchama. "I apologize, I had to go back," he said meekly, and cleared his throat before lying. "The neighbors called and said there was a problem with the apartment's pipes, everything's flooded." "That's fine," Ruchama said, "you don't owe me any explanations." Robert felt her sourness reach him through the phone line. "I probably missed your donuts," he said, and she answered, "You missed nothing, we're catering an event tomorrow for eighty guests, I don't have time for donuts."

Then he called the secretary. "Everything's arranged," the secretary said cheerfully, proud of his achievements, "Baruchin, my driver, will wait for you at the airport, he's a kind man and a big talker, you'll have no problem finding him, he has a huge bald head and a long beard like Elijah's. He'll drive you to the cemetery; the coffin will be waiting, unless there are any bureaucratic issues." Robert said nothing. The cream cake he'd had for lunch was spinning in his stomach. "But you've got nothing to worry about," the secretary said, shoving aside the silence. "I'm sure they won't make any trouble, tomorrow's Friday and people want to hurry home to light the candles and eat some fish. It'll be all right, Robert, trust me and my people." Robert said, "I don't know how to thank you." And the secretary said, "I'd appreciate it if you pulled out of the lawsuit your lawyer has filed against us. I promise the shutter issue will be resolved at some point, maybe even soon. We're like family, we shouldn't air our dirty laundry in court."

The airport was full of Christian pilgrims in long robes, rubbing their beards, their eyes tired from the long flight and their mouths mumbling holy words. Among the black robes it was easy to spot Rochelle, tall and straight in her blue coat, her head towering over most of the other people there, searching for him with red eyes, her face darker than before, her thick hair pulled back, and beside her a tiny child, his hair cropped and his face frowning.

Robert's eyes froze on the child and his heart skipped a beat.

For a moment, he thought he was looking at Hilik as a toddler, on his first day of kindergarten, clinging to Ruchama's leg, refusing to say goodbye and join the other children, who were clinging to their own mothers.

The same pointy face, the same wide and clear forehead scrunching whenever a deep thought passed behind it.

The same shoulders whose width and robustness contradicted his short frame and skinny legs.

The same nose, with the red patches around the nostrils.

And when the boy mumbled a few words of Spanish, Robert was shocked to hear Hilik's familiar voice. His heart was racing. Only the black coat with the gray fur around the collar gave the boy the appearance of a foreigner.

An old vision alongside a new one. A moment of birth alongside a long moment of silence within the tumult of the pilgrims and their welcoming parties.

Only after they'd gotten into the car with Baruchin, the secretary's hardworking, smiling driver, and the boy put his head on her arm and fell asleep immediately, only then did Rochelle say, "He was born on March 15th 1970. I could tell from the very first that he was a sad, anxious child, to this day I don't understand how he was still able to bring so much joy to your uncle's life." Her voice broke as she continued, "Your uncle decided to call him Yechiel, after your father."

Again Robert's heart skipped a beat. He looked at the child sleeping in his mother's lap.

Rochelle avoided Robert's face. Her eyes went to the views of the road leading to Hadera while her palm wiped her son's sweaty forehead. The new Hilik. [6]

Here comes a new Hilik.

They said nothing for the remainder of the trip. Only Baruchin talked and talked, trying to break up with his cheer the lump of tension that filled the car. Again and again he praised Robert's shutters, which covered the windows of his home, as well as those of the other members. He praised the kibbutz secretary and his big heart, "Sometimes even bigger than his brain." One of his hands held the wheel confidently, and the other combed through his long Elijah beard and sometimes ran over his bald head. If not for his military jacket, he might have looked like one of those pilgrims at the airport.

When they left Hadera and turned into the kibbutz's cemetery, which Robert didn't know, Baruchin said with shining eyes, "You should know, I think it's a shame about your sister, I miss her very much." Then he winked and said, "And I'm not the only one in the kibbutz who misses her."

Baruchin parked his car at the edge of the cemetery. A cold wind moved the branches of the trees hovering over the headstones and the paths between them. Rochelle stayed in the car, the New Hilik draped in her lap, sleeping deeply.

Baruchin stood by the gate and smoked a cigarette. "The coffin will be here any minute," he apologized to Robert. "It took them a while to get it out, the procedure states it has to be opened so that they can make sure nothing's being smuggled." For the first time since they'd met Baruchin's smile disappeared. He took a drag of his cigarette and whispered. "I don't want to upset you, but maybe you

---

[6] Hilik is a short form of the name Yechiel.

should know what they saw when they opened it." Robert looked at him alertly, awaiting his words. Baruchin tossed away the cigarette butt. "The *Chevra Kadisha* in Argentina did everything right," he said. "He's bathed and wrapped and ready to be buried, but his whole body is covered in bruises."

"Did you see it yourself?" asked Robert.

"No. It's what they told me," said Baruchin. "They had to check nothing was being smuggled and what they found was the body of an old man who had the daylights beaten out of him." He lit another cigarette and asked, "Do you know how he died?"

Robert shook his head and said, "His wife hasn't told me yet."

Baruchin looked at Rochelle, sitting in the car, with surprise. "She's his wife?" he asked. "I was sure she was his daughter and that the kid was his grandson." He took another drag and his smile returned. "You should find out what happened in Argentina," he said. "We're lucky the guys at the port didn't ask too many questions. That's Friday for you, people hurrying home to read the papers and watch the television."

Along with the coffin came four long-haired and scruffy young men. Baruchin's smile widened. "They might look like a rock band," he told Robert, "but they're only high-schoolers waiting to be drafted into the army, and they're on burial duty today. Believe me, they prefer to be here than on dairy duty or laundry duty." Then he raised his voice and called to the boys. "You can take off the *yarmulkes*, we're doing a secular burial." Robert looked at him with surprise and Baruchin explained, "That's the instruction I got from the secretary, but we can change it if you want. Maybe you can ask his wife, it's not too late, I can easily drive over to the next kibbutz and arrange a *minyan*."

Robert walked over to the car, his steps crunching the gravel. Rochelle sat there, teary-eyed, the tiny child still resting in her lap. "I want to get it over with, I don't care about the ceremony," she whispered, trying not to wake New Hilik, "but I want to ask for something. I don't want the boy there, he's too young, I wouldn't know how to explain to him that his father is in that coffin. He's seen too many difficult things in recent weeks as it is." She wiped her eyes and smoothed her hair as if trying to maintain a dignified appearance for the upcoming burial. "You're the only one here who can speak Spanish, if he wakes up you can calm him and tell him I'll be right back."

Robert nodded silently. He took the seat next to her. Rochelle carefully lifted the boy's head and shoulders and placed them in Robert's lap. The child trembled a little in his sleep, his eyes opened for a short moment and immediately closed, his sweaty head rubbed against Robert's thighs until it found its place and dropped, resuming his slumber. Rochelle waited a bit longer, until she was confident her son was safe and sound, then left the car and walked towards Baruchin and the group of on-duty undertakers.

Robert stayed in the car with New Hilik in his lap. Again his eyes went to the familiar features, again he was astounded at the resemblance. His ears collected the song of the boy's breaths, small and clear, not wheezing or screeching at all. Only the sound of breathing and the black coat distinguished the two children, the two Hiliks, the old and the new. Robert searched for the boy's forehead, gently pushing aside a lock of hair that stuck to it, felt his warmth, caressing him, transferring into his mind tangible proof of this deceptive present that had landed on him out of nowhere.

The funeral took ten, maybe twenty minutes. Rochelle returned to the car, standing even taller and her face darker than ever. New Hilik didn't even open his eyes as he was put back in his place in her lap.

Robert placed a small stone on the mound of dirt under which the coffin was buried, and Baruchin talked and talked, explaining proudly that the hole had been dug in the early morning, and that they made everything run like clockwork. The boys shook the dirt off their hands and disappeared as quickly as they'd arrived.

In the car ride over to Robert's apartment in Tel Aviv, Baruchin said, "Please ask her if everything was all right and if she's pleased with the burial."

Robert asked her in Spanish.

Rochelle said, "Even donkeys get a more respectable burial, the least they could have done was wash up and comb their hair."

"She says she's pleased," Robert lied. "She's very grateful."

"Tell her it breaks my heart to see such a young and beautiful woman burying her husband," asked Baruchin.

And she mumbled in a choked voice, "Why doesn't that man ever stop smiling?"

She stood for a long moment in the center of the large room of his apartment and looked around. New Hilik let go of her leg, climbed on the sofa, lay down and fell asleep immediately. She looked at the windows, examined the few pieces of furniture, lingered on his bed that was pushed onto the balcony. Her gaze was covered in a dim veil Robert couldn't interpret.

Perhaps she expected a large, elegant house. Perhaps she searched for her tiny son's place in Robert's world – seeking a small bed and a squat table fitting his size, and some toys, small cars, a train, crayons and coloring books and colorful Legos.

How could he have known she'd come with a coffin, two suit-cases, and a new Hilik?

Maybe she thought the uncle had told him about their son, may-be even sent him pictures so he could follow his development:

His first bath as a newborn ...

As a one-year-old, crawling on the carpets of their magnificent home ...

At age two, staring at the candles burning on his birthday cake ...

Four years old, building a sand castle with his elderly father on the beach of a picturesque summer town, his skin burned by the sun ...

And now, smiling, a bib wrapped around his neck, dining with the two of them in one of their favorite Buenos Aires eateries ...

Perhaps she thought he'd witnessed their happiness. Perhaps she herself was recalling these pictures and wishing to burst into tears. And perhaps instead she'd break into a bitter laugh, raging at her reversed fate.

To this day, it was unclear what besmirched their happiness, what motivated the long and excruciating four months, at the end of which the uncle had died and Rochelle found herself in a small apartment at the heart of Tel Aviv.

One night, police officers knocked on their door, wanting to take the uncle in for questioning. He was put in a jail cell, and for a week a long list of accusations and suspicions was hurled at him – bribery, embezzlement of government funds, mistreatment of employees, and tax evasion. His wealth was all the proof they needed.

"They must have had an informer," Rochelle said, sitting on the sofa beside her sleeping son, her hand on his head, as if trying to block his ears. "Maybe it was an unfortunate employee who was fired, maybe someone from the local Ashkenazi community who'd been jealous of his success. Your uncle always joked that there was intense competition between his enemies in Buenos Aires. Some hated him for being rich, others for being Jewish, and others yet for being a Jew who was born and raised in Iraq."

He returned a week later. His hair had been shaved because the jail was crawling with lice. His body was covered with bruises. He told Rochelle he'd hurt himself every time he tried to climb up or down from his bed in the cell crowded with detainees and bunk beds. But she knew he'd been beaten, by the investigators, by his cellmates. From the moment he'd returned he was forbidden to leave his home. He spent most of his house arrest with New Hilik. Maybe he knew his days were numbered, maybe he wanted to be consoled. He tried with all his might to put a smile on his sad and anxious son's face, told him funny stories, taught him songs he'd made up, constructed hiding spots with him out of blankets and sheets, and concealed the blue marks on his skin and the trouble that wouldn't leave him alone.

Every two days a different investigator appeared in their house. They'd lock themselves in one of the rooms and, after a long time, the investigator would leave with a small gift. "The house quickly became just a stockpile of gifts. Your uncle gave things away to buy himself some time." First, the safety-deposit box had been emptied of the cash and gemstones that had accumulated in it. Then it was the turn of Rochelle's gold jewelry, later the pieces of art and decor, and finally the furniture and rugs. The last investigators had arrived in small trucks, parked them at the house's entrance, and, after the investigations, loaded them with the dressers, the velvet chairs, even the large plush beds, one of which Robert still remembered well.

The house had been slowly emptied. The uncle and the boy ran through its empty spaces and turned them into a playground of catch and hide-and-go-seek. Their merriment echoed through the large house until they'd fall, breathless, on one of the remaining mattresses, cover themselves with a blanket and fall asleep.

"He kept telling me, 'No matter, all men can be bought with money, and if not with money, then with nice things. We all like to adorn ourselves with the belongings of those we loathe. Their appetite will die out, they'll leave us alone and you'll see how I'll get everything back in weeks and build you a castle.'"

Rochelle moved her hand from the boy's head. She leaned her own head on the wall near the sofa and her eyes rested on the ceiling and the bulb in its center.

"And each time I told him, 'Let's run away. Let's take what little money we still have and go, build a new life for ourselves.' But your uncle was stubborn as a mule. I suggested we escape to Israel, I knew he could use your help. But he wouldn't hear of it."

Finally, the chief investigator himself came to their house. An elegant, wide-shouldered man, with burning hatred in his eyes. The pool of gifts had been cleaned out and the uncle insisted on keeping what little cash was left hidden.

"That's lucky, otherwise I'd have had no way to get out of there."

The chief investigator decided to arrest the uncle again. He spent another week in a smelly cell, again his hair was shaved, again he returned to his empty house with his body covered in black and blue spots and traces of congealed blood. This time he told no stories of falling from the bunk bed. His eyes were extinguished, his voice was weak, his breathing was quick and stifled, trying to overcome the great pain in his lungs, perhaps the result of broken ribs poking him from the inside.

"Yechiel was asleep. Your uncle hugged and kissed him and cried. Then he lay down on the mattress and told me, 'I don't care about the hatred everyone has for me, I'm used to it. Only one thing truly scares me. One day, Yechiel will grow up and find out I bought him, too. He'll hate me too.' I told him, 'He won't find out, you're his father, he loves you and I love you.' He caressed my hand and smiled and said nothing. Then he said, 'If I die, make sure I'm buried in Israel, that's what people like me deserve.' I was angry at him and I cried a little too. He caressed me and calmed me, he said, 'Tomorrow I'll call Robert and take care of everything,' and then he fell asleep and never woke up."

Rochelle undid her hair. She shook her head and scratched it with her fingernails, mussed and aired out her thick hair. For the first time since she'd arrived, her eyes met Robert's and he even saw a little smile there. She said, "I'd very much like to take a shower." Robert stood up and went to the small bathroom. He pulled some towels from the cabinet and turned on the water to test its heat. When he returned he found her asleep next to her son.

He sat on the edge of his bed on the balcony. The sun had set. A small ray of light filtered through the shutters, making its way from the nearby streetlight to Rochelle and New Hilik. Robert watched them, his head clean of thoughts and his body trying hard to keep still, to make no noise, not to wake the two of them bundled on the narrow sofa, sleeping a faint, dreamless sleep. In vain he tried to conjure up the image of his tortured uncle. He sat this way for many hours, his gaze holding on to the two of them, tying them up, protecting them, lest they move in their sleep, lest they fall off the sofa, lest their bodies become covered in bruises.

He sat this way through the long night. A nocturnal sentry with an empty head. He didn't even feel a longing for Ruchama, didn't even think up fragments of poems she'd loved. Only as morning began to break, short thoughts flashed through his mind. Rochelle's life is unclear. When would it be clear. When would it shake off the sand that has covered it. His life is also frozen and blurry, like piles of plastic-covered shutters, awaiting shipment and assembly. You'll even wait an eternity. In the dark of the morning watch, the two looked like Ruchama and Hilik. Hilik the First, who wants to be a book cover. Hilik the First and Hilik the Second. The New Hilik. Yechiel, the name of my dead father. Again my life is like a poem; still, deserted rhymes, a crazy, meaningless poem.

Robert awoke with a start. It was noon. He'd fallen asleep sitting up and now felt embarrassed, like a failed sentry. Strong rays of sun knocked on the balcony's shutters and fell on the sofa. Only New Hilik was lying there, still asleep and breathing quietly. Rochelle was no longer there, only the traces of her long body still engraved in the tattered upholstery.

Robert hopped from his place and went to the bathroom. Then he checked the kitchen. An open box of sardines was on the counter, smelling heavily. Breadcrumbs were stuck to the blue cloth and dirty dishes were in the sink. She'd woken up and eaten a little. And now she was gone, leaving him to watch her son again, his body beginning to stir on the sofa, moans of awakening coming from him, like a waking baby bird, the sunlight making his eyes squint, he sat on the sofa and stretched, loose and blushing, his hair cropped and his face no longer frowning.

New Hilik looked at Robert. His brow furrowed.

It's the first time he's looked at me. I must cherish it.

He's trying to recognize me. Maybe he can see the similarity too. Maybe I remind him of his deceased father. Maybe I remind him of himself. We're all alike, small, short-haired and meaningless. He's looking at me as if wondering about his future.

"I have to pee," the boy said in Spanish. Robert went to the toilet and opened the door. New Hilik got off the sofa, still sleepy, stood on tip-toes in front of the toilet bowl and peed for a long time. Then he returned to sit on the sofa and stare at Robert.

"Who are you?" he asked in a familiar voice. Robert trembled and answered, "My name is Robert." The child nodded and said, "My name is Yechiel." He crossed his legs, leaned his elbows on them and put his head in his hands, as if trying to support his gaze that was fixed on Robert, recognizing the terror that had overtaken him. And then he said, "Don't worry, she only went to get me some food." Robert asked, "Did she tell you she was going?" and New Hilik said, "No. I was asleep." Robert asked, "Then how do you know?" and New Hilik answered, "I know."

A moment later the door opened. Rochelle came in, and her eyes went immediately to her son and smiled. "I'm sorry if I scared you," she told Robert, "I didn't want to wake you." She went to the kitchen and removed a bleeding hunk of meat from the bag in her hand. Robert looked at her with wonder and she explained, "Yechiel hardly eats anything, only meat, I had to go out and get him some, I took some money from your wallet, I apologize, I didn't want to wake you." New Hilik noticed the meat, jumped immediately off the sofa and clung to his mother. "Where did you get the meat?" asked Robert. "It's Saturday, everything's closed." And Rochelle smiled and said, "I walked and I walked until I found an open restaurant, I guess the cook liked me, I think he spoke Arabic, I spoke Spanish, finally I had to make him take some money, he wanted to give it to me for free."

Her hands worked quickly as she spoke. She cleaned the counter of leftover sardines and bread, washed the dishes she'd left in the sink, found a griddle in the cabinet, and while it was heating on the stove, cut a small slice of the meat, chopped it, put it on a plate and brought it near the boy. New Hilik pounced on the rare meat. With his thin fingers he grabbed it and put it in his mouth, chewing and swallowing voraciously, licking the blood from the sides of his mouth. Rochelle cut thick slices and put them on the griddle that had begun simmering and raising happy, fragrant steam. She scattered some salt and pepper and sliced some more meat, which was also swallowed quickly in the child's mouth.

Robert followed the boy's movements with wonder, less than five years old, holding the meat in his oily hands and taking large bites of it. His mother returned from hunting and he was devouring her catch, restoring his strength, wiping the red juice from his plate with pieces of bread. Rochelle fried more meat, added it to Hilik's ever-emptying plate and prepared two more portions, one for Robert and another for herself. The smells of frying and the child's passionate eating created a great hunger in Robert. It had been two whole days since he'd eaten that cream cake. He sat by his new guests and joined their feast.

"Where's my father?" asked New Hilik.

Rochelle's chewing stopped and she said, "He's dead, Yechiel."

"I know he's dead," said New Hilik.

"Then why are you asking?" said Rochelle.

New Hilik cut another piece of meat with his teeth, fixed his eyes on Robert and asked, "And who's this?"

Rochelle hesitated. She put the fork down on her slice of meat, which kept bleeding onto her plate. Her eyes sent a questioning look towards Robert, as if asking, what am I going to tell the boy, how will I explain it. She said nothing, and New Hilik returned to eating his food.

The next day, a new week began. Robert went to school. He spent the previous night sitting up again, this time on the narrow sofa, watching Rochelle and the boy sleeping on his balcony bed, which he'd covered in fresh sheets. He sat at the end of the classroom and stared at the charts in front of him. Thin, black marks outlined the gas compressor, the motor and the air-duct of a foreign-brand air conditioner.

That night he went to the library. As he'd expected, the scholarly teacher sat at one of the desks, preparing Tuesday's lesson. His smile disappeared once Robert announced he wouldn't be coming to his classes anymore. A great sorrow overtook his face. "It's a shame to lose a special student like you," he said. "I'm still looking forward to reading one of your secret poems."

The weeks went by. During the days, he went to school. His head had cleared of shutter thoughts almost entirely and was filled with information about cooling and airing. Then he'd go shopping. He quickly became familiar with the neighborhood's butchers, each day he visited one of them and collected a hunk of meat large enough to satiate New Hilik. At night he'd fall asleep sitting up on the sofa, and when the weekend came near he went to Tiberias. As soon as he'd get on the bus, he'd lock Rochelle and the child in his mind, making himself forget their existence entirely and filling with longing for Ruchama and Shlomi and Old Hilik. Only the back pain that had attacked him after many nights of frozen sitting was revealed to Ruchama's investigating eyes. She knew nothing more, didn't sense it and didn't ask. Robert devoted himself completely to the meals she'd invited him to. His mouth clung to the familiar tastes, collecting more and more of them, using them to bury his new fate deep in his mind. Only on Sunday, when he sat on the bus to Tel Aviv, surrounded by sleepy soldiers returning to duty, only then did New Hilik's face fill his mind. His stomach twisted with worry. When would Rochelle's life clear up, when would it shake off the sand?

One night, she suddenly got up from the balcony bed and sat next to him on the sofa. "When will you stop sleeping sitting up?" she whispered, trying not to interrupt New Hilik's sleep. Robert shrugged. He felt the heat of her body near his and grew tense, trying to push away the forbidden passion that had spread through his limbs. Rochelle put a hand on his cheek. She trembled too, but her eyes never let go of his. In one quick motion she pulled off her nightgown. Robert froze and looked away from her nude body. His body hardened and the back ache pulsed through him. Rochelle whispered, "I haven't been with anyone since your visit. I never slept with your uncle but I was always faithful." Her hands went to him. He could hardly breathe as she removed his clothes. Only when she brought her lips to his did he shake off his paralysis. He jumped away from her, covering his naked body with a blanket, his lips whispering, "I don't want to." Rochelle returned to her bed.

The next day he knocked on the neighbors' door. The withered elderly couple received him gladly. They sat him down in their living room and served him a cup of tea.

"I've noticed that your son hardly comes to visit anymore," said Robert, "I wanted to ask if you'd be willing to rent the small room to me. I'll only come in at night to sleep, you won't even notice me."

To his surprise, the elderly people were pleased with the offer. Their only son went to study dentistry in Europe. "We've invested all the reparations money from the Germans in his expensive school. We could use a little extra income, and maybe with you around, we'll be able to sleep better at night."

In the mornings, he'd study, then go out to hunt a bleeding hunk of meat, dine with Rochelle and New Hilik, study the sad, anxious boy's face, try to teach him some Hebrew, ignore his frowning, his silence and his mother's explanations, "He misses his father, that's why he's sad and upset." Every once in a while he reminded Rochelle to never pick up the phone. And then he'd wash up and go to sleep in the small, stuffy room in his neighbors' apartment. The elderly couple didn't ask any questions. Sometimes they treated him to a cup of tea and some cake, and sometimes they offered him a piece of quality pickled herring they'd found at the Lewinsky Market or dills they'd pickled themselves. Once they told him, "We saw your sister, she was trying to convince her little boy to come out of the apartment but he said no and cried." Another time they said, "She's so tall, your sister, you don't look anything like each other, but the little boy is your spitting image, it's all in the family."

Robert paid them cash. Three or four times he went to see the yellow-faced kibbutz secretary, who handed him a bundle of bills each time and said, "This is an advance, until we solve the shutter issue." He gave a third of the money to the elderly couple, invested a third in the pricey hunks of meat, and used the rest to cover his travel expenses and pay for his two apartments, in Tiberias and Tel Aviv. Ruchama refused to take his money. "I'm doing very well, you take care of yourself and your debts."

One Friday, Ruchama served stuffed fish and a sour soup he especially liked. In contrast to her usual demeanor, she was very kind to him. His heart leaped when she took an interest in his back ache and even suggested warmly, "Don't forget to only take Muscol on a full stomach, otherwise the medicine will cut holes through your belly." Suddenly she turned serious, looked at Shlomi and said, "We have a problem with Shlomi. He doesn't want to go to school anymore."

Robert looked at Shlomi. His eldest son was already at least two heads taller than he was. As he chewed and swallowed, he tried to find himself in Shlomi's face and couldn't. The boy's big eyes looked more like Ruchama's, and so did his tall frame and lanky movements, and even his sharp, determined expression and his pursed lips, swallowing his anger.

Next to him sat Hilik, small and skinny, only his shoulders and his forehead wide and his eyes burning with deep thoughts.

His eyes moved from one child to the other. In his mind's eye he saw New Hilik, risen from that deep, forgotten hiding place. Robert's heart surged and he tried as hard as he could to maintain an amused look.

"What does he need to go to school for anyway?" he said. "He's making more money than I am."

A great disappointment appeared in Ruchama's eyes and she said, "You should be ashamed of the lousy way you bring up your kids."

Again he saw New Hilik, closed up in his Tel Aviv apartment, sitting on the edge of the sofa, refusing to step out the door, eating raw meat and waiting for his mother's life to resolve itself.

"I stopped going to school at a young age, too." Robert said with an apologetic smile.

Ruchama kept frowning. Even when Robert mentioned Shlomi's class bar mitzvah celebration and even when he complimented the delicious meal, Ruchama kept on frowning. And when she said she was planning on taking Shlomi to the doctor to find out why his glands were going wild, Robert said quietly, "What's there to check? He turned out like you, that's better than a midget like me," and again New Hilik's image clutched at his throat. A tiny child, locked in a home that wasn't his and missing a father who wasn't his. If only he could tell her. If only he could consult, ask for her help with a life that had suddenly multiplied. Ruchama got up angrily and put the dishes in the sink. Robert stood at her side and whispered, "What's it going to be, Ruchama? When are you going to let me back in? I've been waiting for you for five years," and Ruchama whispered, "You'll even wait an eternity."

Slowly, sleep started filling his nights again. On his neighbors' son's bed he went back to sleeping lying down, his head pushing into the pillow and his arms spread to the sides, as if prepared to collect calming, forgetful dreams. Until one morning, in the middle of winter, before his neighbors turned on the radio, playing an army march announcing the birth of a new day, they knocked on the door to his room. Rochelle had asked them to wake him. He wrapped himself in a blanket and went out to meet Rochelle, who waited for him on the stairway. "The phone has been ringing off the hook," she said, worried. They went into the apartment. A moment later the phone rang. It was Ruchama.

"I tried calling so many times, why didn't you answer?"

"I stepped outside for some air, what's wrong?"

"Last night we had a storm, we only got the phone line back now, I wanted to call you yesterday but I couldn't." Ruchama stopped, took a breath and continued, "Hilik fell last night and broke both his arms."

Robert said nothing. A faraway pain pricked his arms, a reminder of his distant past when he'd slipped down the stairs in front of his sister, Tehila, and broke both his arms.

Maybe this is a dream. Maybe I'm still asleep at the neighbors' apartment. Again my life is doubled.

"Robert?" Ruchama called. "Can you hear me? Did you hear what I said?"

"Yes," Robert answered, and without meaning to, mumbled,

"even an old vision has a moment of birth."

Ruchama was silent for a moment, and then said, "That's what you have to say right now? I'm telling you your son broke both his arms and you're quoting Alterman? What's wrong with you, Robert?"

"I wish I knew," said Robert. He hung up, got dressed and went to the bus station to catch the bus to Tiberias.

A few hours later he sat across from his son who was writhing in pain. He examined his casted arms, caressed his head, tried to joke, to conceal his unease and his realization that his life was doubling itself so strangely.

"I broke both my arms once too," he told Hilik, "and look at me now, I have excellent hands."

Ruchama lowered her eyes, stifling the sharpened words that wished to come out. Finally she said, "God has a miserable sense of humor."

After Hilik had fallen asleep, surrounded by pillows Ruchama and Shlomi arranged around him, Robert sat in the kitchen. Ruchama made Turkish coffee, poured it and sat across from him. The apartment was quiet and outside, a small wind blew, a pale remainder of the previous night's storm that had plundered the world.

"You look tired," she said, and Robert nodded. "Why didn't you answer the phone? I called many times."

Robert evaded her questioning look and said, "I went on a short walk, it helps with my back."

"I think you've gained some weight," she said and sipped the coffee, which burned her lips. "You even have a little paunch. Maybe it's weighing you down and making your back hurt. You probably eat nothing but bread down there, you should eat more meat and vegetables and less bread."

Robert nodded again and blinked, fighting the tears that were collecting in his eyes. "Don't worry," he said. "He's very young, his bones will heal in no time," and Ruchama said, "I'm worried about Shlomi, too. He blames himself."

She added a teaspoon of sugar to her coffee and stirred it. "You'll have to spend more time here," she said. "You'll have to help me take care of him, Hilik is going to need help eating, getting dressed, bathing, and I can't bathe him, he's too old and he won't let me."

Robert nodded in silence, his eyes dry now.

And then she whispered, "I think someone's cursed me."

"Don't be silly," he smiled. "Who has anything on you, Ruchama?"

"Maybe it's God who's cursed me. Sitting up there, making up curses and rolling around laughing from His miserable jokes, He thinks He's a comedian."

"He's not a comedian," said Robert, whispering too. "He's a poet."

4

ONE BY ONE, THE GUESTS ARRIVED. FIRST HILIK'S CLASSMATES, AND the teachers, even Reuma, Shlomi's teacher, even the principal. She sat on the sofa next to Hilik, who swallowed his pain silently and observed the visitors and the gifts they showered him with. The principal asked short questions and then wore a giant smile and told everybody she was going to retire at the end of the school year so she could visit her son in America for as long as she wanted, and finally alleviate her suffocating longing for her grandchildren. But everyone there knew that the Ministry of Education raised a brow when they'd heard she used to employ children in her private garden, and, after some debate and questioning, decided to make do with a reprimand and early retirement. "It's really about time," Vardina told Ruchama later. "I've never seen such a corrupt woman. She thinks the children are her slaves and tells everyone it's educational punishment. With so many educational punishments, her garden is prettier than those at the Palace of Versailles." And Ruchama said, "How would you know what the Palace of Versailles looks like?" and Vardina made an insulted face and answered, "My mother took me there when I was little, before we moved to Israel." Ruchama sighed and said, "Your imagination has been going wild recently," and Vardina, whose hurt feelings were already coloring her cheeks red, said, "You'd be surprised, I've been to many places in my life, even to the Pyramids. My mom took me all over before she made the mistake of coming to this miserable place, where a school principal makes poor children mow her lawn."

Neighbors came too, and old and new customers, and different acquaintances, even some whose names Ruchama couldn't remember. The falafel vendor brought a bowl full of warm falafel balls, "For the kid to eat and enjoy, falafel is healthy and everyone knows there's nothing like it for healing broken bones," and handed Ruchama a plateful of oiled lemon slices blushed with red pepper flakes.

And Adina from the clothing store came, rubbed the casts on Hilik's arms and tears shone in her eyes. "I remember the day your dad broke his arms like it was yesterday," she said.

And the expert ear doctor came, and his presence brought silence and embarrassed looks, and the quiet workman came, and so did all the medical secretaries Ruchama consulted with, and Baruch from the grocery store, and the woman from City Hall, and Hanna and Ella. A stream of people from all corners and neighborhoods of the city, old women who knew Julia, fish and meat vendors, countless eyes fixing on the cast arms and then continuing to roam the apartment, its walls, its furniture, its windows.

The apartment was flooded with candy. What else could you bring a boy whose arms are in casts? He couldn't hold a book, or draw, or build tiny ship and airplane models from cardboard, or paste stamps into an album. Both his arms were broken, placed on a soft pillow, every little movement filling them with deep pain and making his face pale. But eating – that he could do. And so the table was covered with chocolate bars, bags of toffee and marzipan, lollipops, colorful marmalade, rolls of sweet coconut and wafers coated with sticky chocolate. The generous guests brought fancy boxes of bonbons wrapped in floral paper, and the cheap guests only brought a bag of puffed wheat snacks or a few packs of gum.

"I won't let you gobble up all this candy," Ruchama told Hilik. "It's bad enough your arms are broken. I don't need you spoiling your teeth, too." And Hilik said, "I don't have an appetite anyway."

One evening, after all the visitors were gone, Ruchama scattered garlic bulbs in the corners of the apartment to ward off evil spirits. "What's wrong with you, Ruchama?" Vardina laughed. "When did you become superstitious?" Ruchama said, "I'm worried they're giving us the evil eye. I don't even understand why they all come. The kids from his class, that's one thing, the teachers are one thing, but why did all of Tiberias decide to congregate in my house and act like they came to console mourners at a *shiva*, God forbid."

Vardina laughed again and said, "What don't you understand? They came because they finally have a chance to see how Miss Ruchama lives."

Ruchama's eyes turned into slits. "What do you mean?" she asked.

Vardina tried getting up from the chair she'd sat down on that afternoon. "There's nothing you can do about it, Ruchama," she said. "You've become very famous in Tiberias. The whole city is interested in you."

"Why?" asked Ruchama and anger sounded in her voice, "because of my cooking?"

"With all due respect to your cooking," Vardina said and wiped the sweat from her forehead, "people want gossip. They're interested in the life of a woman who's kept her husband in a separate apartment for the past five years."

Ruchama's eyes escaped Vardina's reproachful look. "Are you serious?" she asked. "That's why they all came?"

Vardina nodded and said, "They're scared of you because you're brave and because you're tall like an antenna and because they also think you're a bit of a witch." Then she signaled to Shlomi who got up, took both her arms and pulled her up. She leaned on his shoulders, dizzy, and began walking towards the door, wishing to return to her apartment and lay her bellies to rest on her comfortable chair. That afternoon, when he'd just returned from school, he went to her apartment and spent a long time escorting her on her journey from the first to the third floor, step by step. Between floors, he set down a chair for her to sit on and rest until her sweat dried and she gave him her arms so he could help her up and keep climbing the stairs. "What did you have to work so hard for?" Ruchama asked her, and Vardina said, huffing, "I wanted to see the boy. Everyone came to visit him and I should stay home?"

Angry tears appeared in her eyes. "Look at what's become of me, Ruchama," she complained. "I'm like your mother Julia, squared." Ruchama waved her hand, trying to fan some good air at her neighbor's blushed face. "You're absolutely irresponsible," she said. "What am I going to do if you have a heart attack on those stairs?" And Vardina said, "Call for a crane."

Robert stayed with them for only two days and then returned to Tel Aviv, to Ruchama's discontent. "How am I going to handle Hilik?"

she asked him angrily. "You should help." Robert answered her in a small, determined voice, "Hilik prefers Shlomi, he won't let me bathe or feed him, I hate to miss school, it's the exam period, and I need that certificate."

When visitors began flooding the apartment, Robert was already in Tel Aviv. Only after hearing Vardina's explanation did Ruchama begin noticing the guests' searching looks. Her eyes followed theirs as they rummaged through the apartment, looking for Robert or for other evidence of their lives, something to hang on to and clarify a mysterious, indecipherable image. A few days later, she decided to cut the flow. Guests knocking at their door were left standing in the stairway. Ruchama opened the door just a crack and only to receive their sweet gifts, to whisper, "Hilik's very tired, he finally fell asleep, I thank you on his behalf," and shut the door in their faces. "Let them poke their noses elsewhere," she said, and added another box of chocolates to the pile, looked at Shlomi and said, "Think, Shlomi, maybe you'll come up with one of your excellent ideas and we can use all this candy for our cooking. Maybe we could melt the chocolate and use it for desserts and cakes, it's a shame to just throw it out."

Those were comfortable days for Ruchama and Shlomi. Most of their orders were postponed because of the shifty weather. In the mornings Ruchama helped Hilik get out of bed, wash his face and put his clothes on. Then she'd sit him down in the living room, bundle him up, place a pillow under his arms, feed him warm honeyed milk and spoonfuls of semolina porridge with melted chocolate that the guests had brought. Another spoonful and another spoonful, until Hilik said, "Enough, Mom, I'm about to burst, I'm going to throw up." When his pain worsened and his face was pale she crushed a small tranquilizer onto a spoon, mixed it with strawberry jam that Shlomi concocted and made Hilik swallow it.

In the afternoon, when Shlomi returned from school, he'd take over tending to Hilik. He embraced him with hugs and tickles, put on silent and entertaining acts, pantomimed impressions of the teachers and neighbors who had visited them, fed him, placed books in front of him and turned the pages, marveling each time at how fast his little brother read. He'd push Ruchama away, tell her in the few whispers he was able to extract from his silent throat, "Let me take care of him, Ruchama, it's my fault he's like this." And Ruchama would say, "I think your voice is getting better, but try not to whisper too much, it's bad for your vocal cords."

Ella took on a mission. Each day she sat with one of the girls from Hilik's class and took down a summary of the classes he'd missed. She sent the notebook over with Shlomi or came by herself and went over it with Hilik. Then they'd have lunch together, which Shlomi insisted on making even if Ruchama had already cooked. Ella treasured every bite, and Shlomi cut Hilik's portion into small pieces, brought the fork to his mouth and tried to ignore the looks his brother snuck at Ella's cleavage and bra strap.

Hanna joined them each time. She arrived in the early evening, when the air turned reddish, kissed and hugged Ruchama like she was her long-lost sister, rubbed Hilik's forehead, touched his casts, sighed deeply and told her daughter, "Come, Israella, you've been here long enough, we don't want to tire Ruchama, her life is hard enough as it is." But then she'd sit down in the kitchen, drink the coffee she brought Ruchama from Brazil, eat a date cookie, tell stories of her overseas experience and keep staring at Shlomi, swallow his body with her eyes, follow his hesitant movements, the sack of skin vibrating beneath her chin, and her eyes trying to catch his. When she finished the coffee she stood up, checked the pots on the stove, tasted their contents with her fingers and told Ruchama, "Your son is a genius, his cooking speaks for him – it sings. It's a shame my Israella has no genius in her."

After they left, Ruchama would smile and say, "Look at that, the Austrian Empress is making herself at home. I just hope she didn't get any sand in the house, I already cleaned today."

One time, Hanna asked Shlomi to join her. Ella stayed with Hilik, going over math exercises with him, and Shlomi followed Hanna to her blue home. She asked him to stand on a chair and help her put old clothes on a high shelf. "With your height," she said, "you can save me a ladder." Shlomi climbed on the chair and reached the shelf easily. Hanna stood at his side, handing him folded clothes in silence. He raised the bundle to the closet, and his legs began shaking. Hanna handed him another bundle and said, "Why are you shaking, Shlomi? You could fall." Then she placed her hands on his knees for support. Shlomi tried hard to calm his breathing, which had turned heavy, and his eyes followed the clothes to the high shelf, escaping her wide-open look. The touch of her hands sent a searing pain through his knees and the shivering moved to his shoulders and neck, spreading a wave of old pain. Shlomi put the clothes in their place and pulled his shirt down to cover the hardening bulge in his pants. When he finished putting all the clothes in their place Hanna gave him her hand to help him down. Shlomi was back on the ground, but her hand kept holding his arm, moving up to his shoulder and neck and then touching his blushing cheek and tapping it encouragingly, saying "Well done, Shlomi, you've been a great help."

Five days after he slipped and broke his arms, Ruchama told Hilik, "Today you're going to sit down on the toilet and not move till you make, you can't keep this constipation up." Hilik said, "I'm afraid it'll hurt, when I push it hurts a lot." Ruchama made him chew two pieces of chocolate-flavored laxative she'd bought at the pharmacy. "No choice, Hilik," she said. "You'll explode if you don't make." The sweet taste made him nauseous and Shlomi put a bowl at his feet in case he needed to throw up. But a few minutes later he got up from his spot in the living room, dropped the pillow and ran to the bathroom. Shlomi ran after him to help him lower his pants and underwear and sit on the toilet. He sat there for a long time, and when he was done Shlomi held his breath and went in to clean him.

Every night, before they went to bed, Shlomi bathed Hilik. He wrapped large plastic bags around his casts, sat him on a stool in the bath, scrubbed his head and his body, dried him off, dressed him, combed his hair and even sprayed a few drops from an old perfume bottle Robert had left in the cabinet near the sink. "I'm so lucky I have you," said Hilik, and Shlomi whispered with effort, "Why didn't you let Robert bathe you?" Hilik said, "I was embarrassed. He had a strange look, like his eyes were new, fleeting eyes." Shlomi whispered, "I don't mind bathing you, you're my brother." Hilik smiled, drops of water falling off his hair and down his face, and said, "Your voice really is getting better."

One morning, before the sun rose, when only a few rays burst beyond the blue mountains east of the Sea of Galilee, Ruchama went to the market. This time, she left Shlomi home to watch his brother. After she left, Shlomi cuddled in bed and closed his eyes, sinking back into a warm sleep. But a moment later he heard Hilik call him. Shlomi opened his eyes. He saw Hilik sitting on his bed, his face pale and his shoulders shaking a little. "I didn't sleep all night," he said. Shlomi cleared his throat and whispered with effort, "Why?" And Hilik answered, "Because I've been hard like a rocket all night long, my balls hurt even worse than my arms, I have to masturbate." Shlomi remained sitting in bed, frozen and staring at his brother with questioning eyes. Hilik kept shaking. "Don't look at me like I'm a spaceman, and don't you dare laugh at me," he said. Shlomi didn't move, only a long, sudden yawn pulled his mouth open. Hilik said, "Mom's going to be back soon, she'll want to dress me, I don't want to stand next to her with my wiener pointing at the sky and tearing up my underwear. You have to help me." Shlomi whispered, "But how?" and Hilik said, "There's a soft, blue towel in the bathroom. Go get it."

Shlomi stood up and went to the bathroom, his eyes fighting to close and his jaw squeaking with each yawn. He rummaged through the closet and pulled out the towel Hilik asked for. "Now spread it on my bed," Hilik ordered, and Shlomi obeyed. Then he continued to follow orders – he removed Hilik's pants and underwear and helped him down on the towel. Hilik said, "Now please leave the room and come back when I call you, and don't you dare laugh at me," and he began rubbing himself against the towel, driving his trembling body back and forth.

Shlomi sat on the cold floor of the hallway, near the door to the room. He heard his brother's small moans, but was asleep in seconds, his head drooping on his shoulder, and woke up only when he heard Hilik call him back. He helped him sit up, noticing his flushed face and his calm breath, and the white drops on his belly and on the towel. Shlomi wiped Hilik's belly, dressed him, washed the towel in the bathroom sink and buried it in the hamper.

When he came back into the room Hilik said, "There's a stain on the sheet, even though I used the towel." Shlomi yawned twice in a row and helped Hilik get up from the bed and sit down in the living room. Then he pulled off the stained sheet, washed that too, put it in the hamper, and lifted the mattress to put on a clean sheet.

Then his eyes fell on a notebook that was hidden under the mattress. He picked it up. It was a thick notebook, the edges of its cover worn from use.

Shlomi opened the notebook. He discovered tight lines of Hilik's tiny writing. His eyes were still glued shut and he had difficulty reading it, but noticed some familiar words. His name was written there many times, and so were the names of Ella and Ruchama and Robert and many others.

Shlomi flipped through the notebook. Words were put into sentences and those floated up to meet his eyes.

The Wednesday wind.

The red plastic roses in Vardina's kitchen.

A room on the Carmel Mountain with a triangle ceiling.

The body of a girl floating in the water. Sugarloaf Mountain receiving lost waves.

Cursed women with scarves wrapped around their necks.

Deborah the Prophetess lighting memorial candles, grieving in her bed.

A storm of noise rising from an ear pump.

The stink of bad meat coming from the kitchen.

A man in torn underwear chasing a terrified lamb.

Drops of blood splattering on a pile of sand.

A blue dress rustling in a silent house.

The Sea of Galilee rising and throwing fish up in the air.

Suddenly Hilik came in. His eyes rested on the notebook and widened with fear. He pounced on Shlomi and hit him with his cast arm. The notebook fell from Shlomi's hand back to its place and the mattress fell too and hid it.

Hilik said, "I won't let you touch that, and don't you dare tell anyone about it, ever."

"But what is it, anyway?" Shlomi asked, whispering through a dry throat.

"It's nothing," said Hilik, tears in his eyes.

"Why are you crying?"

"I hit my arm, it hurts," Hilik cried.

Shlomi quickly spread the clean sheet on the mattress and helped Hilik sit down, carefully placing a pillow under his arms, wiping his tears and watching him with wonder.

When Shlomi returned home from school, Hilik was sitting in his spot in the living room, a big smile on his face and his eyes bright. Ruchama was working in the kitchen, listening to a noisy radio show, her cooking spreading fragrant steam around the apartment.

"Thank you," Hilik said in a quiet, relaxed voice.

"For what?" Shlomi whispered.

"For helping me. I had to masturbate or I was going to explode."

"I noticed that your wiener was turning purple. They're going to have to put a cast there, too."

They both laughed, and Hilik said, "I can really understand what you're saying, your voice is improving and it sounds nice, not chirpy."

They were quiet together, listening to the plates rattling in the kitchen. Ruchama would soon invite them to the table. Thick aromas entered their noses, aromas of chicken thighs stuffed with rice and raisins, of thick bone soup with beans and tomatoes, covered in fresh mint leaves. They breathed in the smells till their lungs were filled, and said nothing.

Until Shlomi raised his eyes to Hilik and whispered, "Are you writing us?"

"I'm not writing anything, my arms are in casts."

"I saw, Hilik."

"You saw nothing."

"Let me read it."

"There's nothing to see. You imagined it."

And again they were quiet, until Hilik asked, "Why didn't Ella come today?" and Shlomi whispered, "She'll come in the afternoon with the Austrian Empress."

Hilik laughed and when he'd calmed down Shlomi asked, "Who do you think about when you masturbate?"

"Different people."

"Ella?"

"Her too."

"You can't."

"All right."

"Promise me."

"I swear."

After they ate and Hilik shut himself in the bathroom, Shlomi went to their room. He lifted the mattress quietly. The notebook wasn't there. His eyes examined the room. He silently opened a drawer and looked, rummaging through the books on the shelf, his hands searching among the folded clothes in the closet. He was filled with wonder again. My brother wants to be a cover. How did he hide the notebook with broken arms? What is he hiding inside that notebook's worn cover?

Then they sat in the living room and ate chocolate and marzipan. Ruchama said, "I found a wet sheet and a towel in the hamper," and looked questioningly at Shlomi. Hilik stuffed his mouth with chocolate and was flooded with shame, and Shlomi said, "Hilik peed a little, so I washed the sheet and changed it." Ruchama said, "Your voice is so much better, I can understand you completely." She removed the wrapping from a new pack of marzipan and said, "I'm crazy about your new voice. It's pretty, like a song."

5

Ruchama's lips touched the steaming cup and took a long, noisy sip of the coffee. "Maybe it's God who's cursed me," she told Robert. "Sitting up there, making up curses and rolling around laughing from His miserable jokes, He thinks He's a comedian." Robert sent dry eyes to the steam rising from his cup. His mouth emanated only a weak whisper, "He's not a comedian, He's a poet."

Hilik was already asleep in the living room, surrounded by pillows Shlomi helped her arrange around him and under his broken arms, his small body saturated with tranquilizers she'd ground into a powder and mixed into jam. Shlomi sprawled out on the rug at his feet, his face long and ashamed, wrapped himself up in a blanket and fell asleep too. Ruchama and Robert sat in the kitchen and drank the coffee she'd made.

She looked at him. His hair buzzed, his temples growing gray, his shoulders a little slumped, perhaps because of his backache, perhaps because of the tiring day, the long ride from Tel Aviv, the sorrow he felt seeing his son's cast arms. Her heart yearned for him. Vardina once told her, "All you have on your mind is the body," in her cigarette-seared voice, when she still smoked ceaselessly, before she'd quit and replaced the cigarettes with unstoppable leftover eating.

His fingers rubbed the rim of the cup and Ruchama was filled with longing. For him, for his body, for his breath in her hair. Five years he's been waiting. She's been waiting too and doesn't know why. Even when she slept with the ear specialist, his begging and tears made her body limp. But her mind was on Robert. Both of them waiting. Five long years. Once they had only a body, and now they had nothing but waiting. Recently, he's been dropping lines of very familiar poetry, which made her wonder. Sometimes she'd close her eyes and imagine him sitting in his small Tel Aviv apartment, his room dark. She'd never visited him there. Maybe his ceiling was shaped like a triangle, maybe his bed was covered with a blue bedspread, and he was holding an old book and wrestling with the words, trying to decipher a five-year silence, his body yearning for her, growing used to the waiting that had become his routine, her routine.

Suddenly Robert asked. "When did Leah Goldberg die?"

"January 15th 1970. Why do you ask?"

"I thought she died on March 15th."

"Why?"

"I don't know, all the dates are getting mixed up."

"But why did you think of March 15th specifically? What happened then?"

Robert said nothing. It seemed his jumpy eyes were searching for an answer, and again her heart yearned. He drank the coffee down. His lips were covered with black grains, and finally he said, "I don't know. I remember a few days after she died, and you shut yourself in the room to mourn, I moved into the apartment downstairs, and for some reason I thought it was March 15th."

Ruchama laughed, though his gaze pricked her and there was something new in it. "You make me laugh when you're confused," she said. "You must be tired, maybe you should spend the night." And immediately she was frightened by her own words, and Robert opened a pair of surprised eyes and asked, "You want me to sleep with you tonight?" And she answered, "Of course not, you'll sleep in the children's room, I just wanted to save you the trip downstairs and I thought you'd like to sleep close to Hilik, he'll probably wake up from the pain soon."

Then she told him about Hanna. In careful detail, she described how she helped her carry Hilik, and how she drove like mad to the hospital, and yelled at the doctors to pressure them, and tried to calm Hilik with funny stories and even sang some Brazilian songs, working her broken bicycle horn voice, stopping once in a while to interpret the foreign language, all to keep his mind off the painful examinations.

As she spoke, Ruchama searched his face for any trace of embarrassment, but found nothing, not even a spark. He listened to her with a sealed face, picking off the coffee grains that had dried on his lips. Finally he said, "I didn't know she was back." And Ruchama said, "So now you know, she's been here for a month, hasn't changed at all, back from Brazil with her strange daughter and brought new appliances from America." Robert shrugged, even yawned a little.

"Maybe you'll want to go to her now," said Ruchama.

Robert raised squinted eyes. "What for?" he asked.

"Maybe you'll want to thank her, maybe you just feel like meeting her for old times' sake."

"Don't be disgusting, Ruchama. I don't care about that woman. You know I'm only waiting for you."

"I don't know anything," said Ruchama, "I have no idea what you do there in Tel Aviv."

"I learn about air conditioners," he said angrily, "I don't hang out with all sorts of doctors, like you."

And all at once his eyes went dark, and she went quiet too. She stood up with a pale face, collected the emptied cups, put them in the sink and said, "You don't owe me anything, Robert." And Robert said, "I'll go sleep downstairs. If Hilik wakes up, send Shlomi to call for me."

Two days later he returned to Tel Aviv. Before he left, he carried the burnt television down to the trash, unplugged one of the three televisions in his apartment and plugged it in Ruchama's living room, "So Hilik doesn't get bored." Then he hugged and kissed his son, apologized, "It's exam period, I have to get back," avoiding his questioning eyes and her raging eyes, and was on his way.

Ruchama wallowed in her anger, complaining wordlessly, suffering from the yearning that had suddenly awoken in her. She only told Vardina about it, and Vardina nodded her large head and said, "That anger has been stuck in your throat for five years, why don't you swallow it already, or spit it out." She patted the arm rest of her chair and said, "I wish I could spit out a little, maybe I'd be less of a cow," and then she raised her voice. "Look at you, you're only thirty-three, a young woman, cooking all day and letting him wait. What do you think you are, a train? How long do you think he'll sit around at the station and wait for you? How long?"

"Why are you yelling?" Ruchama grunted. "I won't have you yelling at me."

"I'm yelling so you can hear me," said Vardina. "Maybe your stopped up ears will finally open."

"It's all your fault. You said all we had was the body."

Vardina was silent for a moment, pondering this, and then said, "I've never said such a silly thing, shame on you for accusing me again."

But shortly thereafter Ruchama's anger dissipated. The waves of visitors storming the apartment ate up all her strength, as did Hilik's needs. The image of Robert bent at the kitchen table, removing the remains of congealed coffee from his lips, moved farther away, and her heart no longer yearned for him.

One day, even before Vardina explained to her what attracted her guests, her sisters came to visit.

Hilik was napping in the living room, Shlomi hadn't returned from school yet. She sat them down in the kitchen. She hadn't seen them in months, and they'd appeared completely changed, as if a hidden hand carrying a paintbrush and some color had erased them and painted new women. At her surprised eyes, the sisters' faces glowed and stretched into smiles. Geula's neck was wrapped with only one scarf, thin and silky, and when she'd removed it Ruchama saw that the swelling had gone down almost completely. Suddenly her pointy chin reappeared, her shoulders separated from the vibrating pillow, her head no longer sunk in between. It seemed to have cracked through, leaning on a fresh neck that gave her an appearance of erectness she'd never had before.

When Ruchama's wide eyes moved over to her other sister, Drora pulled the wig off her head and revealed a scalp sprouting with new hair, small islands of dark and soft fuzz. The red sores that had framed the edges of her scalp, scratching against her prickly wigs, were also gone. Suddenly the skin of her face stretched and brightened and her eyes glimmered within it.

The amazed Ruchama moved her eyes between the two again and again. Their eyes answered with unfamiliar kindness and peace.

"The curse has been removed," said Geula, her face glowing. "We went to a witch and she undid our curses."

"That can't be," said Ruchama. "I don't believe in that nonsense. You must have gone to see a special doctor, and he finally diagnosed your disease."

"No disease," said Drora. "All the doctors we went to were useless. They all just laughed at us."

"In two or three weeks," Geula said excitedly, "I'm going to throw all my scarves into the sea and Drora's going to burn all her wigs," and Drora said, "Or I might sell them, it's a shame to waste the money."

Ruchama offered them coffee and they refused. "We've eliminated coffee completely," said Drora, "and we make tea ourselves, too, with nettle leaves and no sugar." Ruchama made herself thick black coffee, trying to recover from the discovery, while her sisters described their special diet. In the morning, they mashed an uncooked potato, squeezed it and drank its juices. Lunch started with two tablespoons of green olive oil. Then they had a large bowl of small zucchini cooked in water. "No salt, no pepper, no lemon and no onion, no nothing." Sometimes they added some lettuce, and for dessert they chewed fresh parsley. "But only chewing and sucking the juices and spitting out the rest, you can't swallow it." In the evening they were allowed a piece of steamed fish, "without salt or anything," and some more potato juice, and some leftover zucchini from lunch, and all day long the tea with nettle leaves they picked themselves in the field with gloved hands, to protect them from the burn.

"We run to the bathroom all day long, and we have to wake up at least four times a night to get out all the poison we've accumulated since we were born."

"You're crazy," said Ruchama. "I could die it's so disgusting." Drora laughed. "The body is strong," she said. "It needs nothing else." And Geula added, "We need the diet so that the blessing the witch gave us doesn't spoil." But shortly, they promised, when they were done cleansing, and when Geula's swelling disappeared completely and the fuzz grew longer on Drora's head, they'd have a celebration, slaughter a lamb and invite everyone to rejoice with them, even breaking the diet with delicacies.

"And that's what we wanted to talk to you about," Geula said with a smile. "We want you and Shlomi to cook the feast. We'll bring you the lamb once it's slaughtered, and any other ingredients you need, and of course we'll pay, no discounts, we'll even make a donation to the synagogue, and you'll help us share the joy in our hearts with everyone."

And Drora added, "We dream of your food all night long. Each time I have some of that horrible tea I imagine it's your sour soup."

And Geula continued and said, "And with each piece of zucchini I close my eyes and think of your green beet pastry." Drora swallowed the saliva that filled her mouth and whispered, "And your fish with the lemon and the celery leaves and the red peppers, and your lamb stuffed with rice and pine nuts, that's all I think of when I chew parsley." And then Geula shook her sister's arm as if trying to wake her from her reverie, and said, "Enough, Drora, you'll leave a puddle of drool on the table."

"I don't know," said Ruchama, a bit bewildered by the task. "I've postponed a lot of orders because of Hilik, we're about to get really busy." Geula looked at her with determination, even pricking her like she used to, and said, "You owe us, Ruchama, the witch said you had to." And, seeing her questioning eyes, she explained, "That's the only way to remove the curse you put on us, because you started it."

They hadn't met for months. Sometimes she'd notice them when she was out shopping. They'd lumber down the street, carrying their scarf- and wig-covered shame, looking away from passers-by. It pinched her heart. Once she even stood across from them, making them stay put, and offered to have the Passover Seder together, "The whole family, like when we were little, we'll invite Abraham and Yitzhak and everyone's children and have a good time."

Geula and Drora agreed half-heartedly. Abraham and Yitzhak refused vehemently, though Ruchama promised to carefully turn her kitchen kosher and follow all the rules.

Since the death of their mother, the brothers wore *yarmulkes* that grew blacker each year, covering larger parts of their balding heads. They wore black woolen pants, a white shirt and a heavy black jacket even during heat waves, visited the synagogue every day, prayed passionately for each decree. When they met their sister, they looked away, shook their heads and said, "What are you going to do, Ruchama? You're already sinning with Robert, you've forgotten everything mother taught you, you've forgotten you're Jewish." And Ruchama, a little shy and a little angry, looked down at them and said, "Mom was free, she didn't even fast on Yom Kippur. If she saw you in these costumes she'd die laughing." Abraham and Yitzhak sighed deeply, the sorrow of the world on their shoulders, and mumbled, "God have mercy on you and your children, poor babies abducted by a stubborn woman and her idiot midget of a husband," and were on their way.

In spite of their refusal, Ruchama slaved over the Seder dinner. She spent three whole days in the kitchen with Shlomi, concocting delicacies for the holiday table. A soup cooked for hours and strained again and again until it was completely clear and ready to receive matzah balls stuffed with quality meat and chicken livers. Fresh fish from the Sea of Galilee, cooked in several versions, spicy for the adults, sour for the children. And a special stew made of a large fish she'd sliced and given to Shlomi to skin, grind together with onions and garlic and parsley, stuff that back into the skin, then fry it in oil and cook it in a golden sauce whose aroma burst forth from the kitchen, hovered in the stairway, broke into Vardina's apartment, awoke her from her nap and brought tears to her eyes.

But in the afternoon, not long before the time of gathering, when the long table Ruchama had put together was set and shining, Geula called and announced that her entire family was sick. "Coughing and sneezing, burning up." Minutes later, Drora called to report a mysterious stomach flu that had attacked her, her husband Emanuel and their daughters. "We're all vomiting and we have diarrhea," she said and cancelled their arrival.

Robert consoled Ruchama. "No matter, at least we won't have to eat disgusting matzah. Your amazing sauce calls for challah, not this plywood." And he went downstairs to his apartment and brought up a large challah Shlomi had baked for him that morning. He took off his white shirt and encouraged Shlomi and Hilik to do the same. "It would be a shame to stain our shirts with sauce and it would be a shame to miss even a drop of it," he said, and together they attacked the fish, shoving pieces of sauce-laden challah into their mouths, their fingers colored red, and Vardina, who sat at the head of the table, huffing and puffing from the long journey up the stairs, said, "Don't worry, Ruchama, by tomorrow night there won't be even a crumb left."

"Everything you say is nonsense," Ruchama told her sisters angrily. "I'm sick of you blaming me for everything, I'm not to blame for your disease, I'm not a witch and I've never cursed anyone in my life." She sipped the coffee that had turned lukewarm, its grains sticking to her lips. "And besides, I thought you came to visit Hilik, not to put me on trial."

Geula placed a comforting hand on Ruchama's arm. To Ruchama's surprise, her sister's touch felt good, and she went quiet. Then Geula caressed her cheeks. Her fingers were warm and the good smile remained on her lips. "We came because we're worried about you. You'd be surprised, but in spite of everything, we still love you and admire you. You're our older sister, you're our Praying Nasser Ruchama," she said, and her eyes grew moist. "We're worried for you, you're cursed, too."

"Again with your nonsense," Ruchama said and removed Geula's hand. But Geula insisted and held on tightly to Ruchama's arm.

"We want you to go see this woman."

"Who is she anyway? Why would I go see a witch?"

"Don't think of it like that," said Drora. "She's a modern woman, a doctor, she does research."

"So what is she doing in Tiberias?"

"She was born here, grew up in Jerusalem and decided to come back." Geula hesitated and then added, "She's Aisha's daughter."

"Aisha who?"

"Aisha the coal thief, the one who punched you in the stomach and killed your pregnancy."

"Fairytales. Aisha was childless, that stinking wicked woman, no kids, no nothing."

"She wants to meet you."

"Why?"

"Because, that's what she wants. That's why we came."

After they'd left, Ruchama remained seated at the kitchen table, the cup in her hand, a congealed layer at its bottom. She burst into great laughter. Each time she remembered her sisters' whispers, their stories, their beseeching, her laughter grew stronger. The entire morning seemed like a strange play. She bellowed in laughter again and again, until Hilik woke up and she crushed another tranquilizer for him.

All through the day, the moments of that long-lost time returned to her.

She was walking heavily down Ha'Galil Street. A large belly, seven months pregnant.

Her belly hadn't grown as much in her previous pregnancies, nor had she been so tired and slow.

"You must be having a daughter," her mother, Julia, told her. "Maybe even a tall daughter, a Praying Mantis Junior." And she laughed.

She walked down Ha'Galil Street. She could already see the bus stop.

And then Aisha appeared in front of her. Her eyes dark, her hair black and smelly.

"Ruchama, what's going on, you've turned into a pig, what have you been eating?"

And she sent a tight fist to her stomach, sharp and tearing.

And then someone called Robert.

He drove the truck and she sat at his side. And her water broke. And a crumpled baby came out of her.

She was burning with a fever and mumbled verses of consolation, her beloved poets protecting her.

The doctor led her to the operating room urgently. Robert stood over her, pale.

The doctor said, "Take good care of the two you have, because you'll have no more."

And Robert was angry and kicked the doctor out of the room, touched her face and said, "The most important thing is that you get better."

And since that day, she couldn't remember her dreams, not even the bad ones, not even the good ones. She awoke from them to a new day and walked quickly among its minutes.

And every evening after that, Geula called, speaking on behalf of herself and Drora. They'd decided to insist, to keep asking. And Ruchama listened a little, pushed their begging aside and asked to hang up so she could make herself available to Hilik.

Until one morning she woke up early, woke up Shlomi, told him she was going to the market, put him in charge of Hilik and left.

Ruchama climbed the stairs that twisted by a small thicket. The people of the city called the thicket Zvi Forest and some of them warned their small children never to enter it, because wild wolves and rabid jackals were hiding in its depths. Sometimes strange howls were heard, sending chills through both children and parents. Maybe hungry, toothy animals really did roam there, or maybe the howls were made by lovers hiding among the pine trees, who were only goofing off.

Breathing hard, Ruchama looked at the thin clutter of pines and cypresses, wondering how stories have turned this sorry thicket into a scary forest where one could easily get lost, a dark, moist forest, the kind that only existed in Europe or in the horrid tales of the Brothers Grimm, which she'd refrained from reading to Shlomi and Hilik when they were little. Too bad, she thought, we could hike here, sit among the trees, eat sandwiches and fruit, or stand at the edge of the thicket and look at the Sea of Galilee. She stopped for a moment and looked at the landscape in front of her. The air was completely transparent, gray clouds floating over the blue Golan Mountains. Even Mount Hermon was clearly visible.

From the edge of the path she saw Dalia, her sisters' witch. She was bending towards the ground in the garden of her small house in the neighborhood on the hill, a stalky woman whose neck was thick and whose hair was long and red, her dirt-covered hands digging fresh flowerbeds, moving alertly, despite the early hour and the morning cold. There wasn't even a slight resemblance to Aisha, and she didn't look at all like a witch. A large smile spread across her face, as if she'd known Ruchama would come. She helped her hop over the wire fence. "Don't bother going around, you can come in this way," she said.

"I don't know why I came," Ruchama said, and Dalia kept smiling, washed her hands with the hose twisting all over her garden, took Ruchama's arm and led her among the flowerbeds. With pride, she presented her with many fragrant bushes, some familiar to her, and others whose names she'd never heard before. Different kinds of sage, verbena, mint, basil and rosemary, cress, thyme, micromeria, sagebrush, tarragon. Dalia laughed out loud as she explained that za'atar was named *ezov* in Hebrew, that oregano was named simply *ezovit*, marjoram was sweet *ezovit* and lavender was medicinal *ezovion*. "Look how sad our language is," she said, laughing. "They took the word *ezov* and tacked half the herbs onto it." The cold, perfumed air hit Ruchama and made her shiver. Dalia invited her inside. "It's chilly today, let's have a nice cup of coffee and warm up. I haven't had my morning coffee yet."

Her house was simple and clean. Few pieces of furniture, and organized piles of paper and folders with Latin words on them in every corner. An old typewriter stood in front of the window next to a record player and countless records.

The coffee was spiced with fragrant cardamom seeds and Ruchama drank it with fervor, trying to avoid Dalia's eyes that followed her movements as she sliced a cake, put a thick piece on a plate and placed it near her guest. Finally, her eyes fixed on the empty cup Ruchama put on the table. "I never imagined you'd be so tall," she said. "I thought I knew everything about you." And to Ruchama's surprise she began listing what she knew, about Ruchama's childhood, about the laughing Julia, about the bakery in Haifa, about Robert who'd been living in a separate apartment for the past five years, Shlomi who'd grown tall and silent, Hilik who'd broken his arms, the successful catering business and the collapsing shutter business, and her love of poets and books.

"You know all that from reading my coffee?" Ruchama asked, one doubtful brow rising into her forehead.

"No, your sisters told me."

"Then what exactly makes you a witch?"

Dalia burst into laughter. "Is that what Geula and Drora told you?"

"You removed their curse."

"No curse, I just put them on a diet to cleanse their bodies from all the medications and poisons they'd gotten." She tore a corner off the cake, chewed it with pleasure and said, "It's true that I did some tricks for them, I even lit candles and burned incense, but that was just to encourage them. I don't believe in curses."

"Then why did you ask to meet me?"

Dalia smiled, revealing pearly teeth. Ruchama wondered if there was embarrassment in her smile, or only a secret. Pleasant smells of rosemary and mint emanated from her hair and clothes, completely different from the stench Aisha would emanate, the stench of coal, body odor and clothes that had never been washed, until they became inseparable from her body.

Dalia beseeched her to taste the cake she'd made the day before, taking pride in all the good things she'd filled the dough with – tart, unripe plums, carob honey she'd made herself, bitter green lemon peel, pecans and flax seeds. Ruchama bit into the cake and an earthy taste overtook her mouth, along with an unfamiliar sweetness. When she was finished, Dalia cut her another piece. She told her she was vegan, studied the power of plants, leaves, roots and seeds. She'd spent most her life in Jerusalem but came to Tiberias because she missed the place she'd only visited rarely, as a child, to see her mother, "And mostly because my plants are crazy about the basalt earth here, it pampers them and they thrive."

Aisha had given her over to relatives in Jerusalem when she was born. The little clarity she still had made her realize she wouldn't be able to share her odd lifestyle. She lived on the streets, threatened by any offer of a home, rummaging through trash cans, talking brightly to anyone she met, including stray cats and lost dogs. "In her strange way she was a very happy woman. I didn't call her 'mother' because she wasn't a mother. The only true motherly thing she'd done was choosing to get rid of me. And I was happy in Jerusalem."

Dalia only rented the small house at the edge of the neighborhood on the hill during the winter. "In the spring I'll return to Jerusalem, unless I find another house with a garden like this and feel like staying here and spending time with the plants." She spent most of her days squatting on the ground, one of her records always playing in the background and thoughts roaming around in her mind, sometimes making her dizzy and breaking her concentration as she sat at the typewriter, typing her findings. What would have happened if Aisha kept her? Perhaps she'd have learned from her how to speak to animals, perhaps she'd have turned into a scared, bewildered nomad, perhaps she'd have dyed her hair coal-black or gotten pneumonia and keeled over on the shore of the Sea of Galilee and two whole days would have gone by before someone would have stumbled upon her body. And perhaps she'd have been able to cure Aisha of her lunacy, heal her suffering, warm her before her body froze. Perhaps they would have created a special family together, forging a strong pact against demons and ghosts and curses.

Aisha had visions. "The doctors would probably say they were attacks, but Aisha was certain she could see the future. That's why people thought she was a witch," Dalia said and cut another piece of cake for Ruchama. "Maybe that's why they think that about me, too. That's why Geula and Drora came to me to remove their curse. They asked for potions and magic spells, and I gave them a vegan diet, and even agreed to put some fish in their diet, even though it isn't vegan at all, but I didn't want to shock their cursed bodies."

Sometimes Aisha met a familiar person on the street, looked at them and saw a frightening future. That was what she claimed when she told Dalia about her meeting with Ruchama that ended so badly. Dalia was a student at the Hebrew University of Jerusalem. Her reputation preceded her, and she even won a large grant to encourage her research, but she chose to invest it in fixing her mother's life. She came to Tiberias and walked the streets until she found her hiding in a deserted house. She was surprised to find that her witchlike appearance was now very dark, all her insane joy gone. Aisha told her that when she'd met Ruchama—that tall woman whose husband had hair like Samson—she peeked at her face and saw a frightening future. "Inside your belly she saw death," Dalia whispered in a voice that was suddenly choked. "Everything went fuzzy, she didn't even notice you were pregnant. She wanted to warn you but something grasped at her hand and she did what she did. And then she regretted it and suffered till the day she died."

Ruchama felt a terrible nausea crawling from the pit of her stomach and spreading all over her body, bubbling with the three pieces of cake she'd had. She tried to control the terrible anger that threatened to explode within her. "That's what you asked to see me for?" she asked, her eyes burning. "To tell me this nonsense? What do you really want from me, forgiveness for your wicked mother?"

Dalia's lips remained pursed and she said nothing, no longer smiling, only her eyes remained fixed on Ruchama.

"You really called me here so I can remove *your* curse," said Ruchama. "So you can sleep soundly at night, so you can escape the thoughts that make you dizzy." Ruchama took a deep breath, the scents of rosemary and mint enveloped her again and nausea burned her throat. "Your mother was a witch," she said and her lips began to tremble. "An evil, stinking woman who threw you out of her own life and threw me out of mine, and I'll never forgive her." The trembling shifted to her shoulders and then her entire body, and her voice, as she whispered, "If hell exists, I hope your mother is burning there all over again every day. I hope they cook her into a kebab and serve her to the devil. I hope they dig into her stomach and tear out all the insides, like they tore out my one-and-only womb."

And then, all at once, she began crying. It had been years since she'd cried this way. Boiling tears fell out of her eyes and onto Dalia's shirt, and Dalia hurried to her, put Ruchama's head to her stomach, caressed her hair and listened quietly to her wails, waiting patiently until she was finished.

Ruchama cried for a long time, until everything was uprooted.

Before she left, Dalia gave her a large bouquet of fragrant herbs wrapped in the morning paper. The leaves were wet from dew or irrigation water, and the drops absorbed into the paper, painting large stains around the headlines.

Ruchama sat on one of the stairs of the path adjacent to Zvi Forest. Her eyes went to the stained newspaper. It told about the death of Mordechai Namir, whose life work was detailed – a member of parliament representing Mapai, the head of the Workers' Union, former mayor of Tel Aviv. It even told of his widow who was more than thirty years his junior. It told of hard rain and floods in El-Aris, where many Bedouins had drowned.

The weather's so nice, thought Ruchama, how could it be raining in the rest of the country while here it's a different world? And where is El-Aris anyway? Maybe in the Sinai Desert. Egyptian land that Israel has taken and applied its weather to, its rains and floods claiming victims, but coming nowhere near Tiberias.

Maybe we're not even in this country. Maybe we're part of a different country. A country of sun and curses.

And who's this Mordechai Namir the paper is eulogizing, I've never heard his name before.

Maybe Tehila is right when she says I'm detached, stuck in my kitchen with Shlomi, trying to feed the whole world. Tehila has become a politician; perhaps she even met Mordechai Namir. Maybe she fought with him, too. He was mayor of Tel Aviv. There were floods in Tel Aviv, too, the paper has pictures of streets submerged under water, of rivers gushing between houses and people wading through them. I should call Robert, make sure he wasn't washed away, that his apartment hadn't been damaged, tell him I'm not angry anymore, everything has been uprooted.

Suddenly she heard a thin howl from Zvi Forest. She felt chills for a moment. The jackals and wolves from the stories seemed close and threatening. But in an instant she composed herself and laughed. The movement of branches in the wind had turned into a scary howl in her ears. My life has become a joke, she thought, even poorer than God's jokes. It's suddenly full of curses and visions, spells and potions. I've become a miserable character, one who wouldn't even have a place in the Brothers Grimm fairytales.

Ruchama looked up from the paper to the view laid in front of her. Everything was clear and shining. She was filled with wonder.

I've never noticed this view, she thought, it's always been set before me like wallpaper covering cracks and wet stains.

Maybe we'll go to the sea. Maybe we'll sit beneath the trees at Zvi Forest.

I'm only thirty-three. The anger is stuck in my throat, neither swallowed nor spat-out.

I've been dawdling for five years.

I must return Shlomi's childhood, release him from slavery, set him loose, remove the captivating silence from his throat. And I can't have Hilik thinking I'm losing my mind. Maybe I have lost my mind a little. I've become the Wicked Aisha.

I should also send the ear doctor away, give him my blessing and set him free. Remain immune to his tears and begging. Help him save his soul from me.

And next time I feel a yearning, I'll tell Robert to come home.

After she returned and sent Shlomi to school, Ruchama put the bouquet in water. Then she went to tend to Hilik and prepare lunch. She stuffed a chicken with rice and pine nuts and scattered leaves she'd ripped from the bouquet and chopped thinly. She put more leaves in the bone and bean soup, refreshing it with earthy flavors.

After lunch she gave the children and herself chocolate and marzipan and asked Shlomi about the wet towel and sheet she'd found in the laundry, and Shlomi answered, "Hilik peed a little, so I washed the sheet and changed it." She looked in his big eyes and her heart yearned. "Your voice is so much better, I can understand you completely. I'm crazy about your new voice. It's pretty, like a song." Then she announced festively, "Starting today you don't cook anymore."

"Why?"

"Because I want you to have time to yourself, to go out and play, to study, maybe go to the scouts or some after-school activity."

"But what about the cooking? How will you manage?"

"I'll manage. I'll hire more workers. I'll get an accountant. I'm tired of having all the clothes I buy you covered in stains. You're a boy, not an employee."

"But I love cooking."

"So cook sometimes, when you feel like making us something good. And besides, I'm going to revolutionize things. I'm sick of that disgusting mayonnaise, it's old and boring. I'm also sick of checking the meat and the fish. I'm like a wolf." She smiled at Hilik, seeing his joy. "From now on it's just milk and cheese and vegetables and herbs, and those who want meat can go elsewhere."

In the following days, she joined the quiet workman and together they went to visit his relatives in nearby villages. She stood in his sisters' and aunts' kitchens, collecting aromas and recipes and asking many questions. Her notebook was filled with tight handwriting, dozens of dishes passed on from generation to generation, Arabic names she couldn't properly translate into Hebrew. Then she'd return to her kitchen and experiment, frying plants she'd picked, stuffing vegetables and cooking them in goat or sheep's milk yogurt the workman had brought her. She'd chop large piles of leaves, whose smell would spread in the apartment and invade the stairway, infiltrating Vardina's apartment, and she would awaken from her sleep, sniff the air and fill with wonder.

Hilik's arms were healing, and he was able to wave and even write. He returned to school, escorted by Shlomi, insisting on carrying the heavy backpack by himself.

Ruchama felt her life clearing up. She even began feeling a yearning and almost asked Robert to return. But one day, when winter was over and summer began raising its rebellious head, Robert appeared at her doorway, holding the tiny hand of a small, sullen boy. Ruchama looked at the boy and her breath caught in her chest. And Shlomi, whose voice had cleared and thickened, said, "Look, a new Hilik."

6

One evening, many weeks before Ella returned and long before Hilik broke his arms, Shlomi sat in the living room and stared at his idea notebook. As per Ruchama's request, he tried to put together a special menu for a bar mitzvah celebration for Moshik, a boy from his class. "I'm too tired today," Ruchama told him, "sit down and think how we can make that poor kid happy. He deserves our hard work." Shlomi happily agreed because he liked Moshik a lot. When he needed to recruit kids to help with cooking and preparations for generous pay, Moshik was the first to report to duty, his small eyes glimmering and his smile revealing crooked teeth and his entire appearance driving Ruchama into waves of laughter. She'd tell him, "You're a cute kid, I think you're the one they wrote that Purim song 'My Little Clown, Why Don't You Dance With Me' about," and then send him to scrub himself down in the bath. "I don't want you to get dirt in my food," and make him trim his nails, comb his hair and put on one of Shlomi's clean shirts, whose long sleeves she'd roll up until it fit him. Moshik and Genia, who was also in Shlomi's class, quickly turned into experts in scooping out vegetables before stuffing them and cooking them in Ruchama's fabled sour sauce. Shlomi would instruct them in his chirpy voice and watch as they blushed whenever they accidentally touched.

Shlomi stared at the notebook and couldn't think of any exciting ideas. Hilik sat next to him and watched television. The people on the screen were discussing politics, the Agranat Commission and Moshe Dayan, and Shlomi, who was half-listening, thought there wasn't much left in his mind of this war no one could stop talking about. For five years his head had been filled with recipes, menu planning, longing for the girl he loved who went to Brazil and worries about his body, which kept growing as his voice kept chirping and inspiring laughter, so that there was not much space left for the experience of this dark, crowded war. Only whispers of memory sometimes breezed through him.

For example, he remembered standing by the turn in the road near the police station, carrying grocery baskets and watching the lines of trucks leading tanks and cannons to the Golan Heights. Later, Ruchama told him off for taking his time because things were dangerous, and any minute an alarm could sound, sending them to the bomb shelter, and Robert said, "Then stop sending him to the grocery store if you're so worried. I can go shop for you." And she answered, "I don't need any favors from you."

When he wanted to join the high school children who had volunteered to glue paper strips to windowpanes and paint car lights to dim their glow, Ruchama refused vehemently. And on one of the nights they'd spent in the moldy public bomb shelter, Shlomi slipped into a dream he could also remember. In his dream he saw Hilik walking around among parked cars and only painting one of the two front lights. And when he asked him why he only painted one light Hilik answered, "It's in memory of Moshe Dayan." And then Robert was in the dream too, telling Hilik, "You should paint the left light, because Moshe Dayan's eyepatch is on the left," but Hilik insisted on the right light, and Shlomi started folding paper planes and shooting them all over, and a terrific noise roared, a noise of airplanes like in World War II movies, and then he woke up and found that there was a big commotion in the small bomb shelter – the wives of two Canadian UN officers who lived in the neighborhood and had to sleep in the shelter like everyone else, were crying out. They must have been awakened by the sonic booms made by the fighter planes on their way to bomb Syria. The booms shook the shelter and it seemed that the whole of Tiberias was being bombed and would soon be wiped off the face of the earth. The two fair-haired women screamed and screeched with panic, until Ruchama got up from the mattress and slapped them and yelled at them in French, and then told the rest of the people, "I'm sick of their hysteria, the next time they cry like that I'm kicking them out of the shelter," and Vardina said, "Leave those poor women alone, Ruchama, they're worried about their men who are stuck in the war, they don't understand war like we do."

"Then let them go back to Canada and leave us alone," said Ruchama, who returned to her mattress. "There isn't enough air here for everyone anyway."

Shlomi looked at his idea and recipe notebook, trying to ignore the chatter coming from the television. Hilik intently followed what the participants on the show were saying and when Ruchama sat at his side, wiping her hands on a kitchen towel, he said, "They keep talking about self-pity. What's self-pity, anyway?"

"It's what you feel when you remember childhood," Ruchama answered with a long face. "People think it's longing, but they're wrong, because childhood is a crummy thing and when you remember it you feel self-pity."

Hilik looked at her with wonder. "Then why do they talk about self-pity whenever they discuss the war and Moshe Dayan?" he asked. "What does that have to do with childhood and longing?"

"I don't know how to explain that to you," said Ruchama, "but it does," and she stood up and returned to the kitchen, and Hilik smiled and whispered to Shlomi, "She's turned psycho again."

Since then, much time and many plots had passed. Two weeks ago, Robert had replaced the burnt television with one of the three that were in his apartment. During those two weeks, Hilik's broken arms kept healing, and he was able to go to school, insisting on carrying his backpack himself, sitting in classes and painstakingly taking notes and solving multiplication problems. Shlomi would see him during recess, check to see if he was doing all right and gobble the remainder of his white cheese and diced cucumber sandwich. Ella almost always joined him, and always said, "Stop eating your brother's sandwiches, he needs to grow," and Hilik said, "Two bites are enough for me, it's better that he eats it than throwing it in the trash," and then he'd blush and whisper to Shlomi, making sure Ella couldn't hear, to come with him to the bathroom and help him pee, because he still had trouble unbuttoning his pants.

Shlomi sat in class and suddenly remembered Ruchama's words about childhood and self-pity. He wondered why the words she'd said many weeks ago were now echoing in his mind. He sprawled out on the hard, narrow chair, leaned against the wall where their teacher Reuma-Dumba tacked the day's news and felt the tacks against his back. The cutout headlines were changed daily under those copper tacks, "Because times are hard and we need to be prudent, even with tacks," the teacher explained. "Our little country is fighting for its existence. It's important that we practice modesty."

The biology teacher was explaining something about the reproductive system of amphibians, using colorful charts she'd put up on the board. The students listened, riveted. Even Ella listened without moving. Shlomi's eyes shifted among them, trying to evaluate how bad their childhood was.

First he looked at Michal, a thin girl whose fingers were transparent and whose straw hair was attached to her head with many black pins.

Michal threw up every day, and so always carried a large plastic bag, ready to emit the contents of her stomach into it. Almost everything made her nauseous – a sudden chill or a whiff of bad smell, the sound of laughter from a joke or of shouting between fist-pumping boys and hair-pulling, scratching girls. Michal would hear, or see, or smell, and then stick her head in the bag and throw up, growing pale. The students and the teachers were used to it. Each time, the teacher ordered another student to accompany her to wash her face in the water cooler in the yard, and they would perform their task quietly, keeping their distance from her sour smell. Once, Michal threw up on the table. Instead of a sandwich, her mother gave her a small box of meatballs. Michal swallowed one and immediately puked it whole onto the cover of the atlas. The teacher asked everyone to leave the room and within minutes Michal's mother arrived and screamed at Michal until the walls shook. Finally she made her eat the puked meatball and put her hand to Michal's mouth to stop her from throwing up again.

Michal's childhood, Shlomi thought, was pretty crummy.

As was Nisim's, he thought and turned his gaze to the chubby, cropped-hair boy at the front of the row, his eyes fixed on the biology teacher's colorful charts.

Nisim was the friendliest boy in class. His loud flow of words always ended with a burst of hoarse laughter, the kind that made Michal cling to her plastic bag. When they went out for recess, Nisim would join the kids who went to the nearby falafel stand to buy half a pita and swallow it quickly so they could get back to class on time, and maybe even have some time left to play soccer before the next lesson. Nisim only stood there, watching them. He had no money and no packed lunch. His mouth watered and his eyes gaped with hunger. Everyone knew once the children left he went into Moti's falafel stand. Moti closed the door, shut the window and did things with Nisim. In return, he gave him a half a pita stuffed with luke-warm falafel and sauerkraut. Nisim returned to the yard with the pita, sat down and ate it slowly. Sometimes he was late for class, was reprimanded by the teacher and said nothing until the bell rang. Then he'd spring from his seat and run to the water cooler, wash his face, remove the congealed traces of tahini and return to his prattle, jokes and impressions bursting forth like a machine gun.

Everyone knew. Even Shlomi, though he didn't really understand what took place behind the closed window of the falafel stand. But he knew it was bad and wrong, and so he was glad when he heard one of the teachers found the courage to tell Nisim's father, a pot-bellied, irritable bus driver, everything.

Nisim's father exploded. The sweat stains that were always on his light-blue shirt spread until they colored it dark-blue. He took Nisim to the yard of their house, pulled the belt out of his pants and lashed at him in front of his brothers and sisters and even his mother, who stood silently in the kitchen and watched through the window.

But when his wounds healed, Nisim returned to the scene of the crime. Almost every day he'd go to Moti's falafel stand, and this time he'd come back with a whole pita, eat it silently and leave the commotion of the children in the yard. Once, during recess, Shlomi went over to him and offered him a job as one of the cooking helpers. "That way you'll have money," he said, "you can get as much falafel as you want."

A few days later, Nisim joined the group of little workers. He quickly filled Shlomi's chirping orders, while flooding everyone with an ongoing flow of jokes, until Ruchama said, "I want you to work quietly, you've given me a headache with all this laughter." Nisim only worked with Shlomi and Ruchama two or three times, and each time Shlomi gave him an especially generous amount, but Nisim preferred to use it for candy. He kept getting his falafel from Moti his own way, and Shlomi was filled with deep sorrow. He told Ruchama everything. The next day she went to school and disappeared with the principal behind closed doors for a long time. Then she went to Moti's stand. To this day Shlomi had no idea what she told him, but shortly thereafter the stand was closed. People said Moti had died of a heart attack. He fell on the counter, boiling oil spilled on his legs and his face dropped right into the bowl of hot sauce. But he didn't feel a thing anymore. "No matter," said Ruchama, "I hope he's being deep-fried up there." His death was all the talk in the school yard. Children spoke about it with excitement, sharing rumors, and only Nisim sat by the water cooler and said nothing, his eyes gaping with hunger.

And there was Sigal, a long child with a gap large enough to stick a pencil between her front teeth. She was so eager for avocado sandwiches that she was willing to pay a lot for one. She'd taken money from her father's wallet, stolen gum from the grocery store to bribe children, and even locked herself in the bathroom with them and showed them whatever they wanted to see, or let them touch.

Or Doron, the kid with the funny accent and the blue bruises on his body, each time in different places.

Or Shlomit, whose older brother was missing in the war and whose family still waited for some clue of his fate. For two years terrible cries rose in her house at night. She'd fall asleep in class, sleep through lessons and recesses, and the teachers let her be.

And Kobi, who kept talking about his father's journeys, when everyone knew his father had stolen money from the bank where he worked and was in prison. Kobi's mother went to the prison each month but never went inside. She stood outside, in front of the barred window of the cell, and cursed and swore loudly, until the guards came to pull her away.

And, of course, Moshik, whose big smile revealed crooked teeth and whose ears were spread at the sides of his head, giving him the appearance of a clown. Shlomi liked him especially.

Less than two years ago, a little before the war, Moshik arrived in the neighborhood and settled with his three younger brothers in Aliza and Rachamim's home. Suddenly everyone found out that the shouting couple had four children. For five years they'd lived on their own in the neighborhood, avoiding their neighbors' pitying looks. "That must be why they scream all the time," Ruchama used to say, "blaming each other for not having children. I hear their yelling at night and it rips my heart to bits."

Until Moshik and his brothers arrived, no one knew Aliza and Rachamim had left their four children with Aliza's parents in Beer Sheva. Work was limited down south and the shouting couple came to Tiberias to see if Rachamim's truck would find better work up north.

And it did. Rachamim drove it every day, and some nights, shipping equipment and materials for the ongoing construction of military bases and new settlements in the Golan Heights. Robert would often use his services, hiring him to ship shutters, when days were still good, before war ate the country up whole, construction was halted and the north was filled with frozen construction sites and parked trucks yearning for shipments.

Ruchama, like the other neighbors, was amazed. "I don't understand," she said. "Why did Rachamim need five years to find out if he had good work here? I've been watching them from my window for five years, I've never seen them go anywhere, not travel, not visit family during holidays, not to a museum or a celebration out of town. I thought they were miserable, childless people without a soul in the world, only working and returning to their ugly shack. So who exactly raised those kids for them? How can you desert your children for five years?"

The ugly building where Aliza and Rachamim lived contained several irritable families. These families spoke in a myriad of accents, insisting on preserving the sounds of their faraway parents and childhood, the way tilapia fish keep their fertilized eggs in their mouths to protect them from predators.

"Their stairway," Robert said after installing shutters in one of the apartments, "sounds like a radio skit show."

Rachamim turned the building's basement into an apartment and added a small shack, and when Moshik and his brothers arrived he expanded the shack so it contained enough room for the children's mattresses at night. He stretched the borders of the shack until it touched the strawberry tree, where he placed logs and nailed asbestos planks to them. On one side he tore open a window, and on the other he painted a bright window, to make the shack look like a real home.

"Look at him," Ruchama told Shlomi. "He thinks he's Picasso."

But the expanded shack immediately turned into a sound box for

Aliza and Rachamim's yelling, a sort of giant speaker sounding their poison into the distance.

Sometimes, when there was no cooking to be done, Moshik would join Shlomi and Hilik. Together they'd roam the neighborhood, stake out stray cats or compete in tearing down announcements from the bulletin board by the grocery store. Moshik would tell them about missing his grandmother and friends in Beer Sheva, and when they returned home Hilik would tell Shlomi, "That's what Mom meant when she explained self-pity." When screams began rising from the shack, Moshik would cough so loud his ears turned red. But when he realized his coughing didn't conceal his parents' screams he'd beg Shlomi and Hilik to go with him to the construction site at the edge of the far neighborhood that had a view of the sea. They'd enter through a plywood fence, ignore the warning signs and climb to the third-floor scaffolding. Only Moshik jumped down to the sandpile. Shlomi and Hilik held their breath and followed him as he flew through the air for a moment, crying with joy.

Once he was hasty and didn't properly direct his jump, and his leg banged on a plank covered in rusty nails. The nails pierced his skin and his leg bled into the sand. Shlomi and Hilik wanted to run over and call his parents, but Moshik threatened them: "I'll kill you if you call them. They'll kill me if they see I got hurt."

Then he limped to a nearby tap and washed off the blood, waited for it to dry, crying and grabbing his swelling ankle. Each time Shlomi and Hilik tried to get near enough to help him, he drove them away with the nailed plank. Finally he leaned on it and limped all the way home.

Luckily for him, Rachamim and Aliza weren't there and neither were his three little brothers. Shlomi and Hilik stood outside the shack and peeked in quietly. Through the window they saw Moshik applying iodine to his wounds, dressing them with a bandage he found in one of the closets and covering his swollen ankle with long socks, constantly blocking his mouth and stifling his crying, knowing that the echoing shack could spread his voice into the distance, where it might reach his parents who would rush home to punish him. For days he limped to school and back, and made Shlomi and Hilik swear not to reveal his secret.

Shlomi's eyes kept moving among the children, collecting more and more crummy childhoods, making a colorful pile, like the piles of moist clothes Ruchama pulled from the washing machine, dried outside and scattered throughout the apartment.

Maybe I'll take all the kids and put them in the washing machine, thought Shlomi. I'll wash off the dirt and hang them out to dry in the wind. In his mind, he saw his friends hanging from colorful clothespins, and a laugh escaped him. All eyes were on him at once, even Ella looked at him with surprise. The biology teacher asked him what happened, and Shlomi didn't answer, only swallowed his embarrassment.

The teacher returned to her charts and again everybody listened. Shlomi wanted to return to his previous thought and imagine the laundry pile, but it was no longer funny.

His eyes went to Michal and Doron and Nisim and Moshik.

Maybe I'll cook them a big dinner, he thought. I'll invite them over, or to Robert's apartment. He's hardly ever there anyway.

In his mind, he began envisioning recipes for dishes that would make their self-pity disappear.

But Ruchama would say no, he remembered suddenly. She hadn't allowed him in the kitchen for weeks, completely banishing him from his role. No longer using his help, inventing dishes herself, chopping all the green leaves in the world, forcing her customers to refrain from meat and fish. She even hired an elderly clerk to do her accounting.

Shlomi was filled with anger and made a decision. Winter will be over soon, then it will be Passover time, then summer vacation, and he'd announce he wouldn't be returning to school the following year. He'd pack up his things in a large blanket, like Robert once did, and move in with his father. Maybe he'd even convince Hilik to join them. He'd revive Robert's quiet kitchen, go to Haifa and buy pots and pans and everything he needed, and open his own catering business. Only meat and fish. Some of his classmates would go on to high school, and those sick of boring classes would join him. They'd bring their crummy childhood to his kitchen and celebrate together and make good money. All their customers would come with him. Ruchama would be defeated, but he wouldn't give in to her begging. They'd each be in their own kitchen. Maybe she'd have to take Robert back. By that time, he'd have opened his successful air conditioning business. He'd collect his clothes again and pack them in a blanket and return to his old home, and Ruchama wouldn't tell him to even wait an eternity anymore.

And then he was flooded with pity. He was overcome at once and tears came to his eyes. Pity for Robert, pity for Ruchama. Maybe their childhoods were crummy too. Maybe they were still trapped.

His eyes kept wandering around the classroom, and as always, they landed on Ella. Leaning forward, scouting the teacher's charts, one eyebrow arching into her forehead, the strap of her bra peeking out from the shirt falling off her shoulder, her sleeves pulled to the tips of her fingers, hiding the scratches on her wrists.

In recent days his voice had become better. Words started hatching from his throat, sometimes whispered, sometimes hoarse. Ella encouraged him to speak, touching his neck, closing her eyes and listening.

They spent most of the day together. In class, sitting at the end of the row. In the yard, on the stone wall. In his home, nodding silently when Ruchama begged him not to overwork his vocal cords. And in her blue home. Hanna treated them to sweet tea and gave Shlomi her looks, until Ella said once, "Careful, or your eyes will get stuck," and Shlomi was surprised to find a red blush spreading through Hanna's cheeks and down to the vibrating sack of skin under her chin. But most of the time she was out of the house, working late, accompanying new immigrants, helping them find their way in this difficult place. Ella and Shlomi would get comfortable in the blue living room, do their homework together, sometimes going to the kitchen and enjoying dishes Shlomi invented.

"Why do you hate your mother?" he asked.

"I don't hate her," she answered.

"Do you miss your dad?"

"I don't remember him at all," she answered. "I only miss you."

She told him about Rio de Janeiro and about her house that was surrounded by a high fence and a barred gate. A driver took her to school in a car filled with sour air. She wasn't allowed to crack a window because of stoplight thieves staking out cars, poking arms in through the windows and tearing off jewelry, handbags and even clothes.

She told him that through her bedroom window she could see the beach, and taught him words like *Copacabana* and *obrigada*, whose sound made him laugh and reminded him a little of Robert.

"I only miss you, too," he said.

"Do you love me?" she asked once, and Shlomi was surprised.

"I've loved you before I even knew you," he whispered, and she said, "How is that possible?" and then kissed his lips.

She told him about candy made of guava and coconut, about black bean stew, and about meals so spicy you had to bite into a cool orange wedge to keep your mouth from burning and about one dish Hanna would buy her at the market, a sort of ball, like a falafel but huge, opened when steaming hot and filled with small, burning, spicy sea creatures. She'd eat it up with pleasure and Hanna would look at her with wonder and say, "You'll turn into a little African boy."

One day, Hanna asked Ruchama to let Shlomi sleep over. "I'm going to Jerusalem for two days and I'm afraid to leave Israella alone." Ruchama hesitated, suggested Ella sleep at their apartment, nodded when Hanna explained Ella had trouble falling asleep outside her own home, and finally consented. She put pajamas and a tooth brush and a clean school uniform in Shlomi's bag and said, "I agreed because I owe her and because I trust you that there will be no funny business, you have school tomorrow and you need to go to sleep early."

First they sat in the living room and were silent for a long time, embarrassed as if they'd just met. The silence of the apartment was familiar as well as new. Then they went into the kitchen and only had water and returned to not speaking in the living room until Ella got up and turned off the lights. "I want to tell you things," she said, "and it's better in the dark, the light scares me."

She told him about the nanny she had in Brazil, Christina, a thick-browed heavy-set woman who'd lumber around the house, cooking and cleaning, floating like a dark ghost doing her chores, and sleeping at night in her small room. That way, Hanna could devote herself completely to her work, sometimes returning late at night, sometimes leaving for several days for an assignment in Sao Paolo. Once in a while, Christina acceded to Ella's begging and let her go out to the beach for a while, buy an ice cream cone, sit on the sand and watch the children playing soccer. Each time she'd give her a little of her own money or look the other way when Ella stole money from her mother's hiding spot, and they both swore to keep it secret from Hanna.

One day Christina said, "You owe me a lot of money and it's time to start paying." She threatened to tell Hanna everything and even embellish. Ella was only eleven, terrified of her mother's threats of sending her to boarding school in Israel, alone, and of her screams at night. With no other choice, she gave in to her nanny. And so, every few days, while Hanna was working at the agency, Christina would welcome men into their home—young men and adults, sometimes wrinkled elderly men—undress Ella and seat the guests in front of her. They'd fix her with hard eyes and touch themselves. Christina would stand in the corner, watching that they didn't get too close, and with a face twisted with distaste collect the money they handed her.

Christina's customers multiplied. Many were already familiar to Ella, though each time she tried to shut her eyes hard and let her thoughts carry her elsewhere. When she opened her eyes she met their look, which scratched and tore abysses into her body.

One day, Ella told Shlomi, she took a metal ruler and tried to cut herself with it. Christina dressed her bleeding wrists and Hanna only took a quick look and said, "Why aren't you more careful, you only give me trouble," and shortly thereafter Christina disappeared, never to return.

When she was finished telling her story she put her hands on her eyes, her head bent and her breath thin. He got up and turned off the lights in the kitchen, hallway and bathroom. Only a few moon rays filtered in through the windows and turned the apartment even bluer than usual. Shlomi pulled her hands off her eyes, leaned closer and kissed her lips. Then he pulled her up gently and led her to the kitchen, feeling around in the dark with his long arms, trying to identify the dangers the darkness had waiting for them. He warmed milk in a small pan, added honey and stirred, his movements quiet in the dim light from the open fridge and the stove's flame. He fed her sweet milk and had some himself. She drank it down, smiled and whispered, "Shlomi, you made me a land of milk and honey." He kissed her again, a long kiss this time, giving in to her tongue and lips, tasting the sweetness of the drink. Ella put her head on his chest. "I was very moved when you let me dress you without even blushing," she said, "I don't want to be shy with you either."

In the darkness of her room they took off all of their clothes. Her body emanated a heat that burned his palms. They lay in bed under a thick blanket, shaking with cold, their bodies touching, her mouth fluttering over his, his hand hovering on her belly and breasts, touching the thin hair between her thighs for a moment, her hand moving on his neck and face and waist, touching his penis for a moment. Their touch was careful and hesitant, full of desire but also deterred by the unfamiliar feeling, their fingers searching for new things.

A great embarrassment took over and their movement stopped. They lay on their backs, their arms crossed, waiting in silence for their breathing to settle.

"We talked so much," she said, "that we forgot our Bible homework."

"No matter," he answered hoarsely. "We can copy it tomorrow at recess, you can copy it off Shlomit and I'll copy it off you."

Ella laughed. "Why Shlomit?"

"Because she sleeps all the time anyway, you can easily steal her notebook."

"Does she even do her homework?"

"Her mom does it for her."

"Really?"

"Everyone knows, even the teachers, but they let her be and let her keep sleeping because her brother is missing."

Ella fell asleep, her limp hand still in his and her breathing quiet. But Shlomi's body was still strained, his thoughts running and his penis swollen and hard.

Slowly, he got out of bed, careful not to wake Ella. He walked quietly on the cold floor and stood in front of the toilet, trying hard to pee. Maybe my wiener will deflate and I'll be able to sleep, he thought and tried again, but couldn't.

He left the bathroom, felt the chill of the apartment while his body still burned. His feet took him to Hanna's room. He stood in the doorway and was suddenly plagued by the image of Robert and Hanna sitting on the big bed. His eyes went to where there was once a small window looking into the bathroom's balcony. The window had been sealed shut when Hanna renovated the place, and only small bumps marked its spot. That was where he stood then, watching them through the bars. The slap he'd gotten from Robert had sent the image far to the back of his mind but didn't erase it, and here it was again – the blue darkness. His father, Ella's mother, both naked, she was crying, her shoulders shaking, her nipples pink, a thicket of light hair below her stomach.

His body was taut. He tried to pull away the image, throw it back in its place, but it wouldn't go, and only aroused him more and more, spilling into the memory of her hands on his ankles when he helped her get clothes out of the closet. His hand went to his penis and began rubbing, squeezing and moving like he sometimes did in bed at night, like Hilik taught him, like the doctor recommended. His eyes closed, a sharp pain burst from his neck and down his back, and then a stream of white drops flew out of him.

Shlomi leaned on the door frame. All at once his body had grown limp, even his breath relaxed. He looked at his hand, and saw his semen in the dark. This was the first time it had appeared. I have white drops too. And why is there no joy?

Despite the relaxation in his body, he was filled with shame. He returned to the bathroom, wiped himself off with toilet paper, and then got dressed and returned quickly to bed. He was tormented for a long time before he finally fell asleep.

When they woke up in the morning Ella asked, "Why are you dressed?" and Shlomi answered, "I was cold in the night," and she said, "I didn't feel a thing, I slept like a dead person."

The teacher folded her colorful charts and began writing down the homework on the blackboard. Shlomi opened his notebook. Winter will be over soon, then it will be Passover and then summer vacation. Maybe I can have my own kitchen in Robert's apartment. Maybe I'll have the entire class over for a big meal. They'll all come and bring their crummy childhoods along. I'll feed them and make them special drinks. Land of milk, milk and honey. Land of milk, milk and honey. There's a song in my head. But why is there no joy?

7

ON WEDNESDAY, MARCH 19TH 1975, A WEEK BEFORE PASSOVER AND about three months before his fourteenth birthday, Shlomi slept with Hanna.

Some would say he lost his virginity that day. His body was mature and developed, his limbs no longer tripping him over when he walked, his posture robust, small patches of hair on his body and face, and his voice thick and stable – but his soul was still chirpy and dawdling, like a bird flying between walls, crashing into transparent windows, chirping and yearning, seeking a remedy, wandering from slumber to slumber and from longing to longing.

About three months before his fourteenth birthday, Shlomi slept with Hanna. White drops came out of him, were absorbed in her body and impregnated her.

Had Robert known he would have thought – once again life is like a poem, once again it is singing itself, rhyming and multiplying and doubling.

Had Ruchama known she would have burned Hanna's house down along with its two residents.

*

In his Tel Aviv apartment, Robert sat with New Hilik and taught him Hebrew words. The child refused to leave the apartment and wouldn't give in to Robert's temptations – we can eat ice cream, go to the playground, climb a multi-colored ladder and jump down to the sand, spin on the merry-go-round, swing on the swings, walk to the Mediterranean beach and look at the gray waves. New Hilik stood firm in his refusal, never moving from the chair by the kitchen table. Across from him was a plate with the remainder of meat from that day's lunch and in his mouth were new words in a funny language.

Despite his insistent refusal, he no longer frowned. With each day he grew softer, even smiled, especially when he raised his eyes to Robert and asked for more and more new words.

Rochelle sat on the sofa, pale. She wasn't feeling well, had a burning in her throat and her nose was red and inflamed. For two days she'd tried unsuccessfully to reach her aunt in Paris on the phone.

And Robert, he was in a wonderful mood. That morning he'd received his test scores. His efforts had come to fruition. He'd even been gloriously praised. The program principal told him, "I was surprised, I didn't expect a guy like you, coming from Tiberias, to get these grades." He presented the framed certificate with pride to his elderly neighbors. They hugged and kissed him, pouring onto him all the longing they'd accumulated since their only son had gone away to school.

Robert meant to go to Tiberias a day early, arrive in the late afternoon and show the certificate to Ruchama and the children, but at the sight of New Hilik's smile and in response to his begging for new words he changed his plans. He'd go the next day. Rochelle wasn't feeling well. He'd spend today with her and New Hilik. In the evening, he'd make the boy dinner, tell him a funny story that rhymed and put him to bed, and would never know that at that very moment, Shlomi was sleeping with Hanna, his life disintegrating.

*

Ruchama stood in the kitchen, chopping leaves. She planned to make a special soup to celebrate Hilik's casts being removed. A hot, sour soup where chopped fennel bulbs would swirl alongside strips of green onions, garlic, coriander, dill, mint and tarragon. Then she'd rip pieces of goat cheese, ball them and coat them with flour, fry them in oil and drop them in. The brown coating of the cheese would burst in their mouths and its soft contents would crumble, staining the green soup with white pools. If Robert was early and came today, she'd invite him to join their meal. They'd praise Hilik together, show their admiration for his quiet suffering, and compliment Shlomi on his devotion to his brother, his resourcefulness and his healthy voice.

Ruchama shook the water off the tarragon stems, picked off the leaves and quickly chopped them. A strong aroma emanated from them, reminding her of the smell of arak liquor. She smiled. *Artemisia dracunculus* in Latin, also known as dragon wormwood, these were scary words attached to such a fresh and innocent herb. Even its bitterness was innocent, peaceful, jubilating. If Robert came she'd pour them both a glass of arak she kept in the kitchen cabinet. They'd sip it and she'd congratulate him for graduating from air conditioning school. He'd probably call soon to tell her about his grades and she'd be pleased even if they weren't high, and happy for him and his new future. She might even pour some arak for Shlomi and Hilik. They were big boys, they could have a drink, warm up and cheer their hearts.

*

Hilik sat in the living room, examining his arms, impressed. They'd suddenly revealed themselves to him after many long and painful weeks. They were very pale, their skin slightly wrinkled. Once in a while he went to wash them in the sink. He washed them again and again, enjoying the feeling of water that his skin had almost forgotten.

From the kitchen came the clinking of Ruchama's pots and the green aromas that had recently been filling their home on a daily basis. It's too bad Shlomi isn't here, that he's late coming home from school. Today he will go to a scout meeting for the very first time. He and Ella had decided to join. Since being sent away from Ruchama's kitchen he'd become afflicted with a lot of free time. He no longer walked around in stained clothes, and the scratches on his hands were gone. If only Shlomi were here. They'd stare at Hilik's arms together, laughing at the way they looked, like an old lady's legs. But Shlomi would only come in for a moment to change into his khaki uniform and then run along and return only late that evening, Hilik thought, and he didn't know that when darkness descended, his brother would sleep with Hanna, his beloved Ella's forty-two-year-old mother, and his life would crash into transparent glass.

*

In her blue home, Hanna hosted two new immigrants from Russia. She served them sweet tea and date cookies Ruchama had given her, and told them in fluent Russian about the terrorist bombing that took place two weeks before at the Savoy Hotel in Tel Aviv. They listened to her silently, terrified. Earlier, they had shared their anger for having been sent to a place as miserable as Tiberias. They felt humiliated, having thought they'd be housed in Tel Aviv, by the sea, or at least in Jerusalem, where the air was cool and not stifling. Hanna explained that Tiberias had a sea too, a fresh-water sea no less. She opened a window to let in some of the wind that went wild outside and said they had excellent air there too. "Above all else," she whispered, as if revealing a secret, "terrorists don't come to a place like Tiberias. You can live here in peace. You should be grateful and shut up."

After saying goodbye to them, she ironed the khaki uniform and scout tie she'd bought for Ella. The school day would soon be over and she'd come home frowning, as usual, pick at the meatballs and potatoes, and then go with Shlomi to their first scout meeting.

Steam from the iron burned her eyes. Again she felt loneliness weighing her down, hurting her like an over-stuffed backpack whose straps she couldn't remove. Occasionally she would go over to Ruchama's, have coffee and giggle as if her life were pleasant, as if her eyes couldn't see the tall woman's impatience. She thinks I don't know she can't stand me. She thinks I can't feel her son's looks, almost as tall as her, fixing on me and shaking up what I thought had burst five years ago.

On weekends she stayed away. She knew Robert came in from Tel Aviv. His eyes would collapse her if she saw him. And on other days, when she stopped by for a short visit, she saw her reflection in Ruchama's glasses. Her slender neck, her eyes, still beautiful, the skin loosening under her chin. She also saw the eyes of the woman who couldn't stand her through those glasses, recognizing in them a yearning similar to hers. She'd only felt his touch for a few moments. Moments that had temporarily erased the memories of horror that had been engraved in her. A frightened childhood in hiding places, great hunger. At night she woke up, her body returning at once to its skinniness, to its pain, and she yelled, remembering that Shmuel was dead and wouldn't come to calm her down, wouldn't remind her that there was no more hunger, that there was a present, that she had a daughter. The pretty and frowning Israella.

Hanna turned off the iron and went to heat up the lunch she'd made for Ella. Maybe she'll like the food and we'll have a nice time. Maybe she'll want my company, she thought, and didn't know that in only a few hours a new fetus would be forming inside her womb.

*

Vardina also sat in her living room, her limbs loose in the chair that had long since grown shabby. The Kurds used to live here. She hadn't seen them in a long time, hadn't gone out in a long time. Robert bought their apartment and switched it with hers so she wouldn't have to climb the stairs to the second floor. Since then, the pain had spread from her knees to the rest of her body, which had grown swollen. How badly she wanted to go out. To wear something nice, put some makeup on and comb her hair. To go to the playground and watch the children and toddlers climb multi-colored ladders and jump joyfully down to the sand, spin on the merry-go-round screeching its endless tune while the wind reddened their cheeks.

But only her eyes went on their regular walk. Again she looked at the plastic roses. They'd been covered in a thick coat of dust. Their redness had grayed. She kept forgetting to ask Shlomi to take them down and wash them. That kid is so tall, he may not even need a chair. Then her eyes went to the phone, waiting for it to ring, for another order to come in. She'd haggle, prolong the conversation, take down the details and make an offer.

A spicy aroma came from Ruchama's kitchen, down the stairs, into her apartment and surrounded her. Ruchama was experimenting again. She thought she was a scientist. And customers were complaining. They wanted meat. They wanted blood. What was she doing up there now? It smelled strongly of arak. Maybe she'd broken a bottle and spilled the liquid, its smell reaching all the way down here. Let it be cleaned quickly, let it not leave a puddle, don't let that poor boy slip again. He'd only gotten his casts off today and before he went upstairs he came in to show her his very white arms. That boy spread more light than a reading lamp.

If Mom were alive she'd look at me in shock, Vardina thought.

"What's become of you Rosalina?" she'd say, using the Romanian version of my name. "How many bellies can one woman carry?" Maybe she'd slap me, like she used to, a double slap, her hand hitting one cheek and coming right back to hit the other. One quick, sharp motion, like a trained ballerina. "You should be ashamed of yourself, Rosalina," she'd tell me, "you should have gotten married and had children," and I'd say, "How could I, I had to take care of you," and she'd make a face and say, "Stop blaming me for everything. Soon you'll blame me for becoming big as an elephant."

Vardina's ears pricked up. She thought she heard a sound in the stairway. Maybe it's Shlomi coming home, maybe he'll come in to ask how I'm doing, and I'll ask him to take down the roses and clean them, I like his company. And maybe it's Robert, coming home early from Tel Aviv. Maybe he'll come in and make us both coffee, and I'll tell him of Ruchama and her experiments, his eyes and his silence telling me about his longing.

The noise grew louder and clearer. It was only the Wednesday wind, roaming the stairway, disguised as people. A clever wind, a con-artist, Vardina thought, and didn't know that when the smell of arak evaporated and the wind calmed down, Shlomi would come to her home and, rather than taking down the roses, would fall into her lap and cry his eyes out.

*

Shlomi and Ella left school in a glorious mood. The day after tomorrow would be the first day of their Passover break, and just minutes ago Reuma-Dumba announced that the general knowledge exams would not be taking place this year. In just a few hours they'd be in a special scout meeting. The troop would receive new members in a festive ceremony, words would be lit up in flames when darkness descended, and rumor had it, the head of the group himself would call each new member to a secret talk and have them swear their loyalty to the country, the city and the troop, forever and ever.

"What nonsense," Ella said. "How do they expect me to swear to something when I don't even know what it is?" Shlomi bought them each a chocolate marshmallow treat in the kiosk that until recently housed Moti's falafel stand, and said, "We don't have anything better to do anyway."

Moshik asked to walk home with them. His walk was stable, his limp completely gone, and the clownish smile was on his face as always. He was sorrier than anyone that Shlomi had been sent away from Ruchama's kitchen. He missed the money, as well as the baths Ruchama made him take and the moments he'd touched Genia, who worked alongside him, in a flutter.

"Where's Hilik?" asked Moshik, and Ella explained that he'd gotten his casts off and had to miss school. "Lucky him," he said and swallowed the half of the chocolate marshmallow treat Shlomi handed him.

Moshik touched his heart. He joined them almost every day, blushing as he walked next to them, slowing down his steps on purpose, as if trying to stretch out time. Sometimes he'd tell them stories, wanting to surprise them, to have them look at him and be impressed by the unbelievable details he made up about himself. "You don't have to lie," Ella once told him, "we love you just the way you are," and Moshik blushed.

When they neared the alley they used to take as a shortcut, Moshik stopped and signaled to them to be quiet. A cat stood on one of the trash cans, rummaging through garbage, its head lowered into the can, its tail wagging. A different smile appeared on Moshik's face. Ella looked at him, her eyes suspicious, but before she was able to say a word, Moshik pounced on the cat, grabbed its tail and pulled it hard. The cat cried. Moshik began spinning it in the air, his laugh competing with the cat's howls and with Ella's screams. Two or three spins, and suddenly the cat flew off and only its tail was left in Moshik's hand, bleeding.

Ella jumped on Moshik and began hitting him – his face, his head, his shoulders, and he laughed, a screechy and distorted laugh, not even trying to defend himself from her blows, his body erect as in a military march, still holding the twisting tail. She kept hitting him until Shlomi grabbed her and pulled her away. Moshik threw the tail in the trash can and left quickly, his laughter still echoing in their ears.

Ella couldn't calm down. Her hands hit the air as if Moshik still stood before her. Her eyes searched for the vanished cat, and only the few drops of blood on the asphalt attested to what had happened.

"The cat ran away," Shlomi said, but Ella kept looking. "What are you going to do?" he asked, "find it and glue on its tail?"

She collapsed on the sidewalk, her head in her hands.

"You need to watch out for that boy," she whispered. "He's completely demented, he'll kill someone someday."

And Shlomi thought about Moshik's crummy childhood and the shack where his parents' shouts echoed in the distance.

Only two days before, as they walked home from school together, Moshik walked between Shlomi and Ella, holding onto their arms for a moment, like a child asking to be lifted in the air, and said, "Maybe we'll start a kibbutz together, only for children. We'll open a stuffed-vegetable factory, Shlomi will invent the recipes and only we will be able to work there, no parents and no teachers, and people will come to buy our food from all over the country."

Shlomi and Ella laughed. "That's all I need," said Shlomi. "If Ruchama hears I'm going to join a kibbutz she'll hang herself."

Now he found it hard to believe they would ever have moments like that again. Ella was so angry she would probably push Moshik away. Maybe she'd even punish him, tell the teacher about the brutality Shlomi refused to see. He wanted to protect Moshik—"He only wanted to impress us, I'm sure he didn't mean to rip off the tail," he said—but Ella was still shaken up.

She got up and they started walking home again. Ella said she couldn't go inside, Hanna had the day off and she didn't feel like answering her annoying questions, and if she served her the sweet meatballs and the pale potatoes she'd throw up.

Shlomi suggested she come over and she refused. Then he suggested they go to Vardina's, have some tea, relax and then each go home to get dressed for scouts.

"She scares me," said Ella. "She has clairvoyant eyes." A smile finally appeared on her face. "Besides, I'm afraid one day she'll explode."

Shlomi laughed. "If she explodes our building will be ruined," he said, and Ella said, "Not just your building, the whole neighborhood would be ruined, the whole city, the whole country, the whole Middle East, even Europe will be ruined, there will be a holocaust," then she got scared of her own words and said, "Thank God my mom can't hear me talk about the Holocaust like that, she'd go nuts."

"The important thing is you've calmed down," Shlomi said.

When they crossed the street Ella remembered that right there, in the six-story building with an elevator, lived their crybaby second grade teacher.

"Let's go visit her," she suggested. "I heard she had a baby."

Shlomi was taken aback. The last time he was at her house, over five years earlier, he was pricked by the eyes of her dead twins. Their pictures hung on the wall, what remained of their belongings on a nearby dresser, a sort of monument in the center of the house that made its inhabitants walk around with lowered eyes. He remembered he'd come to pick up his report card but instead found himself reading newspaper headlines aloud, proving that the words had finally fallen on his head, like she'd promised. Since then, he'd seen her sometimes at the grocery store or at school, and each time her eyes were red and moist.

She hadn't come to school recently. People said she was pregnant. Despite her age and her gray hair, she'd decided to say goodbye to grief and give herself to belated motherhood. She even took down the pictures and the mementos. An army beret, a wrinkled envelope, a chewed red pencil, a black recorder.

"You need a lot of courage to do that," Ruchama had said about that, and Vardina put her hands together and said, "That's not courageous, it's irresponsible. She's too old. She might have a mongoloid or a baby with one short leg. And then who would she blame? She wouldn't be able to blame the army anymore." Ruchama rolled her eyes, blew air out noisily and said, "God forbid, just don't give her the evil eye now."

The crybaby teacher opened the door and her eyes were immediately filled with tears. She hugged them, sat them down in the living room, poured lukewarm juice into glasses and sat across from them. "You're so beautiful it hurts my eyes," she said, grateful for their surprise visit. "You were beautiful in second grade too, but now you've become man and woman."

She wiped her tears, encouraged them to drink up and asked Ella about Brazil and about returning to Israel. The whole time, Shlomi's eyes searched for the pictures, but they were gone, along with the dresser.

Only later, when she invited them to go quietly into the room where her baby slept, Shlomi had noticed the pictures hung over the baby's bed, as if he was put in the care of his dead brothers, watching him and protecting him from evil. The second grade teacher's tears poured again, and Shlomi was surprised to find that Ella was tearing up as well. She looked at the baby lying on his belly from between the bars of the bed. "One day I'll be a mother too," she whispered.

The baby woke up. The crybaby teacher picked him up. He didn't look like a mongoloid, thought Shlomi, and both his legs were exactly the same length. The baby was blushing and calm, and only his mouth opened and closed with the effort to find a nipple to nourish it. His hands twirled in the air, drawing invisible circles.

Then the teacher handed him to Ella.

Ella sat down, breathless, and looked at the baby. "Do you want to hold him too?" the teacher asked Shlomi, and he was frightened, and even took two steps back. "No way," he said, "I'm scared I'll drop him, he's so small."

His eyes went to the pictures of the twins again, examining the faces that were mirrored in their new brother. The baby's room carried their death, he thought, and maybe their lost lives would be revealed in the baby's forming soul.

Shlomi trembled and turned back to the baby. Was he really calm? Was this true peace or was he just tired? Just born and already weighed down by their smiles. Couldn't yet stand and already bent down. And his arms weren't drawing circles. They were fighting, trying to push away what this room summoned for him.

"Look at that, he's smiling at you," said the teacher, but Shlomi thought, he's crying for help, he's asking Ella to help him escape.

He remembered Moshik again and his heart contracted.

And who will save him? Who'll help him escape that shack that spreads its poison to the distance?

The whole thing lasted two, maybe three seconds, in which the cat's body spun in the air before it detached from its tail and shot like a cannonball into the road.

No more than three seconds, but they played out in his mind and he didn't understand why he suddenly felt his gaze had changed.

Something about it had grown sharper and thicker, like his healing voice, like his shooting height.

When they left the teacher's house a strong wind was already blowing. Ella took his hands and they ran together, the wind scratching their faces. Before they parted she suddenly came near him and kissed his lips, and then ran down the path and was swallowed inside her building.

Shlomi closed the door behind him and dropped his backpack. Hilik was sitting in the living room, waving his fixed arms like two white flags. Shlomi went over and touched his arms carefully. "Don't be scared," said Hilik, "it doesn't hurt at all anymore, they even did an X-ray and saw that the bones were completely healed." Shlomi smoothed his fingers over his brother's arms excitedly and said, "They're wrinkled, like an old lady's legs," and Hilik whispered with a smile, "Now I can masturbate in peace. I don't need your help anymore."

Shlomi laughed. "Now you can keep writing in your secret notebook," he whispered.

"There's no notebook," said Hilik. "You imagined it, you had a dream or a *fata morgana.*"

Shlomi made a face. "Don't start with your big words," he said and took a deep breath. "It smells like arak here. Where's Ruchama?"

Hilik pointed to the kitchen. "In her lab." Then he peeked at the clock and added, "You should hurry, or you'll be late for the scout meeting."

Shlomi went into the kitchen. A hunger was bothering him. Ruchama stood there, concentrating, her brow wrinkled, and tasted the green soup boiling on the stove. She handed him a spoonful of boiling liquid.

"What is it?" he asked.

"Taste."

Shlomi tasted with the tip of his lips and tongue. A pleasant sourness filled his mouth and exasperated his hunger. Ruchama looked at him, waiting to hear his opinion.

"Did you put arak in this?"

"No arak, there's tarragon in this."

"But what is it, anyway?"

"It's soup. You eat it with fried goat cheese."

"Too bad," he said and returned the spoon.

"Why?" she asked, disappointed.

"Because it could make a terrific fried fish sauce. As a soup it's boring."

"Imagine it with fried cheese."

"I imagined and I was bored. And it stinks of arak, too."

Ruchama covered the pot and turned off the stove. "It's a shame I let you taste it," she said and a bitter disappointment sounded in her voice, "I forgot you don't show an ass unfinished work."

"You're an ass yourself," Shlomi said angrily, and Ruchama looked at him, her eyebrows rising over her steam-covered glasses, and said, "Don't talk to me that way, Shlomi, I'm still your mother, even though you're as tall as an electrical pole, and don't raise your voice at me."

In a moment Shlomi forgot his hunger. He turned to leave the kitchen but Ruchama stopped him. "When are you getting back from this meeting?"

"I don't know, why?"

"I want you here for dinner, maybe Dad'll come too."

"Since when do you care so much about him?"

"You're raising your voice at me again. Why?"

"That's what I feel like doing," he said and left the kitchen and walked quickly to his room, passing by Hilik and his white arms. The ironed khaki uniform waited for him on the bed.

Ella waited for him on the stone wall. Together they walked to the meeting point, frowning and silent. One look was enough for them to understand they'd had similar experiences, each with his or her own mother – Ruchama and her strange soup, Hanna and her sweet meatballs. "I'm starving," said Shlomi. "I'm still nauseous from that chocolate marshmallow," answered Ella, and the two returned to their silence.

The Wednesday wind hit them, their khaki uniforms were thin and they felt a chill. Something's about to happen, Shlomi thought, and maybe it already has.

This day is new and something in it is changing.

Within minutes they reached the edge of the new neighborhood that looked out over the Sea of Galilee. A few houses whose construction had been frozen, surrounded by fences with signs warning of danger to infiltrators. Until recently, Shlomi used to come here with Hilik and Moshik. One day, Shlomi thought, people will live here and see the incredible view from their windows, the Sea of Galilee shining like in Rachel the Poetess's poem: just reach out and touch it. The people living here won't have to go up to the roof to look at the sea.

Almost all their class members were there, waiting for the meeting to begin. The sound of Nisim's laughter and coughing echoed from all directions. Michal clung, as usual, to the plastic bag. Even Shlomit came, surprisingly alert. And some children came from the other school, the one next to City Hall. Most of them were used to these meetings and the rest were new members, excited and chilled from the wind.

Moshik wasn't there. Maybe he decided to stay in the shack and help his little brothers with homework. Maybe he didn't have a uniform. Maybe he was embarrassed and scared that Ella would pounce at him once she saw him.

The meeting point was right at the end of the neighborhood. A dirt path led from the spot to the hills over the sea. In the horizon, they could see the Arbel Cliff, towards which they were meant to climb – crossing the field, walking past the Bedouin encampment and continuing up the mountain until they reached a hidden field, where the fire writing and the secret ceremonies would await.

But soon the plan was cancelled. The wind changed it, as usual, drawing paths to a new future with a cruel hand.

At the end of the path were several counselors, and leading them was a sturdy, short-haired guy. When they neared, they saw the counselors' faces had fallen. The guy, who introduced himself as the head of the group, spread his arms in sorrow and announced that the meeting was cancelled. "The wind is very strong," he said. "The structures and the fire writing we made for you have collapsed."

Protests were sounded and he hushed everyone. He apologized again and again and explained, "It's very dangerous up there, I can't be responsible for it, we'll have to postpone the meeting until Saturday." And then he signaled to the counselors and together they turned to the road and walked back to the neighborhood. Before they disappeared, the head of the group turned and called to them, "It's best that you go home, it might start raining soon, I don't want you getting wet."

But the group didn't heed his advice. "I'm not going home now," said Nisim. "While we're here we can at least take a walk," and one of the kids from the other school said, "Yes, we'll have a walking meeting, we don't need his favors."

The wind kept whistling as they turned and began walking down the path. Shlomi and Ella looked at each other wordlessly and decided to join. They walked at the end of the line, listening to the funny songs the veteran members sang. The new members mumbled with them, trying to chase down the surprising lyrics – "In a minefield a group of scouts is marching, in a minefield they march all day, oh-oh-oh, boom there goes my leg, oh-oh-oh, boom there goes my arm."

Ella made a face and whispered to Shlomi, "Maybe we should go back, this is stupid," and Shlomi whispered back, "Soon, we don't have anything to do at home anyway."

They walked for only two or three minutes before the thing happened.

The two veteran boys who led the group stopped when they noticed a donkey standing at the edge of the field, eating grass. Deep, bleeding scratches stood in relief on its stomach and legs. It must have been whipped, and now it stood in the peaceful green, letting the wind dry its wounds.

The two boys thought the donkey must have escaped the Bedouin encampment and had to be returned to its owners, and began throwing stones at it.

Ella tried to stop them right away. "Leave it alone," she yelled. "It could be a wild ass. It's dangerous to provoke it." But they laughed and continued, more children getting carried away with them.

They all stood in a line, cheering, and threw small stones at the donkey. First it only flapped its tail, as if trying to shoo away a pesky fly, but when the excited children began throwing heavier and sharper rocks, it stood straight, looked right at them and began braying. Its cries were deafening and overtook Ella's shouts. "Stop it, stop it, it'll attack us," she yelled and started hitting the arms of the stone throwers. "Do something, help me," she yelled at Shlomi, but he just stood in back, his body frozen and his eyes caught in the donkey's gaze. It seemed to Shlomi that the donkey was looking only at him. He shuddered. A moment later the donkey was galloping at them, its brays now screeches and insanity in its eyes. All at once, the children's laughter turned into screams of terror. They began running. Shlomi grabbed Ella's arms and pulled hard, forcing her to run after him. But the donkey was quick and nervous like a predator fighting for a pray. It broke into the group of kids, its legs kicking and punching and its mouth biting, its teeth piercing, injuring and tearing off pieces of khaki soaked in blood.

And then, suddenly, it stopped, took off down the hill and disappeared.

The counselors ran to them from the edge of the path. They had heard the screams and turned back, terrified at the sight of the children lying on the ground, hurt and crying.

Shlomi only got a small bruise, but it had knocked him down and separated his hand from Ella's. He found her passed out, a lot of blood flowing from her shoulder, her shirt torn and revealing deep bite marks. A large chunk of her flesh was almost torn off. Shlomi leaned towards her and put her head in his lap. Her eyes opened and closed intermittently, but her gaze was dull. His hand fastened the torn flesh to her shoulder, trying to attach it back and stop the flow of blood staining her new khaki uniform.

An hour later they were at Poria Hospital. The head of the group sent one of the counselors for help. Three ambulances came and carried all the children away.

Worried parents began showing up. Shlomi was the only one who hadn't called home, and when one of the nurses recognized him and offered to call Ruchama he asked her not to worry her. "I don't want to scare her, nothing happened to me." He dictated a number to the nurse and asked her to call Hanna and tell her gently that Ella was hurt. Ella was too weak to dial herself.

The whole way to the hospital, and later, Shlomi kept his hand against her wound, until she was taken on a gurney into a room to have her wound cleaned and stitched and to get tested and scanned. Even before, in the ambulance, she was already awake. Her shoulder burned with pain, but Ella had stifled it and even smiled at Shlomi and whispered. "I told you it was stupid, we should have gone home." Then she giggled and added, "A cat and a donkey, this day is crazy." And when they were almost at the hospital her face darkened for a moment and she said, "Twice today you stood still and didn't move and only looked on, like you were a lighthouse, you forgot you were a kid."

When Hanna arrived Ella was already bandaged. The tranquilizer she'd received made her drowsy and she sat comfortably on the bench, her head leaning on Shlomi's shoulder and her eyes shut. Hanna's face went white like a wall. She sat at her daughter's side, took her into her lap and caressed her head. Ella opened half an eye and said, "Careful not to touch my shoulder, it hurts like hell."

And then Hanna looked at Shlomi as if just noticing him. "I should have brought your mother along," she said. "I'm sorry I didn't think of it, I was so scared, I drove like mad."

"That's all right," said Shlomi. "I didn't want her to come, nothing happened to me anyway."

"You're covered in blood," said Hanna and her eyes went to his stained clothes. "That's my blood," Ella said sleepily. "Shlomi held me the whole way here."

Hanna tried choking down her tears. Her pale woolen dress was covered in blood from Ella's clothes. It was like the children's story of the little girl who ruins her dress helping an old man carry a sack of coal, Shlomi thought and smiled to himself. Then he looked at her, her straw hair done neatly, her slender neck, above which the skin at the edge of her chin vibrated, and her icy blue eyes. This is the first time, he thought, I've ever seen her cry.

The sun had already set by the time the three of them got into the car. Shlomi sat in the backseat, Ella sprawled at his side, her head on his shoulder. Hanna drove with concentration, every once in a while checking on them through the rearview mirror.

"I won't let you go home like that," she said. "Ruchama might see all that blood on your clothes and have a heart attack."

Shlomi looked at her questioningly.

"Come to our place now," she said. "I'll clean your clothes and then you'll go home as good as new."

"How?" Shlomi whispered.

"I'll quickly wash your clothes. We have a dryer from abroad. It'll all be dry in an hour. At our apartment everything is modern."

Shlomi helped Hanna put Ella in bed. Then he waited outside the room until Hanna finished cleaning her, putting on her pajamas and tucking her in. Ella opened her eyes and complained of pain. Hanna said, "It's best you go to sleep," gave her water and two pills. She fell asleep shortly thereafter and Hanna turned to Shlomi and said, "Let's clean your clothes."

She filled the tub with hot water and sprinkled some powder into it. Shlomi stood next to her, trying to escape her eyes and quiet his trembling.

Hanna asked him to take his clothes off, but he froze in place. She asked him again and he didn't move. She came near him, he could feel her breath on his face, sent soft hands towards him, and began unbuttoning his shirt, gently releasing his hands from his waist, removing the thin khaki shirt and then the white undershirt, which was also stained with Ella's blood. She soaked his clothes in the water, shaking them well so they absorbed the suds.

Hanna waited for a long moment, letting Shlomi free himself from his frozen state. The water grew red. She came near him again, and again he felt her breathing, and this time it was quicker. She unzipped his pants and pulled them down his legs. His hands went to his crotch immediately, trying to hide the bulge in his underwear. Without a word, Hanna helped him pick up one foot and then the other to release his pants and soaked them in the water as well.

For the first time, he raised his eyes to her. Her face and neck were blushing and her eyes avoided his. Her hands ran over her dress, checking the blood that had already congealed and darkened on it. She grabbed the ends of her dress and pulled it slowly over her head, remaining in only a thin, almost see-through slip. His hands clung fiercely to his underwear. He was afraid of what happened only recently, when he spent the night with Ella and stood naked at the door to Hanna's room.

Hanna leaned towards the water, shook the clothes and scrubbed them until they grew brighter. She pulled out one item of clothing at a time, wrung it hard and put it in the dryer. When all the clothes were inside, she shut the dryer door and turned it on. The clothes beat against each other and it hummed and shook the bathroom.

Hanna stood across from Shlomi. Now her eyes tied with his. His entire body was hard and contracted and his hands wanted to hold her, to touch her waist, to run down her neck and her breasts. Suddenly he took off his underwear and stood against her completely naked and shaking. She took off her slip. Her nipples were as pink as he remembered. She clung to him, her head reaching his neck, her mouth searching for his, and he lowered his head to hers, tasting her lips, the taste of clear water, a certain saltiness, maybe from the tears that were flowing from her eyes again, her belly against his penis, their hands lost on each other's bodies, the dryer's hum covering the sound of their breathing. Hanna laid him down on the cold floor and lay on top of him, her breasts rubbing against his chest and her hand taking him and putting him inside her. In a second he exploded within her. All the white drops burst from him and into her.

*

Robert called Ruchama only after New Hilik fell asleep. He asked Rochelle to stay quiet, but his request was redundant. She lay silently on the sofa, burning with a fever and shaking under the covers. In a weak voice she thanked him for giving her a pill and some water and asked that he spend the night with them. She was worried that Yechiel would awake in the night and she wouldn't be able to go to him, so weakened was she by the fever. Sometimes the child had nightmares. He'd sit up in bed in the middle of the night and call for his dead father. Robert consented. It was already late, and he would go to Tiberias the next morning. He'd tell the elderly neighbors he wouldn't be staying with them that night and spend his few hours of sleep in the wide bed in the balcony, next to New Hilik. Should the boy wake up and cry out, he'd calm him and rub his forehead until he fell asleep again, and allow his mother to heal.

Ruchama picked up and he immediately heard sourness in her voice. She seemed to be disappointed. She mumbled something about a special soup she'd made, thinking he'd come early and be there tonight to see Hilik's healthy arms and tell them about his test scores and his certificate. Her mumbling and the disappointment in her voice moved him, were pleasant even, but again he had to lie, tell her something about important errands he had to run, settling his debt, saying goodbye to his teachers and fellow students, picking up the paperwork he had to submit to the employment service. He really did have to do all these things, but was finished before noon, and since then he'd been here, teaching little Hilik new words, listening in on Rochelle's attempts to call her aunt in Paris, and tending to her illness. He'd been lying for two months, hiding his two guests who'd arrived suddenly to double his life.

"Shlomi went to a scout meeting and hasn't returned yet," said Ruchama. "The wind is going wild outside, I'm worried."

"He's a big boy," said Robert. "You don't need to worry about him. The wind won't blow him away."

"When will you be here?"

"Tomorrow, I'll leave in the morning."

"That's too bad, Hilik was waiting for you. He's been sitting in the living room all day, looking at his arms."

"He's a big boy too."

When he hung up he stood by the balcony shutters. New Hilik was sleeping deeply, his breathing peaceful, his arms spread to the sides. I exhausted him today, thought Robert; he might not even feel me sleeping next to him. The light of the streetlamp cast a blue shade on the heavy trees of Gordon Street. Robert saw them standing still. Strange, he thought, in the north the wind is blowing and worrying Ruchama, and here, nothing, the air is still.

He turned off the light, lay next to the sleeping child and fell asleep, his arms spread to the sides like his son's.

*

Ruchama put the phone back in its cradle. Her head hurt. Maybe because she'd shut all the windows against the howling wind. The air in the apartment was still and stifling. A strong smell of arak still filled the kitchen and the living room.

"You want some soup?" she asked Hilik who sat in the living room, staring at the television, every once in a while looking at his white arms. "I'm not hungry at all," he answered. She returned to the kitchen and lifted the pot's lid, letting loose some more of the aroma that made her nauseous. The soup was lukewarm; the green leaves had blackened in the yellowish liquid and looked to her like seaweed moving slowly among the rocks at the beach she used to visit when she lived in Haifa. Sometimes she'd go to the port, stop and watch the waves breaking on the rocks and shaking the limp seaweed.

She picked up the heavy pot and poured its contents into the sink. She collected the black leaves so as not to cause a blockage and threw them in the garbage. Then she washed her hands and took a painkiller.

As she passed by Hilik on her way to bed she told him, "Make sure Shlomi eats something when he gets back, he hasn't eaten all day, I hope they at least gave them some refreshments at the meeting," and Hilik said, "Of course not, it's a scout meeting, not a party."

"Make some sandwiches, there's cheese and cucumbers in the fridge," she said and went to bed.

*

Hanna dried the hair of her washed head, absorbing the water into a towel quickly so as not to get her nightgown wet. The apartment was cold and the steaming shower hadn't warmed her body. Shlomi had left. His clothes were still a little moist when he put them on quickly and vanished.

On the tips of her toes she went into Ella's room and saw that her eyes were half-open. Hanna put a hand on her forehead. "I think you're getting a fever," she said. "Maybe it's an infection." Ella didn't answer, only lay on her side with effort, careful not to let the bandaged shoulder rub against the sheet, and closed her eyes.

Hanna went to her room and lay in bed. Her hair was moist and cold. She covered herself with the thick blanket, trying to stop the shaking. With her teeth chattering, she wished to feel something new in her body.

Shlomi's eyes as he moaned underneath her.

Another chill.

Maybe she should turn on the radiator.

She got up, wrapped in the blanket, and returned to Ella's room. "I want to give you a pill. We need to lower your fever."

Ella hummed something, her eyes shut.

"And you had nothing to eat today. Maybe I should warm up some potatoes and meatballs for you."

Ella lifted her body a little and whispered, "You're interrupting my sleep," and put her head back on the pillow.

Hanna's hands lifted the blanket a little, her eyes inspecting the sheet and the pajamas. She had to make sure the stitches hadn't opened. That blood wasn't leaking. Those doctors were bad. They may not have stitched her up properly. She couldn't let her get an infection.

She went to the kitchen. Maybe I'll make some hot tea. My entire body's shaking.

His hands on her waist. Her belly rubbing up against him.

She's chilled now, too.

Maybe something new is developing in her. She waits.

She'll have hot tea and go to sleep.

Her room is freezing. The kitchen is warmer.

Sitting on the chair in the dark, wrapped in the blanket. Thawing.

Her eyes closing.

*

When Shlomi came in, Vardina was still in her chair, alert and smiling. After finishing dinner, she shut all the windows and turned on the radiator and the radio, which was playing Hebrew songs she loved, quiet and wistful. This winter had started late, she thought, and now it can't make up its mind to end.

The radiator slowly thawed out the air and the songs pinched and warmed her heart. When she heard the small knock on the door she knew immediately it was Shlomi, returning from the scouts and wishing to share his experience with her. But this time his face was long, his hair was wild and his lips were pursed.

"What's wrong, Shlomi?" she asked. "Did someone annoy you at the scouts? Wasn't the meeting good?" but Shlomi didn't answer, only looked at her with hard eyes. She invited him to sit by her side, surprised when he drew back as she put a warm hand on his knee.

"Why are your clothes wet?" she asked. "Did it rain?"

Shlomi nodded, his shoulders slumped with exhaustion.

Vardina offered him tea and cookies, and he said no.

"I can see you're not in the mood for talking," she said. "That's all right, sit with me and listen to the beautiful songs." She turned the radio up and thought about ways to improve his mood. Whenever he felt blue he came to her for funny stories, and she gladly obliged.

"You hear this singer?" she asked with a smile. "Her name is Netanella, a strange name, and everyone on the radio says she's a genius. But I think she sings through her nose. She wants to be special so she sings through her nose instead of her mouth." Vardina joined the singer in a nasal voice, mimicking her style – "*Away ... away ... on the water floating, she's still waiting ...*" she burst into laughter, amused with herself, but there was no smile on Shlomi's face.

He's really sad today, she thought. I should try harder.

"You should know," she turned to him as if revealing a secret, "I saw Netanella on television, singing this song in last year's Song Festival. I saw her pinching her nose with two fingers to get that special voice. One day she'll be a rich and famous singer and she won't have to pinch her nose anymore. She'll pay someone else to do it, and that'll be his job, to stand next to her on stage and pinch her nose as she sings, *high, high, over the Gilboa Mountains.*" Again she laughed but stifled it quickly when she saw that Shlomi wasn't moving, looking down at the floor with a sealed face.

"You want to tell me what's wrong?" she whispered worriedly.

"Nothing."

"Then why are you sitting there like a statue? You're scaring me."

Shlomi said nothing and Vardina felt her worry deepen and turn into anxiety. Something's happened to the boy.

"I have an idea," she said finally with a forced smile. She suggested that Shlomi climb on a chair and bring down the plastic roses from the tops of the kitchen cabinets. "They used to be blood-red, and now they're gray with dust. It's time to clean them." Shlomi looked up at the plastic roses. His eyes narrowed. "I even remember," she said, "how one time your girlfriend wanted to wear one of the roses in her hair and her mother got mad. I think that was when everyone came over to watch the festival on my television. That was an excellent festival with beautiful songs, and no one sang through their nose."

And then, all at once, Shlomi burst into tears. His whole body shook and his tears washed his face and his shirt. Vardina was scared. She sent her hands to him immediately and pulled him close until he put his head in her lap. His trembling shoulders were locked between her bellies, her hands caressed his forehead and wiped his tears. He sat like that and wept in her lap for a long time.

*

There was a boring show about Passover on television. Hilik tried to follow the speakers who told stories from their childhood Seder tables, joking about matzah and constipation. He finally fell asleep with his head on his white arms. He awoke when he heard noise coming from the kitchen. A voice read a biblical verse, while on the screen a finger moved across the holy passage. Broadcasting would soon end for the night.

Hilik turned off the television, went to the kitchen and found Shlomi there. He must have come in quietly, careful not to wake him. His eyes were red and lifeless.

Hilik wanted to ask about the meeting, about why he'd come home so late, about what made him cry. But Shlomi's eyes made him retreat.

Maybe I'll ask him tomorrow, or the day after. I'll wait for Shlomi to calm down. Something definitely happened to him, and now it's raging inside of him. Winds are blowing in there, wilder than the one we had today.

But he must be hungry.

Without a word, Hilik opened the kitchen cabinets and began pulling out the sweet gifts he'd received when he'd broken his arms – loads of chocolate bars, rolls of marzipan in transparent wrappers, bags of candy and pralines, meringue kisses, banana and coconut treats and marmalade. He spread them all on the table in front of Shlomi's surprised eyes and quickly unwrapped everything, his hands taking pleasure in their renewed freedom.

"Eat," ordered Hilik.

And when he saw his brother hesitating he sat at the table too, broke off a piece of chocolate and began chewing voraciously, encouraging his brother to follow suit.

Shlomi started eating. At first he only took one piece of chocolate and a small bite of marzipan, and then more and more. He ate and ate. His mouth was overflowing with sweetness. He ripped off chunks and shoved them in his mouth, chewing and swallowing and biting again.

Hilik looked at him. His voracity pinched his heart and he didn't know why. He got up, poured milk into a tall glass and handed it to him. Shlomi drank it all up and went back to his gorging, devouring, his mouth bleeding chocolate. Hilik refilled his glass with milk and sat down next to Shlomi. His hand went to his brother's forehead and moved the hair that had mussed there, then returned to his forehead and stayed there, as if checking his temperature, as if supporting his head so it didn't fall.

Thus they sat for a long time, Shlomi filling his mouth with sweets and sipping the milk, and Hilik at his side, hand on his brother's forehead, not letting go.

8

IN THE FIRST WEEK ROBERT INSTALLED TEN AIR CONDITIONERS. IT seemed that the new business that was launched with a storm of excitement was going to be successful. Robert offered lavish discounts, newcomer prices and payment plans. But the sudden departure of winter and its replacement with an irritating heat also helped him seduce customers. "Good," said Ruchama. "People are sick of their own stench. I've told you many times before, you have a special sense for these things."

Equipped with the money he'd made, he got in his old truck and went to visit the yellow-faced kibbutz secretary. He wanted to pay him back for all his help in recent months, but the secretary, whose suddenly-gray hair made his face even yellower, laughed and said, "Absolutely not, we had a deal, I gave you money and you cancelled the lawsuit." Finally he consented to Robert's pleading and agreed to send three trucks to pick up all the shutters from the kibbutz's cancelled order. "That way I'll have more room for the air conditioners," Robert said graciously. "It's better you have the shutters than me just throwing them out."

Ruchama's face soured. "It isn't enough that crook ripped you off and put you in debt, but then you end up giving him the shutters for free." And Robert lied to her again: "He promised to pay me when the kibbutz gets its act together, and I believe him."

The factory was emptied of the piles that had filled it for months. Robert dismantled the machines and placed their dusty components in one of the corners of the factory floor. He drenched the concrete floor with water and scrubbed it until it shined, and then placed the air conditioners in its center, packed in cardboard boxes and tied together. Robert looked at the pile of cardboard cubes that only took up a small part of the floor. He smiled to himself. There used to be a giant monument here, many blocks of plastic-wrapped shutters, and now it was barely a tombstone. He remembered the scholarly poetry teacher. The man was sure Robert was an anonymous poet whose shutters and air conditioners were private metaphors, testaments to his secret poetic sensibilities. Robert laughed. What would the teacher think now, had he stood by his side, staring at the pile of cardboard. There used to live here a long, convoluted poem, bursting with rhymes and similes, like a clumsy, dusty ballad. And now, upon this shiny floor, a short, purposeful poem had been born, quick as an arrow and sharp as a blade. Modern.

During those first days, Hilik helped him. It was Passover vacation and Robert suggested, "Why don't you come help me instead of being bored, it'll help strengthen your weaky arms after the cast," and Hilik said, "It's weakly arms, not weaky arms," and Robert, who remembered New Hilik whenever he looked at his son, trembled for a moment and thought, I don't need to teach him any new words, he knows the entire Hebrew language already.

But Hilik had trouble performing the chores Robert gave him. Installing a new air conditioner entailed breaking a hole in the wall. With stable, precise motions, Robert outlined and then chiseled. He asked Hilik to mix cement and whitewash in a pail to create concrete mixture to spread at the openings of the hole in the wall. The cement and whitewash spilled out of Hilik's hands. He always used either too much or too little water. Concrete sprayed on the floor. But Robert smiled and encouraged him, correcting and cleaning up after him. Each time Hilik would say, "I'm sorry, I don't have good hands like Shlomi," and Robert soothed him immediately: "Your hands are terrific and I'm happy you're helping me."

Once, as they were collecting the tools and the new air conditioner blew good air that dried their sweat, Robert asked, "Why is Shlomi sad? What's with him?"

"I think he's worried about his girlfriend," said Hilik. "She's hurt."

Then he told him what little information Shlomi had volunteered the day after the scout meeting. He'd heard the rest at school right before the Passover vacation. Everyone was talking about the donkey that'd gone wild and wounded kids and about the ambulances that took them away. "Nothing happened to Shlomi," he said, "but Ella was hurt in the shoulder and got an infection."

"Are you kidding me?" Robert said. "Since when do donkeys go wild?"

"I guess it was a wild donkey. It was hurt and the kids hurled stones at it."

"Hurled? What's hurled?"

"Threw stones at it," Hilik explained.

"And why didn't you tell me? Why didn't Mom tell me?"

"You were busy with the air conditioners."

Robert nodded and sighed. "The important thing is Shlomi wasn't hurt."

"I think there are other things bothering him, but he won't tell," said Hilik.

"He'll get over it, he's a big boy," Robert said and sighed again.

And another time, as they unloaded the cardboard cube from the truck and carried it up the stairs, Hilik suddenly said, "Mom talks about you a lot." Robert stopped, the air conditioner almost dropping from his hands, and Hilik continued. "I think she misses you." Robert looked at him and remembered New Hilik again. The two were so alike and so different. The younger one frowning, the older one smiling.

It seemed the air conditioning business was on track, but at the end of the first week, sales came to a halt. Maybe because of Passover expenses, which caused people to put an end to their passion for renewal, and maybe Ruchama was right when she said, "Don't forget where you live, people hardly have money to feed themselves here, how do you want them to pay for this luxury?" Robert nodded despairingly and said, "What am I going to do now?" and Ruchama answered, "It's enough for you to sell one unit a week, you don't need to be Baron de Rothschild." And a week later, when Robert said, "Maybe I should call the kibbutzes, offer some serious discounts, they get hot in summer too," she answered immediately, "But this time make sure to get paid up front."

Then suddenly she said, "I want to buy an air conditioner too, no discount."

"Are you crazy?" said Robert. "What are you talking about, buy? Just ask me and I'll install as many as you want."

"I want one in the kitchen and one in the living room, but I'll pay every last lira, up front."

"Forget it, Ruchama, I won't take your money."

"Then I'll go to someone else, you watch out."

"Why do you suddenly want an air conditioner? You were always against it."

"I'm hot, and I can afford it, I have enough money."

"I can't have you paying me," said Robert. "We're still married, though I've been waiting for you to take me back for over five years."

Ruchama went quiet. Robert saw her lips moving, like the words were hesitating to come out. After a long moment she said, "I'll go to your competition tomorrow and order air conditioners. I swear I will if you won't let me buy them from you."

Robert stood in her home for an entire day, chiseling and spreading and tightening and checking and cleaning. Hilik helped him as best he could. He stood beside him silently and handed him tools, his lips blushing and his eyes growing excited each time Ruchama gave Robert something. Once she made him coffee. Once she made him take a break and eat cookies, fresh from the oven. Then she made a large lunch, even cooked fish, veering from her recent habits for his sake. And after he'd swallowed all the bread soaked in red sauce, he went to the kitchen and helped her clear appliances and dishes so he could chisel comfortably.

That night the new air conditioners were already working and filtering out the smell of cooking that had filled the apartment. Shlomi was out all day. He said he was going to meet friends, returned only in the evening with a long, pale face and whispered, "It's so cold in the apartment," and went to take a hot shower. Ruchama told Robert, "I'm worried about him, he walks around with a sour face and showers three times a day, he keeps bathing, I don't know what's wrong with him." And Robert said, "Don't worry, he'll get over it, he's a big boy."

The Passover Seder took place about a week after he'd returned to Tiberias and about two weeks before he installed Ruchama's air conditioners. They did not celebrate together. Ruchama was very tired. She'd cooked for her customers for two days straight. People who were too lazy to handle the holiday meal ordered immense amounts of food from her, if they could afford it. Ruchama filled large trays with stuffed fish, made giant pots of bone soup with small float-ing meat and matzah-meal dumplings, and vegetables cooked with a multitude of green leaves, as had become her habit. After the cus-tomers came by to pay and pick up their orders, Ruchama lay in bed and slept through the holiday.

Robert cooked a meal for Shlomi and Hilik. He asked questions and was answered with silence, and chastised Shlomi for pecking at his food and for his face having turned pale and skinny, and Shlomi only said, "I don't have an appetite," and sat in front of the televi-sion.

Robert filled a plate and went downstairs to Vardina's apartment. She was happy to see him as always. Though she'd already eaten the delicacies Ruchama had sent her, her eyes widened with gluttony at the sight of the food heaped on the plate. "When did you learn to cook like this?" she asked, her mouth watering, and Robert smiled proudly and said, "I cooked the whole time I was in Tel Aviv, I had no choice, I had to eat something." As she sat in her chair, Vardina immersed herself in the plate, biting into the meat and praising the taste. "That's how I like it," she said with her mouth full, "when you leave the blood there, not dry the meat out and turn it into rubber."

Then she insisted on getting up and with great effort made them both tea. Amused and breathless, she told him about the singing competition she'd recently watched on television. "I even thought of having guests over, like I used to for the Independence Day festival," she said. "And this time it wasn't just any festival, it was Eurovision, half the world watches that." She sighed and continued, "But I'm too tired to entertain these days, I can hardly get up to go to the bathroom."

She told him about the Israeli singer and her eyes lit up. "I think he was the cutest and the best singer, I've always liked him, even when he was in the Navy Singing Troop." "Who was it?" asked Robert, and Vardina was amazed. "Shlomo Artzi represented us. Where do you live, Robert?" And when Robert shrugged, she wagged a thick finger at him and said, "You should be ashamed of yourself, not knowing who Shlomo Artzi is, the whole world knows but you." Robert said, "That's all right. He doesn't know who I am, either."

Vardina served him a cup of tea and kept telling him about the competition. She even jumped around a little, trying to demonstrate the singer's body language, describing in detail the white shirt he wore, the popped-up collar over a black vest, and the heart-shaped pendant on a chain around his neck. "I wish he'd worn a Star of David," she said sorrowfully. "He is representing our country, after all." And then she sat down in her chair, breathing heavily. The sudden sorrow had molded into her face. "But my favorite is Mike Brant," she said, pondering. "If they'd have sent him we would have won. They should have sent him. He's still an Israeli, even though he's been in France for years. His real name is Moshe."

Robert had drunk half of his tea. He saw tears peeking from her eyes and she wiped them with a handkerchief she'd tied to her wrist.

All of a sudden she said, "Don't lose hope, Robert. I know she loves you. It's just that her heart got tied up a bit and she became tangled. But I feel it'll happen soon. Believe me, because I know her better than anyone, she's like my daughter and my sister and my mother, combined. You should know even that ear doctor doesn't come around anymore, she only misses you all day. And you, you sit quietly and wait, until some day ..."

She asked Robert to add sugar to her tea. "I forgot the sugar in all the excitement," she said, "I made a sad tea, and I like it sweet and happy."

Exactly a month later, Vardina passed away. Robert found her sunken into her chair, holding onto one of the plastic containers with Ruchama's leftover cooking. No one knew what made her heart stop beating. Maybe a piece of potato got stuck in her throat. Maybe she was shocked by the radio announcement of Mike Brant's death, or maybe she was overcome by the sorrow of Ruchama having told her tearfully, the day before, about New Hilik and about her decision to detach herself from Robert forever.

Five days before Vardina's death, Robert sat on the factory floor. The radio played cheerful morning songs and he covered the disassembled machines with plastic sheets, wondering if an order was going to come in. He was energized and ready to get to work.

When the phone rang, he hurried to the office with excitement, thinking his prayers had been answered and that a customer was calling to order an air conditioner. But to his surprise, he heard the voices of the elderly couple, his Tel Aviv neighbors. It sounded like they were standing cheek to cheek, holding the phone between them, wishing to share the conversation.

"I'm very sorry to interrupt you," said the old man, "but I didn't have a choice." And his wife added, "We're very concerned, you'd better come here."

They told him they'd been hearing the little boy crying in the apartment next door since the previous morning. At first they thought nothing of it, the crying was quiet, almost shy, but at night it grew louder. It seemed the kid was standing on the balcony over-looking the street and weeping. They couldn't go back to sleep. They knocked on the door twice, and then he went quiet. From behind the door they asked where his mother was, perhaps she'd gone out and never returned, perhaps something had happened to her and she couldn't come to the door. But the child didn't answer. And when they returned to bed he burst out crying again, his voice hoarse, bleating words they couldn't understand. And early in the morning, when a small mayhem broke in the stairway because other neighbors were angry about losing sleep, the child went completely quiet, and the apartment had been silent ever since.

"No one's answering," said the old man, and his wife continued worriedly, "Something's wrong there, tell us what to do, we can call the police or you can come quick."

Robert locked his air conditioning factory and ran out to Ha'Galil Street where he hailed a cab, paid the driver double his normal fare and instructed him to drive to Tel Aviv as fast as he could.

Within two hours he sprang into the building on Gordon Street with shaking legs.

Rochelle had disappeared. It was as if the earth had swallowed her whole, along with her clothes, which she'd packed in one of the large suitcases.

When Robert opened the door, he found the child balled on the sofa, his body trembling and his eyes swollen with tears. New Hilik sat up, and when he saw Robert he broke into a soundless cry, only weak whispers leaving his throat. Robert thanked the elderly couple and shut the door at their wondering faces. He examined the apartment quickly and noticed a suitcase was missing. Then he saw that the clothes had disappeared from the closet. On the table were two plates of fried meat that smelled old. Rochelle had made New Hilik his meals, waited for him to fall asleep and took off, he realized, trying to push away the waves of sourness rising from his stomach.

Robert sat down and took the child in his arms. He held the child for a long time, trying to quiet his mute weeping, until he calmed down a little and told him in whispers that when he'd woken up the previous morning he found his mother gone.

At first he thought she'd gone shopping as usual, but when he saw the meat and the empty closet shelves he was filled with terror ...

She never came back. Just got up and left ...

She had been silent for two days. He thought she was sick again, her throat hurting. She hadn't even talked on the phone. When he asked her to play with him she pushed him away and sent him to bed ...

He bathed by himself and put himself to sleep in the large bed, practicing new Hebrew words ...

He stood there waiting for her by the balcony shutters until he choked with tears. He watched the path leading into the building ...

He hadn't touched the meat. Hadn't answered the knocks. He was scared.

She left him and didn't come back ...

Robert pulled New Hilik to him. His clothes were wet. He must have wet his pants, perhaps from fear, perhaps from not wanting to abandon his post on the balcony. He gave him a bath and helped him into clean clothes, and made him eat some bread, cheese and chocolate and drink a whole glass of milk. New Hilik was thirsty and hungry and exhausted. The entire time he clung to Robert with a strong grip, his fingernails piercing the man's waist, never letting go.

When he fell asleep, Robert carried him to the bed and closed the shutters, blocking the afternoon sun from waking the boy.

Robert turned the apartment upside down. He looked in every possible corner. She could have left a letter, or at least a note. His hands felt through the clothes, rummaged through the drawers, searched between blankets and under furniture. The only trace of her was a pile of files on the kitchen table. She'd been postponing their submission to the Ministry of Immigrant Absorption to settle their status as *aliyah* immigrants for months. His eyes ran over the empty forms. She hadn't even put her name on them.

Among the forms was New Hilik's passport. Hers was gone.

Robert tried to push away the image that appeared in his mind – Rochelle at the airport, standing tall in her blue jacket among pilgrims in black, waiting for her life to clear up. And now it had. It was no longer covered in sand. She took her passport and her clothes and she took off. For months he'd been wanting to ask her when her life would clear up and hadn't. Ever since his course was over he visited the apartment once a week at most, lying to Ruchama, making an excuse and going to Tel Aviv, placing some money in Rochelle's hands, spending time with New Hilik, trying to convince the stubborn boy to get out of the apartment, and returning to Tiberias. And that whole time her life had been growing clear and she'd been making plans.

He looked among the notes by the phone again. They were all his. They had the numbers of his classmates and of wholesale air conditioner marketers in his own handwriting. He shuffled through them, thinking he might find her aunt's number in Paris. Maybe she went there. But how did she pay for the ticket? Maybe she had some diamonds saved in a hiding place, assuring her she'd have a way to get up and go. She'd come to bury her husband, to place her son in his real father's hands and to disappear.

A great fear overtook him. He didn't even know her aunt's name. He remembered he'd never looked at Rochelle's passport. Did it have her current name or her maiden name, which he didn't even know. It suddenly was clear to him that he knew nothing about her. And moreover, he realized he wasn't surprised. As if he'd known that one day she'd disappear just as she appeared. And maybe he even wanted her to. He never asked any questions, never pressed her to make a decision, only let time pass. Maybe he wanted her to see for herself. To realize that time went by here like an imperceptible gust of wind, not strong enough to remove the sand from her life. To realize that this was no place to live. This was a place to wait. Like eternity. Maybe he wanted her to up and go and leave his new son, to whom he'd already grown attached.

Robert sat in the kitchen chair and forced himself to take a deep breath. The fear that had overtaken him had morphed into a paralyzing horror.

Relax, Robert. Take a deep breath. Be rational.

Another breath.

Another breath.

Maybe she'd only gone on a short trip. She'll be right back. Maybe she went to run some errands and needed her passport, and then got stuck. Maybe lost. Maybe she'd met someone violent. Maybe she was in a car accident. Wounded. Hospitalized. But she could have asked to make a phone call. Why didn't she? Maybe she was unconscious. But what did she pack a suitcase for? She took everything. She escaped. Otherwise she wouldn't have made the boy one or two days' worth of meals. They called him rather than the police. What would he tell the police if they came? And Ruchama. He'd have to explain. What would he tell Shlomi and Hilik. You have a little brother. His mother ran away and left him here, abandoned him. I'm his real father. All I wanted was to make my uncle happy. His pleas broke my heart and I obliged. I took his diamonds. I only wanted to make him happy. But Ruchama would never believe it. I knew you'd do that, she'd say. I knew you'd punish me for no longer having a uterus. That terrible woman punched my belly, killed my baby, made me barren, just like my beloved Rachel the Poetess. And now you came and punched my soul. You'll even wait an eternity. And what about the little boy, New Hilik, abandoned by his mother. I was abandoned too, more than once. Again life is being multiplied.

Again horror swirls in his head, making him dizzy.

He's sweating. Take a deep breath. Can't.

Maybe she'll call soon, having reached her aunt's house, and explain everything. How long does it take to get to Paris? And maybe she flew back to Argentina. I should wait. You'll even wait an eternity.

Robert waited two days. During those days he kept searching for a clue to explain, even partially, this meaningless act. He even called the kibbutz secretary, swore him to secrecy and shared what had happened with him. The Yellow Face pulled all his strings at the airport but came up empty. Then he checked the hospitals and finally told Robert, "You don't have much of a choice, you have to call the police."

When he wanted to leave for a few minutes to get some groceries, New Hilik stood in the doorway and blocked his way. Robert suggested he come with him but the child refused and clung to him, piercing his nails into Robert's waist and whining. Robert raised his voice, even threatened to punish him, until the child had to give up.

For the first time since they'd landed in Israel with the coffin, New Hilik left the house, and with his hands holding tightly onto Robert's fingers, he walked to the grocery store and back. He was pale, his eyes hurt from the strong sun. And when they returned with the groceries, he lay down on the bed in the balcony and fell asleep. Robert tried to rouse him to eat something, but the short journey had depleted the child. He slept on his stomach, his face buried in the pillow, and once in a while raised his head and asked, "Is she back?"

When night fell, Robert sat on the sofa and brought the phone close. I'd better do it when she can't see my face, he thought, and dialed Ruchama's number. He'd only spoken to her once since coming to Tel Aviv, on the evening of the day he'd arrived and found Rochelle gone. He'd had to lie. He told her there were problems with the pipes again and he'd been called to Tel Aviv, and would only return when he could find a solution that would relieve the neighbors. Ruchama encouraged him. "No matter," she said. "It's best you just get rid of that apartment, it's given you nothing but trouble, and the course is over anyway." Since then, two days of terror and sleeplessness had passed. It was time, Robert told himself, and called.

"How are you?" asked Ruchama. "Are the pipes fixed?"

"There's no problem with the pipes," Robert answered, "I lied to you."

She fell silent and he took a breath.

He asked where Shlomi and Hilik were.

In a weak voice she said they'd gone downstairs to his apartment to watch television.

Robert alerted her that their conversation was going to be long, that he had a lot to tell her, and asked if she had time.

He told her everything, keeping nothing to himself. The details poured out of him, as if wishing to liberate themselves from their five-year-long imprisonment:

The airport and the red cop. The delay in getting to Buenos Aires.

His old uncle's tears and his requests, which he'd agreed to out of weakness or frivolousness, or perhaps generosity.

The five years of torment. The longing and the silence and his self-sentenced abstinence.

Their sudden arrival with the coffin. The elderly couple that enveloped him in warmth.

The frowning child who was his son.

Her disappearance.

And the entire time he spoke she said nothing. He heard only her breaths, steady, even calm. The breathing of a person in deep sleep. As if she'd fallen asleep and was now dreaming his words.

Robert was finished. They were both silent.

New Hilik suddenly woke up, sat up in bed and began crying. Only then did Robert hear her breath contract, as if she'd risen from sleep into a frenzied wakefulness.

"Why did you tell me all this?" he heard her whisper. "You could have kept lying." And a moment later she slowly placed the phone back in its cradle.

Robert went to New Hilik and rubbed his head. The boy's crying stopped and he went back to sleep. He called again, but Ruchama didn't answer. His body was burning and he stood in the shower under the cold water. Then he packed up all of New Hilik's clothes, and a decision was reached in his mind. He'd sell the Tel Aviv apartment as soon as possible. If Rochelle suddenly returned, her life would be her own to fix. He wouldn't abandon New Hilik to her whims any longer. He'd put another bed in his apartment. Shlomi and Hilik lived at Ruchama's anyway and only came over to watch television. He'd contact a lawyer about untangling this mess tomorrow. Teach the kid more Hebrew and make him forget his mother. Appoint Shlomi and Hilik as his older brothers. Hilik will help him with new words. And Ruchama? He would no longer lie to her or hide things from her. He'd keep yearning for her and would ask for nothing.

A warm wind blew through the windows of the bus that took them home from Tel Aviv. Winter was over. New Hilik sat silently by his side, taking in the view. He didn't even ask questions, didn't cry and never mentioned his mother. When they got to Afula the bus pulled over for a small break and the child drank up the entire bottle of orange juice Robert got him and ate half a pita with falafel.

The whole way there, Robert's mind stirred with familiar words and searched for neighboring ones to provide them meaning. This was the scholarly Hebrew poetry teacher's habit. Sometimes he'd play around with words and their neighbors and Robert did the same now, perhaps wishing to alleviate the beating of his heart. Before, he'd played with the word shutters—shutter, shudder, shatter, shitter, shot-her, chateau, shuttle, subtle. Then he tried to play with the phrase air conditioners—condition, conditioning, conditionary, dictionary, conviction, convection, convict, convent, cogent—but found no meaning and his heart kept beating as they drew closer, and only relaxed when the Sea of Galilee appeared beyond the bus windows, a blue floor across the landscape.

When Ruchama opened the door her eyes went to the child and froze. He clung to Robert's leg and frowned. Shlomi and Hilik sat in the living room silently, amazed. Ruchama had told them earlier that their father was on his way, asked them to wait for him and for the explanations he'd make himself.

Shlomi gave the child a long look and said, "Look, a new Hilik."

Hilik looked at his tiny double and said nothing. Only his eyes widened.

With the child in his lap, clinging and piercing, Robert spoke to his two older sons. This time, he kept some things to himself. Their eyes made it harder for him, as did Ruchama's eyes that were fixed on the child. Suddenly he noticed New Hilik smiling at her. Maybe her height and her dark hair reminded him of his mother. Maybe he found her thick glasses funny. He smiled at her and hid his face in Robert's shirt, and smiled at her again and hid his face again in a kind of mischievous game. Her lips trembled and her eyes grew moist.

"Did you feed him?" she suddenly asked.

"I got him some falafel in Afula."

"Does he speak Hebrew?" asked Shlomi.

"A little," said Robert, "only what I've taught him," and he looked at Hilik, whose eyes were lowered to the floor.

"I'm sorry," whispered Robert, "I wish I could turn back time."

Without raising his head, Hilik suddenly asked, "What's his name?"

"Yechiel," said Robert. "My uncle named him after my father, may he rest in peace."

New Hilik got off his lap and walked towards the aquarium. His face went to the glass and his small finger tapped on it, trying to awaken the fish.

A taut silence was drawn between them, only the child's tapping was heard. Shlomi moved his eyes to Ruchama, awaiting her words.

And she took deep breaths, another and another, and finally said:

"My entire life, people have been telling me I'm an electrical pole, tall like a giraffe. And suddenly I feel small, like a match, like that dwarf in the movie I took you to see once, hiding in a donkey's ear." A small, bitter smile appeared on her face. "I've become Thumbelina. I've always wanted to be tiny."

She took another deep breath, and then looked up at Robert.

"You, Robert, stay in your apartment and raise your son," she said. "And I'll stay here, in my apartment, with my children. You won't come up here, and I won't go down there. We'll run into each other on the stairway once in a while and we'll each go our separate ways. I'll go downstairs and you'll go upstairs, or the other way around, I'll go upstairs and you'll go downstairs."

She turned to Shlomi and Hilik.

"And you two," she said, "he's your father and this boy is your brother. You go see him as often as you want. But you have to swear to tell me nothing. Because if you tell me, my ears will plug shut. I can already feel them closing up, I can hardly even hear myself."

New Hilik kept tapping on the aquarium glass, frustrated by the fish ignoring his calls.

"I'm sorry, Ruchama," whispered Robert. "You won't see me again if you don't want to, I know I deserve it. But I want you to know I'll keep waiting, even an eternity."

And Ruchama raised her voice, "Shut your mouth, Robert." She stood up, went to the kitchen and locked herself in.

Robert opened all the windows of his apartment. The air that burst in was warm but refreshed him and New Hilik. By evening he managed to clean the entire apartment, arrange the boy's things in the closet and change the sheets on the large bed in his room. The child would sleep with him for now, until the longing and the nightmares went away, and then he'd get his own bed, and a small desk, and a place to keep his toys.

To his surprise, New Hilik was in high spirits. He jumped from window to window, drinking in the views of the neighborhood, roaming the rooms, checking every corner, and constantly giggling and chattering excitedly.

Robert drew a bath and sat him down, scrubbed his head and said, "From now on we speak only Hebrew." Then he dressed him in warm pajamas, closed some of the windows because it had grown chilly, and sat him down in front of the television.

Though the air was cool, his body was burning up with sweat. He showered again, trying to wash the day off. In his mind thoughts and plans flew about, mixing with moments from his difficult conversation with Ruchama. Robert wished to relax and began memorizing details from air conditioning class. One teacher asked students to refrain from saying "air conditioning," and to opt instead for "climate control." "Air conditioning is for idiots, anyone can do that," he said, enraged. "We're going to do climate control, which is important and takes expertise and intelligence." And to prove his point he told them the history of this great invention that had changed the world and challenged God's exclusive ability to control nature and the weather. Robert remembered stories of the first air conditioning units installed in hospitals to heal patients suffering from malaria and other ancient diseases that had since disappeared from the world. He chuckled under the cold water. The teachers wanted to excite them, to make them feel the profession was designed to redeem people's misery. For months, they shared their noble thoughts with us, tested our ability to feel, to recognize from afar human situations that involved sadness and pain and to reveal the great knowledge they imparted to us – the miracle of the compressor, the magic of the condenser, the surprising secrets of the carburetor. Benevolent pipes within which gas turned into liquid, heat was pulled away and a soul-enlivening chill was born. Different types of compressors and condensers. And different types of carburetors. He needed to know everything in detail. To know intimately each bolt and each connection and each twist of a cable or a pipe. Like a brilliant brain surgeon.

What did I learn all that history for? All I need is to break open a hole in the wall, push the cube inside and hook it up to the electricity. No one here has enough money to order a serious system, with tin trenches to integrate into the house's structure. No one will ask me to take measurements and figure out climate control. And some of these cheapskates prefer to save and make do with installing the air conditioner in a window, they don't even care about the view. And I oblige. I put the cube there, tighten it and seal the hole, removing landscape and sunlight.

I have to act. I'll go to the printer's, to clothing stores, I'll explain that if they air condition their changing rooms they'll get more customers walking in for cool air who'll end up enriching their poor wardrobes.

Robert closed the faucet and remained standing in the tub.

What's become of me? First, I blocked their view with shutters and now I'll block it with air conditioners.

The scholarly teacher was wrong to make a poet out of me. A poet wouldn't seal off people's homes, wouldn't place them inside of cubes, concealing their childhood landscape.

My childhood hid itself from me. It got up one day and left, secreted away from me. And I, vengeful man that I am – bearing a grudge against fate, taking my revenge upon the world, encouraging the world to hide and push away the landscape of its childhood, to eliminate and ignore.

Robert dried his head with a towel and looked at his body in the mirror. Thin, with wide, strong shoulders. A small, slightly protruding stomach. Tiny. His penis falling on his thigh. Like a meaningless image, he remembered the poetry teacher's favorite expression. Like a meaningless image. It's been months since he'd so much as touched himself. Since Rochelle undressed before him and lit in him a forbidden lust, since then he refused to submit and continued spending his nights in the small room of his neighbors' apartment, since then he hadn't touched himself, hadn't fallen apart. Maybe I should have succumbed to her. Maybe she would have stayed.

When he came out of the bathroom he was surprised to find Shlomi and Hilik sitting in the living room with the new boy. In the hours that had passed since they'd first laid eyes on him, their shock had transformed into a hesitant curiosity. They spoke to him and asked questions. Hilik's eyes were still wide. The child smiled at them and tried to pronounce the fractured Hebrew words he already knew, behaving as if they'd known each other for years. Perhaps Shlomi's height and dark face reminded him of his mother. Perhaps Hilik's appearance reminded him of his deceased father, or of Robert, or maybe of himself. There was not a trace of a frown on his face. His eyes were lit up, they looked like Hilik's eyes.

When he came into the living room, a towel wrapped around his waist, the three boys went silent.

A moment later, Shlomi showed him a pot of stew and explained that Ruchama had cooked it and sent it down, "So you can give the kid some proper food and not just omelets and falafel." The rest of the stew, Shlomi said, she took down to Vardina's place after saying, "That poor woman needs to eat too, I've neglected her for too long," and since then she'd been locked in her neighbor's apartment.

Hilik looked at him and said, "We don't know what to do now." Robert sat down at his side on the bamboo sofa, hugged him and said, "Don't do anything. Whatever will be, will be."

New Hilik looked at him too, his eyes squinting at the wet spot he'd left on the sofa, and finally he smiled and said, "You're cold Robert, wear something warm."

And at night, when his eyes refused to close, he played with words to wear himself out. He remembered the scholarly teacher, who said in one of the classes, "Pay attention to the word 'yearning.' It's a strange, unusual word, it's not even pleasant to the ear." He kneaded the word in his mouth, distorted his lips and his voice, mocking the ridiculous sounds. The students burst out in fawning laughter and began pronouncing comparable words, strange and amusing. Even Robert smiled from his seat at the end of the room. Yearning, burning, spurning, churning, mourning, turning, yearn, yelp, help.

Only the next night did he gather the courage to go downstairs to Vardina's apartment. He wanted to explain himself, to find solace in her words. He knew Ruchama had been to her place the day before, bawling. Her head was in Vardina's lap, he imagined, and her tears were absorbed in the woman's dress as her hand caressed her hair.

The living room was dark and it took him a while to notice her figure. The radio played Mike Brant songs between expressions of sorrow over his sudden death. Had he fallen? Had he jumped? Vardina was sunken into her chair, still, and in her hand a plastic container filled with leftover cooking.

In order to get her body out of the apartment, Robert had to call in five men to join him and the paramedics. The doorway was too narrow and Robert had to break the wall and expand the window overlooking the yard. Once there'd been a pile of sand there that Ella jumped onto from the roof of the building.

A great sorrow blew through the entire building, from its foundations, through the apartment on the third floor, where Ruchama locked herself in her room, and all the way up to the roof, where Shlomi stood, his arm linked with New Hilik's, both of them looking down at the giant elephant body carried out through the hole in the wall. The sorrow moved in waves, spread out and rested upon the entire neighborhood. Neighbors stood and watched from afar. If not for the sadness choking their throats, they might have laughed at the strange image – burly men fighting the giant body of a woman, silently clearing her from the building through a shattered wall, placing her in Robert's old truck, leaving behind them a dark apartment with a shabby chair and a radio that was still playing, because no one was brave enough to turn it off and silence the clear-voiced singing.

9

VARDINA'S LIFE WAS SHORT. THE GREAT CROWD FILLING THE CEMETERY on the shore of the Sea of Galilee would have been amazed to find that she was only fifty-five when she died. People thought she was an old woman and treated her with the kind of respect reserved for village elders. Her immense body was ageless. The skin on her face was tight and shiny, maybe because she was always sweating, and her voice was scorched, though she'd quit smoking four years before and had replaced cigarettes with endless munching on Ruchama's cooking.

Her life was so short and so lonely, thought Ruchama, refusing to accept that she'd been abandoned again, deserted by her best friend, who left her with loneliness as an inheritance.

Many came to pay their respects. Even Adina from the clothing store swallowed her anger for the filching of her silent workman and came to mourn. A great big crowd — it seemed the city had emptied of its inhabitants — all gathered by her grave, most of them her friends and acquaintances, but also several curious parties, wanting to see how the undertakers would deal with the dimensions of the task at hand.

The two lives of Vardina. In the first she was her mother's only child. The two of them lived in Bucharest, and their lives were good and full of plenty. More than once Vardina sighed with the memory of the cream and cherry cakes whose flavor she'd longed for her entire adult life. She never experienced any harassment. She didn't remember anyone mocking them for being Jewish. They hid nothing and were ashamed of nothing. Maybe that's why when she grew up and became a woman she was always suspicious of Jewish refugees and Holocaust survivors. She'd often told Ruchama, "They invent most of their stories to get pity and money and apartments," and Ruchama would cover her ears and say, "My ears hurt from listening to your nonsense. I hope you make sure not to talk this way outside. One day you'll be stoned to death."

Her father died when she was two years old. Her mother removed all his pictures from the house. She told her he died of a disease. Another time she told her a wild horse trampled him. And when she was nine a neighbor in Bucharest told her that her father had been murdered by a devout shoemaker. Her father had bragged and taunted him, cursing Jesus and the pope, until the Christian attacked him and shattered his skull with a cobbler hammer.

Her mother responded derisively. "Your father was agnostic, he didn't care at all about popes or rabbis, he died because he was sick of living," and said no more.

When Vardina was seven, her mother befriended a lonely elderly Christian man who claimed to be a descendent of ancient Romanian aristocracy. Almost every night a car pulled up outside their house to drive Vardina's mother to his mansion on a secluded hill on the outskirts of the city. Vardina herself never visited there. Many nights she stayed home alone but never feared, for the neighbors were kind and made her feel safe. She read till the late hours of the night and ate as she pleased. Despite her young age she was already fluent in two languages, reading and writing in Romanian and French. She was especially passionate about the news and the exciting stories published in Zionist journals. A Jewish newspaper vendor whose stall stood by her building always gave her any Zionist publications and had long talks with her about the redeemed Promised Land. And that's how she came up with the idea of coming to Israel, long before the idea became her mother's sudden decision.

One day, when she returned from the girl's school she hated, because everyone there mocked her fat body, she found a large wooden trunk, in which most of her clothes and possessions were already packed. That very night they went on a long train journey. The trunk was sent to her mother's acquaintances in Jerusalem, and the two of them, dragging small suitcases, began drifting from city to city across Europe. "We need to spend most of our money first," said her mother. "I have too much, I don't want to get to the Holy Land rich, they'll talk about us and won't let us be true pioneers."

And the money was spent in fancy hotels, in beautiful restaurants and luxurious sleeper cars. Vardina didn't understand where the money had come from. Her mother seemed to be escaping some unknown danger. Once she told her it was an inheritance she'd gotten years before. Another time she said she'd sold a piece of antique jewelry. And once, in one of the exquisite cafés in Paris, she told with pride that she'd won the money as an award in her youth, what for, she didn't say. She refused to talk about the elderly aristocrat. When Vardina's questions continued even later, she told her, "Stop asking, just be happy we're in Israel, you got what you wanted."

Her mother didn't like Jerusalem. It was too crowded and she didn't like the way it smelled. Moreover, the very day they arrived she began quarreling with the acquaintances she'd shipped the trunk to. In her opinion, the chisel marks she found on the wood attested to attempted theft. And so, only a week after they arrived in Israel, she took the trunk and Vardina and moved to Tiberias. She told her daughter, "Smart girls like you should grow up by the sea and not by walls and a smelly market and uncultured people."

On their way, she announced to her daughter that from that point on her name would be Vardina. She was starting a new, Hebrew life, with the Hebrew equivalent of her name, and would leave the name Rosalina behind, in Bucharest, along with the cream and cherry cakes.

It was 1930. Vardina was ten years old, a pudgy, energetic child who quickly learned how to chat in Hebrew and a little bit in Arabic, when she spoke with the Arab vendors in the old neighborhood of Tiberias, where she and her mother lived. Since she was already fluent in French, she quickly became the teachers' pet at the Alliance School. The principal, a stern, hard man, forbade children from speaking Hebrew and demanded they speak French even during recess. Those who failed to do so were punished with a ruler on their knuckles. Needless to say, Vardina was never punished. She was often appointed as the student officer, taking down the names of insubordinate children. Loyal to the principal and his rules, she found a way to get back at the kids who mocked her and her weight.

Four years after they'd settled down in Tiberias came the great flood. Vardina's mother ran a small but beloved and popular sewing supply store. From all over northern Israel, customers traveled to buy her sewing needles, knitting needles, buttons and pins. The shelves were covered with pretty articles of clothing she'd found in

Haifa. Customers praised her good taste and bought scarves and hats, embroidered gloves and silk shirts, slips and colorful socks. When Vardina returned from school she'd report to the counter and help her mother. Her mother told her, "Stop haggling so much, we have enough money to live well, the store is for our souls, the main thing is that customers enjoy themselves." And customers shopped and enjoyed themselves, addicted to the stories the mother invented about her European experiences and sharing their troubles with her.

But then came the flood and everything turned on its head. Water drenched the lower city, leaving many families homeless and taking many others' lives. The store was completely flooded. The shelves were torn off the walls and the products flew away with the water. Her mother tried to protect what little she could, fought against the flow and finally was pulled away too, her head banging on the basalt walls.

She was unconscious for days at the Scottish Hospital, Vardina at her side, tending to her and stroking her arms. When she opened her eyes she said, "The clothing store's gone, that's a shame, but don't worry, we still have enough money left." Only later did she realize how badly she'd been hit. Her lower body remained completely paralyzed and she could hardly move her arms.

Vardina didn't go back to school. From age fourteen on, for twenty years she devotedly cared for her mother, until the day she died. They spent most of the time locked in their house. Vardina carried her, bathed her, dressed her, fed her and listened to her words that had grown bitter. Vardina hardly saw anybody, but rumors of her dedication reached all the city people's ears.

Five years before her mother's death, Vardina suggested moving her to a home. "I'm twenty-nine," she said meekly. "I don't have a profession yet, I haven't met a man yet." "You don't need a profession," her mother said drily. "We have enough money." And suddenly she began crying. "If only you knew what I had to do for that money," she said. "You'll never know what I went through for you, and now you want to throw me to the dogs." Then she raised her partially-paralyzed arm with effort and slapped Vardina.

Vardina never brought up the subject again. When she sat down in the evening and swallowed whole loaves of bread with butter or chopped liver, her mother would say with disgust, "What's become of you, Rosalina, who would want to marry an elephant like you? How are you ever going to have children?"

The two lives of Vardina. The first ended when she was thirty-four, with the death of her mother. In the second life she had Ruchama, and she had Robert and Shlomi and Hilik, and they were her entire world.

Between one life and the next, from the day her mother died to the day she met Ruchama on the stairwell, she found herself drifting, working a little, and mostly subsisting on the money she had left over from her mother.

And she met some men. They were all taken by her sense of humor, impressed with her big heart and her broad mind, but she pushed all of them away, protecting the pleasure of her solitude. Vardina was a virgin till the day she died.

About four years before she passed away, she met a man and thought, I'm going to have someone too.

Mr. Rott was a clerk at the Health Maintenance Organization offices, a quiet and gentle man whom everyone knew. He'd come to Israel with his wife, who, like him, was saved from death in the extermination camps. They lived in a small house near the Arab cemetery. His wife was hardly ever seen, spending most of her life in their shuttered house. At night the neighbors heard her nightmarish screams and fragments of the soothing words he told her. In the mornings he'd come to the office red-eyed and dejected, and when anyone dared ask he'd smile sadly and say, "She's in longing, it's hard for her." They had no children.

Mr. Rott was an excellent and efficient clerk, though he only had one arm. He lost his left arm in unknown circumstances, but he moved the right one with wondrous force, using his stump and even his jaws, filing forms in numbered folders with precision, after filling them out in his handsome handwriting. The neighborhood children called him Trumpeldor and giggled, but never to his face[7]. Some said

---

[7] Joseph Trumpeldor was a Zionist activist who lost his arm as a young man in the Russo-Japanese War, and died in Israel during the battle on the settlement of Tel Hai in 1920.

that the original blue number was tattooed on the arm he'd lost and that Mr. Rott himself had carved it into his remaining arm.

"If the story's true," said Ruchama, "then that man is the greatest romantic I've ever met. He didn't want his wife to be left alone with her blue number, the kind only the miserable human powder have."

Vardina laughed loudly and said, "Nonsense, the blue number is always on the right arm," and Ruchama sighed and said, "You don't understand the Holocaust at all."

Finally, when his wife's state worsened, Mr. Rott had to put her in an insane asylum. All at once the windows of his home were pushed open, and his eyes were no longer red.

At the time, Vardina suffered from a painful swelling in her legs. Switching to the apartment on the first floor helped only slightly. She required special bandages, and Mr. Rott took it upon himself to handle her matters. She'd limp to the Health Maintenance Organization, and despite her pain continued to laugh and make jokes, which filled him with wonder. "I've never seen someone as brave as you are," he told her and used his one hand to fill out the forms for her and made sure to send them and call in every day to speed up the process of approving her request.

When the bandages arrived he called and asked for her permission to deliver them personally. To her amazement, Mr. Rott insisted on bandaging her legs with his own hand. Vardina was excited, and acquiesced. He spent a long time leaning at her feet, his one hand wrapping the bandages around her ankles and knees, holding its end with his teeth. When he was finished, as blushing and breathless as she was, he complimented her well-groomed feet and her bright red nail polish.

He visited her each night, had dinner with her, drank tea, and helped her change the bandage. On one occasion, he came equipped with special oil and, to her amazement, asked to massage her aching feet.

His hand felt good and Vardina was pleased beyond belief. His touch was new and surprising, and she closed her eyes and let him undress her, marveling at his quick movements. When she opened her eyes, she saw him standing in front of her, completely nude, his eyes fixed on her huge breasts and large stomach, mumbling words of admiration for her voluptuous body and his penis was stiff and pointed forward. She'd never seen such a thing. She breathed and shook, allowing his hand to travel over her body until she felt something explode inside and a great sense of peace spread through her. Her body lay loosely on the large chair as Mr. Rott rubbed his penis between her feet until his semen sprayed over her swollen ankles.

Words escaped her, and so she consented silently when he asked to sleep at her side that night. She stayed up, watching him, incredulous that her fate had summoned this for her. She remembered she'd once told Ruchama, "You and Robert, all you have on your mind is the body," and smiled to herself, about to understand something that had no words yet. She wondered what Ruchama would say when she told her, if she ever did. She might laugh at her, might encourage her, might warn her against this man who'd fallen in love with her feet. Rosalina finally found herself a man. Went to the Health Maintenance Organization and found a Trumpeldor.

Mr. Rott slept on his side, his eyes closed and his stump exposed. For the first time in her life, a naked man slept by her side. For the first time in her life she herself slept naked. It was also the first time she'd touched herself, careful not to disturb him, until she felt that same trembling, became peaceful and fell asleep.

Early in the morning, she woke up and limped to the bathroom. A moment later, Mr. Rott woke up and surprised her by clinging to her under the hot water. He burned with passion again and whispered in her ear, "I want to really sleep with you," and she mumbled shyly, "I'm a virgin."

Mr. Rott turned quiet. It seemed he was scared. He got dressed in silence, but before he left he asked if he could return at lunch time. Vardina nodded excitedly.

At noon he asked to cut his workday short. It was Holocaust Memorial Day and his boss understood and let him go and be alone with his painful memories. Mr. Rott hurried home, bathed, put on cologne and rushed over to see Vardina, who was waiting for him.

On the stairs, he met Shlomi who had just returned home, wearing a white shirt for the Holocaust Memorial Day ceremony that was held at school. Shlomi, who knew Mr. Rott from the organization, smiled politely and chirped, "Happy holiday!"

Mr. Rott was astonished. He stopped Shlomi firmly with his one hand and asked him to explain his greeting.

Shlomi was confused, but finally said, "Today is Holocaust Memorial Day, and that's your holiday," before running for dear life.

Vardina's attempts to explain and appease did no good. "He's a little boy, he's not even ten yet," she said. "He just tried to be nice and made a mistake." But Mr. Rott was enraged and demanded to see Ruchama.

He screamed at her for a long time, chastising her for how badly she'd brought up Shlomi. "You should be ashamed of yourself," he yelled. "Is this what we deserve after all our suffering? To have a stupid, ignorant kid laugh at us?" Ruchama stood across from him in Vardina's apartment, her head bowed. She apologized and promised to punish Shlomi, but Mr. Rott wouldn't let it go.

"I'll punish him myself," he said.

"What will you do to him?" Vardina cried. Till that moment she'd been waiting quietly for things to calm down.

"I'll show him, telling me 'happy holiday' on Holocaust Day," announced Mr. Rott. "I'm going to give him a slap in the face."

Vardina's face turned white, the blood pumped through her aching knees. "Get out of here," she told him, "right now."

He looked at her questioningly. "Are you sending me away?" he asked.

"Take your feet and get lost," she yelled, "And don't show your face here again."

Mr. Rott froze in place. His eyes filled with sadness. He nodded again and again and finally told Ruchama, "I promise you, I'm going to complain about him at the Ministry of Education, and I'll complain about you, too."

Vardina lumbered towards the door, opened it and said, "If you dare complain about that kid and if you even touch him, I'll go to your workplace and tell everyone how you planned to celebrate Holocaust Memorial Day. I'll shame you so badly you won't dare leave your house again."

Mr. Rott looked at her for a long moment, tears in his eyes, and then walked out the door and never returned.

When Ruchama asked, "What was he doing here, anyway?" Vardina said, "He delivered the bandages I ordered." And when the door closed and she was left alone she sank into her chair and wailed.

Ruchama punished Shlomi. She ordered him to stay out of the kitchen for two weeks and devote most of his time to the books she'd borrowed from the library. Shlomi obeyed with unusual discipline and read about the Final Solution, about the Nazis and the death camps. He was sick with regret for insulting the gentle, miserable handicapped man.

Vardina cheered him up. When he tired of the dark books he'd go downstairs to her apartment. She'd feed him tea and cookies, tell him her funny stories and play a trivia game with him. To help him memorize his materials, she suggested they add a Holocaust category to their game, swearing him to secrecy. For E they wrote down "Eichmann," for B they wrote down "Buchenwald." For K, "Kristallnacht." G was the easiest letter. It had many possibilities – ghetto, Goebbels, gas chambers.

She never saw Mr. Rott again. Since he left, she sank into her chair more and more often. The bandages didn't help and her pain worsened. As catering orders rushed in, her fridge filled up with leftovers. Ruchama and Shlomi did wonders in their kitchen and Vardina gave herself up to the abundance. And so her body became bloated, and when she died Robert had to break through the window to get her body out and lead her to burial.

*

A day before she died, Ruchama came to see her and told her about New Hilik. She sat at her feet, put her head in her lap, wept for a long time and broke Vardina's heart.

After Ruchama left, Vardina went to the fridge, took out a plastic container full of delicacies and sat back down in her chair. The radio kept reporting Mike Brant's sudden death and playing his songs. Sorrow is coming at me from all directions, Vardina thought and began chewing. All at once she felt light. To her surprise, she was satiated. Even her knee pain was gone, replaced with a pleasant tickle. She blushed, thinking about things she wanted. The radio played a cheerful song, "*Elle a gardé ses yeux d'enfant ma mere,*" sang Mike Brant, *my mother's eyes remained the eyes of a child*, and suddenly Vardina smiled. If she hadn't been so shy she might have started dancing.

10

SHLOMI LAY ON THE ROOF AMONG THE WATER HEATERS, HIS ARMS resting on the edge of the concrete, his head leaning forward and his eyes staring at the pile of sand that remained ever since their beloved neighbor passed away.

After her funeral, Robert made sure to fix the wall he broke. Shlomi and Hilik helped him unload the blocks from the truck, take them to the yard and place them near the sacks of cement. New Hilik was appointed to keep an eye on the toolbox. One of the neighbors, a building contractor, volunteered to provide the necessary mortar. Thus, with the help of his three sons, Robert took charge of the task. The wall had been fixed, the window replaced, Robert even spackled and painted and cleaned, but the sandpile remained in place. Only a small part of it was used and the rest stayed, like a strange monument, a large sand belly lying in the yard for almost eight months.

From his spot on the roof the pile looked to Shlomi like a warm yellow bed. He was plagued with a strong urge to jump down to the sand, float through the air and crash into it. Just as Ella did, years ago, before she ever went to Sugarloaf Mountain. Maybe he'd break open his own leg, a splintered bone peeking out. Maybe his entire body would shatter, his limbs scattering in all directions, and the yearning would drop out of his heart and he'd finally have peace and quiet. Maybe then his mind would finally stop taking down and gathering and collecting things that had been and things that were only now hatching, fragments of speech and shrapnels of crying, swirling fumes of rage and tight waves of longing, and countless words, sandpiles of words.

And then, as he watched the sand, he heard a small chirp. His mind noted that as well. It was a baby's cry, coming from Ella and Hanna's building. The baby was only born two weeks before and now he was crying, letting his mother know he was hungry. And Hanna quickly warmed up some milk, put it in a bottle and would soon feed and tend to her new son.

Shlomi had left her apartment a few minutes ago. She even let him hold the baby and he felt a longing in his heart. Then he left, upset, and went upstairs to lie on the roof, his eyes clinging to the sandpile and his entire body filled with yearning. Yearning for Ella, whom he hadn't seen for months. Yearning for Hanna, whom he only had once and since then had longed for to no end. And a sudden yearning for the baby who was now crying.

From elsewhere in the neighborhood he heard the radio. Someone was speaking about 1975, which was coming to an end. They mentioned a man named Carlos who, only yesterday, masterminded a terrorist attack at some important event in Europe, and they said his hostages were now being flown to an Arab country and that their lives were in danger. One speaker claimed that this event symbolized and summarized the entire year, a cursed year of confusion and poverty, of urges undermining the logic of the entire world. He sounded worried, his angry voice overtaking the others, growing grating and violent. But then the radio was turned off and Shlomi's ears tuned in once again to the baby's crying.

A little over nine months had passed since the donkey had gone wild, wounding Ella. The next day, Shlomi went to school, sick to his stomach due to the chocolate he'd gorged on the previous night. It was the last school day before the Passover vacation and all the kids were talking about the crazy donkey, sharing rumors and transforming the animal into a horrific beast. Some claimed their parents were going to demand that the police put the dangerous animal down. Some announced they would not go to scout meetings anymore because of the irresponsible counselors. In the lower classes, teachers instructed students to paint pictures and write get-well-soon cards for the students who were still in the hospital.

Shlomi sat in his place at the end of the row and refrained from speaking. He was silent even when asked to share his experience. Ella wasn't at school and he was worried. Now and then, images of the previous day appeared in his mind, but he pushed them all away – the cat flying through the air, the dead twins smiling over the baby's bed at the crybaby teacher's house, Ella's shoulder ripped and bleeding in his hands, Hanna's naked body lowering onto him.

At recess, Shlomi took his bag, snuck through a hole in the back fence and left school. He ran the whole way and knocked on her door. He knocked again and again but there was no answer. He climbed on the stone wall and peeked inside Ella's room. Her bed was empty and unmade. He waited for hours, until he saw Hanna's blue car approaching and parking alongside the path. Hanna got out and walked toward him.

Her eyes were red. "I had to take her back to the hospital," she said. "She's burning up, she must have gotten an infection." Her shoulders were slouched tiredly and her eyes escaped his. "I only came to pick up some things, then I have to get back."

"Can I come with you?" he asked.

"You shouldn't."

"Why?"

Hanna hesitated. She looked at him for the first time, and they both shivered. "Go home now," she said in a stifled voice, "and don't come back." For a moment she touched his cheek, and then she turned around and went inside, closing the door behind her and not opening it again, even as Shlomi knocked again and again and begged her to.

Day after day, all throughout the Passover vacation, he appeared at their door and kept trying. At first he'd stand on the roof, on the lookout, and when he saw Hanna returning from the hospital he'd hurry down the stairs, run down the path, knock on the door, only to be ignored. Only once did he hear her say, "Please leave." Another time he cornered her in the stairway, blocking her way. "I just want to know how Ella is. I want to know if I can visit her," he begged, and she said, "Israella doesn't want to see anybody. Stop giving me a hard time, Shlomi. I have it hard enough as it is."

He spent the rest of the vacation lying around the living room, staring at the television, or wandering the neighborhood. Once he even went to Moshik's shack and called to him from outside. Moshik opened the window and said, "My parents won't let me out." And when Shlomi told him, "Ella's in the hospital," Moshik answered, "I don't care about the two of you anymore," went back inside and shut the window.

When the unease expanded to block his lungs, he asked Ruchama to let him help her cook, but she said, "No, no, go play with your friends and forget about the kitchen."

He spent the Passover Seder at Robert's. Ruchama was tired from all the cooking and went to sleep. The fried meat Robert cooked bled on his plate and eliminated what little appetite he had.

"You're just pecking at it, you hardly put anything in your mouth," Robert scolded. "You've become as thin as an African boy and pale as a wall. What's with you?"

Shlomi apologized and sat in front of the television. Then he went up to Ruchama's apartment and took a long shower, his third that day, scrubbing his body and trying to empty it of unease.

The Passover vacation was over. Ella hadn't returned to school. The seat next to him remained orphaned, his ears blocked out the teachers' words and he returned his high school prep test sheets blank. Reuma-Dumba gave him a letter to pass on to Ruchama, in which she expressed her worry regarding his grades, but Shlomi tore the letter up. In the long hours he spent sitting still, his back rubbing against the thumbtacks, he tried to figure out why he'd been locked out, why she was ostracizing him. Occasionally, to calm his nerves, he pulled out recipes from the shelves in his memory or invented new ones, but his mouth remained dry and flavorless.

On Holocaust Memorial Day, while the school held a morose ceremony, Shlomi snuck out again to lurk for Hanna and force her to speak with him. A wire from the opening in the fence caught on the sleeve of his white shirt and made a small hole. This angered him, and he grabbed the sleeve and tore it off. The whole way to Ella and Hanna's house he kicked stones, crushed flowers and overturned garbage cans. He punched at the closed door, too, pummeling with fists and feet in his rage, and only stopped when he heard the voice of Mrs. Katz. The old teacher was frightened by the sounds and had gone out to the stairway. "Is that you, Shlomi?" she called from upstairs. "Why are you making so much noise? And why is your shirt torn?" And Shlomi ran away.

He went to Vardina's next. He knew he could hide from Ruchama's questions in her home. When she opened the door she noticed the torn sleeve and his face trembling with anger.

"What's wrong, Shlomi?" she asked, worried. "Did you get into a fight?"

"Yes," he said and fixed her with a burning glare.

"Who with?"

"Nobody."

"And why are you looking at me like that, like some sort of crazy animal? Stop making those mean eyes or I'll punish you right now."

"How exactly are you going to punish me?" he muttered.

"I'll sit on you." Vardina smiled. "I'll squish you till you scream with pain and beg me to get up before I turn you into a pita."

All at once, he thawed and burst into laughter.

Then she ordered him to get her sewing kit from the cabinet, and with a skillfulness that surprised him, reattached the sleeve and even sewed the small hole.

"Why don't you tell me what's been eating you lately," she suggested, and Shlomi shrugged. "Are you worried about going to high school and taking your exams?" she asked and didn't wait for an answer before adding, "Don't worry so much, not everyone has to go to school. What you know about cooking nobody could ever teach."

The next day, Robert came by and installed two air conditioning units in Ruchama's apartment. When Shlomi returned from another silent school day the project was underway. Hilik helped Robert and Ruchama cooked a lovely meal. The apartment was filled with forgotten aromas and excitement, but these were lost on Shlomi. He ate a little, announced he was going out to meet friends, and left.

That morning, when Reuma said Ella was recovering and her mother asked to refrain from visiting her, he made a decision. He'd make his own way to the hospital and surprise her. His heart told him she was lying there, waiting for him. Hanna was the one stopping him, pushing him away.

He ran up the main road, turned near the soccer stadium, skipped up the stairs alongside Zvi Forest and stopped for air only when he reached the edge of the hill. He only stood there for a few seconds, breathing the air and watching the sea and the pine thicket, where Tiberians claimed frightening jackals and other animals were hiding.

Maybe two hours had passed since he'd left the apartment. He crossed the upper city and the fields and finally made it to Poria Hospital. His clothes were soaked through with sweat and his face flushed with excitement.

Ella lay in a hospital bed with her eyes closed. Her room was small and clean and had only one bed below a large and sunny window. Shlomi sat down quietly, careful not to wake her. She'd lost some weight. Her pale pallor suited her, emphasizing her long lashes. Shlomi wanted to touch her, to feel the heat of her body, to press his lips against it, to embrace her shoulders and hold her close to his heart. He breathed carefully. Heavy odors of cleaning substances and the sour smell of a hospital.

Ella shifted. She opened her eyes and looked at him immediately, not the least bit surprised to see him, as if he'd been sitting there for days or even weeks. Her eyes rested on him but were aloof and distant, and she said nothing, even when he smiled and asked how she was.

Then she pulled over a tray of food. She ate her lunch silently, her eyes and hands busy with the cold soup, the white mash and the gray meatballs, ignoring him completely.

When she was finished eating, she got up, picked up the tray and left the room. Only then did Shlomi see that her shoulder wasn't even bandaged. The hospital gown was too big for her and fell off her wounded shoulder, exposing it. Only a twisted scar remained, and some yellow iodine stains. He kept sitting there, breathless, alert to anything that would help him understand.

When she returned to the room she sat on her bed and looked at him.

"You're sweating," she said finally. "How did you get here?"

"I walked," he said.

"It's very far," she said, suddenly tired.

"That's all right, I wanted to see you."

"You're a stupid boy," she said, and Shlomi looked at her face, trying to find a spark or a smile.

She got up again and locked herself in the bathroom adjacent to the room. Then she came out, washed her hands in the sink and sat back down on the bed.

"That day with the donkey ruined me," she said tiredly. "It hurt at night and I was cold. I only pretended to sleep so she'd leave me alone."

She went silent. Tears appeared in her eyes. She blinked, trying to dry them, her eyes turned to the window, no longer looking into his.

"But I couldn't fall asleep. Because it hurt like hell, and also because the dryer was making a terrible noise and shaking the entire apartment. Maybe I was asleep and only dreamed I wasn't, I don't know, maybe I was having dreams I didn't want."

She looked at him again, her eyes cool.

"Finally I couldn't take it anymore. The wound was burning like a bonfire. I wanted to ask her for a pill but I found her asleep in the kitchen, on the chair, wrapped in a blanket. I didn't want to wake her, so I swallowed all the pills I could find, and only then she woke up and took me straight to the hospital. Too bad. I wanted to sleep so badly and they wouldn't let me."

Her words pounded him. A pain shot from his neck down his back.

Ella lay down and covered herself. "Now leave," she said. "She'll be here soon."

"I'll come back tomorrow," he whispered.

"No," she said.

"Why?"

"I don't want you to."

And before he left her room she said, "Don't save me anymore."

And he hadn't seen her since.

He ran the whole way home and arrived in the evening, his clothes drenched in sweat. The new air conditioners were working, the living room was clean and Ruchama and Robert were standing around, smiling. Shlomi whispered, "It's so cold in the apartment," and locked himself in the bathroom to wash his body in boiling water.

Then he lay down in bed. The apartment was quiet. Robert had gone back downstairs, blushing and hopeful, and Ruchama, no less moved, went to the kitchen to wash the dishes.

Hilik sat by him, looking at him with worry, and said, "You're overdoing it with the hot water, your body is red like a monkey's ass," and Shlomi said, "I like it like this."

"You went to see her in the hospital, right?" Hilik asked and Shlomi didn't answer. "It's about time you explain to me why you've been acting like a psycho," Hilik said resolutely.

"Leave me alone," Shlomi muttered and looked away.

"You're not leaving me much choice," said Hilik, determined, and turned to leave the room.

"What are you going to do?"

"Talk to Mom. It's about time she knew you were a psycho and took care of you."

"Don't you dare, Hilik, if you go talk to her I'll finish you."

Hilik turned to leave again, but Shlomi grabbed his shirt and pulled hard. Hilik was pulled back and fell over, his head banging the wall. He got up immediately, pounced on Shlomi and began hitting him with both hands. Shlomi slapped him. Hilik lost all control, climbed on top of him, scratching and kicking and punching, and Shlomi kneed him in the belly.

They wrestled like that until Ruchama heard them yelling and came over and ripped Hilik away from Shlomi and shouted at both of them.

"Since when do you fight?" she asked after they'd calmed down a bit. "What are you fighting about all of a sudden?" and they said nothing.

Only after she'd left the room, Hilik said, "I'm not talking to you anymore."

He hadn't seen Ella again since visiting the hospital. And that entire time, and even now, lying on the roof, her cold eyes pierced him and her words bubbled within him. At first he wanted more than anything to ask what they meant, but with time that feeling transformed into a lump of anger and hatred. How could anger and resentment live inside of him alongside his longing, moving together within him in an exhausting storm?

The passing days only added more quandaries.

For example, the day New Hilik suddenly appeared and Robert sat them down in the living room and told them confusing stories.

And the day Vardina died.

And the day Tehila came to visit and Ruchama told her Hanna was pregnant. They whispered in the kitchen and suddenly Ruchama began weeping. And Shlomi, from his seat in the living room, could hear Tehila appeasing his mother. "Enough, Ruchama, don't exaggerate, not every pregnancy you see is from Robert," and Ruchama answered through her tears, "I don't know him anymore. He must have seen her and lied to me like he did all the other times. He's punishing me for being defective."

Days of quandaries, longing and hatred. And all of them went by so quickly. Almost every day he went up on the roof to look at Hanna going out and returning home, and every day her belly was bigger. One day, his teacher, Reuma-Dumba, told him that Ella had gotten better and returned home, but wouldn't be coming to school anymore. The school year was almost over, and next year she would transfer to a special boarding school in Jerusalem. "It's a place for excellent children," said the teacher. "Israella took some exams and she is a gifted child, we're all very proud of her."

They celebrated their elementary school graduation in a big ceremony. Ruchama made all the refreshments herself, and again she didn't succumb to Shlomi's begging to help her. At night, the whole class climbed to the peak of Mount Tabor to watch the sunrise together. Shlomi agreed to link arms with Genia, and even acquiesced when she clung to him and rubbed up against him. But Ella's words kept pecking at him through the summer vacation and the first months of ninth grade.

Shlomi was accepted to the mechanics and metalworking class, a class where the weak students from all the city's elementary schools were collected. When Ruchama came in to complain, Reuma-Dumba told her, "You should be grateful we didn't hold him back a grade with his low marks."

Ruchama, still weak and pale since her life had been overturned and Vardina had died, said meekly, "But it's a class that doesn't even take the matriculation exam, how will he make it without matriculating?"

"He wouldn't have passed the exams anyway," the teacher said. "But don't worry, he has excellent hands, he can be a locksmith or work on air conditioners with his father."

Shlomi sat in the back row in high school too, leaning against the wall. The classroom was more spacious than the one he'd had in elementary school, but cheerless, the walls devoid of decorations and thumbtacks and the windows barred. During recess he'd sit in the corner of the hallway, chewing on a white cheese and cucumber sandwich and looking at the students. His old classmates had grown all at once, their arms and legs sprawling and small mustaches adorning their faces. But they were scattered in different classes and barely spoke to him. Moshik went to a different high school. Sometimes he saw him on the street, folded inside himself and wearing a *yarmulke*, according to his new school's rules. Once or twice, he noticed Shlomi and asked if he had a job for him in Ruchama's cooking business, and told him that after school he had to work as a porter for measly pay to help out at home.

Ruchama abandoned her attempts and returned to her old meat and fish stews. Shlomi no longer tried to convince her to let him cook again. She hired two helpers, women wearing headscarves who obeyed her every word. Robert ran around with his air conditioners. The rough summer brought a blessing to his expanding business. He enrolled New Hilik in a nearby kindergarten. Sometimes Shlomi agreed to drop the boy off at school in the morning, pick him up at noon, and stay with him until Robert returned from work. Shlomi made him lunch, impressed by his appetite for meat, listened to his amusing chatter and wondered silently at how this new boy was able to spread light around him. Whenever he saw Ruchama in the stairway, he jumped on her, hugging her with his thin arms, forcing her to bend down to him and wetting her cheeks with kisses. And when he called her name, his Rs rolled like Robert's. Rrrrruchama. Rrrrrruchama.

He hardly saw Hilik. His brother spent most of his time outside the house, concentrating on the eighth grade or scout meetings, and he was even appointed assistant counselor, and spent the rest of his time helping Robert with the air conditioners, fighting for attention, threatened by a small, heart-tugging double.

And now Shlomi lay on the roof, looking at the sandpile below, his heart wishing to jump, float in the air for long seconds and crash.

That morning he'd gone to the grocery store and heard the neighbors talking. Some of them were speaking of Carlos's terror attack the previous day. Others mentioned Hanna, the Polish woman who worked at the absorption center and had a baby a few days prior. "It's a crying shame," one neighbor said. "Look what's become of us, a widow giving birth without a husband, even the gentiles would be appalled." And she sighed deeply.

After school Shlomi returned to the roof to watch over the path to her building. A few minutes later, he saw her stepping out of a cab with the baby in her arms, wrapped in a blue blanket.

Shlomi waited a little, and when he felt his lungs about to burst he got down from the roof and went to knock on her door. This time she opened it, her face bright and smiling and even the sack of skin stretched out and no longer vibrating, and invited him in.

The baby was on the sofa, his eyes open and his face calm. "Look at his beautiful eyes," she whispered. "All the doctors and nurses said they'd never seen such a long baby."

She picked him up, careful not to unwind the blue blanket. "I haven't bought him a bed yet," she said and brought the baby to her face, breathing his scent and checking his temperature with her lips. "Israella is very busy at her boarding school in Jerusalem and can't come help. But I'm doing all right. He's so calm and nice."

"What's his name?" he asked.

"Shmuel," she said, "for my late husband."

She ran her lips over his small lips again, her eyes closed, beaming.

And then she asked Shlomi to sit down and put the baby in his arms.

To his surprise, his breath relaxed at once. The touch of the baby spread a pleasurable sensation in him and his body loosened, as if all the tension accumulated and hardened over the past months had been sucked out. He breathed him in, the scent of soap and sour milk, looked at his face, seeking and finding similarities to himself, strong and clear.

A new Shlomi.

His head was emptied of noises. His eyes were linked with the baby's cloudy gaze and only looked up at Hanna when she said, "I'm not staying here."

She sat next to Shlomi and told him she'd decided to move to Haifa. "The air is good and it's a nice place to raise kids."

Shlomi trembled, hesitated for a long time and then asked, "Do I need to go with you?"

"Why?"

"Because of the baby," he whispered.

Hanna laughed and placed a soft hand on his shoulder. "Of course not," she said. "You need to be here and help your parents. Don't worry, I'll do fine." Then she added, "You aren't even fifteen yet, Shlomi, it's best if you forget a little, you remember too much, it's unhealthy."

Before he left, when they stood by the door, he asked her, "When the baby grows up, will you tell him about me?"

Hanna didn't answer, only ran her hand down his neck, kissed his cheek and shut the door behind him.

He sat on the stone wall and the noises returned to his head. Ella's cold look, the words she'd spoken. She was in pain that night. The sound of the dryer kept her from sleeping. She got up and looked for her mother.

He remembered their visit to the crybaby teacher's house. He wouldn't hold the baby then, afraid he'd drop him. And now his hands were longing, asking him to let them hold the new baby, protect him from pain. His hands wanted out of his body, his legs threatened to run into hiding, and his eyes wished to close forever. Every part of my body wants something different, he thought. They're all fighting and rumbling. Ruchama once told me, "You're like a poem with too many tenses." I want to break all the tenses apart so they scatter. I'm a child and I have a child.

He rose with effort, walked the path, climbed the stairs and went out onto the roof, where he lay on his stomach among the water heaters, his head bent forward and his eyes fixed on the yellow sandpile.

The chirping of the baby he'd just held in his arms sounded from Hanna's apartment. From another direction came the harsh words of a radio. Then the radio was turned off and only the crying went on.

"Don't save me anymore," she'd said.

Shlomi closed his eyes.

If he'd opened them and looked down, to the yard, he'd have seen many things:

Hanna standing on her balcony, dusting off a suitcase, preparing for a trip.

Hilik leaving for a scout meeting, quickening his steps.

Robert and New Hilik in the yard, looking for an anthill.

Ruchama helping the quiet workman carry the stews she'd cooked.

Robert standing right in front of her while she treated him as if he were air, ignoring him.

But the child made that difficult, running to her and hugging her, rolling her name around in his mouth. Rrrrrruchama, Rrrrrrrruchama.

Without a choice, she patted his head, her lips trembling.

Robert pulled the child away from her, took him inside, and Ruchama continued helping the workman. Suddenly she stopped; maybe she'd heard the baby crying.

If he had opened his eyes, he would have seen how from above it seemed that everyone could see everyone else, but he would have immediately understood that this was not the case; there were plants in the way, and fences, and building corners obstructing views. Only from above did his world look flat and teeming with action.

His eyes remained closed and just the chirping cry sounded in his ears. The touch of her lips still warm on his cheek. She has a new baby, a new Shlomi, a newborn. One day he'll grow up and will never know I am his father.

All of a sudden he opened his eyes, stood up and jumped forward.

He floated through the air for several seconds. His arms spread out, hitting the wind.

This is exactly what she'd felt back then, when she jumped, years ago, before she went to Sugarloaf Mountain.

Wind blew alongside his body, nice and cool, a multitude of smells flowed into his nose.

The day Ella returned the world was scorching and filled with sand. And now Shlomi was falling onto the sandpile. Suddenly he smiled to himself, in midair. *From right to left only sand.* Sometimes Robert sang that song for them and made funny faces, rolling his Rs on purpose. *Rrrrrak khol va'khol,* only sand and sand.

Rrrrrrruchama. Rrrrrrruchama.

As he landed, he remembered; it all flew through his mind. Her blue car. Thunder and lightning. A howling cat. A crazy donkey. Hilik waving his white arms and then widening his eyes at his new brother.

New Hilik. New Shlomi. New Hilik. New Shlomi.

His legs hit the sandpile and sank. His body was thrown forward, feeling the sand's warmth, his clothes were covered in sand that went into his eyes and nostrils.

He felt no pain.

No bones were broken, no blood flowed. The soft sand accepted him like a cloud.

My body is iron, he thought, refusing to fall apart, trying to teach me a lesson.

I won't wait an eternity anymore.

He got up, shook his clothes and went upstairs.

*

Ruchama finally caved. For two weeks she begged him, even tried dragging him out of bed in the mornings, but Shlomi insisted. "I'm not going to that stupid school anymore, and don't try to make me, Ruchama, I'm stronger than you." She asked Hilik to speak with him, and that didn't help, either. Then she tried to entice him, promised she'd let him cook again, but he was intent and determined, "I want to open my own business and move away, I'm sick of this place."

"You're scaring me, Shlomi," she said. "You've become hard."

"I don't care," he said dryly.

Left without a choice, she called Robert, shared what had happened with him and finally gave in.

Shlomi agreed to the condition his parents set. Together they would find an evening school and he'd promise to study seriously and do well on matriculation exams. If he worked hard, he'd be able to complete the course in two years, maybe less.

In early 1976 Shlomi and Robert went to Tel Aviv. Robert helped Shlomi arrange his clothes in the familiar room in the elderly couple's apartment. He paid them generously and they promised to take good care of the tall boy with the pretty eyes who had suddenly appeared in their lives.

Then he enrolled him in evening school, paid the entire tuition in advance and told him, "I trust you to keep your promise."

When they finished having lunch at a restaurant in the Yemenite quarter Shlomi suddenly got up from the table and walked confidently into the kitchen. In front of the cooks' and manager's amazed eyes he took some vegetables from the boxes and demonstrated his abilities. Before the manager was able to protest, the vegetables were already emptied and ready to be stuffed. His quick hands moved as in a magic show, all his yearning burst onto the work counter, and the manager had no choice but to set the terms of his employment.

In the mornings, before the sun even came up, he'd report to the restaurant and pounce on the fresh produce that came in from the nearby Carmel Market. Not a week had gone by before the menu was updated with new dishes he'd invented or extracted from his memory. Customers sang his praises and the restaurant manager, still amazed at The Wonder, which was how he called Shlomi with a smile, doubled his salary.

In the evenings he'd wash up quickly in the restaurant's sink and hurry to school, then back to his room. Within two weeks he convinced Robert to let him stay in the small apartment which he hadn't sold and was just collecting dust. The elderly couple, who'd grown attached and were very sorry to see him go, helped him move his things and give the neglected apartment a thorough cleaning.

Shlomi painted the walls and used the money he made to buy new furniture and a small television. The only old item of furniture he kept was the bed, which he moved inside from the balcony, arranging a nice sitting corner in its place.

His lungs opened and his mind grew clearer.

On weekends he'd go to Tiberias, listen patiently to Ruchama as she begged him to come home, consult with her on cooking and exchange recipes. Then he'd play catch for a while with Robert's new kid, and spend the rest of his time with Hilik, who helped him with school work.

Occasionally Noam, the manager, gave him the day off, begging him to go out for a bit, maybe even to the beach to woo pretty girls. But Shlomi devoted all his spare time to school and to planning new dishes, which he experimented with in his small kitchen, inviting the elderly couple to taste and marvel.

On one of his days off, he went to Ella's boarding school in Jerusalem. The secretary told him with excitement that Israella and her classmates were guests at a special Knesset committee meeting and were then invited for a tour of the studios of Kol Israel public radio, and might even visit the national television network studios in Romema. Shlomi thanked her and declined to leave a message or a note.

The following day, he took the train to Haifa. He'd gotten Ilan na's address beforehand by calling the absorption center in Tiberias, and they happily obliged. He saw her from a distance, stepping out of a tall building in the Neve Sha'anan neighborhood, pushing little Shmuel in a colorful stroller, smiling, her straw hair blowing in the wind and her lips mumbling children's gibberish, inviting bursts of laughter from the child. Shlomi didn't approach her and Hanna didn't notice him. His arms wanted to hold the baby again. His body wanted to explode. Finally he got hold of himself, went to the train station and returned to Tel Aviv.

One day, Tehila came to visit. She surprised him, walking into the restaurant and asking for someone to summon him from the kitchen. Shlomi was happy to see her and filled her table with goodies. The other diners recognized her from her appearances on television, in which she decisively articulated her political doctrine and cried out in the name of the oppressed. Noam shook her hand warmly. "It's an honor," he said, excited. "We all hope you get into the Knesset in the next election and can represent us. We need more good people like you." And when he realized she was Shlomi's aunt he put his hands together and said, "You're a family of pure gold."

When the turmoil died down, Tehila asked Shlomi to sit with her for a bit. They drank mint tea and Shlomi told her about school. She listened with a smile and finally said, "Ruchama sent me to try and convince you to come home, but I see you're happy here."

Before she left, she suddenly remembered something and asked, "Did you hear about what happened to Moshik, the neighbor's kid in your class?" and then she told him of the event that shocked all of Tiberias. A few days prior, Moshik woke up in the middle of the night. His father had come home for a short break from reserve duty. Moshik picked up his father's army rifle and fired off rounds at everyone in the house. The neighbors heard the shots and hurried over. When they managed to break the door down, they found Aliza and Rachamim and the three little boys dead, punctured through with bullets. Moshik sat on the floor in the corner of the shack, the gun still in his hands, staring into the air.

Shlomi was silent. He looked at Tehila and refused to believe it.

Finally he asked, "How could I have not heard anything? The papers didn't say anything about it, and it wasn't on the news."

Tehila sighed. "That's the way it is in small places like Tiberias. They hush everything up, maybe out of consideration for whatever family poor Moshik still has left, or maybe out of shame that the city has people like him."

She finished the last drops of her tea, smoothed her hand softly over Shlomi's face and said, "And maybe Tiberias is in a different country altogether, a country they don't write about in Israeli papers, a hot, sweaty country where the air stands still and people fight to walk through it, one step and then another, like in a pool of sand."

Part 3

1983

1

Hilik was killed on a Wednesday in the middle of spring.

News of his death only reached Shlomi at night, many hours after he was already cold and wordless.

That morning, Shlomi turned to Noam, who had once been his boss in the Yemenite quarter and who at some point over the years had made Shlomi a full partner in the restaurant, and said, "So strange, I feel like the weather's been cancelled." Noam laughed and Shlomi explained, "I'm not kidding, I really can't feel any weather, no wind and no rain and no heat and no hail or haze. My skin can't decide if it's cold or hot or anything."

"You've been talking too much nonsense lately," Noam said and chuckled. "I think you haven't been getting enough sleep. You'll end up cutting off your finger, you're so tired."

At noon, Ruchama called and they discussed cooking. She asked Shlomi to get a few bunches of green garlic at the Carmel Market, because she couldn't find any at the Tiberias Market, and had sent the silent workman to the Arab villages of Kafr Kana and Maghar and even to the Nazareth Market and he'd returned empty-handed. Shlomi promised to get some and send it over and then told her about the missing weather.

"Here the wind is out and about just like any other Wednesday," Ruchama said, "It's lucky I took the laundry down in time, or the wind would have ripped it away along with the clothesline."

The two didn't know that at that time, Hilik's body was being evacuated in a helicopter. A bullet had penetrated his skull and killed him in one quick moment.

The only one who knew anything was Tehila. She sat with her party members in their office in the Knesset building. As they heatedly discussed the vote that was to take place later that day, the party secretary came in and told them of an accident that took place in southern Lebanon, two soldiers killed. Tehila still didn't know one of them was Hilik. Only hours later, when the heavy sensation was stifling her throat, she called her friends in the Ministry of Defense. They made some calls and confirmed her fears in small voices. During a routine reconnaissance tour, Hilik's platoon was caught in the midst of friendly fire. Another platoon was conducting improvised training in a nearby shooting range without giving necessary notice. A sudden strong wind must have hindered the stability of those firing weapons or shifted the bullets from their planned course.

Tehila pulled all her contacts in order to delay the message from reaching Ruchama and Robert. She wanted to pick up Shlomi in Tel Aviv and bring him over to Tiberias so that he could be with his parents in that terrible moment.

A little before midnight, she appeared at the restaurant, her face long, and told Shlomi, "You be strong now." Shlomi felt her words knocking on the door to his head, entering, and being pushed out immediately, his body rejecting them like rotten food.

Hilik was twenty-years-and-five-months-old when he died. In the noontide of his days.

Shlomi was nearing his twenty-second birthday.

A wind blew only in Tiberias, and quieted down as evening descended. Weather had departed from the rest of the world, covering its face, making itself scarce.

Perhaps it was ashamed of the sudden gust of wind that drew the bullets away from their destination.

Perhaps it was tired.

Perhaps it held its breath so as not to interrupt the sky from exalting and sanctifying.

*

Shlomi sat in the car as Tehila drove, his body still as rigid as it had been the moment she gave him the news. The two made their way along the coastal highway in silence.

Before they left, Shlomi called Noam and asked him to finish closing up the restaurant. Noam was struck with sorrow. Like everyone else in the restaurant, he knew Hilik well and loved him dearly. He hugged Shlomi and wept on his shoulder, and Shlomi felt his breath growing harder, his eyes as dry as the desert sand, while a sharp, shrieking whistle installed itself in his ears, going on and on and never ending.

At that very hour, the announcement delegation already stood at Ruchama's door. Tehila's pleas had helped only a little. The announcement was delayed for several hours, but when the on-duty commander's shift was over in the Tiberias City Officer Unit, the next on-duty commander insisted on completing the assignment according to procedure. "I don't know who this Tehila is," he said, "and I don't care about politicians and won't let them interfere with my procedures."

Ruchama opened the door. A male and a female officer stood there, along with a military doctor, a male and a female soldier. She looked at them, her eyes long and open, put on her glasses, and her eyes became spotlights at once. Their faces were forlorn and their mouths dammed, trying to contain their message just a minute longer before opening up and letting the bad words rush out and hit her.

To their surprise, Ruchama stood tall and held her head even higher than usual. She asked them in. "First sit down and have something to drink," she said, "and not one word will leave your mouths before you finish drinking."

Helpless, they sat down. Ruchama prepared black coffee and the silence was broken by the squeak of the spoon stirring the pot. She served the coffee very hot and sweetened and ordered them to drink. They sipped it and it scorched their tongues. She ordered them to drink again and they did, their tongues burning and their mouths on fire. Then she made them eat date cookies. They ate and ate, and when they were finished they collected the crumbs with moist fingers. And that entire time she stood over them, her hands on her hips and her spotlight eyes torn, moving among them and preventing the bad words from being said.

And then she went over to the door, opened it, and sent them away. They wanted to stay a moment longer, said they had to deliver a message, but Ruchama began yelling, demanding that they leave her home immediately. "You drank, you ate, you've had enough," she screamed, "and now you get out of my house." She slammed the door behind them, locked it and refused to open it again.

Hearing her screams, Robert went out to the stairway. He raised his eyes to the top floor and discovered the embarrassed group, all standing silently, looking at him, as if asking him to help them and take the load of the message off their shoulders. The young female soldier tried to hide her tears behind the doctor's back. The male soldier at her side seemed familiar to him, maybe he'd been in Shlomi or Hilik's class. Before they could take one step towards him, Robert went back into his apartment, slammed the door and locked it twice. They knocked on his door again and again, asking him to open it, but only a small rustle came from inside. New Hilik woke up, noticed Robert standing frozen at the door and heard the people knocking from outside, begging him to open and let them deliver their message. New Hilik, already thirteen, immediately understood the severity of the night he'd awakened to. He sat on the bamboo sofa in the living room. The sofa screeched, and that was the only sound the delegation of announcers in the stairway heard.

Finally, they gave up and went downstairs to the yard. They stood there to wait for Shlomi and Tehila, knowing they were on their way.

They stood and waited for a long time, darkness all around them, only the lamp at the entrance to the stairway spreading a small ring of light.

Wondrously, neighbors began showing up. First one and then another and another. Coming, looking, reading the delegation members' expressions silently and standing in the yard, a great sorrow burdening them. It was night, the air weatherless, standing still, as if holding its breath. And the neighbors arriving, another and another, wearing pajamas and robes, the harsh news hovering from gaze to gaze, not a word spoken. Standing and grieving wordlessly.

When Shlomi and Tehila got there, a large crowd had already gathered. It seemed all the neighborhood residents, and those of the nearby neighborhood as well, had collected around the team of announcers. Shlomi's eyes went to the group in uniform and noticed Nisim, his classmate, the one who used to hole up in Moti's falafel stand and leave with an appetizing half-pita. He was a soldier now. Still stocky and no longer joking, his eyes lowered, avoiding Shlomi and standing next to a crying, bird-like female soldier. Next to him stood all the others, surrounded by countless people. All the neighbors who had visited when Hilik's arms were broken, bringing gifts and candy, now stood in the yard, weeping in complete stillness. As in a silent film, their bodies were twisted, their eyes shed tears, and not a peep left their throats. They knew Ruchama and Robert had yet to receive the official message and would wait until Hilik's parents were told, and only then would they let out their cries.

Shlomi asked Tehila to wait until he called her. Then he climbed the stairs, opened Ruchama's door with his key and went inside.

All the lights were on. Ruchama had set three giant pots on the stove to boil water. Maybe she meant to cook some soup for all the city's residents. The washing machine was on, and even the dishwasher that Shlomi made her buy to lighten her load. The entire house was buzzing with electricity and glowing with light. Ruchama stood in the middle of the living room and gave him a new look. Then she turned off all the appliances, and the gas burners and the lights. The stillness outside overtook the old apartment. A pale light entered through the windows, casting a blue tinge on her face as she told Shlomi, "I'm not stupid, I've understood everything. Tell them they can leave," and then she went to her room, lay in her bed and closed her eyes.

Before he went down to the yard to ask the soldiers and the gathering to quietly disperse and leave them alone, he knocked on Robert's door. New Hilik opened it, his eyes wet with tears. Shlomi entered. Robert still stood frozen at the doorway, as if they were in the midst of a human chess game.

"Shlomi, what's wrong?" asked New Hilik, and Shlomi answered, "Hilik died."

2

SEVEN YEARS HAD PASSED SINCE THE DAY SHLOMI INVADED THE restaurant's kitchen to demonstrate his abilities. Noam still talked about his surprise at the sight of the Magic Show, which was what he called the moment when Shlomi poured his yearning out onto the filthy work counter. Noam never imagined the boy was only fifteen. Maybe because Shlomi was very tall and had to bend his neck when he entered the kitchen. Maybe his deep voice confused Noam, or the seriousness of his eyes and the precision of his motions, motions containing his many years of cooking. And maybe because Robert stood by his side, skinny and small, embarrassed by his son's sudden actions. Noam never imagined that the small man with the rolling Rs was the father of the long, broad-shouldered youth. He was entirely submerged in Shlomi's burning eyes as they turned the dirty kitchen into a shimmering stage.

It took three or four days before Noam realized that his new employee was in fact an overgrown kid. He was worried at first, afraid of the authorities, and started to check if a special employment permit was required. But when diners began storming the place and raving about the delicacies the boy produced in the small kitchen, his worries were alleviated. He even let Shlomi design a new menu, revive old dishes and invent new ones, using the restaurant as a sophisticated research lab.

Shlomi had him spellbound. Before he came, bringing new spirits with him, the restaurant was wallowing in the sadness that had overtaken Noam after the death of his parents. He was an only son. Bonds of love tethered him to his old parents, whose entire world was the restaurant. They'd built it, cooked the food themselves and cheered up their customers, until they'd fallen ill and soon perished, first his father and, shortly thereafter, his mother. "My parents died of exhaustion," Noam told those who came to console him, and his heart almost burst with anger at himself. He was left alone, twenty-five years old, surrounded by a shrinking crowd of customers. Sorrow and dirt clung to the place and the food no longer brought cheer, but rather drove people away.

Noam would look at Shlomi with admiration and once told him, "You've brought my soul back, you cheeky kid, Og King of Bashan," and patted the back of his neck with great affection. On one of his visits, Hilik whispered in Shlomi's ears, "Watch out, he might eat you up. He's completely in love with you," and Shlomi twisted his face and said, "You talk too much nonsense. He's like my older brother." Hilik laughed and said, "Let's be very clear on this, Shlomi. I'm your only brother in the whole world."

Noam had seven good years. The partnership he wisely nurtured with Shlomi secured the restaurant's fortune. The place grew and became a center of attraction for politicians, journalists and senior military officials. Tehila's frequent visits helped, too. Even before she became a member of parliament, she used to hold her meetings there. The people she brought fell in love with the place and began eating there regularly. All of their attempts to meet the new cook and praise him to his face failed. Shlomi made sure to stay behind the kitchen doors, away from the tipsy tumult around the tables. Seven years at that counter, many hours a day, and from there to school or his apartment, with short visits to Tiberias once in a while.

For Ruchama, these were seven bad years. First Vardina passed away. Then Shlomi moved to Tel Aviv. A year later Hilik decided he wanted to go to military boarding school in Haifa.

All her attempts at convincing him to stay were for naught. "What do you want with the army?" she told him. "You're a boy who loves words, your body is small and weak from all your illnesses. How will you manage with the drills and the marches and the running?" Hilik insisted. His success as a scout counselor filled him with enthusiasm. "I'm sick of words," he told Ruchama. "I want to strengthen my body."

But Shlomi knew that more than anything, this was his brother's way of distancing himself from New Hilik. The little boy whose funny accent brought a storm into Robert's life and took away most of his attention. Robert did his best to devote time to Hilik. He brought him to work, patiently taught him to assemble air conditioners, but when they returned home and New Hilik ran into his arms, Robert's flesh bristled with excitement. The new kid would ramble on about the events of the day, filling Robert's ears with his rolling Rs, and Robert would giggle and reply with his own rolling Rs, another R and another R, cackling like two strange birds, speaking a non-existent language only they could understand. And the whole time Hilik would look at them with an impassive face and unload the work tools from the truck.

When Robert asked him to teach the new kid Hebrew, the way he taught Shlomi when they were little, Hilik refused. He also refused to watch him, or to take him to kindergarten, play with him or feed him. The forced presence of a little brother rendered him mute. Whenever he saw him, he'd open his eyes wide and stand at attention. Their resemblance seemed to erase him.

Shortly after Shlomi left, the infections returned to Hilik's ears. Again he had to spend long days in bed, again he was rushed to see experts who sucked the puss from his ears and caused hallucinations and dizziness.

Shlomi understood that his brother's desire to leave home was meant to save his soul and his ears.

Hilik enlisted in the military boarding school, his hair was buzzed and his body quickly became firm. In his khaki uniform, he looked like a miniature soldier. His eyes and his smile shone again and his ears healed completely.

Ruchama remained alone. Most of the kitchen work was performed by the cooks she'd hired, supervised by the silent workman. The workman took on more and more of her management duties, and his complete loyalty freed up more and more of her time for herself and her solitude. She refused to see the ear doctor and he finally decided to move south. Since then, they hadn't even talked on the phone. She met Drora and Geula occasionally, listened impatiently to the unending stories of their miraculous recovery and their longing for Dalia, their fairy godmother who'd gone to a renowned research institute in America and hadn't been seen or heard from since.

"Some say she took her own life," said Drora and wiped away a tear, and Ruchama nodded and nodded and said nothing, waiting for the moment when the two would get up, leave her apartment and return to their families.

Ruchama was surprised anew every time a small yearning for Hanna appeared suddenly in her throat. She would miss her visits and the flow of her speech and even her screeching voice, the sound of a broken bicycle horn. Ruchama wondered why she'd disappeared without saying goodbye.

During her seven bad years, Ruchama felt herself slowly sinking into loneliness and solitude, like Vardina, as if her beloved neighbor had left her her life's essence. Each time she felt lonely she remembered that on the floor beneath her lived her heart's desire with his new son, and her heart burned stronger. Each time she felt lonely she reminded herself of her two children who lived far away from her, one in Haifa, the other in Tel Aviv, and her soul almost burst with pain.

Seven bad years, and the last one the worst. A war broke out in Lebanon, and Hilik, by then an experienced soldier, found himself in the heart of danger. Ruchama's solitude and anxiety were now joined by alert waiting for the cursed years to be over. But who could have known the seven bad years would end with Hilik's death? How could she have guessed the following years would be even worse?

When Hilik died, Ruchama was only forty-one years old, her electrical pole body still erect and tall, her breasts stable and her curves beautiful, her eyes spewing sparks behind her glasses and a wild mane of hair on her head. A young, large and beautiful woman whose life was old and lonely.

And as for Shlomi – the seven years that had passed were neither good nor bad.

Shlomi saw how his actions made Noam happy, and saw Ruchama's pain on the other hand. He saw Hilik grow and develop and generously spread around him the excess energy he was filled with. Shlomi also saw Robert and New Hilik, and their cackling Rs made him feel nothing but indifference.

Everyone was growing and being grown around him. The restaurant prospered, Noam's joy grew, Ruchama's pain grew, Hilik's spirits and vitality overflowed, and Robert's business multiplied, almost as much as his eternal longing for Ruchama. Even Tehila – her circles of influence expanded, as if she were a small rock thrown into the sea of politics and raising waves within it.

Shlomi's seven years were a sort of time capsule he'd entered and then gone still. From outside, his life appeared to gallop and spin. He cooked like four people. He drank up his studies and completed his matriculation exams successfully within two years. With the money he'd saved, he bought the elderly couple's apartment. The longing for their son, who'd opened a dental clinic in Rome, suffocated them and they decided to join him. Shlomi paid them and still had enough left over to connect the two apartments into one big apartment and build a large, state-of-the-art kitchen to house his cooking experiments. From the outside, his life seemed to burst with action. Noam asked him repeatedly, "When do you even sleep?" but within his capsule, Shlomi felt his eyes were closed most of the time, his mind thrown between the images fixed inside of it.

Images of Ella, especially the one in which she sends him away, asking him never to return.

Or images of Hanna, especially the one in which her body is splayed over his and he's exploding inside of her, and the one in which she places little Shmuel in his arms and he looks at him dully.

And many other images passed in their midst.

His mind shifted between them, crashing into one and being pushed towards the next.

His life seemed like one long slumber, in which his brain dreamed the images and was thrown between them, and at the same time his hands moved and cooked as if they had a mind of their own.

Hilik spent most of his time off from boarding school at Shlomi's. They met at least once a week. Shlomi fed him and bought him clothes and books, and Hilik helped him study for his exams. After connecting the neighbors' apartment to his own, Shlomi turned the elderly couple's bedroom into Hilik's room. He expanded the window looking out onto Gordon Street and the room was filled with sunlight and the whispers of trees. He bought a bed and a wardrobe and covered the floor with light carpeting. Ruchama slept in this room when she came to visit, and Robert sometimes did too, when he came to Tel Aviv for business. But Hilik was the main tenant.

Sometimes he asked Shlomi, "When will you finally tell me what happened that time, that day?" and Shlomi said, "A donkey went crazy and I was scared, that's all."

Hilik didn't let go. "But why didn't you see each other anymore after that, you and Ella?" He insisted. "And why did she leave?"

"Because," Shlomi said drily. "We were little kids, what difference does it make?"

"And why don't you have a girl?"

"Because I don't have time."

"What's going to be the end of you, Shlomi, you're twenty years old and still a virgin," Hilik said and Shlomi was silent. "I regret teaching you how to whack off, you have to stop doing that and meet someone," and Shlomi stayed silent.

Ever since the night he'd slept with Hanna, he'd had no other women, and hadn't masturbated either. Sometimes he'd begin rubbing his morning erection, but then the images appeared in his mind and a sharp pain burst from his neck. The sorrow of longing softened him. He didn't tell Hilik or anyone else about it, didn't even talk about it with himself.

Hilik was the opposite. His life stormed with action as well, but he didn't sleep through it, but rather lived it fully, body and soul. At boarding school, and later in the army, he was admired by his friends, teachers and commanders. Each time he came to visit Shlomi he'd go out on the town, return in the middle of the night with a giggling girl, a head taller than him or more, and they'd shut themselves up in his room until it was flooded with the morning's light. The next night he'd return with another, and Shlomi would be filled with wonder.

"How do they even let you into those places?" he asked. "You look like a sixth-grader."

And Hilik laughed and said, "Join me once and see for yourself, I'm unstoppable."

And a few times, he did join him, but only when the clubs called to report that Hilik was dead drunk and he needed to be picked up. Shlomi would take a taxi or ask Noam to help him rescue Hilik and pay for the damages he'd unwittingly caused. When they arrived home, Shlomi would bathe him and put him to bed, like he often did when Hilik's arms were broken.

"I have to burn myself out, that's the only way I can get some sleep," Hilik said, wrapped in shame, and Shlomi ran his hand on his brother's cheek and said, "That's all right, as long as you don't throw up, I don't care about the rest."

About three years after he'd arrived at the restaurant in the Yemenite quarter, Shlomi was drafted into the military. Without hesitation, Noam contacted the senior officers who were his regular customers. "I'd have no choice but to go out of business," he warned them. "If he goes into the military you'll have no place to eat." The officers used their influence and it was finally agreed that Shlomi would go through a truncated basic training, then be stationed in a position that would allow him to leave each day at noon. When she heard about this arrangement, Tehila made a face and told Shlomi, "I don't like all these perks. The papers will say I used my connections to get you an office job." Noam answered angrily, "Don't spoil this, Tehila, not everything is about your politics." And Shlomi only shrugged indifferently and returned to the kitchen.

Basic training went by like a quick, prickly gust of wind. The weeks passed before he could figure out when he was awake and when his eyes were closed, dreaming about everything that was happening. Due to a shortage in firearms, the soldiers in his platoon were equipped with broomsticks, and shooting lessons were constantly postponed. Most of his time was spent walking in line, obeying the commander's rhythmic barks with everyone else, the slippery stick leaning on his shoulder, recipes racing in his mind and his heart full of worry for the fate of the restaurant. Noam used Shlomi's absence to temporarily close it for renovations and cleaning. He refused to share his plans with Shlomi and only said, smiling, "When you get back you'll have a big surprise."

In the third and last week of basic training, the promised weapons finally arrived and were dipped in vats of black oil and entrusted to the soldiers. The sight of the gun gave him chills, and he saw in his mind's eye the image of Moshik shooting his entire family, one by one, their blood spraying on the walls and the sounds of explosions bursting inside the shack, as if within a giant sound box.

The commanders and platoon soldiers called him Aulcie Perry, and when he squinted they explained that his height reminded them of the gifted basketball player. Shlomi nodded, though he knew none of the terms that were tossed at him from all sides. They spoke with longing about Maccabi Tel Aviv and the European Cup, mentioning names he'd never heard, such as Brody and Aroesti, Berkovich and Silver, Varese and Boatwright. As their excitement grew, Shlomi realized just how distant he was from the life bubbling around him. He suddenly realized he'd unintentionally recreated the city of Tiberias in the kitchens of the restaurant and his apartment. In the years since he'd left Ruchama's home, he walked the streets of his new city, wandered its boulevards, paced its beaches, worked and studied, but his mind remained enveloped and disconnected.

"At least read the paper," Tehila once told him. "Listen to the news on the radio. You live in a covered pot and your life looks like soup." And Ruchama, who'd just come to visit, defended him, "Leave him alone, what good would headlines do him? You ought to take a look at yourself, because you'll end up alone in the grave with your newspapers and radio and political parties."

"I'm happy like this," answered Tehila. "It's my choice."

And Ruchama nodded derisively and said, "Don't try to fool me, Tehila, I wasn't born yesterday."

"And what about you?" Tehila answered angrily. "You're alone too."

"That's right, but I don't lie and say I'm happy and I don't make speeches."

The day after he finished basic training, Shlomi reported to the restaurant. The walls had been repainted, the floor tiles replaced, the furniture reupholstered in cheerful colors, and even the kitchen had been spruced-up. It had been enlarged, with new shiny stainless steel counters and sinks. But Shlomi couldn't see any of this. As soon as he stepped inside, Noam saw his paleness, went over and immediately put his hand on Shlomi's forehead. He was burning up, his breathing heavy and his eyes rolling around in their sockets. A moment later he collapsed on the floor and passed out. Noam took him to the hospital, where he lay for an entire month. Complications from pneumonia, with meningitis on top of it all. He was unconscious for some of the time, and Hilik and Ruchama sat at his side until he was better and his mind was clear.

Shlomi didn't tell a soul, not even Hilik, that he'd met Ella the night before he fainted, and stayed at her apartment in Jerusalem. It was a frozen, horrific night, and by the time he arrived in Tel Aviv the next day he already had a fever.

Shlomi told no one, not about this meeting, nor about the previous ones.

Three or four times she'd called him, asking questions. Three or four sour conversations.

Anger could be heard in her voice, and even ridicule and hatred, but beyond that, he could sense her need to hear his voice, her longing.

She wanted so badly to kick him out of her life, and couldn't.

They'd met three times, too. In their short meetings, a great lump of unease accumulated until it finally burst on that cold night in Jerusalem.

A month passed until he healed completely, but in light of his shaky health, he was discharged from all military duties.

And thus, two months after he'd been drafted, Shlomi returned to the renovated restaurant and to his life's routine. In the corner of the kitchen he placed a radio and listened to it as he cooked. He wanted to thaw the disconnect, and mainly he wanted to hear Ella, who'd been drafted into the army radio service. She began as an announcer, then became a reporter and an astute interviewer and quickly turned into the station's star. Tehila told Shlomi that despite her young age, Ella was feared by politicians. Her direct questions scared them and their stuttering responses exposed their lies.

Sometimes Ella would host nighttime broadcasts where she hardly talked and mostly played music. Shlomi would listen then, too, waiting alertly for her to play a song from that 1969 Song Festival. In front of the images of that festival, staggering on Vardina's new TV, the two of them had sat on the floor, and Ella had picked up one of the plastic roses and placed it in her hair.

One day her voice disappeared from the radio. Tehila told Shlomi she'd been removed from the station because of brash questions she'd asked the army Chief of Staff during a special interview, questions about his symbolic disciplinary measures taken after the Yom Kippur War. "It takes a lot of guts," said Tehila, "to ask a man like Raful if the time he spends collecting empty cartridges and chasing bare-headed soldiers isn't dealing with nonsense."

He hadn't seen her since that night in Jerusalem. He hadn't heard her voice since she'd been removed from the radio.

Seven years had gone by for Shlomi in Tel Aviv, neither good nor bad. And at their end, Hilik's death upended the world.

3

Before the funeral, Robert asked Shlomi to view Hilik's body. "Maybe they made a mistake, I don't believe a word they say," he said.

Hilik's commanders had sat down with them earlier and explained everything. They described in detail the shooting drill that took place near the platoon's reconnaissance route, tried to explain the faulty coordination, shook their heads again and again and claimed that, even now, no one knew why the bullets had veered off course. The bullet that killed Hilik went in through his ear and out the back of his neck. "In the middle of a sentence he suddenly fell down," said one commander.

Shlomi wanted to ask what his last word was, but kept quiet. He even shrugged and smiled to himself, as if this were all a prank, as if knowing he'd soon wake up from this nightmare.

He looked at Ruchama. She sat on the edge of her bed and looked at the group of men, and it seemed a smile would soon appear on her face as well. She was also convinced she'd wake up to her previous life at any moment. Only Robert stood by the officers, his mouth gaping and his head moving back and forth slowly, never stopping, like a stubborn pendulum. Shlomi looked at him too, trying to stifle a giggle that almost escaped his throat. The image reminded him of those little plastic dogs pasted to car dashboards. Whether the car was tearing through the road or whether it stood still, the plastic dog keeps nodding, acquiescing to its fate.

And then, without closing his eyes, Shlomi imagined the flight of the bullet. Moving through space, gliding on the wind among mountains and rocks, bushes and furrowed hills, and suddenly hearing from a distance the words simmering in Hilik's head. The bullet is filled with curiosity and instantly changes its course and flies happily towards the source of the sound. Once, when they were very little, Hilik told him of the words spinning in his head. Not yet seven, he already knew how to read, and would dig into Ruchama's old books and pull out meaningless words, falling desperately in love with them. Fire and duskiness and gloom and treetop and fig leaf and udders and evil and sourness and thrust and torrent and cleaver and darkness and annihilation. "When I grow up I want to be a cover," he said from his sick bed, his nose running and his ears plugged with cotton balls. A scorched and screeching *kover*, pronounced with an extra hard "k," a cover snorting and gurgling with disease. The bullet heard the simmer of his words and came to his head. It must have passed by the many tiny scars in his ears from all the times a tube had been inserted to suck out an infection. The bullet continued its journey to the brain, collecting there all the words Hilik loved. The boy who wanted to be a cover was left emptied of words, the bullet took them all.

Shlomi wanted to ask if they'd found the bullet. Maybe he could read the millions of words collected in it. Maybe it contained Hilik's secret, maybe it described the hiding place where he'd once buried his story notebook, whose existence he'd denied ever since. "There's no notebook," he repeated. "You imagined it."

*

Even as Shlomi looked at Hilik's body, his mind refused to validate the truth of the moment. The shiny stainless steel table the body had been laid on reminded him of the restaurant's kitchen after renovation. Today, four years later, the steel was already scratched and dull with scrubbing.

Hilik's head was bare, his eyes shut, his naked body covered with a gray sheet. In the center of the sheet was a bulge, stretching the fabric and turning it into a small tent. The Military Rabbinate official accompanying Shlomi gestured towards the bulge, embarrassed, and said, "It's natural, it happens a lot, I apologize, it must make you uncomfortable," and Shlomi said, "Why would it make me uncomfortable? He's my brother." The Military Rabbinate man ran a hand through his beard. "People don't usually understand it," he said. "They think the deceased has come back to life. Some even see it as a sign from above, God have mercy on their souls. And I explain to them: it's physiology. Something happens to the body at the moment of death. It collects blood into the genital region and things stand up. That's all. But they refuse to accept it, because their grief is too much to bear."

Then he left Shlomi alone in the room with his brother's body.

Shlomi looked at the pale face. He had a hard time feeling the grief the man had spoken of, and wondered why. His dead brother was laid out before him. His death was a known fact. There was no mistake. But there was no grief, his eyes were completely dry, his breath calm, as if his body refused to take in what his mind was reluctantly beginning to.

Shlomi pulled off the sheet and looked at Hilik's body. It was clean and whole. He'd bathed him so many times, when his arms were in casts, when he'd picked him up from his nights on the town, drunk and dizzy. Shlomi laughed at the sight of the erect penis. "Even death doesn't stop your wiener from getting hard," he said out loud and continued to laugh, playing along with Hilik's amusing prank. Shlomi didn't need the Rabbinate's explanations, he'd already heard about this phenomenon on a radio show discussing the body's idiosyncrasies. But still, he knew this time the reason was different. He knew his brother and knew that, even dead, his body was still swelling over with cravings and desires. Even after long marches, even exhausted from drills or his nightly outings, even then, his vigor was wondrous and his appetite huge. The boy with the sick ears, the boy who gave his older brother his cheese sandwiches and date cookies and only collected the crumbs for himself, that boy went out to eat the world up in large bites. He devoured and read and thought and recorded and wrote and scampered and arranged and helped and taught and joked and trained and marched and ran and climbed and danced and drank and charged and masturbated and flirted and made love and never stopped for a moment. And now his soul has departed and his body was confused and restless and his wiener was hard.

Shlomi looked at Hilik's face. He looked serene, smiling even. He's also laughing at his body's shenanigans, thought Shlomi.

He touched the fingers of his hand, which were rigid and cool, and wanted to cry.

What am I going to do without you?

And why do you make me laugh when I want to cry for you?

*

All through the funeral, laughter stood at the tip of his throat and threatened to burst out until he finally gave into it. Most of the time he tried to bury his eyes in the ground and stifle his giggles. Wherever he looked, he found something that tickled him. Robert, still moving his head like a pendulum, or Ruchama's strange new walk. She suddenly seemed like a giant praying mantis, throwing her limbs around, her lips pulled into her mouth, as if she'd just finished gobbling up her prey and was trying to keep her mouth shut so the animal couldn't jump out and escape.

Tehila's huge sunglasses brought to mind pictures of scowling movie stars and made him want to laugh. So did the neighbors' wails and the soldiers' rigid movements as they aimed their weapons to the sky and shot into the air in honor of the deceased, and even the wooden coffin in which the body was carried. Shlomi imagined Hilik inside, smiling mischievously, his penis still hard, rubbing against the cerecloth pleasurably.

He wanted to be a cover, and now he was covered in cloth ...

Hilik would have liked that play on words.

If he were by his brother's side, they would repeat these words over and over, covered, cerecloth, covered, cerecloth, ccccccccccooooovered, ccccerecccccccloth, cccccccccooooooovvered, ccccc, oooo... and go wild with laughter until Ruchama yelled from the kitchen, "You're giving me a headache, if you don't cut it out now I'll either throw you or myself out the window."

And then the thing happened. Ruchama went to the open grave, carrying a cardboard box filled with old books. Shlomi recognized the disintegrating covers. They were the books of Hilik's fort, the books he'd pile up in bed, surrounding himself with them like a wall and breathing their dust into his gurgling lungs. All at once, Ruchama threw the books into the grave. The covers hit the coffin and a cloud of dust rose from the hole. Everyone present watched her with wonder, and only Shlomi blocked his mouth with the palm of his hand, lowered his head and burst into uncontrollable laughter, spewing stifled sounds, his shoulders shaking. Fortunately, everyone thought he was choking with tears, and Tehila came closer with her silly sunglasses and put a consoling hand on his shoulder.

He told her the truth later, apologizing, and she told him, "You must not realize what's happened yet. It's natural. The tears will come at some point. In the meantime, laugh all you want. What do you care?"

When the ceremony was over and the crowd dispersed, Shlomi remained standing at the side of the grave for a few more minutes. I've never been here before, he thought, though in his imagination he'd visited from time to time, after Ella's father was buried. From the military plot, he could see all the way to the Sea of Galilee, resting at the bottom of the hill. He remembered the day they sat on the beach of the overflowing sea, waiting for Ruchama's prophecy to come true, for the waves to throw fish up in the air. From afar, they saw a group of fishermen and police officers pulling the body of one lovesick girl out of the water.

And already another picture rose – Ella sitting by his side at the school principal's house, surrounded by their classmates, all watching Prime Minister Levi Eshkol's funeral. Ella whispering in his ear, "Half my ass is freezing on the floor, and the other half is sweating on the carpet," and Shlomi laughing. Even then, everyone thought he was crying for the prime minister being led to his grave.

These images were burned into his mind. They'd float up occasionally, making him yearn till his throat constricted. Yearning for Ella, yearning for Hanna, especially for the moment she'd put the baby, Shmuel, in his arms, the new Shlomi, his spitting image.

Faraway images, different but similar, like rhymes in a poem; in one, a body is drawn out through a window; in the other, a dead girl is pulled out of the water; in a third, drums thunder and a coffin is lowered into a grave in black-and-white.

And now a fourth image joins. Hilik's funeral. A light wooden coffin. Robert becoming a pendulum. Ruchama turning into a praying mantis. The dust of crumbling books. Cries of anguish. His desperate battle against laughter. Ella far away. Hanna farther. Hilik too. What am I going to do without you?

In light of this picture, the others grow pale and dim. Suddenly a small cry begins tickling his throat, but then retreats back to where it came from.

*

After the funeral, Robert's head stopped moving. He went into his apartment, and in front of New Hilik's worried eyes, took a large blanket and put most of his clothes inside. He tied the ends of the blanket together, loaded the bundle onto his back and went up to Ruchama's apartment.

Years had gone by since he'd last set foot there. He went inside wordlessly and turned to the old children's room, dropped his bundle on the floor and sat on Hilik's bed. Ruchama followed him silently. Within seconds, she'd untied the blanket, collected the pile of his clothes and arranged them in her bedroom closet. When she was finished, she changed the sheets on her bed and added a pillow and blanket for him.

Then she lay down in bed and told him, "You can stay here, but I won't have your son Yechiel in this apartment. Find someplace else for him. My Hilik is dead, I don't want a new Hilik."

Robert nodded and lay by her side. Within seconds, their arms intertwined and their two bodies gathered together, looking for a moment as one, and then they broke into quiet tears.

They stayed that way all night, gripped in their tears.

They didn't talk throughout the *shiva*, only exchanged looks and small gestures, like a gentle and well-coordinated dance. The way they carried themselves around the apartment, among the visitors and among themselves, indicated that they were completely devoid of words now, left only with the body.

Within days, Robert's hair grew long. After two or three weeks it touched the middle of his back, spilling down and covering the back of his neck and part of his shoulders, strewn with thin strands of gray.

*

As soon as they returned from the funeral, Shlomi stormed the living room and began preparing for the *shiva*. He cleared out furniture, placed mattresses along the walls, removed pictures, covered the television, obeyed the orders Abraham and Yitzhak, Ruchama's brothers, gave him at the cemetery. He placed a long table along the entrance wall, and put cups and napkins there, alongside bottles of juice and cookies Geula and Drora had brought.

Noam arrived later and helped him with other arrangements. Visitors were pouring in and Shlomi greeted them, apologizing for Ruchama and Robert, who were still lying together in bed, weeping.

Ruchama's brothers took it upon themselves to lead the prayers. They made Robert pull himself from Ruchama's arms, get out of bed, wipe his tears, put a *yarmulke* on his head and a prayer book in his hands, and sway at the right moments.

Once, when he was bringing dishes into the kitchen, Shlomi heard Abraham whispering to Geula and Drora, "This is her punishment for all her sins, if she'd listened to us and repented she'd still have the boy." Drora whispered back, "It's never too late to fix things. Look, she took Robert back," and Geula wiped her tears and whispered angrily, "Stop this nonsense. This isn't punishment. It isn't even the curse that used to plague her. That boy was like an angel and God wanted him all to Himself," and then she was silent because she saw Shlomi standing at the kitchen doorway and listening to them. She walked over and took the dirty cups from him, offered him some coffee and the cookies she'd bought. Shlomi refused. In his mind, he saw Geula and Drora during the days of the curse, lumbering down the street, one wrapped in scarves and the other scratching under her wig, and again he had to work hard to stifle a laugh.

The visitors filled the apartment with delicacies and it was saturated with familiar aromas. It seemed the many visitors wanted to repay Ruchama for all the food she'd made to please them over the years. When the sun began to set there was no more room. Rows of pots and pans bursting with goodness lined the kitchen, and Shlomi asked the silent workman to give most of them away to the less fortunate. Until then, the workman had sat in the corner of the kitchen, his face as pale as a wall, unbelieving and unbreathing. Shlomi's request brought him back to life. "At least now I have something to do," he said. "Otherwise I'll lose my mind, I'll never be able to understand how they took that child from us." Shlomi had never heard so many words leave the man's mouth at once.

Noam helped the workman load the pots and pans onto the old truck and joined him on his mission. When he returned Shlomi told him, "I want you to get some sleep. You don't look good," and Noam answered, "This day killed me, I loved your brother so much."

Shlomi made up the large bed in Vardina's old apartment. When she'd died, all her possessions had been entrusted to Ruchama, until Shlomi and Hilik grew up and could use them. Ruchama insisted on keeping the apartment just as it was, and even made sure to clean it once a week. She tried to alleviate her longing for her giant neighbor by scrubbing the floors of her apartment and wiping the dust off the plastic roses that still decorated the kitchen cabinets. Sometimes she used one of the rooms to store things she couldn't find room for in her own apartment. Old pots and serving dishes, old pans from the catering business that had since been replaced, and old books, piles of books that were no longer needed after Hilik went to boarding school.

Noam collapsed on the bed in his clothes and said, "Don't worry about the restaurant. Nothing will happen if we close up for a week," and Shlomi said, "I think I'll have to stay here for a while longer after the *shiva*. We'll need to find a solution." Noam yawned, kicked off his shoes and said, "I'm not worried. We'll find a way. The only one I'm worried about is you. You keep running around. You haven't given yourself a chance to fall apart. I haven't seen you shed one tear. I'm scared for you."

Only late at night, after he'd washed all the dishes piled in the sink, cleaned and straightened up the living room and forced Ruchama and Robert to eat a few slices of bread with white cheese, only then did he remember New Hilik and go downstairs to Robert's apartment.

The boy sat on the squeaky bamboo sofa in the living room. His eyes were puffy. It seemed he'd been crying most of the day. "I'm sorry, Yechiel," Shlomi said, "I had so much to do I forgot about you."

"It's all right," said New Hilik, his Rs rolling quietly.

He's already thirteen, thought Shlomi. As usual, his eyes took in the complete resemblance between him and his dead brother. This time he felt a chill and lowered his eyes.

"Why didn't you come upstairs to be with everyone?" he asked.

"I don't want to hurt Ruchama. That's why I didn't come to the funeral, either," the boy said with a dry throat. "I know we look exactly the same. It was always hard for her to look at me, even when I did everything I could for her to take pity on me and give me some attention." His eyes searched for Shlomi's and he added, "Now it would hurt her even more to look at me and remember. It must be hard for you to look at me, too."

Shlomi sat by his side. He put his hand on the boy's head and caressed his hair. He was touching New Hilik for the first time. It was the first time he was close enough to smell his scent, and it was familiar, Robert's eucalyptus shampoo.

At first, New Hilik froze, his entire body attentive to Shlomi's hand, surprised and then instantly clinging and submitting and even resting his head on his arm.

"Why did you cry?" asked Shlomi.

"I didn't cry."

"Don't try to fool me, Hilik," said Shlomi and patted his shoulders. "Your eyes are puffy like balloons."

"You called me Hilik," the boy said, surprised. "You always call me Yechiel."

Shlomi said nothing.

A moment later, he got up and suggested they move to the kitchen. "I'd better eat something. I haven't had a thing in two days, and you must be hungry too."

New Hilik hurried to the kitchen, trying to get there before Shlomi. "I'll make you some food," he said and began pulling groceries from the fridge. "You go take a shower and freshen up."

The bag of Shlomi's clothes that Noam brought from Tel Aviv was still in the apartment upstairs. Shlomi thought he'd stay in his and Hilik's old room, but, seeing New Hilik's puffy eyes, he decided to stay in Robert's apartment. He took a shower, wrapped himself in towels and sat down to dinner. New Hilik placed a plate before him, half a loaf of bread stuffed with steaming, fragrant contents. While Shlomi had been in the shower, he'd fried thin slices of bleeding beef and stuffed them into the emptied bread along with tomatoes and onions and hot peppers and a few tablespoons of tahini. The meat's juices were soaked into the bread, and when Shlomi bit into it, they spilled into his mouth and filled it with an intoxicating taste. For himself, New Hilik made a plate of just meat, which he ate with his fingers. "You only eat meat?" asked Shlomi with his mouth full. "I'm used to it," New Hilik answered with a smile. "But sometimes, when Dad makes me, I eat some fruit and vegetables and drink a little milk." Shlomi chewed voraciously, enjoying every crumb, licking his lips and his fingers. New Hilik was hungry too, and he devoured the meat, letting the blood drip from the sides of his mouth. Shlomi tried to imagine the boy with a white cheese and cucumber sandwich, and that made him laugh. In his mind he saw Hilik standing by the water fountain in their elementary school, handing him the sandwich Ruchama had made, reminding him to bring the wax paper home for future use.

Suddenly New Hilik said, "What am I going to do, Shlomi?" His fingers placed the meat back in his plate and his face grew long. "Dad went up to Ruchama's," he said, his throat dry again. "He's been waiting for this his entire life. I know he won't come back here and I won't be able to go up there because Ruchama won't have me, so what am I going to do now?"

Shlomi stopped chewing. His heart went out to the boy sitting across from him. New Hilik's face grew even longer, and he continued: "One day my mother got up and left me, disappeared. I know that, even though Dad keeps making up stories, that she was sick and died. Then you went to Tel Aviv and Hilik went to boarding school. He never forgave me for looking so much like him, so he just ran away. And now Robert's left, too. Where will I go? Where will I grow up?"

His tears spilled on the plate, watering down the pool of blood that had formed next to the meat.

"Don't worry," said Shlomi. "I'm here." He picked up the stuffed bread, bit into it and said, "And now eat and stop whining, you're too old for tears. I guess you turned out emotional, like our dad."

*

On one of the *shiva* days, the yellow-faced kibbutz secretary came to console Ruchama and Robert. Tehila was there too, but her presence didn't embarrass him at all. It seemed the past events that had made her leave the kibbutz had been completely erased from his mind, or, if not erased, had left no lasting impression on him, not even a shadow of regret or a hint of a pang of conscience. Tehila, on the other hand, had trouble disguising her loathing, but the yellow face sensed nothing of it. He sat on a chair across from Ruchama and Robert, reclining limply on their mourners' mattress, and fascinated the other visitors with amusing stories of his past, stopping only to swallow another date cookie or take another sip of the coffee Shlomi had made him. Now and then he sent Robert a little smile, accompanied by a hidden wink. He might have wanted to cheer him up, or might have wanted to signal that he knew how to keep a secret.

Ruchama never met his gaze. Maybe because she had no interest in the tales he told and in life on her hated kibbutzes, and maybe because of the tranquilizer Tehila gave her. "You have to get out of bed," she had told her and Robert. "People keep coming and Shlomi has to handle everything."

In recent years, the secretary's hair had gone completely white and his face had grown yellower. Deep wrinkles plowed through it, and when he spoke the hair resembled stalks in a field, fidgeting nervously in the wind. When he was finished telling stories, he began discussing matters of utmost importance with Tehila. He presented his opinions at length and chastised her and her friends in the Knesset. She answered curtly, evading his questions as best she could. First, he spoke of the war in Lebanon and of the inquiry committee. "Even though I'm a kibbutznik," he said, "I think that committee should be ashamed of what its members said about Arik Sharon, Hero of Israel." He wagged his finger threateningly. "Saying he should be removed from office because of a massacre we weren't involved in? Hypocrisy will be the end of us," he said. "Look at what happened to the Americans in Beirut two weeks ago. Seventy people the terrorists killed, just put a bomb in the embassy, right under their noses. But they never learn. They were hypocrites and they'll stay hypocrites forever, just like the rest of the world. We saw how they said nothing during the Holocaust, knew about all the horrors and kept their mouths shut. Closed their eyes and let the Jews burn."

Then he complained about how hard it was for kibbutzes to survive. "Is that why you're selling shares on the stock market? Is that part of your socialist dream?" Tehila asked with a small, stinging smile. "We're going to the stock market because we have no other choice," he answered irritably. "It's a shame people like you don't look out for us. What did we even send you into politics for?"

Tehila's eyes bugged but she held back. The yellow secretary added, "If you had a smidgeon of integrity you'd make sure the kibbutzes get the money they deserve."

"Why do you deserve it?" Tehila asked, trying her best to stay restrained.

"We built this country. There'd be nothing here without us," he answered. "We've sacrificed so many members, lost so many in the wars, we deserve it."

He was silent for a long moment and then looked at Ruchama and Robert, smiled sadly and said, "Now, after your son has been killed, you in Tiberias know what we've been dealing with our entire lives. Now you're like us, now you're true Israelis."

For the first time since the secretary had arrived, Ruchama raised her head and fixed her eyes on him. She nodded while the other visitors said nothing, hardly breathing.

"Thank you," she finally said weakly. "Thank you so much for your approval." She took a deep breath, her eyes still fixed on him, and said, "My family's lived in this country for centuries. It's really about time someone like you finally accepts us. I truly thank you."

She shook a little and Robert put his hand on her, trying to prevent the unavoidable. He and Shlomi, from his seat at the edge of the mattress, felt the lava burning inside her.

She nodded again, the glasses dancing on the tip of her nose, and then whispered to the yellow face, "And now, after you've cheered us up, I ask that you finish your coffee and get out of this house. Get out of here and go back to your Israel. This is a different country."

The secretary listened to her with shock and then let his eyes escape her. He put his cup on the table, trying in vain to catch Robert's eyes, so he could help him decipher his wife.

For a moment, it seemed his lips had curled into a short smile, maybe an awkward smile, maybe a smile of contempt.

He leaned forward to get up from the chair.

And then it happened.

All at once, Ruchama pounced on him from her seat and punched his face.

The secretary screamed, surprised, and before he'd finished screaming Ruchama sent another blow, and a moment later she was on him, her legs and arms flying every which way, tearing his clothes, pulling out his hair, punching him mercilessly, biting and slapping, screeches and cries leaving her throat and shaking the house, escaping out the windows and spreading through the city.

The yellow face tried to protect himself with his shaking hands. The visitors watched them with gaping mouths. Long seconds of confusion and shock went by until they got a hold of themselves and leaped forth, trying to pull Ruchama away from the man, who was already bruised all over, his clothes torn and his yellow face bleeding.

The secretary ran away.

Tehila and Shlomi dragged Ruchama to her bedroom and tried to give her some water and calm her down. But her screams didn't stop. She screamed until her throat broke, hitting herself, pulling out her hair. And only when the doctor came and gave her an injection, only then did she stop, lay down with her head in Robert's lap, as he caressed her hair and wiped away her tears.

They never saw the yellow secretary after that. He never set foot in their country again.

A few days after he was beaten by Ruchama, he noticed the skin on his face had begun to peel, leaving infected, bleeding blisters. The doctors diagnosed a sudden sensitivity to sun. The sensitivity had been latent for years, and suddenly erupted. "It might be your age," said one doctor. "You aren't a young man anymore."

The secretary had to leave his position and stay at home. During the day, he drew all the shutters Robert had once installed for him, blocking out the sunlight. Only when darkness descended he'd leave his house and sit on his stoop, watching the kibbutz members pacing the paths, deterred by the blisters on his face, looking away and hurrying off. The doctors gave him a special ointment that colored his face gray. He was no longer yellow, no longer a secretary. Months later, when the stock market crash almost did the kibbutz in, he locked himself inside in the evenings too, and no longer showed his face in public. First Ruchama beat him. Then her curse was laid upon him, and finally he was shrouded with great shame.

After Ruchama went to bed, Shlomi began cleaning the apartment. Tehila helped with some of the dishes. "I admire your mother," she said. "I've been dreaming of punishing that man for what he did to me for years, for how he used me and then threw me out like a dog. I almost applauded when she beat the hell out of him."

Robert stood there, watching them silently, and nodded when Shlomi said, "I'm going to sleep downstairs. I don't want to leave Yechiel alone."

Tehila said goodbye and gave him a quick, firm hug, almost official, trying to keep her tears at bay and conceal her sorrow, and then she went back to Jerusalem.

Shlomi took his bag of clothes and went downstairs to the middle apartment.

New Hilik was waiting for him at the table, had cooked him another delicious meal. This time he chopped the meat and cooked it slowly with garlic and tomatoes and potatoes. Before filling the plates, he scattered minced parsley and a few refreshing drops of lemon juice on the food. While doing this, he told Shlomi about the rehearsals his class was having for the approaching Shavuot ceremony. He was meant to have a solo number, but there was one line where the Rs rolled on his tongue and all the children started laughing. New Hilik laughed too, and nobody could stop laughing until he got a different role, one with no Rs.

With a wild smile, he sang the words of the song to Shlomi and illustrated the problem. "*Bikurrrrrey katzirrrrrr ...*" Shlomi laughed.

Then they ate. They soaked the sauce into pieces of bread. The stew was spicy and burned Shlomi's throat as he told the boy about what had transpired earlier. He described to him the face of the beaten secretary and they both laughed out loud, the red sauce streaming down their chins and staining the tablecloth and their clothes.

*

One morning, Shlomit, Shlomi's elementary school classmate, the girl whose brother was pronounced missing during the Yom Kippur War and who used to fall asleep in class, came to visit. It had been ten years since the war, and there was no chance of finding her brother. "But I've made my peace with his death," she said, and Shlomi looked at her with gaping eyes. Shlomit had become a beautiful woman. Her eyes had opened and grown alert, she was all freshness, as if she'd woken from a long slumber. I wonder what prince kissed her and blew away her crummy childhood, Shlomi wondered, but was too shy to ask. She took his hand and held it in her lap all through her visit. Her touch felt good, arousing even. He tried hard to focus on her eyes and not give in to the urge to look at her neckline and her bare shoulders.

In those far-off, sleepy days of eighth grade, she told him, she'd visit the principal's home every day. The principal had decided to help her through that rough period. "She helped me with homework and mainly taught me to sing. I sang and she accompanied me on the guitar," she said, "and she talked to me, about my brother, about my crazy home, and about you."

"About me?" he asked, surprised.

"Yes," she said. "She thought we should be friends, that it would help both of us. I have no idea why. Maybe because she could tell I had a little crush on you. She'd always bring it up and then laugh and say, 'Maybe you'll start a duo, Shlomi and Shlomit, like those popular singers Ilan and Ilanit.'"

They both laughed. She strengthened her hold on his hand.

"So why didn't you do what she proposed?" he asked.

"I was shy," she said. "And besides, there was Ella, that strange girl who hardly ever came to school, and for you she was everything."

She asked if they were still in touch, Ella and he, and Shlomi moved his head lightly, signaling neither yes nor no.

"Today I know," she said, "that what made me most tired was insisting on not crying. I thought if I screamed at night like my mother and cried like her it would be like acquiescing to God to take my brother away. I thought it would be agreeing to his death. I wish I'd had someone to release me from that thought. Even the principal, with all her good intentions and her big heart, even she encouraged me to hope and believe and kept telling me, 'Don't cry, Shlomit. You have nothing to mourn. You need to believe he'll come back and you'll see it'll happen.'"

Before she left, she told him she lived next door now, in the building where Hanna and Ella used to live. She'd recently bought Mrs. Katz's apartment, after she'd passed away. Shlomit had installed a few ovens, and made a living baking and selling cakes. Her military service had turned her into an experienced pastry chef, her baked goods were loved and popular and it made her very happy. She invited him to visit her and got up to leave. On the refreshments table, she placed cakes she'd made. The apartment was filled with the scents of cinnamon, chocolate, vanilla, almonds and sour plums. The cakes were gone within minutes. Even Ruchama and Robert gave in to temptation and shared a small piece of almond cake.

*

Soldiers came to the house every day, each time a different group of Hilik's friends. Shlomi knew them all from the times they'd gotten unexpected leave and Hilik brought them to the restaurant in Tel Aviv. Shlomi would encourage them to eat more of the delicacies he made them, until they were about to burst. Then they'd go out, taking in every minute of freedom before returning to South Lebanon. They'd arrive in Shlomi's apartment before sunrise, shower and sprawl in every available corner, sink into a quick sleep and depart in the morning, leaving Shlomi with mountains of dirty towels.

They came to the mourners' home bathed and silent, holding in pain and confusion, staring at Ruchama and Robert and not knowing what to say. Only one of them, tall and slender, his face as white as a wall, told Shlomi what had happened.

When the shots had begun sounding, they'd fallen to the ground immediately. The platoon commander had realized an error was being made and ordered them to hold their fire. He tried to contact the platoon training in the shooting range. He yelled into his device, "Cease fire, you morons, you're range-finding us, cease fire right away, idiots." And suddenly Hilik said, "I want to see," and stood up. His friends tried to stop him, pulling him back down, but Hilik fought them off and said, "They aren't shooting anymore, I have to watch," and stood up again and his eyes opened wide. Something out there filled him with wonder. He managed to mumble excitedly, "I've never seen anything like this," and before he was finished speaking, he was hit.

None of them knew what Hilik wanted to look at and what his eyes saw before the bullet hit his head.

Right after he collapsed, another bullet hit a second soldier, though he was hiding behind a rock. "Nothing that happened there made any sense," the soldier told Shlomi, shaking his head as if searching for words, and said nothing more.

Shlomi continued looking at the pale soldier, waiting for more words to interpret and knowing none would come. He was filled with a gigantic anger that grew larger and larger until his face turned red.

If Hilik were here, he thought, I'd beat him until he begged me to stop.

I'd break your retarded arms again.

I'd slap your stupid little face,

Scratch you,

Kick you in the stomach until you threw up.

His rage burned for hours. At night, after Ruchama and Robert went to bed, waiting for sleep to descend and let them escape into dreams, Shlomi began looking for Hilik's story notebook. He'd asked about it many times and Hilik had denied its existence. But Shlomi remembered the sight of the notebook under the mattress. A thick notebook, the edges of its cover worn from use, containing countless tight lines of his tiny handwriting, miniscule, miniature letters, as if he wanted to hide them from an intruder, to turn their existence into nothing but a hint, until they curled into themselves and disappeared. His name floated among them many times, and so did Ruchama's and Robert's, and Ella's. He remembered well how the lines flew up into his eyes, until Hilik came into the room and hit him with his cast arm. That notebook must be hidden here. It's been hiding in silence for eight years, waiting for its owner to redeem it. Maybe he'd written more, maybe he'd written about himself. If Shlomi could find it, he might find some meaning, some solution.

Shlomi looked through all the closets, rummaged through drawers, moved furniture quietly and searched behind and underneath it. He groped pillows and mattresses, his fingers seeking a lump to signify the existence of the notebook. He opened and shook the books that were still left on the shelves, waiting for the notebook to fall from between the pages.

Ruchama and Robert looked at him indifferently from their bed. He told them he was looking for photographs and they shrugged, letting him search the bedroom. They showed no resistance when he lifted the mattress they were lying on and searched and touched and looked and found nothing. He tore the kitchen apart too, looking inside the large pots, separating pans, until the noise woke Ruchama up.

"What photo are you looking for?" she asked.

"Something of Hilik's," he answered.

"Some of his things are in Vardina's apartment. I put them there a long time ago," she said and went back to bed.

On his way downstairs he picked up New Hilik and asked for help with the search.

Together they went into the familiar apartment.

Everything was in its place. The chair where Vardina used to sit, where he once put his head on her leg and cried. The plastic roses. The opening Robert widened to pull her huge body out of there.

The large bed was unmade. Noam, who'd slept in it a few days prior, had gone on his way without making it.

"I've never been here before," said New Hilik. "Dad told me a lot about Vardina, but Ruchama wouldn't let us in here."

In the other room were many boxes. Shlomi opened and looked through them thoroughly. When they reached the boxes of Hilik's old books he felt something fluttering within him, like a small bird flapping its wings against the walls of his stomach. He shook the books and flipped through them, and then handed them to New Hilik for a second check. An idea came to him. Perhaps the notebook had been split into individual pages, each concealed elsewhere. Perhaps a sophisticated act of concealment had taken place here, something Hilik had learned from one of the many suspense novels he'd read. He knew Shlomi had seen the notebook, knew his denial wouldn't make him forget it. Maybe he scattered the pages, just as he'd once scattered notes with words all through the apartment, to help Shlomi learn how to read and write. Maybe he'd divided his notebook into separate paper notes, meaning to use them to teach Shlomi a new language, present him with a mystery to solve, to make everything clear.

But there was nothing but dust.

When he opened the last box, he felt another chill. There were some of Hilik's old textbooks and school notebooks, from before he'd transferred to boarding school. Shlomi checked notebook after notebook. Third grade math and geometry. Fifth grade English. Biology and Israeli geography, both from fourth grade. What did he keep all this for? Why did he feel the need to collect evidence, to prove that he'd had a childhood, that it still lived in a box as well as in his mind?

A picture of a wagtail bird.

A multiplication table.

An illustrated paper on the Bedouins in Israel.

Shlomi flipped through them, tense, his eyes carefully examining the contents, careful not to miss anything. New Hilik sat in the corner of the room and watched him quietly, letting him be.

Between two textbooks, Shlomi was surprised to find the recipe notebook, in which Ruchama had collected all of his cooking inventions, and in which, when he was able to write, he'd added some too, or glued in recipes he'd written earlier, on notecards.

On the cover, Shlomi recognized Hilik's handwriting:

Save this! Until some day when Shlomi might need it.

Hilik had surrounded the words with a red rectangle, turning them into a warning sign.

He hadn't collected this evidence for himself alone. He'd kept the recipe notebook along with his school notebooks, thinking maybe, some day, he'd have to tell Shlomi, "Look, you had a childhood too. It's kept for you here, and if you've forgotten it, just reach out and touch it."

Shlomi flipped through the notebook, wandering among familiar recipes. Some of them were even adorned with pencil marks, instructing the proper way to plate the dish. He followed his handwriting from page to page, the way it hardened and stabilized, the letters growing lucid and the words clear.

The final pages made him smile. They reminded him of Vardina's Holocaust games. From the day of the incident with Mr. Rott and until her death, they'd wink to each other on every Holocaust Memorial Day and exchange a surreptitious "Happy holiday!" One day, when the cooking business was already thriving, Vardina proposed to Shlomi that they collect recipes together and write a cookbook. "The entire country would want to buy this book," she said, and even presented him with a French book she'd bought that had dozens of illustrated recipes, arranged in chapters by subjects. "We'd divide the book into chapters according to holidays," she'd said, excited about her own invention, "recipes for Passover, recipes for Rosh Hashanah, Purim cookies, dairy dishes for Shavuot." Shlomi told her, "As long as we also have a chapter for Holocaust Memorial Day meals." While they rolled around laughing, the two began devising recipes: frozen beets stuffed with snowflakes, dried bread in dirt sauce, and an entire chapter dedicated to rotten potato peels.

Shlomi put the recipe notebook back and continued to rifle through the box.

There were grammar and art and geography notebooks too.

But he couldn't find the one he wanted. Neither whole nor in separate pages.

Maybe he really had just imagined it.

And then he recalled that some of Hilik's books had been thrown into his grave. A cloud of dust rose as Ruchama tossed in the books of his fort. Perhaps the cloud covered the lost notebook as well.

Shlomi closed the boxes and returned them to their place. Then he went up to Robert's apartment with New Hilik. The aroma of the roast the boy had made earlier and had just taken out of the oven emanated from the kitchen. The steaming hunks of meat fell apart as they poked their forks in them. The potatoes were slightly scorched, but they were also swallowed eagerly.

When they finished, New Hilik opened two chocolate bars, broke them into pieces and placed them near Shlomi.

"What notebook were you looking for?" he asked.

Shlomi didn't answer. He looked at the chocolate pieces, put one in his mouth, and another, and another. Again he felt a small cry tickling his throat, and again it disappeared. His eyes remained dry, his throat choked with sweetness and only his stomach grumbled with anger and yearning.

4

TodayImadeupthelongestwordintheworldandnowI'vewrittenitdowninthenotebook

Pain again, both my ears, stronger in the left, throbbing in the right
    (bobbing, robbing, mobbing, lobbing, sobbing)
My secret, I won't tell, I won't let the cat out of the bag
    (hag, nag, lag, rag)

<u>Words I hate:</u>
Order
In order to
Accuracy
Focus
Bubbling
Bullet
Fermenting
Droppings
Sandwich
Genius
Worm
New
I

The first line of the poem looks at the second line and sees a rhyme. The
first line says proudly: the second line is my daughter (or my son).
My father looks at us and gets confused — which one is the second line,
Old Hilik or New Hilik? Which one of us is the real rhyme? The real
rrrrrrrrrhyme.
Only one of us will remain in the poem. Rrrrrrremain in the poem.
I choose one word and send it to circle the Earth and then come back here
and hit one of us.

Only one will remain. Old Hilik or New Hilik.
And I'm here, turning my life into words in a notebook. Words words words.

No More
I'm sick of words
I want to be just a body

I flip back through the pages and I'm stunned. I wrote I so many times. I and I and I and I.
Tehila once said the world had fallen in love with the word I. It's a dangerous disease, she said. A plague that broke out in the kibbutzes and spread everywhere.
I wrote too much I, I and I and I and I. And now I'll erase the dangerous word ~~I~~.
And then ~~I'll~~ burn it.

~~I~~.
~~I'll~~ *erase.*
~~I'll~~ *burn it.*
~~I'll~~ *write and erase and burn all at once.*
~~I~~ *open the drawer, ~~I~~ find matches, ~~I~~ rub the match against the rough paper just like ~~I~~ rub myself against the blue towel, ~~I~~ start a fire, ~~I~~ bring the paper closer, ~~I~~ keep writing, ~~I~~ light the top edge of the page, ~~I~~ look at the flame searing it, ~~I~~ pull my writing hand away, ~~I~~ make it smaller on the paper so it doesn't burn, ~~I~~ see the fire chasing my hand, ~~I~~ feel the heat and the burn …*
~~I~~ *have to stop writing or my hand will burn,*
~~I~~ *write words quickly,*
~~I~~ *escape the fire,*
~~I~~ *write fire and duskiness and gloom and treetop and fig leaf and udders and evil and sourness and thrust and torrent and cleaver and darkness and annihilation and…*
~~I~~ *write cov*

5

Two weeks after the *shiva* was over, Shlomi called Ella. She was surprised at first, even had trouble answering, her voice a little nasal, maybe she had a cold, maybe she'd woken from a frenzied sleep.

"I have to bring you back into my life," he said and she laughed and coughed, embarrassed by his sudden honesty.

"Everything in my life is numb," he continued. "I move and respond and do things and talk and cook, but everything happens inside this sleep that suffocates me. Just like back then, when you went to that place near Sugarloaf Mountain. I slept for five years then, and now it's been eight. I've turned into longing. Longing with legs and arms."

Beyond the static on the phone, he heard her blow her nose.

"Are you sick?" he asked.

"Not anymore. I was," she answered.

"Is that why you didn't come to the *shiva*?"

"I couldn't."

"I waited for you," he continued. "I hoped you'd come."

"I really couldn't," she whispered. "I'm sorry about Hilik, I loved him very much, I read in the paper that he'd been killed and my heart broke for you and Ruchama." She said nothing for a moment, took in some air, still surprised. "I didn't think you'd ever call me again," she said.

"I want to see you," he heard himself say. "I want to be with you, I want to love you, I want to know everything, I want to sleep with you, I want to forget everything."

To break the silence that had fallen, he told her of his efforts to reach her. First, he'd called the apartment she'd gotten in Jerusalem after she left the boarding school. Her landlord told him she hadn't heard anything in years. Then he tried at the radio station, where they refused to answer his questions. With no other choice, he asked

Tehila to pull some strings. Everyone remembered the radio's energetic star, and especially her brash interview with the Chief of Staff that led to her removal from the station, but no one knew where she was now. Finally, he'd decided to call Hanna, after finding her number in the phonebook.

"I didn't know you moved to Haifa," he said.

"Two years ago," Ella answered, "when her health began getting worse, I had to be here to help her."

"How is she now?" Shlomi asked, and Ella went quiet, a long silence, even her breathing was swallowed in the line's static, or maybe she wasn't breathing at all.

"I thought you knew," she finally said.

And then she told him of Hanna's death earlier that year, over four months ago.

Her demise was long and slow, Ella said. In recent months, her neck had become very swollen and all her hair had fallen off. And not because of chemotherapy, which she'd decided to avoid altogether, it had just fallen off by itself. Then she'd lost her sense of touch. "I had to tie her arms to keep her from doing dangerous things without noticing. In the end she lost her voice too, whispered a little when she had to, and most of the time said nothing, until she died."

Shlomi listened to her, images running around in his head.

"Where's Shmuel?" he eventually asked.

"He's here with me," she answered, "a sweet, quiet boy, looks just like you did when we first met in the yard. It's uncanny."

"I want to see him."

"Why?"

"I want to see you and him, I want you two to come."

"Why, Shlomi? What for?"

"That's what I want."

*

Five years before Hilik died, the phone rang in the restaurant and Ella asked to speak with him. Shlomi was seventeen, hidden in the kitchen, submerged in his yearning capsule. It'd been a long time since she'd sent him away from the hospital room and asked him never to return. They hadn't seen each other since. He'd gone to her boarding school in Jerusalem once, wanting to see her, and failed.

Noam handed him the phone and said, "Someone named Israella wants to talk to you."

Maybe someone was pulling his leg, thought Shlomi, maybe it's Hilik, playing a prank. Otherwise, what were the odds of her introducing herself as Israella, the full name she hated, only Hanna insisted on using it, and what were the odds of her calling at all after she'd kicked him out of her life?

He dried his hands again and again, taking the phone.

"I'm sorry if I'm interrupting," she said. Her voice hoarse, her words rushing out and knocking on his ears.

She asked how he was. Showed some interest in the restaurant.

He answered in few words, mostly listened, trying to follow the changes in her voice.

"I called to talk to you about Moshik," she said.

She told him she'd been getting letters from Moshik for the past year. At least once a week he wrote her a long letter from prison, detailing his routine, describing his cellmates and the rehabilitation process. At first she was surprised and didn't write back. With time she'd grown used to his letters, even waited for them, something about his writing touched her heart. Sometimes he mentioned books he'd read and what they made him think. Sometimes he quoted poems, burrowing into them and analyzing them until he was able to summarize the psyches of their authors with few words. "He's changed a lot," she said. "It's hard to recognize that stammering, needy, crazy boy he used to be. He writes like a poet and not like a cat-tail-ripping-psychopath." She finally gave in and wrote back.

"I wanted to ask you to join me," she told Shlomi. "I'm going to visit him next week."

Since he'd been imprisoned, Moshik hadn't received any visitors. His dead parents' family ostracized him completely. Even his grandmother from Beer Sheva, who'd raised him until he moved with his three brothers to the shack in Tiberias, even she erased his existence altogether. The letters he'd written to her all came back. A few months ago, as part of his rehabilitation, he went to visit the cemetery where his parents and brothers were buried. Accompanied by his devoted psychologist and a warden, he stood in front of the five graves. By chance, his mother Aliza's two younger brothers arrived at the same time. They must have come to clean the headstones, as was their weekly custom. They noticed him and pounced. His escorts tried to rescue him from the two brothers' wrath, but they were also beaten mercilessly. Sprawled on the ground, as his two uncles pummeled him, breaking his ribs, kicking and spitting, Moshik cried, "Forgive me." He shouted again and again, but his apologies faded beneath their hate, their yells and their beating. Eventually they let him go, let his escorts carry him away, warning him never to show his face there again.

"Why do you want me to join you?" asked Shlomi.

"He asked," she answered. "He misses you a lot. He's written about you many times, he's very fond of you."

Her speech turned soft, the hoarseness disappearing. Maybe she's actually talking about herself, he thought. He suddenly felt a strange peace descend on him and spread pleasantness through his body. Just like on the day Hilik broke his arms, when she helped him take off his wet clothes, dried him and dressed him up.

They met in the central bus station.

"I didn't think you'd keep getting taller," she said as she'd looked him over with a smile. Her excitement was evident, despite her efforts to act indifferent.

Her hair had grown longer, slightly darker, and shinier, it looked nothing like Hanna's straw hair. She was tan, her lips slightly chipped from the dry air, hadn't gotten any taller, only rounder and more erect, her walk dancy and more refined, as if she'd just gotten out of ballet class. Five or six freckles, an eyebrow arching into a furrowed forehead, her shirt falling off her shoulder a little, revealing a bra strap. He instantly wanted to lean his head on her, to breath in the scent of her hair. His entire body yearned. He felt his hands longing, demanding him to let them leave his body and go to her. He'd felt something similar before, but could not remember when and where.

"You aren't talking again, just like you used to."

"When?"

"The first time we met."

"I don't remember."

"Liar."

"I don't always have something to say."

"And here I thought your voice might be gone again."

On the bus, she pushed herself against the window. Perhaps she wanted to stop her body from touching his. He pulled away too, gluing himself as best he could to the back of the seat.

There's so much I want to tell her, he thought, so much I want to hear.

I see her searching too, she'll turn her head to me soon and her mouth will spill out all the words she's kept from me, and I'll drink them in passionately.

What she's learned, what she's done, who she's met, what she's thought about, what's gone through her mind. What she remembers and what she forgets. What gnawed at her mind and kept her eyes from shutting at night, and what woke her up in terror when she could finally fall asleep. And is she in a time capsule too, a longing capsule? And why did I let her go, why did I do as she said, why did I agree to be banished from her room and her life? Why did I let Hanna sleep with me on the cold bathroom floor, in front of her shocked eyes, why didn't I stop her from taking away the little boy who is my son?

Suddenly Ella turned to him, took his hand and put it on her cheek. She rubbed her face against his surprised hand, her eyes shut tightly, blocking the tears that were threatening to burst. Her lips touched his fingers, feeling their heat and clinging to them.

"I'm sorry," she said after pulling away at once, "I couldn't stop myself. I've been dreaming of this moment for years."

"Me too," said Shlomi.

"I know," she said and dried her eyes, "otherwise I wouldn't have let myself grab your hand like that."

"I thought you hated me."

"You're a stupid boy, always were."

"I thought you'd never forgive me."

She was silent for a moment. "I really won't forgive you," she said, "even if I wanted to I couldn't."

"I'll wait for you."

"Why?"

"Because. I have no other choice."

And they said nothing more until they arrived. Sat quietly on the bus to the prison.

Again life is like a poem. An evil, cruel and sour poem. Two people going to visit a prisoner in jail, and they themselves are the prisoners, while he's a free man. They are imprisoned in their love, finding no forgiveness, a life sentence. They'll even wait an eternity.

They were seated in a rather small, windowless room. Within a few moments, Moshik was brought in. Without hesitating, he hurried over and pulled them into a long hug, one arm wrapped around Ella's waist, the other raised and working to grip Shlomi, who was a few heads taller than him, by the neck.

Small and skinny as he used to be, only his shoulders had widened a lot. He smelled nice and clean and his clothes were new and carefully ironed, in complete opposition to the ratty, stained clothes he used to wear. Whenever he laughed, he covered his mouth with his hand, trying to hide the fact that some of his teeth were broken or missing. Several small scars adorned his face, mementos of the beatings he'd taken from his uncles, and his ears protruded from his shaven head even more than before. "I think you're the one they wrote that song 'My Little Clown, Why Don't You Dance With Me' about," Ruchama used to tell him. He remembered that when he noticed their eyes on him. "With this bald head," he said, "I look even more like a clown, or like that cartoon elephant who can fly with his ears." And when his laugh subsided, he said, his eyes sparkling, "But you two stayed beautiful, you're even more beautiful than you used to be."

He spoke for most of their meeting. Maybe he noticed their embarrassment and wanted to make it easier for them.

He asked how Ruchama was and reminisced about the days when she'd force him to bathe so he could work in her kitchen.

"She didn't always trust me to do it right," he said. "Sometimes she'd come into the bathroom and scrub my head, really scratch my scalp with her nails, and then towel me down and check me all over, looking for lice, and towel me down again really hard, until the towel turned into sand paper. It hurt a little, but I didn't care. I wasn't even embarrassed when she came into the bathroom when I was half-naked."

He giggled again, even blushed a little.

"And then we started working in the kitchen and scooping out vegetables," he continued, "everyone working quickly, and I sank into my imagination. I imagined the three of us living together in one house, cooking, I was your little boy. You, Shlomi, taught me how to invent dishes, and you, Ella, scrubbed my head and helped me clean my ears, like Ruchama. One time I even told you we should start a kibbutz together with a stuffed vegetable factory that would serve the entire country, but you laughed, even though I was serious."

Moshik went quiet for a moment.

"Sometimes I dream of Genia, too," he said. "I remember our hands touching when we worked together in Ruchama's kitchen. I used to tremble with excitement, I was so shy. Until one time I noticed Genia blushing too, and that sometimes she touched me on purpose. I think about her a lot, but I know there's no chance. I don't even try writing her because I know she won't answer."

Images were fixed in his mind too, thought Shlomi, and they came back up on him too, taking up space and blocking new images from getting in.

"Why don't you ask me about that night and about the shooting?" Moshik suddenly asked. "You can ask if you want, I can handle it." But Shlomi and Ella didn't say a word, their embarrassment only growing.

"Everyone asks," he finally said, "and I tell everyone I don't remember and don't understand what came over me. I don't just say that, I really think a demon took over. But all the boys and young men that come in here look at me with admiration until I blush. It makes me very uncomfortable. I'm even scared to tell my therapist about it because it might be snitching and they could get punished. One of them even told me once that he admired me for having the guts to do what everyone wants to do but can't. I think he's crazy, his words even made me feel sick, but I have to say the only thing I really remember of that night is that it was suddenly quiet. That shack, from the moment I got there, was like a beehive. And suddenly it was quiet. I remember thinking at that moment, that's it, it'll stay quiet, and something inside of me relaxed all at once. I'm ashamed of it. I didn't even tell my therapist, I don't know why it's suddenly come out now. Maybe because you've freed yourselves of your parents, like me. I wish you'd have taken me with you. I wish I'd had the courage to run. Maybe I wouldn't have been overcome by that insanity … I'm sorry to be like this. You must think I'm crazy and a terrible murderer, but it's important for me to tell you the truth, because you were the people I've loved most in my life, you and my grandmother and Ruchama and Genia, and Hilik, who has the best heart of all hearts. It's a shame you're so far away from one another. How can you be in Jerusalem while you're in Tel Aviv? A love like yours can never happen again anywhere in the whole world. If I get out of here one day I promise to do whatever it takes to get you back together."

Before they left, he asked them if they forgave him.

"What for?" asked Ella.

"For that cat," Moshik answered. "It really was cruel of me, but the therapist says the insanity must have already started back then."

A few months later Ella called again and asked Shlomi to join her for another visit. "His therapist called me," she explained, "said it's important to him to talk to us himself. It would help him know Moshik better. He also said he's been doing much better since our last visit, and that it brought light and hope into his life."

Shlomi hesitated. "You have to come," she begged. "I'm afraid of seeing him without you, he's completely nuts."

They met on the bus again, and again they burrowed into their silence and kept their distance. This time she didn't take his hand, barely looked at him, a great gloominess covered her face.

The visit was short. Moshik had the flu and only stood in the doorway, greeted them and hurried away, careful not to let them catch it. Then the kind therapist came in and asked some questions, mostly looking them over with his smiling eyes. Then he told them of the prison's intention to let Moshik out for a short leave. He carefully asked if they'd agree to keep him company and maybe even host him. "If there's no other choice," he said, "I'll take him home with me. I'd even be glad to, but I think he'd rather be with you. You're the only people from his previous life who are willing to be in touch with him."

When they were on their way back, Ella suggested that Shlomi come to Jerusalem with her. Shlomi was surprised but agreed immediately. The gloominess left her face all at once.

They got off the bus in the central bus station and walked to the Old City. Ella told him about the boarding school and her decision to leave. Shlomi told her about the restaurant. They exchanged experiences from their matriculation exams, laughed about the fact that they both chose an external path and had taken exams on the exact same dates and times. When they reached the alleys of the Old City, Ella directed them to special places she loved. A stall in the market that sold colorful mats and beautiful scarves, and a special alley, on one of whose walls funny faces were painted, and a hidden, dim restaurant, where they ate hummus and drank lemonade.

From there they walked to her home. Ella introduced Shlomi to her landlord. The stocky woman widened her eyes and was impressed by his height. Then they locked themselves in her room. Ella distorted her voice and her face in a funny impersonation of her landlord, and Shlomi burst out laughing, carrying her away with him. Together they lay on her bed, laughing and laughing, and then Shlomi leaned over and kissed her lips.

She accepted his kiss at first. They tasted and sucked, their eyes closed. A long minute.

And then she pulled away.

Tears rose in her eyes suddenly and she told him Hanna was sick.

They'd recently found out. She'd have surgery soon, and treatment. Her time might be measured. She might come out of it and live. The many question marks.

Ella tried to stifle her tears. "I've been praying for her to die my entire life," she said, "and now I'm suddenly terrified it might actually happen."

All at once, she became weak and put her head on his stomach. "I tried killing myself so many times to punish her, and here she is, winning again."

Shlomi put a hand on her forehead, trying to console and calm her, but had trouble concentrating. Hanna's face floated against him again, the straw hair, the vibrating sack of skin below her chin. The old and familiar pain shooting from her neck. Her lips smiling at him as he took clothes from her hand and put them on the top shelf. Her eyes swallowing him at the kitchen table at Ruchama's apartment. Her body shaking with tears as she sat on the edge of the bed, Robert by her side. Her hands grabbing his shoulders and shaking hard until his neck screamed with pain.

And in the midst of all this rose little Shmuel's face as he'd recently seen him, sitting in his stroller and laughing at the baby gibberish she spoke to him. Brrri brrra puttttabrrra putttabrrrrina puttttabrrra …

"What about Shmuel?" Shlomi asked.

Ella pushed his hand away and sat up. The gloominess returned at once and her eyes were prickling slits.

"I go to see her every two or three days," she said coldly, "take her to her tests and help out with Shmuel, don't worry."

"I want to help," he said.

"No need," she answered immediately. "We're doing fine."

"I'll go there tomorrow."

"What for?"

"I want to see her and Shmuel.'

"Don't you dare, Shlomi," and her eyes were already burning.

"Why?" he asked, his voice almost pleading.

"You've abandoned him once," she answered. "You've left him in the hands of that monster and took off. Now you leave him be. He's a sensitive child, not even four years old. He doesn't need you coming and going, stay away from there."

Shlomi was surprised by the force of her anger, the sharpness of her words, the fire her eyes blew at him. "You're accusing me for something that happened when I was a little kid, Ella. We were both little kids, what could I have done?"

"You're so stupid, Shlomi," she said. "We were never kids, neither you nor I. We were robbed without even noticing it. I warn you, if you go there, you'll never see me again. Stay out of it. That boy is a happy child. He's happy with what he's got, leave him and her alone."

Shlomi got up as if to leave. "Then why did you tell me all this?" he asked.

"I don't know," she whispered. "Ever since you've come into my life everything has gone crazy."

He sat at her side again, curling her up in his arms.

"I curse the moment you came over to ask me to come to the Sea of Galilee," she said. "I curse the moment my father left me alone with her yelling. She's done nothing but compete with me my entire

life, jealous of me because I didn't have to go through the insanity
of the camps, like her, and then fighting me for you. It took so long
until I finally found you, and then she came and swallowed you up.
She wanted to punish your father because he was the only one who
wouldn't let her swallow him. I curse all the times you came to save
me. I already told you – don't save me anymore."

Shlomi consented to her demand. He didn't go to Haifa and didn't
call. He dived back into his work at the restaurant, and, as always,
suppressed his longing and his worry amidst the clamor of the pots
and the compliments of the guests, until it turned transparent, like
the air.

Months passed before she called again. It was a day before Shlomi
was drafted into the military. Ella was short and sour, said nothing
about Hanna and Shmuel, only wanted to notify him of Moshik's
first leave.

"They approved a twenty-four-hour leave," she said, "and I agreed
to let him stay over with me, my landlord is going to be out of the
country anyway."

"I'm being drafted tomorrow," said Shlomi. "I don't think I can
join you this time."

Basic training lasted three weeks, and when it ended, he went on
a short break. When he reached the central bus station in Jerusalem,
he remembered it was Moshik's day off. He hesitated for a long time
and finally decided not to get on the bus to Tel Aviv.

He walked to Ella's house, and by the time he got there he was
wet with sweat and the rain that had begun pouring. January 1980
in Jerusalem was especially cold.

Moshik opened the door, very happy to see him. He hung onto
his neck, excited about the way he looked in uniform.

Ella was surprised. She pricked and ridiculed him at first. She
laughed at the sight of his buzzed hair and the uniform that was too
small for him, twisted her face at the smell of gun oil on his body
and sent him to take a shower. Shlomi had no clean clothes and so
she searched her landlord's closets and found a heavy woolen robe.
Shlomi scrubbed his body, watching the black water that dripped
from it. Only when he felt his body had completely thawed, and that
the stench of guns was replaced with a lemony scent, and that his

excitement was diminishing a little, only then did he turn the water off and towel himself dry.

He sat with them in the kitchen. In the checkered robe soaked with the smell of an old closet, Shlomi felt like a kid in a costume. Ella wore a short-sleeved light blue dress. She looks like a nurse, he thought and smiled to himself, a tough, impatient nurse, just returning home from work not having had a chance to take off her uniform. First, she must feed her household, the old man in the checkered robe, and especially the kid with the protruding ears, wearing new clothes, sitting at the table, trembling with excitement. Maybe once he's fed and satiated she'll pick him up and dance with him. Wanting to lift his spirits, they'll hold hands and skip and sing, "My Little Clown, Why Don't You Dance With Me."

Ella warmed up the dinner she made. Meatballs in a sweet sauce that reminded Shlomi of Hanna's gray meatballs. She served them with browned potatoes and a tomato and cucumber salad to which she added lots of chopped parsley and cilantro and mint and squeezed an entire lemon.

Moshik told them about the food in prison. Everyone there complained, but he was happy. He complimented Ella on the meal, and soaked the meatballs' cloudy sauce in pieces of bread.

Shlomi told them about basic training. Moshik and Ella laughed as he demonstrated how the soldiers in his platoon marched with broomsticks rather than guns. When he told them he'd been nicknamed Aulcie Perry, Moshik choked with laughter, until they had to pat his back again and again and give him some water.

Ella told them she'd been accepted to the army radio station. "They want me to be a reporter but I want to play songs at night," she said. "I don't sleep anyway."

She suggested they go to a movie, but Moshik preferred to stay in. 'It's nice and warm here," he said, "and I have the two of you to look at. That's better than the cinema."

Ella opened the cabinet below the sink and brought out an old bottle of brandy. "The landlord probably doesn't remember she has this," she said and poured some into glasses.

Slightly off-balance, they opened the pull-out sofa in the living room and covered it with bedding. "The two of you will sleep here," said Ella.

She was suddenly dizzy and she lay down.

Moshik sat on the edge of the sofa, a small distance from her feet. His eyes shone with excitement when Ella reached her arm out to Shlomi and pulled him to her until he was sprawled, his head leaning on the armrest and her head resting on his stomach.

It seemed Moshik was holding his breath. His wide-open eyes followed Ella's hands as they searched for Shlomi's neck, pulled his head to hers, her lips clinging to his for a long kiss.

Without pulling away from his lips, she took off his robe and then removed all her clothes until she was naked.

Shlomi looked at her bare body and trembled. The exhaustion and the brandy pulsed in him, but his hands gripped her and pulled her close, his lips traveled all along her body, tasting and sucking. All his longing rose and erupted. Moshik's gaze had completely slipped his mind, as if he weren't sitting there on the edge of the sofa, choked and excited, watching them like they were a dream come true.

Suddenly, Ella pulled away from Shlomi.

All at once, she began pulling Moshik's clothes off and covering his face and neck with kisses.

Moshik froze. The sudden touch of her hands hit him, loosened him completely, and he accepted her.

That whole time, her eyes were fixed on Shlomi. A narrow, searing and painful look.

The image of the two of them suddenly reminded him of Robert and Hanna, sitting nude on her bed, she crying in his lap.

A long moment passed before he came out of his frozen state. He got up from the sofa, went out to the porch and sat on the cold floor. In nothing but underwear. A winter wind and some rain. He stayed that way all night, shaking and wondering.

He only went inside at the first hints of morning. Moshik was sprawled out on the sofa, sleeping in the nude, breathing heavily. Ella was sitting by his side, curled up in the woolen robe, avoiding Shlomi's eyes. He quickly collected his clothes and his backpack and left.

When he entered the restaurant in Tel Aviv he was already burning up, and he collapsed there.

He didn't tell anyone about that night, not during the month he spent lying in a hospital bed, and not afterwards. But the images kept coming. Her blue dress being thrown to the floor. Her breasts heavy and beautiful, her nipples pink, like Hanna's. Her lips kissing him and in one sudden moment moving over to Moshik. Her eyes punishing and being punished, and Moshik's ears sticking out and blushing more than ever, his nudity revealed behind her hands traveling over him.

And Shlomi pondered and wondered. Why did she punish him that way? Why did she punish Moshik, herself?

Ella didn't call again, but he heard her voice on the radio. The wonder slowly disappeared, the anger and the insult evaporated, and their place was taken by the familiar longing. When she played a song from that long-lost festival, he felt the longing grow and suffocate him. She missed him too, he'd tell himself, one day I'll call her and she'll come.

Almost a year after that night, Shlomi received a letter from Moshik. He wrote at length about his experiences, about books he'd read and films they showed in prison. His writing was enthusiastic, just like his speech. Towards the end of the page, the letters grew narrow and crowded and he wrote, "Our night together was the happiest night of my life. I only regret one thing – drinking that brandy. Maybe it was spoiled, and maybe I'm sensitive to alcohol, all I know is that the brandy made me forget everything that happened after we finished eating. I must have fallen asleep."

At the end of the letter, Moshik suggested coming to the restaurant on his next leave. But Shlomi didn't respond, and they never saw each other again.

*

Four years had passed since that night, four long years of numb yearning, until he called her after Hilik's *shiva* and said, "I want to see you and him, I want you two to come."

And they came.

6

EACH TIME ROBERT OPENED HIS EYES HE SAW RUCHAMA BY HIS SIDE, her thick hair splayed on the pillow, her eyes closed, her breath unsteady. She sleeps and dreams of Hilik. Sometimes she mumbles in her dreams. Sometimes her eyes well up without opening.

And Robert thinks, if I could hear fate laughing my ears would explode in a moment. The walls would crack and the ceiling would fall on Ruchama and me. Here, my dream has come true and I've returned home, to Ruchama. But the house is sour and Hilik is dead.

Ha-ha-ha-ha, its laughter hurts my ears. The walls will soon fall on us.

Almost thirteen years had passed since he'd migrated to the downstairs apartment. She always told him, "You'll even wait an eternity."

Well, this is what the eternity looks like, thought Robert.

Ruchama's eyes shut, both of them in bed, getting up once in a while, bathing, peeing, eating some bread, lukewarm tea, returning, the shutters drawn, the ceiling bluing with dimness. This is the eternity.

Robert looks at Ruchama and wonders, what else do my eyes see?

They see in her the dead Hilik but also New Hilik, sitting in the apartment downstairs, waiting for him. The little boy doesn't know his father won't be coming back. His father is now caged within this eternity and will therefore abandon him. Just like his mother once abandoned him. Got up one day and went off to her eternity.

Robert looks at Ruchama and sees Shlomi, too. The two look so much alike. He's tall too, lighthouse-tall, pretty eyes, imbuing confidence. He can be trusted, I'll leave the boy to him.

He remembers Rochelle too. She is also tall, her head sticking out among all those pilgrims at the airport when she came to bury his uncle. She buried him and disappeared. Deserted her son, and now he was doing the same.

Again, life is rhyming.

He looks at Ruchama and sees his great love, now his curse.

And the same goes for Ruchama. Each time she opens her eyes she sees Robert. Usually he is awake and watching her. "You have to get some sleep," she says and he smiles a little, says, "I've slept enough," and his eyes turn red and his tears spill and soak into the pillow.

What does Ruchama see when she looks at Robert?

She sees Hilik, skinny and short and broad-shouldered like him. The two look so much alike.

Sometimes she gets up and looks out the window. Down in the yard, on the stone wall, sits Shlomi, and alongside him New Hilik, and her stomach contracts. The two look so much alike. Hilik and Hilik, the old and the new. The dead and the living. I'm better off blind, she thinks.

She once saw a TV show about genetics. They showed a picture of little strands inside the cells, carrying everything within them, the past and the future, diseases and hopes and heartbreak. DNA, that's what they called it on the show, and even demonstrated through funny drawings how it generously spread itself and its charge. Those strands passed from generation to generation, and each time they forced people to encounter again what they'd preferred to forget. If only I could forget Hilik, she thought, maybe I'd be able to breathe. But Robert is lying here by my side, and beyond the window my eyes see New Hilik. How can I forget?

Vardina once told her, "People look at each other and only see themselves." Ruchama remembers well how Vardina took a puff of her cigarette, coughed a little and continued speaking. "You, for instance, look at me and see your mother," she said, "maybe because I'm a big fat bear like she was, or maybe because I'm also giggly. Sometimes you get absolutely confused and take out all your tantrums on me. You forget I'm not your mother, and that your mother is dead." She sighed deeply and added, "That's how people are, they only see what's convenient for them."

Ruchama smiled. "And what do you see when you look at me?"

Vardina looked at her and pondered, as if she were seeing her for the first time. "I see the Land of Israel I dreamed of when I was a child in Bucharest," she told Ruchama, "and I see the tall beautiful woman I so wanted to be, and I also see the daughter I could have had if I'd been a a little luckier."

People look at each other the way they read a line in a poem, thought Ruchama. I read one of my favorite poems and suddenly remember my past. Again and again I read and wonder, what is it in the words of this poem that reminds me of my parents' house, my childhood dreams, the moments when the pebbles on the beach scratched my bare feet and my mother called from a distance, "Don't run, the stones will tear your feet apart," and told my brothers who sat at her side, "Look, look at that child, like the Tower of Babylon she's going to be, her head in the sky and her feet bleeding."

When Ruchama opens her eyes, she looks at Robert and reads him like a poem. Her life reflects back from his image. Maybe someone will make a TV show one day, explaining that life itself has genetic strands, DNA. Maybe those strands are buried deep in the center of the Earth, maybe they're in the sky, held by the hand of God. Life has genes too, and it multiplies itself. And maybe these genetic strands carry an ancient curse, passing it on from generation to generation, multiplying and scattering it.

Life is a poem. The poem is a curse. The curse is my tragedy. I cannot forget.

One day, Ruchama got out of bed. She looked out the window, knowing she'd see Shlomi and New Hilik sitting on the stone wall, as was their custom. But to her surprise, there were four of them – Shlomi and New Hilik, and next to them a woman and a child. Ruchama recognized Ella right away, looking like her mother, the phoenix in a sandstorm, but younger and thicker. Her eyes went to the boy and widened. He looked just like Shlomi when he was seven or eight. Uncanny. Four of them sat there – Shlomi and New Hilik, Ella and New Shlomi, looking like a family, a new and quiet family, sitting on the stone wall and peacefully greeting a nice night.

7

New Hilik opened the door for Ella and Shmuel. The stories Shlomi had told him about her and their shared childhood filled him with curiosity and he waited for her expectantly. One might assume the loneliness that had been forced upon him ever since Robert locked himself up in Ruchama's home had also created in him an excitement for their visit. Something new is about to happen, his face said. He looked to Shlomi like a person sitting across from a movie screen, waiting intently for the movie to begin, to escape from his anxiety and answer questions that have yet to be asked.

And indeed, New Hilik sat in the living room and bit his nails. An open book was placed on his lap, but his eyes kept going to the door and saying, Let it open and let the guests come and bring a different air with them.

When he finally opened the door, his eyes went to little Shmuel and his smile was immediately gone. He gave him a long look and then looked at Shlomi and returned his eyes to the boy at the door and again to Shlomi.

He seemed to understand everything.

It was hard not to notice the similarity between the two. Despite the age differences, they looked like two copies of a single original, in different sizes.

A day before, New Hilik looked at old pictures of Shlomi. There were very few pictures, one taken even before Shmuel, Ella's father, had suddenly died. Ruchama and Robert had befriended Hanna and Shmuel back then, and during one dinner together, Shmuel had pulled out his camera and taken a photo of everyone present. Ruchama and Robert and Hanna sat at the table, smiling, a little shy. Little Shlomi and Ella and Hilik stood behind their backs. Shlomi looked a little sleepy, Ella made a funny face, and Hilik looked at her and laughed. And now, before New Hilik's eyes, was a perfect copy of Shlomi as he looked in that picture, even wearing the same expression, a little sleepy and shy.

But New Hilik wasn't laughing, rather watching with wonder.

Shlomi too, though he was expecting the resemblance, glared, amazed. And the boy balled his little body further, and his hand gripped Ella's.

Ella herself had trouble moving, this was the first time she'd seen New Hilik.

It was hard to tell whose shock and embarrassment were greater.

Much later, Ella told Shlomi that the strange moment of meeting reminded her of a TV show, where moments of surprise and awkwardness are disguised by the laughter of an invisible audience. But when she stood at the doorway and held Shmuel's hand, no laughter was heard. Even their breathing was barely heard, only their eyes moved from one to the other, a magnificent, silent dance of eyes.

New Hilik was the one to finally break the frozen moment. He walked over to Shmuel, took his hand and invited him to his room. "Come on," he told him. "I'll show you my coin collection, and if you get hungry or thirsty just tell me." And Shmuel followed him.

*

Day after day goes by, and the days are good.

Yechiel and Shmuel's rolling laughter would wake Shlomi and Ella in the morning. They opened their glued-shut eyes, their arms linked, her body against his, holding and not letting go.

And the two children would laugh for hours. Enjoying the sudden vacation. "The summer break will start soon anyway," said Shlomi. "It wouldn't hurt them to miss a little school. It's more important that they get to know each other." Ella agreed and the children cheered.

At noon, they'd spread a blanket on the floor and sit down to devour the delicacies that Shlomi or New Hilik had cooked. Sometimes they cooked together while little Shmuel ran among them, handing them dishes, stirring, even kneading dough with large motions, solemn.

In the late afternoon, they'd go outside and sit on the stone wall. The air was no longer scorching. It cooled down as the sun grew red and finally disappeared. There was digging underway in the road close by, an improvement to the neighborhood's sewage system, but by the time the four of them sat on the wall, the machines were already still. They watched and breathed in the scent of moist dirt.

At night, the children would sit up in bed, New Hilik reading Shmuel a thriller, reading and reading until Shmuel's eyes closed.

One night, when he was finished reading, he went to Shlomi and whispered in his ear, "He can't read or write at all."

Shlomi shrugged and said, "So what."

New Hilik became upset. "He's in second grade and can't even read one word."

Shlomi smiled at him. "So maybe you can teach him," he said, and Hilik answered, "You're the one who should teach him. You're his father."

Shlomi felt awkward and said nothing, and Hilik continued, "One look is enough to know you're his father. The question is when will you tell him, he needs to know, too," he added and returned to his room, pulled the covers tight over Shmuel, curled up in bed and fell asleep.

Each night, after the two children fell asleep, Shlomi and Ella took their clothes off and clung to each other in the large bed. Kissing and caressing, heating up, but stopping their lovemaking, pulling apart before they could fully merge.

"I'm not ready yet," said Ella, "and neither are you. We'd better wait and not burn out our longing too quickly."

Shlomi told her he'd only slept with a woman once. They both knew what he was talking about, and that time brought a similar pain to both of them.

They would heat up and stop, calming themselves down with long conversations, holding each other all night long, even after they'd fallen asleep. He told her about the restaurant and Noam, about Hilik and the *shiva*. She told him about school and the radio station, about moving to Haifa and living with little Shmuel.

They didn't talk about Hanna at all, and never mentioned Moshik or that cold night in Jerusalem.

Another day went by, and another. Only six days since the two had arrived, but it seemed like a lifetime.

Shlomi examined Shmuel, looking at him again and again, his soul growing more and more attached to the child's. Something in his expression wounded him. His large eyes reminded him of Ruchama, lending him the appearance of a lighthouse as well.

And more than anything, New Hilik filled Shlomi with excitement. The boy was happy. His joy was so great and contagious that Shlomi felt they'd begun speaking a different language, a new and unfamiliar language, inventing itself as it left the speakers' mouths.

At the end of the *shiva*, Shlomi had to return to his apartment and job in Tel Aviv and begged New Hilik to join him. "What do you care?" he told him. "Your class is doing nothing but rehearsing for the end-of-year play anyway. You can spend some time with me instead."

New Hilik hesitated. Ever since Robert brought him to Tiberias, he hadn't left the city limits, even dodging field trips with various excuses. Shlomi continued to beg and New Hilik finally consented.

Noam welcomed them at the restaurant with great excitement. After they ate, they walked to Shlomi's building. On their way, they passed by a school. The school day had just ended and the children swarmed in the yard, refusing to say goodbye. "If you agree to move to Tel Aviv and live with me," said Shlomi. "You can go to this school, I'm sure you'd have fun, look at the kids and you can see for yourself they're happy."

New Hilik lowered his eyes and said nothing. Perhaps he was surprised to discover the thoughts racing through Shlomi's mind.

Shlomi presented his apartment to the boy with a flourish, trying to ignite an emotion in him, gauging once more how the boy felt about moving in with him in Tel Aviv. He couldn't leave him alone in Tiberias. But Yechiel's face was long. He looked at the apartment in silence and then sat in front of the television and claimed to be tired. Shlomi asked if it would be all right for him to pop by the restaurant alone, to go over some urgent matters with Noam and do some shopping. Hilik encouraged him to go out. "Don't worry about me, I'll just rest."

But in the afternoon, when Shlomi returned, the boy was gone.

Shlomi was filled with worry, but shortly thereafter the phone rang and New Hilik announced that he'd returned to Tiberias on his own. The Tel Aviv apartment had stirred some bad memories in him. He even remembered a night he'd spent standing at the window, weeping and calling back his lost mother. "Don't worry about me," he told Shlomi. "I can be here on my own, you go back to your restaurant and I'll manage."

Shlomi summoned Noam to drive him back to Tiberias. On their way there, he told him, "I'm not so sure I can come back to the restaurant. We need to figure out a real solution. I can't abandon that kid, he's my brother." Noam nodded understandingly, and when they arrived and found New Hilik in his bed, crying quietly, he told Shlomi, "You stay here as long as you need and don't worry about the restaurant. I'll take care of everything."

From day to day, the boy grew stronger, and when Ella and Shmuel arrived, his happiness was complete. Seeing his joy, Shlomi thought, this boy spreads light, like a reading lamp.

One morning New Hilik told Shlomi, "Shmuel told me about his mother and I understood she was also Ella's mother."

Shlomi tried to maintain an indifferent expression, but the boy's glum face made it harder. "I look at Shmuel," said New Hilik, "and see your whole life story in him and it hurts my heart." Shlomi smiled with an effort and said, "Don't pity me, Hilik," and Hilik answered, "I'll pity you as much as I want and whenever I want, I'll pity you from today all the way to tomorrow or even the day after that," and when he said "tomorrow" and "after" his Rs rolled so much that they both burst out laughing. "Tomorrrrrrow … Afterrrrrr …" they told each other between blasts of laughter.

*

And on the seventh day, a Wednesday afternoon, they decided to go to the Sea of Galilee. They wanted to see if the water was rising like it had back then, throwing fish up in the air.

The wind was raging as usual, and Shlomi forbade the children from going in the water before the sun set and calmed the waves. He told them about the wind's ability to go wild and even decapitate people. New Hilik and Shmuel listened and laughed. Then they went to skip stones on the water.

Shlomi set up a small pit and started a fire. He placed a gridiron over the flames and grilled meat. Ella's face grew very gloomy and Shlomi became alarmed. Her silence was foreboding.

The wind spun among the coals and the meat was charred. He placed the parts that had been grilled well on the children's plates, and they went and sat at the water's edge. Ella and Shlomi followed them with their eyes as Hilik taught Shmuel how to bite into the meat and then tip the plate and drink the red juice, swallowing it with one gulp. Shmuel obeyed and glowed.

Ella's eyes grew even darker.

"This kid is coming between us," she suddenly said. "I can never love you as long as I see him in front of me."

"I don't understand," said Shlomi.

For the first time since they'd arrived at the beach, she looked directly at him. "What do you see when you look at him?" she asked.

Shlomi hesitated, but her eyes didn't let go. "I see a little boy," he answered, "a boy who's mine and whom I'd like to make happy so he doesn't have a crummy childhood."

Ella laughed and tears appeared in her eyes. "You've always been a silly, emotional boy," she said. "Maybe that's why you can see things just as they are, without evasion or beautification. I wish I could be like that a little, but I can't. When I look at that boy I see different things, so many things that I'd rather be blind. And that's one thing you can't save me from, Shlomi."

The kids had moved farther away, their laughter barely audible anymore, only the whispered sounds of the surf and her words.

"I've been punishing you ever since that night. Even if I try not to, I'll still punish you. My soul has been cursed and broken for a long time, I can't be with you and raise a boy who's my brother and your son."

Ella took his hand and held it in her lap. "I look at him and see too many things," she said. "He looks just like you, he's named for my father, it's getting me confused. When he looks at me, I know I remind him of her. He even gets confused sometimes and calls me Mom. Try to understand me, Shlomi, I could never love you as long as he's in front of our eyes." She wiped her eyes. "It's scary how much Yechiel looks like Hilik. It's scary because Hilik is dead and you insist on turning us into a family of ghosts."

"Everything is new, Ella," Shlomi said angrily. "Everything is brand new, everything is beginning now."

Ella looked at him, surprised by his anger and determination, yearning for him and pulling away. His eyes wounded her, open and lit.

"We'll go back to Haifa tomorrow or the day after," Ella whispered, "back there we're just two orphans from the same mother, I'm the older sister and Shmuel is the little brother and that's it. We're almost used to it and we're almost happy. Tomorrow or the day after we'll go back, and if you want you can visit us sometime."

Tomorrrrrrow ... Afterrrrrr ... Shlomi mumbled to himself.

The wind had weakened. Shlomi saw the two boys remove their sandals and walk barefoot in the shallow water, enjoying the chill. If Ruchama had been here, he thought, maybe she'd call out, "Get your feet out of that ice water before your toenails fall off."

*

Everyone fell asleep before nighttime. New Hilik didn't read Shmuel the rest of the story because their eyes closed as soon as they got into bed. Ella fell asleep in the large bed and Shlomi lay down on the squeaky bamboo sofa. Surprisingly, his breath was calm.

He woke up to the smell of heavy aromas filling the building. The aromas pulled him off the sofa. He left the apartment and followed them to the upstairs apartment. When he went in the kitchen, he saw Ruchama cooking. Three bubbling pots stood on the stove, spreading strong aromas, spicy and sour, green and red. She looked at him beyond the glasses, not at all surprised to see him there in the middle of the night, as if she'd known he'd come. Without a word, she pushed a pile of vegetables towards him and he began skillfully scooping them out.

They stood like that for hours, cooking silently, like they used to, even the silent workman appeared after a while, depositing overflowing boxes he'd collected according to Ruchama's list, and disappeared into the night. They cooked and cooked and said nothing, and only Vardina was missing, sitting across from them and explaining what to do with mayonnaise, and Hilik walking around the apartment, his fingers pinching his nose to block the smell.

In the middle of the night, they heard the neighbors' voices.

"Ruchama, Ruchama ... "

She opened the window and looked down. Some neighbors were standing in the yard.

"We're not complaining," one of them said, "but it's impossible to sleep with these smells."

"It smells so good," another said. "I woke up in tears, tears coming down and my stomach grumbling."

"What did you put in there?" the first one asked. "We've been breathing your cooking for years, but this time my whole body is shaking. Please close your window so we can go back to sleep. We have work tomorrow."

They sat at the table only when the night began to wane. Ruchama made black coffee and placed a plate of date cookies, warm from the oven, in front of them.

"What's his name?" she asked.

"Who?"

"Your son."

"Shmuel," he whispered.

"Did she make you do it, Hanna?"

"No."

"But you were just a boy, not even fourteen."

"So what."

"And why didn't you tell me? You could have at least told Hilik, it would have made it easier for you."

Shlomi shrugged and sipped his coffee.

A few years earlier, Hilik saw Hanna in Haifa, Ruchama told him as the coffee's steam clouded her glasses. Hanna was walking down the street, the little boy holding her hand. Hilik saw the boy and understood everything right away. After he told Ruchama, she was filled with rage and curiosity and went to Haifa, wishing to see for herself. But even before she could leave the bus station, she'd decided to go right back home.

"I was afraid," she said. "That woman is a phoenix in a sandstorm. She stole everything from me, even you." Ruchama removed her glasses and wiped the steam with the edge of her dress.

"I didn't know Hilik knew. He never said anything," Shlomi said with wonder.

"Because I asked him to keep quiet," she said, "I wanted to protect you. I always wanted to protect you and I've never succeeded, that's my curse."

"That's enough, Ruchama," he exploded with rage. "There are no curses, everything is new."

They drank silently. A moment later, Robert joined them. He woke up, staggered to the kitchen in his underwear and sat by Ruchama. She collected him into her lap with her long arms.

When Shlomi got up to leave, Ruchama told him, "Please call me Mom. I don't want you to call me Ruchama anymore. I'm your mother."

And Shlomi smiled and said, "All right."

Shlomi's mother rested her head on Shlomi's father's shoulder. They both closed their eyes, probably pondering the eternity they still had to live through.

Shlomi's mother, Shlomi's father, Shlomi's mother, Shlomi's father, he mumbled to himself, walking down the stairs. Shlomi's mother, Shlomi's father.

*

When he went into the kitchen, he saw Ella curled up on the chair, her eyes squinting, a little shaky. She suddenly seemed like a terrified animal. He prepared some coffee and made her drink a little. Then he leaned over and kissed her lips.

"All right," he said. "Go back to Haifa, but leave me Shmuel."

Ella flinched. "Why?" she asked.

"That's what I want."

"You're crazy. How could I?"

"We have to break the curse," he whispered in her ear. "He's my son, I'll take care of him."

His gaze blinded her and she closed her eyes. "I can't," she wept.

Shlomi pulled her onto his lap. "Go back to Haifa, go to Sugarloaf Mountain if you want. Everything is new now. I'll get a lawyer to take care of everything. I'll raise both of them, New Hilik and New Shlomi, until they're happy."

He kissed her lips again, left the kitchen and went to sleep.

*

When he woke up, she was gone. She'd collected her few items of clothing and gone, leaving Shmuel there.

It was early morning. He'd only slept for an hour, maybe a little longer. His eyes were still glued shut as he watched Yechiel and Shmuel, sleeping in their beds, side by side.

Shlomi stood among the old bamboo furniture in the living room and wondered at the meaning of the peace that had suddenly descended upon him. He even felt relief, like he'd really wanted her to go.

His wonder grew. Most of his life, at least the life he'd recorded in his mind, he prayed for Ella to be by his side, to return from all the Sugarloaf Mountains she'd escaped to over and over, to hold onto him and not let go, to forgive him, to let him save her again, to love him. He'd been waiting and praying most of his life.

Suddenly he remembered two lines from a poem he'd seen in one of the books Ruchama loved. Several times when they were still very small, Hilik had picked up that book and drawn over one of the poems with colorful pencils, until he'd covered it almost completely. Only two lines remained visible, untainted by color:

Because I pray that you'll be mine,
Only so I can forget you.

Ruchama had gotten upset. She yelled and yelled, promised all sorts of punishments, shook her finger in front of Hilik's terrified eyes. When she calmed down she asked him why he drew on the whole poem and only left those two lines bare and clean, and Hilik answered, "Because it's silly and funny."

I've been praying my whole life, Ella, that you'll be mine, only so I can forget you. Silly and funny.

My mistake is suddenly clear, bare and clean among the colorful drawings.

I've been wrong most of my life, thinking my love for you was the center, the essence of my story, my poem.

Ella was a place to run to. A shelter that was sometimes open to me, and I went in because I wanted out of the rooms where my life rustled. Maybe I thought I'd find my childhood there, in her blue home, on the Jewish Agency bed, between her beautiful arms, one scratched with lines like a notebook. Maybe she ran to me from her mother and the screaming, ran from human powder, from her dead father whose body they had a hard time pulling out the window.

The mistake had been so great, thought Shlomi, but how could I have known? What am I, Deborah the Prophetess?

Where is my life, he wondered, in the places I run from or in the places I want to reach? I spend most of my time knocking on doors. The door to Ruchama's room as she mourned her poets, the door to Robert's apartment as he waited an eternity among the bamboo furniture. And the door to Hanna and Ella's home. I kick it and bang on it with my fist and yell and beg, until Mrs. Katz-fart comes out to the stairway and shouts, "Who's there? Who's making all that noise?"

The elegant Mrs. Katz. The famous math teacher, revered by the city's children, had been forgotten in her final years. No one greeted her, no one looked at her in awe, no one was scared she'd fail them on a math test. No one even remembered how once, in the middle of class, she let out a little fart that miraculously made everyone fear her even more. Maybe it made her human, someone to laugh at too, more than just to fear the future dictated by her grades. But all that was completely forgotten once she retired. Sometimes she'd visit the school. The new teachers didn't recognize her. The guard at the entrance would interrogate her, asking insulting questions and checking her small bag, as if she'd hidden a bomb there, as if this old lady had come to act as the biblical Samson in her old workplace, to blow up the building and cry, "Let me die with the students."

After a while, she stopped going out altogether, and one day she turned on the gas on her stove and sat in the kitchen until her eyes closed. Some claimed the window was open because she was cooking soup and wanted to air the room out, but then a pleasant wind came in to caress her face and she sank into a sweet sleep, never noticing that the wind had blown out the flame on the burners. Gas flew in and filled the room and Mrs. Katz-fart never woke up. Shlomit bought her apartment and baked cakes in her kitchen, spreading scents of cinnamon and almonds.

Suddenly, standing among the old bamboo furniture, his love for Ella seemed pale and dull, like a piece of clothing forgotten on the clothesline, blowing in the warm wind, losing more and more of its color, becoming thin and perforated and finally crumbling into the air.

He was seven and a half when he'd first seen her. Before he'd turned fourteen he'd slept with her mother, and nine months later, his son was born. The son was taken from him as well, and now had been returned. If life is a poem, he asked, what is its meaning? Maybe Ruchama would be able to interpret it, she understands poetry. If she read it, her love of poetry would awaken and maybe she'd help me understand. Or the crybaby teacher who also taught literature. Maybe she'd read it and understand why it was even written, why it was structured as it was, a verse and another verse, a home and another home, a floor over another floor, a yard by a yard, people rhyming with each other, signifying and symbolizing and likening.

Suddenly his love for Ella seemed thin and distant, like Hanna's straw hair, blowing in the wind, streaked with gray. We don't know how to love at all. Any of us.

Only Hilik knew, and his life had been abducted.

If Hilik were alive, he could have helped interpret the poetry of his life. He really did understand words and sentences, knew how to study stories and poems and extract flavors and smells and meanings.

If he were here, he would have explained it.

Hilik, my beloved, my brother.

Suddenly a great weakness overtook Shlomi's body. His legs shook. He collapsed on the floor. All at once his tears broke out, a great flood. He'd never cried like this before, not even back then, when he'd wept at Vardina's, his head on her elephant legs and his tears staining her dress.

My little brother. My beloved. My life teacher.

Everything is new. And what am I going to do without you?

Yechiel and Shmuel woke up with a start when they heard his crying. They came over and looked at him with worry. Yechiel held Shmuel's hand, and their faces were filled with sorrow for the good dreams that had been taken from them, or maybe for Shlomi, bawling on the floor.

He wiped his eyes and stifled his tears.

"Everything's okay," he said and asked them to go back to bed.

They are so much like us, Hilik, you and me.

Maybe everything does need to be new. Maybe we can fix it now, prevent their crummy childhoods.

Life is a poem and the poem is putting me to the test now, asking me for the last line, or maybe the first.

*

When he felt his tears coming again, Shlomi left the apartment, closing the door quietly behind him, careful not to wake the children, and went up to the roof.

The sun was peeking from behind the blue mountains. Its rays fell on the Sea of Galilee, transforming it into a shimmering mirror. It's so early in the morning and it's already hot. It's going to be an aggressive summer. Heat waves will attack the city, the winds will cover it with sand, shutters will be drawn, air conditioners will be turned on, darkness will calm things down, walls will turn blue, and a new air will enter the houses.

Every other time Ella had left, he'd slipped into a slumber right away, but now he felt more awake than ever. His eyes were still dripping but his entire body was alert. His ears heard everything, his eyes saw everything. Even his nose smelled all the scents. The scents of a still morning, the scent of moist dirt from the dug-up street, and tender scents of burnt sugar and lemon peel from the nearby building. Through Mrs. Katz's bathroom window, he'd watched Ella standing on the roof, right where he stood now, and he'd tried to stop her from jumping off.

Today, he promised himself, he'd find a lawyer to take care of Shmuel's situation. He'd speak to the kid first, gauging his readiness. New Hilik would help Shmuel relax and adjust to his new life. Then he'd suggest to Noam that he close the restaurant and come work with him here. He'd give him Vardina's apartment. Everyone would cook, make people happy on their special days with their food. Maybe they'd invite Shlomit to join them. The memory of her good eyes filled him with yearning and again he breathed in the sweet scents coming from her home. She would probably agree. He'd have Ruchama make the children white cheese and diced cucumber sandwiches. He'd teach Shmuel to read and write using paper notes, and protect New Hilik from stupid wars.

Shlomi stood on the roof, among the antennae, the water heaters and the black bits that, to this day, Ruchama was sure were mouse poop. They had lain right here, he and Ella, two seven-year-olds, and watched the struggle to remove a body through a window. Then Ella had gotten up, shaken off the dust and dirt, run down from the roof, down the stairs and along the path until she reached Hanna and clung to her, so she wouldn't yell, so her throat wouldn't break.

Strange, thought Shlomi, people always say your entire life flashes before your eyes before you die, moments floating into each other, fighting their way upstream and amounting to one second in which the soul leaves the body and then nothing.

Strange, because it's the exact opposite for me. My entire life is flashing before my eyes, one image after the other, a moment before I begin living, a moment before my breath is born.

His eyes were dry. He went downstairs to his apartment, looked at the two children, New Hilik and New Shlomi, sleeping deeply and dreaming meaningless dreams, their breathing steady and only slightly squeaky, and began collecting words and writing them on countless paper notes.

Tel Aviv, May 29th 2010

Author's Acknowledgements

Einat Glaser Zarhin; Daniel, Ori and Rona Zarhin; Shulamit Zarhin; Ayelet Menachemi; Shiri Artzi; Dalya Yaloz; Iris Mor; Bina Pe'er; Yardenne Greenspan; New Vessel Press; The Institute for the Translation of Hebrew Literature; Kneller Artists Agency Ltd.: Arik Kneller, Talya Akerman, Adi Muvchar and Yuval Horowitz.

And a great thanks from the bottom of my heart to Ronit Weiss-Berkowitz, editor of this book in the Hebrew original, who is a lighthouse.

This book contains quotations from the following poems and songs:

Kinneret/Rachel
The Oak Tree/Yoram Taharlev
On the Way Back/Ehud Manor
A Ballad for the Medic/Dan Almagor
Prague/Shalom Hanoch
My Poems Limp Towards you on Crutches/Nathan Alterman
(from *Stars Outside*)
My Eyes Swear They'll See You Again/Nathan Alterman
(from *Stars Outside*)
Moon/Nathan Alterman
(from *Stars Outside*)
Old House and Pigeons/Nathan Alterman
(from *Stars Outside*)
The Pigeon's Poem/Shimrit Or
Elle a gardé ses yeux d'enfant /M. Jourdan – M. Brant

COCAINE BY PITIGRILLI

Paris in the 1920s – dizzy and decadent. Where a young man can make a fortune with his wits … unless he is led into temptation. Cocaine's dandified hero Tito Arnaudi invents lurid scandals and gruesome deaths, and sells these stories to the newspapers. But his own life becomes even more outrageous when he acquires three demanding mistresses. Elegant, witty and wicked, Pitigrilli's classic novel was first published in Italian in 1921 and retains its venom even today.

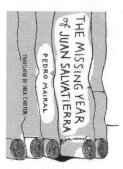

THE MISSING YEAR OF JUAN SALVATIERRA BY PEDRO MAIRAL

At the age of nine, Juan Salvatierra became mute following a horse riding accident. At twenty, he began secretly painting a series of canvases on which he detailed six decades of life in his village on Argentina's frontier with Uruguay. After his death, his sons return to deal with their inheritance: a shed packed with rolls over two miles long. But an essential roll is missing. A search ensues that illuminates links between art and life, with past family secrets casting their shadows on the present.

FANNY VON ARNSTEIN: DAUGHTER OF THE ENLIGHTENMENT BY HILDE SPIEL

In 1776 Fanny von Arnstein, the daughter of the Jewish master of the royal mint in Berlin, came to Vienna as an 18-year-old bride. She married a financier to the Austro-Hungarian imperial court, and hosted an ever more splendid salon which attracted luminaries of the day. Spiel's elegantly written and carefully researched biography provides a vivid portrait of a passionate woman who advocated for the rights of Jews, and illuminates a central era in European cultural and social history.

KILLING THE SECOND DOG BY MAREK HLASKO

Two down-and-out Polish con men living in Israel in the 1950s scam an American widow visiting the country. Robert, who masterminds the scheme, and Jacob, who acts it out, are tough, desperate men, exiled from their native land and adrift in the hot, nasty underworld of Tel Aviv. Robert arranges for Jacob to run into the widow who has enough trouble with her young son to keep her occupied all day. What follows is a story of romance, deception, cruelty and shame. Hlasko's writing combines brutal realism with smoky, hardboiled dialogue, in a bleak world where violence is the norm and love is often only an act.

THE GOOD LIFE ELSEWHERE BY VLADIMIR LORCHENKOV

The very funny - and very sad - story of a group of villagers and their tragicomic efforts to emigrate from Europe's most impoverished nation to Italy for work. An Orthodox priest is deserted by his wife for an art-dealing atheist; a mechanic redesigns his tractor for travel by air and sea; and thousands of villagers take to the road on a modern-day religious crusade to make it to the Italian Promised Land. A country where 25 percent of its population works abroad, remittances make up nearly 40 percent of GDP, and alcohol consumption per capita is the world's highest – Moldova surely has its problems. But, as Lorchenkov vividly shows, it's also a country whose residents don't give up easily.

To purchase these titles and for more information please visit
newvesselpress.com.

New Vessel Press